*Acclaim for*

# THE PHOENIX CYCLE

"*Phoenix Fire* is an intense sprint that kept me guessing with the turn of every page! Grimm brilliantly tackles the heart topics of family, sacrifice, and belonging. Readers, dust off your shelves."

— **NADINE BRANDES**, award-winning author of *The Nightmare Virus*

"A gripping page-turner that transports readers through time as its mystery unfolds, Grimm's *Phoenix Fire* is unlike anything I've ever read. Beautiful, romantic, and absolutely fascinating, this is storytelling that readers won't soon forget. Sign me up for book two. I'm hooked!"

— **JILL WILLIAMSON**, Christy Award–winning author of *By Darkness Hid*

"This tale of mystery, identity, and discovery starts with a bang and never lets up. S.D. Grimm deftly balances a twisty plot with a heartfelt emotional journey, and Ava's story is sure to captivate fans of *Supernatural* and *Buffy the Vampire Slayer.*"

— **LINDSAY A. FRANKLIN**, Carol Award–winning author of *The Story Peddler*

"A flare of adventure, a spark of romance, smoldering ancient magic, and high stakes combine in this absolute gem of a story. The Phoenix Cycle is a unique read that will keep you reading late into the night— and well worth it! Highly recommended for any fan of YA fantasy."

— **JAMIE FOLEY**, award-winning author of The Katrosi Revolution series

# PHOENIX FIRE

Books by S.D. Grimm

**Children of the Blood Moon**
*Scarlet Moon*
*Amber Eyes*
*Black Blood*

*Summoner*

*A Dragon by Any Other Name*

**The Phoenix Cycle**
*Phoenix Fire*

THE PHOENIX CYCLE BOOK 1

# PHOENIX FIRE

## S. D. GRIMM

FAYETTE
PRESS

*To Cilia,*
*one of the sweetest,*
*wisest souls I know,*
*because this one is her favorite.*
*I love you, "cister,"*
*and I appreciate you more than you know.*

# IF MY FOSTER FAMILY FOUND OUT

I was reliving someone else's memories, they'd ship me off to a new home before I could say *insane*.

That made it even more important to save face during this otherwise perfectly normal "family" dinner.

The last thing I heard was Mrs. Fields asking Mr. Fields to pass her the salt. Then laughter and singing that wasn't happening in this room—only in my mind—drowned out everything else.

I'd tried to focus on the shiny mahogany of the dining room table. The taupe placemats beneath our dinnerplates. Square. They were square plates. None of my other foster families—and there had been many—used square plates. That was my first inkling that I might—just *might* have finally found a place to belong. Squares in a world of circles.

But I was wrong. The Fieldses—Dave and Jean—were as normal as any rich suburban family. Three-car garage. Purebred dog with some fancy kennel name. Micro-fiber sofas in a living room that was just for show. The exquisite leather couches in the family room with the big—no, huge—TV were for lounging. They even had non-pasteurized milk delivery. And yet, somehow, they'd taken me in with my black-rimmed, smoky-eyed makeup, tattooed shoulder—courtesy of a foster sister in a previous home—purple-streaked hair, and rebellious nature without blinking.

And they made me feel welcome.

I placed my palm flat against the perfectly polished table. Spread my fingers over the dark wood. And tried to stay grounded in this world. This life. This reality. But deep inside, my I started to burn, my lungs choked on a non-existent fire, and my mind tried to tear me away from the scene in front of me. The happy couple chuckling over meatloaf, actually saying things like "how was your day" and caring about the answer.

Not again. Not now. I could not afford to ruin this.

I fought it, because as far as I could tell, normal people didn't have memories of things that never happened to them, and that was exactly what was going to happen to me any second.

The first flash hit hard: Yellow ribbons in my braided hair, obstructing my vision as I looked over my shoulder. White streamer in my hand as I followed the other girls circling around a maypole. We were singing a song. And though I'd never heard of a maypole before, I suddenly knew what one was.

In the strange other reality, I giggled. A happiness bubbling up in my chest that didn't belong—because this wasn't me. It wasn't *my* memory. I had to get out of the house before the Fieldses saw me lapse into an episode—as I'd taken to calling them. They were coming more frequently now, and the only way I knew how to calm them was to get out and race to the woods.

Another flash from the vision exploded into my senses. Laughter still in my lungs, I gazed across the field, through the endless parade of young girls racing the maypole, and my eyes landed on a young man with piercing blue eyes. I gasped.

*I* knew that face.

As in, real-me knew that face.

*STOP!* I cried out in my head, imploring my brain to work right. To condemn this madness.

"Stop what? What's wrong, Ava?" That was Jean's voice.

My fork clanked against the edge of the square plate so loudly, I flinched. And I stared at Jean as the memory in my skull begged for me to stay. Pleaded for my attention. The blue eyes were last to melt away, and I was left looking at Jean's concerned expression. Both of them watched me as if frozen in time. As if they knew I was crazy.

The memory inside my head fought back. It would take over all my senses soon. And if I'd actually yelled out loud moments ago—I was done here. They'd ship me off to a new place. How could I have allowed myself to hope?

Jean's apologetic smile didn't mask her worry. "Ava? Don't you like the meatloaf? You don't have to eat—"

"I-I have to go." My voice came out rough.

"Now?" Mr. Fields's voice held a slight edge to it.

"Y-yes." I stood, accentuating my point. And my cloth napkin fell onto the plush, cream rug. So normal. So refined. So opposite of everything I was. A broken plate that didn't belong anywhere but the trashcan.

I headed toward the front door.

"Ava!" Jean and Dave's voices overlapped. Jean's sounded concerned, but Dave's came out stern. I knew that tone.

My heart sank. I'd overstayed my welcome, just like every-where before.

And it hurt. Because even though I'd tried not to let them, this family fanned the flame of hope in me. Hope that I could . . . maybe . . . belong here . . . someday.

I slipped on one of my tennis shoes, squeezing my eyes shut and embracing the single thing that would keep the tears from falling—my anger.

Sure enough, they followed me into the hall. Even the dog. I scoffed, stomping my heel into the other shoe. The fact that I'd made it to the night before my second year in a row at the same school seemed an impossible feat. Well, almost second year. I'd come in the middle of sophomore year last year. But still. The fact that I lived with a family who tolerated me and gave me my space seemed more impossible. Yet here I stood on the threshold of walking right out the front door on all the security they dangled in front of me—at least until I turned eighteen and had to find my own way.

"Do not leave this house." Mr. Fields' warning sent a flare up my spine. My anger latched onto it and snarled.

I looked up at him, glare heating my gaze. Totally unprovoked, and I knew that. But the glare came anyway. Defense mechanism extraordinaire.

A challenging smirk playing the corner of my mouth. And I prayed I'd be able to control my tongue. "Watch me."

Why couldn't I just control my tongue?

"If—" He started forward, but Mrs. Fields held out her arm to stop him.

"Ava." She stepped toward me, extending her hand over the glossy solid-oak floor between us as if reaching across a divide. I wanted to grab it. The worry in her eyes looked genuine. But accepting that connection screamed *risky* . . . in case I got attached just to be shipped off again—after all, they'd wanted younger kids. Not me. "We just want what's best for you."

Ha! Every parent in every foster home said that. And seriously, they didn't even know me. How could they possibly decide what was best for me?

She stopped moving toward me, hand still extended, as if asking me to make the decision to trust her. To return.

Where had trust gotten me so far? I looked right into her compassionate eyes, and another vision flickered in my mind. Fear steamrolled the action I wanted to take. "And you're the expert in what's best for me?"

Mr. Fields held up a finger. "Just where do you think you're going, young lady?"

Oh no. He'd said "young lady." That was sure to make me listen. I rolled my eyes, but inside I wanted to crumple. Perceived threats typically tempted me to act out in ways contrary to how I felt. Showing affection made me vulnerable. Showing anger—that was my protective armor. And it fit like a leather glove that said I was in too deep to back down now. So instead of crossing the invisible threshold back toward their promised forgiveness, I narrowed my eyes further. "None of your business."

"Listen here—"

"Dave." Jean's voice warned him to calm down. Then she looked at me. "Ava, your safety is important. We just want to know where you're going."

"For a run."

"It's dark." Dave's exasperation poured out in his tone.

"And?" Stupid tongue. Stupid girl. Why was I doing this?

"We just don't want you to be alone." Jean's soft voice pleaded with me.

Alone. Really? Why did no one seem to understand how fully capable and self-sufficient I was? Why did I have to prove it when my whole life up to this point no one cared where I would end up at eighteen? My hands balled into fists as tears threatened. "I can take care of myself."

They stood there, looking stunned.

Jean's quiet voice broke in. "I don't know why you push us away."

The words speared my heart. But why expect her to understand? What in her perfect little life with expensive, matching couches and luxury items like throw pillows had ever given her cause to imagine someone wanting to push people they cared about away? Nothing.

I turned toward her and her "help me understand" expression. "I just want to go for a run. *Alone.*"

Mr. Fields's voice remained calm and collected. "We need you to understand that living under our roof means you obey our rules. You can't just jump up in the middle of dinner and announce that you're leaving."

There it was. The ultimatum. The inevitable threat. I crossed the buffed oak floor to the double-paned front door, touched the handle and paused, my thoughts wrestling. I could apologize. Let them win. They'd likely smother me with hugs. They might even take me into the kitchen and place a bowl of ice cream in front of me. A scenario I'd dreamed of many times.

I closed my eyes. Who was I kidding? I was old enough to know what real life looked like, and that wasn't it.

My chest clutched, and the memory that wasn't mine fought the edges of my mind. In a moment I wouldn't be able to contain it. I'd be lost inside of it. They'd see how broken and crazy I truly was.

I opened the door.

Mr. Fields promised what I feared. "Ava, don't you dare leave this house."

I faced him. "Or what? You'll send me away?"

He opened his mouth in stunned silence. I slammed the door behind me and raced out into the night.

Summer heat still lingered in the humid air as dusk took hold, but inside my brain it was spring. Cool. Bright. Colorful. So real.

Not yet. I pushed against the unwanted memory.

Free of the confines of the brick and mortar that housed expensive furniture and immaculate rooms, my walls wanted to crumble. End-of-summer air filled my lungs. Sweat dripped down my back. The rhythmic sound of my shoes hitting the pavement joined my breathing, and the trees beckoned me ahead. Soon the crunch of dirt and gravel would echo under my shoes, and trees, with their cooling mists, would surround me. Wrap around me like a security blanket. Hide me from prying eyes. Keep the world from seeing my pain. My brokenness. The memory pounded on my senses. Burned hot in my mind. I needed the woods. I needed to be alone. No witnesses.

The memory could overtake me there, and everything would be okay.

And why wouldn't the woods be my safe place? I'd been found here. A four-year-old, lost and alone, walking away from a fire. I might not remember anything about my life before that moment, but dozens of foster homes since? I remembered them.

The forest remained my only constant.

A rabbit bolted, its lean body rushing in zigzags as it ran past. Headlights left a golden gleam on the outline of its lithe form. One thing separated me from the dirt road surrounded by trees and the heartbeat of freedom: this road.

As I crossed into the cover of trees, my mental barriers burst open, and the strange vision overtook me.

The maypole. My braided hair. The laughing girls. But the boy standing on the opposite side of the meadow—I knew him from school. Okay, I didn't *know* him. I'd seen him in the halls. Recognized him when I'd seen him running in the woods a bunch of times this summer. At least twice a week. Always at night. And he always disappeared right after I spotted him.

But I remembered those eyes.

The vision seemed to stutter and restart once. Twice. Three times. Waiting for me to let go of reality and let it play out. Too tired to push against it, I let it show me.

Laughter continued as girls wrapped their streamers around the pole, but I'd walked away. The piercing blue eyes pulled me in. A little dizzy, I staggered toward him. Hope seemed to bloom in his expression like an opening dandelion. But suddenly someone else stepped in front of me—a young man.

"Where are you off to in such a hurry?" His voice was musical. Kind. He knew me, and I felt a familiarity with him. But I tried to look around his chest to see the blue-eyed boy. And he was gone.

Disappeared. Not unlike his real-life self.

And the vision melted.

Exhaling shaky breath, I took stock of my surroundings. I'd kept running somehow—making my way through the maze of trees. And I'd ended up here. Of course I was here. I'd come back to my beginning. To the place they'd found me almost thirteen years ago.

Trees still bore the scorch marks—as if they'd survived an explosion, at least that's what the fire department had said. The girl who walked unscathed out of an inferno—that was me. And after years of floating from foster home to foster home, I'd made my way back to my roots.

I sank to the ground, buried my face in my hands, and let sobs wrack my body. That vision or memory or whatever it was had been too hard to stave off. I almost hadn't made it. And I'd caused so much damage to get free. The Fieldses would never forgive me for this.

A stick snapped. I wiped tears off my face and looked around, heart revving into a faster beat. "Who's there?"

Probably some deer or rabbit . . . right? I rubbed my hands over my upper arms and stood, peering through the trees to catch any sign of movement. Nothing. But I heard a shuffle behind me, coming from deeper in the woods.

Yeah. Not staying around for whatever that was. I tore off back toward the road, my shoes hitting uneven ground. Crunching twigs and underbrush. I tripped, again aware of how insanely bizarre it was that I'd made it this far into the woods while blinded by a fake memory.

Why couldn't I be normal?

"Ava!" My name filtered through the forest, and that hope I'd trampled during my run dared to rise.

I stopped dead in my tracks. "Mr. Fields?" I whispered his name to myself first. Then I shouted, "Mr. Fields!"

"Ava!"

Was that Mrs. Fields too?

I stood there a moment, listening to their voices pierce the night. They . . . they'd come after me? My stupid, stupid hope grew wings.

Something behind me hissed, and I turned toward the sound. A deep growl gave me goosebumps, and a creature shrieked. Nope. Not staying for the witching hour. I raced toward the road again, but a snarl, loud and rumbling, filtered through the trees. Underbrush crunched.

"Dave? Jean?"

A throaty snort responded. Then thumping footsteps. My heart jumped as something crashed from the darkness between branches. I ran.

I was imagining this, right? This wasn't real, right? Nothing was chasing me. Right? I risked a glance over my shoulder.

Two yellow-beacon eyes flickered back at me. I screamed and ran faster.

In a whirlwind, I spun back to watch where I was going. A tree blocked my way. I dodged it somehow, but something caught my shoe, jerking my leg to a halt. The rest of me kept moving. Arms out to catch my fall, I slammed into and skittered over the ground. Sticks and pebbles cut into my skin. And I struggled to get free. The panting behind me grew louder. And I swore I heard a growl. Panic flooded my senses. I got free and dashed forward, half tripping over my momentum. Something roared, like a mountain lion—but they didn't have those around here.

"Ava!" I heard the sound of a car and raced toward the road, but something smashed into me. I whirled around as I skidded forward and fell to the ground.

Whatever it was galloped on, and car brakes screeched.

Headlights blinded me.

I shrieked, throwing my arms in front of my face.

Tires slid.

The SUV swerved on the dirt road.

It headed right toward me.

"Ava!"

Someone's hand gripped my arm and yanked me backward. I tumbled into another human being. Unyielding arms squeezed me close and guided me away from the inevitable crash.

The awful crunch and squeal of bending metal ripped through the night. I peered through the arms shielding me to see the SUV slam into a tree sideways. No. No, no, no. I knew that car. And I glimpsed the driver. New fear—primal—gripped me. I screamed Dave's name and pushed against the wet T-shirt of whoever protected me. His hold encircled me and pushed me closer to the ground. Shards of metal and glass rained against leaves and tree trunks, leaving gashes in the bark. Pieces had to be hitting the guy who held me. I closed my eyes and covered my ears. This could not be happening.

"Dave!" I didn't recognize my hoarse voice until my outburst hung in the humid air.

An instant later, my protector let go and pressed a phone into my hand. It was ringing.

I looked up, for the first time catching his face. Sweaty, brown hair. The same Mercy Falls T-shirt he always wore out running. He was missing his signature geek glasses, but I knew those piercing blue eyes.

Wyatt. Wyatt Wilcox.

The guy from the vision.

Of course he'd be running tonight too.

He pointed to the phone. "It's 911. Get out of the road." Then he raced toward the wreckage. Fresh blood on the back of his T-shirt glistened in the streetlight.

"911, what's your emergency?"

"I—I just witnessed a car crash." I tried to stand, but my whole body shook, and I knelt in the packed dirt. Something sharp bit into my knee. I shifted my position, too weak to rise on shaky legs.

"Miss, is anyone hurt? Where are you?"

Her barrage of questions continued, along with that soothing voice of hers. I couldn't form words. I had to see if my foster father was alive.

Wyatt pulled the door to the SUV, and it snapped off with a huge *crack*. A bloody arm reached out of the vehicle and grabbed Wyatt's shirt.

"Hey, Coach Fields." Wyatt calmed him. "Just relax, and don't move. Okay? Help is coming."

Help was coming. My stomach roiled.

The Fieldses would never forgive me now. And I couldn't blame them.

DRIED BLOOD I'D FAILED TO SCRUB AWAY remained underneath my fingernails from holding Mr. Fields's hand. I gripped the paper coffee cup, watching the liquid tremble with my shaking. My pulse pounded in my throbbing knee—from where I'd knelt on a shard of glass or something—keeping me aware of the slow passage of time. The heavy smell of antiseptic stung my nostrils every time a nurse walked past. How long was Jean going to keep me waiting out here before they told me what state Mr. Fields was in?

This was all my fault.

The fight. The visions. The running away—again. And they'd actually come after me.

I could almost imagine them as my parents. Almost allow myself to hope the word "adoption" would come up. But after tonight, that dream was dead.

I always ruined everything.

"It's not your fault," Wyatt's steady voice reminded me for the third time.

How did he keep doing that? Knowing when I started blaming myself.

I looked at him, sitting next to me, watching me with those big blue eyes—brighter in this light. I don't think I ever noticed the color behind his glasses before I'd seen him in that vision. Then again, I'd never really looked.

His elbows rested on his knees; his hands cupped together under his chin. Red stained the front of his shirt where Mr. Fields had grabbed him. He wore a hoodie now that covered most of it. He zipped it up higher.

I stopped staring and focused on my coffee cup. "It *is* my fault."

"Something was chasing you. That's what caused Coach Fields to swerve. Not you."

"But then I made it worse."

He tipped his head up, and I followed his gaze. Jean walked toward me. I barely registered Wyatt sliding the coffee cup from my hands as I sprang out of my chair. "How is he?"

Jean wrapped her arm around me. Her red-rimmed eyes made it clear she'd been crying. "Dave's going to be okay. He cracked a few ribs, and they cleaned and stitched up the gash in his arm. He's really lucky."

"Does he hate me?" My voice shook.

Jean smoothed my hair and squeezed my hand. "Oh, sweetie, of course not." She smiled sadly and brushed my tangled hair out of my face. "I think you should head home and get some rest."

My throat felt tight. "But Mr.—"

"Is asleep now. He'll be here till tomorrow."

"I'm so sorry!"

Jean pulled me into a hug. "This wasn't your fault, okay? Something was chasing you."

"But . . ." My heart stuttered in my chest. Who told her that? I—I'd been so shaken when she and Dave showed up at the crash site. And the ambulance came. And I'd been swept off into Wyatt's car—which he'd said wasn't far away—and he'd followed Jean and the ambulance . . . Wyatt must have told her everything while we were still at the scene. I didn't remember speaking in coherent sentences.

Jean extended her hand, and Wyatt shook it. I didn't realize he'd followed, but knowing he stood behind me made me relax for some reason.

She motioned to me, but her gaze stayed on Wyatt. "I'm glad you were with her. She's been insisting that she's not running alone when she takes off at night, but I had my doubts."

"Oh, I—" I stopped myself. This could be good. If they thought every time I raced out of the house for a "run" that I was meeting Wyatt and not actually alone . . .

"Jean, this is Wyatt. He's a friend from school." I glanced over my shoulder in time to catch Wyatt raise his eyebrows. I stared at him, pleading.

He recovered quickly. "Nice to see you again, Mrs. Fields."

"We know Wyatt." Jean smiled at me like she knew something more was going on between us. "He used to play on the lacrosse team." She patted his arm. "We've missed you."

Right. He'd called Mr. Fields *coach*.

"I'll give you a ride home, Ava. Just give me a minute to settle things here." Jean's voice wavered.

"I-I can take her home—if you need to stay, I mean." Wyatt looked at me. "If-if you want."

I glanced at Wyatt. There was no reason for him to be stuck in this mess. But I was still shaken, and having him here helped. Perhaps because he'd protected me. I caught myself staring at him, and my face flushed as I turned away.

Memories of the accident came careening back. Cars screeching, metal bending, glass shattering. I squeezed my eyes closed.

"I'll go home with you, sweetheart." Jean wrapped me in a hug, and my knees weakened.

"No. I'm okay." A lump in my throat made my voice squeak. Dave was her husband. She should be here with him. And I really didn't need anyone. "You stay. I'll be fine."

She looked at Wyatt. "Will you stay with her? Just until we get home." What?

"I—yeah." Wyatt looked at me, eyebrows raised as if asking what I thought. "If that's what you want, Ava."

"Umm, sure. Thanks." I swallowed the lump in my throat and turned to Jean. "And thank you." I didn't really know what else to say besides "for not kicking me out tonight."

"Take Dave's keys. I have mine." She dug them out of her purse. "And thank you." She smiled sadly as she passed the keychain over.

Wyatt tipped his head toward the exit sign, as if asking whether I was ready. I nodded and followed him to the parking garage. The stupid pain in my knee made me walk a little slower. I needed to get peroxide on that. No way I'd ask here, though. They'd likely put me in a room and make me see a doctor. I'd had enough poking and prodding as the girl who'd walked away from the inferno to remember that I hated hospitals. Thank goodness my black pants hid any evidence of blood.

Wyatt leaned a little closer. "If you don't want me to stay at the house with you, then I'll just go home. If—if that's what you want. I won't tell if you don't."

I glanced over at him. Took in his lean, surprisingly muscular frame, the concern shining in his expression. "You were spectacular tonight."

His eyes met mine and seemed to smile. "You actually shouldn't run alone—especially at night."

"Are you seriously lecturing me right now? Because I've seen you running alone on numerous occasions."

"You've seen me?" He seemed surprised.

"Is that why you don't wave back?"

"That's a wave? Because I thought it was just the way you let your hands flop all over when you run."

"I do not let my hands flop all over." I made to shove him, but his arms flew up protectively to block me, so I refrained. "Good reflexes."

He shrugged.

"Thank you for helping my foster—er—Dave."

"Anyone would have done what I did."

"Anyone? No. I don't think so. You were—amazing." Images of Dave out of it and panicking shot through my mind. Wyatt had calmed him. Gotten him to relax. Gotten me to relax when I saw my foster dad all banged up and bloody in the car. "And thanks for not ratting me out to Jean—about running alone."

"*Amazing* is overselling it. But you're welcome." One side of his mouth curved up in a smile.

Wyatt Wilcox. I'd seen him around school enough. Easy target for bullies, but he seemed nice. "Why don't you play lacrosse anymore?"

He looked a little surprised by my question but brushed it off with another shrug. "Not really my scene now."

"Not good enough?" I shot him a smirk to let him know I was teasing. "Let me guess. Your arms flop all over when you run, so they benched you."

His chuckle radiated warmth . . . and carried the small edge of an almost growl in it that I found surprisingly pleasant. "I suppose I deserved that."

I laughed, and it felt good. Like something wound tight inside me uncoiled.

The parking garage was pretty empty, making finding Wyatt's ancient Toyota easy. He clicked the unlock button, and the car's lights flashed. Memories of tonight rushed back. Headlights swerving. Metal bending. Glass shattering. Shaking, I looked down at my hands. The bloodstains on my shirt, brown in the pale-yellow light of the parking garage, stole my breath.

My thoughts started spinning. What I was seeing—my hands, Dave's blood—changed like someone shook me back and forth so hard I couldn't focus. Not again. Not right now. My knees grew weak, and then I didn't feel anything. Cut off from everything around me except my thought. Then I saw it. Another vision. One of those strange memories. Not mine. Someone else's. But I got to play the main character.

I was staring at my hands—but they couldn't be mine, right?— and someone's blood. Lots of blood, dark and wet. And I was crying someone's name over and over while I knelt beside a boy I didn't know. He lay on the grass, motionless. My throat burned. I could barely breathe. And something deep inside of me ached, as if my heart had been torn to pieces. Shredded. Hot tears coursed down my cheeks in the weird vision, but I felt them.

*"Cade! Don't you die, Cade. Caderyn, I'll never forgive you if you leave me!"*

Even though it wasn't my memory, the pleading voice within it was mine.

# 3

## CADE

I LEANED BACK AGAINST THE Challenger's passenger seat and cracked one eye open to glance at the guy driving. Nick. I remembered his name was Nick. I remembered what he looked like—I even had memories of him as a much younger kid. The thing was, none of these memories came from my lifetime— I'd only met Nick three weeks ago.

"How's your head, Caderyn?" Nick asked as he guided the Challenger around a turn headed toward the dark, gaping mouth of a cemetery.

"It's Cade." I sat up. "A cemetery? You sure this is the place?"

"This is the place." He pulled the car forward past the sign and turned off his headlights.

"What are you doing? You can't see a thing!"

Nick didn't take his eyes off the road. "I can see."

"Where are we?"

"A cemetery."

"I meant what city."

He chuckled. "Little beach town near Lake Michigan. Where the water's salt-free and freezing for at least half the year."

"Haven Beach?"

He paused a beat. "Yeah."

Of course he'd bring me here. I knew this place. Well, I knew it in name. I'd been found here. I squinted and peered out the windshield. The sliver of a moon did little to light our way. "I'm pretty sure being in a cemetery after dark is illegal."

"Since when does that bother you?" Nick eased the car down a slope that could not possibly be a real roadway and parked.

"Since never, but how do you know that?"

"I told you. I'm your brother."

So he'd said. Eight years older. "Yeah. I remember that much."

"You do?"

I held up my hand to stop that train of thought. "Okay, wrong word choice. I remember you telling me, but no, I don't recall you being my brother."

We sat in silence for a minute, each staring at one another. Well, I thought Nick was looking at me, but the dark made it hard to tell. Oddly enough, it seemed as though the warm glow of morning might be starting to leak onto the horizon. That, or my eyes were adjusting really well.

A sudden thought made me sit up straight. "Can I . . . do I have superpowers or something?"

Nick laughed. A real honest laugh, and it sounded so familiar. Comforting in a strange way. "You can see me?"

The more I focused, the more I could see. Weird. My heart pounded, and I couldn't stop staring. I breathed in deep to try to calm my nerves so Nick wouldn't notice. "Y-yeah."

"You don't remember this place yet?" Nick motioned with his chin for me to peer out the windshield.

Towering trees stretched over weathered and crooked gravestones. The place had a kind of peaceful feel to it. But I didn't remember—oh no. A wave of pain, like a splitting headache, pulsed into my skull. Stronger with each heartbeat until I buckled over and cupped my head in my hands. The pain settled behind my right eye and reached pulsing veins over the whole side of my head as a vision infiltrated my brain. Great. Here we go again. I hoped Nick had a puke bucket handy.

The visions always came with sudden vertigo—and they hurt.

Then I saw myself. My hands, covered with dirt, wrapped around a wooden handle. I stabbed a shovel into the ground, and the tip sank deep. I wiped sweat off my brow. Brow? Where the heck had that word come from? Nick worked beside me. He looked younger, and his clothes . . . What was he wearing? Something from the 1800s? These visions just got weirder. And more painful. *Breathe through it.*

Thankfully, it drifted away, taking the throbbing ache with it. Eyes closed, I leaned back against the seat again. Then I cracked one eye open.

Nick sat there, puke bucket in one hand and a water bottle in the other. I could clearly make out the deep crease between his eyebrows that belonged to his concerned face. I knew this because something in my brain said I'd seen the expression a million times before. Yet I also knew—logically—I'd never seen it before three weeks ago.

He handed me the water bottle.

"No thanks."

"It usually helps you when you're hydrated."

In that case, I downed half the bottle. Then I faced my brother. "How much do you remember?"

"Everything." He paused and smiled. "I think."

"For how long?"

"It took some time to sort the memories and get myself in a position to find you. So I got a steady job and the house. And now I have to wait for your memories to start returning."

"And Ava?"

"She turns seventeen in a few months—same as you—so she should start remembering any day now."

I glanced out the windows again, simultaneously dreading the memories and wishing they would hurry up and return. "And we just look for the girl buckling over in pain every few hours?"

Nick winced.

Even if I only just started remembering him, I knew my brother was hiding something. "What?"

"You're the only one who gets the headaches."

Perfect. "What does that mean?"

A smile lit Nick's eyes. "It means you're a wimp."

"Shut up." I punched my brother's rock-solid arm. "You never answered the superpower question."

Nick laughed again. "Cade, you were born to hunt monsters. Don't you think you were also granted some special skills?"

This very strange situation just got a lot cooler. "So, all those weapons in the trunk. We get to actually use them?"

His smile grew contagious. "Do you *remember* using any of them?"

I shook my head, but I wouldn't mind having those memories back right now.

"I thought this would be a good place for a lesson. Just let me know if you start having a memory."

"A lesson? As in, you're going to teach me?"

"Yes."

"Sweet. Let's start with the nunchucks."

"No way. We start with those, and you'll have more than your memories giving you a headache."

"AVA?"

Wyatt's voice called me out of the strange memory, and I realized I'd leaned against his car to remain vertical. My pulse raced, and my hand left a sweaty print on the dull reddish hood.

Wyatt stood next to me, his eyes searching my face. "You okay?"

I shook my head but pushed myself off the car. Had I said anything? Done anything weird? How long had I blanked? I stared at him, willing him to answer those questions even though I'd never ask them aloud.

He didn't.

I swallowed, realizing my mouth was dry. "Yeah. I think I'm just tired." I held out the keys with a trembling hand. How could I get this weird memory thing to stop? What was wrong with me? Suddenly, I wanted nothing more than to be as far away from this hospital as possible.

He guided me to the passenger side. Then he opened my door, watching me the whole time. "You sure you're okay?"

I certainly wasn't okay, but I wasn't ready to share this information with anyone.

"I'm fine." I slid into the car, ignoring the stab of pain in my knee, and he closed the door behind me.

The ride to my foster parents' house remained quiet except for the radio. But each of Wyatt's glances in my direction spoke volumes. I just didn't know what they said. He either thought I might stab him if he looked away for too long, held honest concern for me, or guessed I might pass out and didn't feel like carrying me inside if I were a heavy sleeper—which I wasn't. At least the ride lasted long enough for me to calm my jittering nerves.

He pulled into the driveway, and I pushed the garage door opener from Jean's key fob. Ajax's monster German shepherd head popped up between the curtains in the front window.

Wyatt pulled the car into the garage and turned off the ignition.

"You don't have to stay," I said without making eye contact.

"O-kay."

It almost sounded like a question.

Neither of us moved to exit the car, and I took a chance and gazed up at him. I didn't need him to stay. I was fine on my own, which no one seemed to understand. But I sort of wanted him to stay. Tonight's events had left me shaken.

His eyes flicked to the door leading into the house. "Are you going in?"

I should, but I stayed rooted.

"Ava?"

"Yes. Thank you." I unbuckled my seatbelt as Wyatt popped out of the car.

Before I could open my door, he got it. I stepped out and looked up at him, rubbing my arm. "S-so you're leaving?" Why did I suddenly not want him to?

He paused for a heartbeat, a slight squint to his concerned expression told me he was having as difficult a time reading me as I was him. "Do you need me to stay?"

Need? No. I didn't *need* anything from anyone ever. That was the point of everything. "I can't ask you to do that. It's getting late. How far away do you live?"

"It's no trouble. I'm two blocks away."

"Oh." Duh. That explained why we ran in the same places.

He offered me a strange smile. "You sure you're—"

"Don't ask if I'm okay again. I'm not. You were there tonight. It's not something you can just be okay with. But I'll be fine."

"Good enough." He seemed to want to say more but then closed his mouth and shook his head.

"What?"

He let out a nervous laugh. "Mrs. Fields wanted me to make sure you're all right, so how about I just . . . leave you my number?"

I leaned back against the car. The garage lights had started to dim, but I could still see his shy expression and the slight reddening on the tips of his ears. One seemed to stick out from his head slightly more than the other, giving him an endearing and perfectly imperfect look. The garage door closed on its own, the lights blinking out. I could still make out his silhouette.

"Wyatt?"

"Yes?" In the dark I could hear the smile in his voice. I walked to the wall, and in my fumbling to find the light switch, I accidentally hit the door-open button. The lights turned on again anyway. I faced him. "Is that an attempt to give me your number?"

He laughed nervously and rubbed the back of his neck while he studied the ground. "Did it work?" He glanced up at me.

I shouldn't get attached to anyone. But I was nearly seventeen. I'd likely be on my own in a year. Maybe it was time to start making relationships that might last. Not that this one would. Just the thought made the possibility of making friends more real.

Something about him made me feel comfortable. I pulled out my phone. "What's the number?"

His eyes widened for a moment, then he rattled off the number, and I entered it into my phone.

"You going to call me with yours?"

I pocketed my phone and smiled. "If I need to."

"Fair enough." He grinned, and something inside me melted. "Night, Ava." He headed around to the driver side of his car as the light started to dim again.

I stared at his back as he walked away, and a memory slammed into me—one of my own. He'd run to Dave's mangled car, and I'd seen blood on his T-shirt. He'd shielded me. He wore his hoodie now, but I distinctly remembered seeing blood. Why hadn't he said anything? Did he hate hospitals, too? I couldn't let him leave injured—I clutched my hands to my chest, and my throat tightened—especially if he'd been hurt on my behalf. I picked up my cemented feet and followed him. His dark-blue hoodie made it hard to tell if any blood had soaked through.

"Wait, Wyatt."

He paused, expression expectant.

A deep, ferocious barking came from the house, Ajax keeping watch.

I stepped in front of Wyatt. "You got hurt at the accident site."

"I'm not hurt."

Something heavy seemed to settle in my stomach. "I saw the blood on your shirt."

He unzipped the hoodie to reveal darkened blood on the front of his T-shirt. "Coach's blood got on me. I—I didn't get hurt."

Not possible. I glanced down at my throbbing knee. The black yoga pants hid signs of a wound, but I'd knelt in shards of car parts that had pelted him as he'd shielded me. There was no way he'd escaped injury. Why would he lie? My heart beat faster. I nodded slowly and darted behind him. Sure enough, a couple spots of dried blood on his hoodie called his bluff. "There's blood on your shirt. You afraid of a little hydrogen peroxide?"

He whirled around, facing me and backing up a step, skittish suddenly. "Ava, I'm fine."

The sensation of tiny pinpricks flushed through my veins, and I felt dizzy. I had seen the blood. I'd—black spots started to overtake my vision. He wouldn't lie about this, would he?

He faced me and gripped my upper arms, offering steady support. "Ava?"

Slowly, the spots started to clear, and I stared into those eyes. What was wrong with me? Had I imagined that, too? I backed away from the comfort of his touch. "My mistake. Everything happened so fast."

A crease formed between his eyebrows. "You sure you're okay alone?"

"Yeah." I pointed my thumb over my shoulder. "I should get Ajax to calm down."

Wyatt studied me through squinted eyes. "He's not barking anymore."

Right. Of course not. I swallowed through the tightening in my throat. "Okay. I'll see you tomorrow?"

He nodded once, still watching me like I might topple over. "You call me if you need anything. Okay?" He smiled, weak and unsure.

Need anything. Yeah. What? A sanity check? Absolutely. But not something I wanted to share with anyone, no matter how comfortable they made me feel. I managed a strangled answer. "I will."

It seemed to appease him enough to reluctantly get in his car and leave, but he knew something was up, which made the need to figure it out before Jean got home doubly urgent.

# 5

CADE

MY ARM STRAINED AS I HELD THE BOW
and arrow steady. Aimed at the target Nick had placed against a
crooked tree between two crumbling headstones.

"Now." Nick's voice remained calm, but I nearly jumped. My shot
went wide.

Dang it. Not that I expected to be good my first time, but something
in my competitive nature *wanted* to rub Nick's nose in a bull's-eye.

Nick chuckled, aggravating the desire to get it right this time.

I lowered the weapon and turned on him. "You try shooting arrows
at a target in the dark!" As soon as I said it, I regretted my challenge.

Nick simply held out his hand for the bow. I smacked it into his
palm. Smoothly, with practiced skill, he raised the weapon, nocked
and arrow, and held. "Say when."

Good. At least he'd give me the chance to wait until his arm was
shaking and then yell "now" loud enough to startle him. I opted for
"Fire when ready."

With a soft hiss and a hard *thwap,* the arrow found its target.

Dead center.

Of course.

He handed the bow back to me. "You used to be a better shot."

"Ha. Ha." Grumbling, I raised the weapon. Took aim.

"Breathe in. Hold. Then out." Nick's voice became a piece of my concentration, and I closed my eyes while I drew in a breath. I felt the foam grip against the crook of my thumb. Felt my muscles pull back the arrow. I'd never done this before, but I *knew* this feeling. I couldn't explain it.

My eyes popped open, and instead of focusing on the competition, I let myself *feel* what I was doing.

"Now."

This time, my brother's command was the fire at the end of a fuse. I let the arrow fly.

*Thwack!*

"Yeah! That's what I'm talking about!" I pivoted to give my brother a high five. He put his hand up to meet mine. "Did you actually just smile?"

"Get your arrows." He nodded toward the target, but the smile stayed. "And do it again."

For whatever reason I wanted to make sure that tiny show of pride in my brother's grin would be the first of many. Three bull's-eyes coming up.

I jogged toward the target and gathered those arrows first, then went for the one that had missed. As I bent down to pick It up, marveling at the pure awesomeness of my newfound night vision, something *whooshed* by me. Every hair on the back of my neck stood straight.

Slowly, I plucked the arrow from the gravel. *No sudden movements.* The thought pulsed through my brain like a mantra.

"Cade?"

I turned to look over my shoulder and nearly jumped. Nick was closer than expected. His eyes scanned the tree line around the graveyard.

"Did you sense it?" he asked.

"What is *it*?"

"Not sure yet. But it's close. Help me." He started back toward the car.

I jogged to catch up. Nick opened the trunk and handed me a shovel.

That earlier vision flashed through my thoughts, but I didn't want to dwell on it. A memory right now would not be a great idea—not if whatever-*it*-was still lurked in the shadows.

I held up the shovel. "What's this for?"

Nick's answer was to walk twelve paces from a massive oak tree and stab the ground with his shovel. I followed suit. So it was going to be just like that stupid vision.

Nick excavated his side of the hole twice as fast. Every time I dumped a shovelful of dirt onto my growing mound, it seemed like Nick's pile had collected twice the amount.

I wiped sweat off my forehead. "What are we digging for?"

Just then, his shovel thudded into something.

Together, we pulled out an ancient-looking—well, there was no other way to describe it than *treasure chest.* What the actual heck?

Nick unwrapped cloth from a padlock, then pulled a key from his pocket.

"This is so cool." I couldn't stop myself from saying it. And I didn't care. My life had just gotten infinitely better.

The lid squealed as Nick folded it back, allowing me to peer inside.

"Whoa! It's an antique armory!"

Nick smirked. "I'm gonna need you to curb the excitement just a little."

"Why?"

"Because," his face grew serious, and I decided my brother might be a real-life Batman, "we're going hunting, and I need your head clear."

"Aww, yeah." I rubbed my hands together. "What are we hunting?"

"A wraith." He started pulling supplies from the chest. "And you're going to do exactly as I tell you." He paused to give me stern eye contact.

He officially needed someone to loosen him up a bit. But I wasn't gonna play Robin for long. Sidekick wasn't really my style. I'd be his equal soon. The Nightwing to his Bat. And it looked my chance to prove myself had arrived.

I STEPPED INSIDE AND DROPPED JEAN'S keys into the drawer of the little table by the door, trying to make sense of everything. My mind had captured a clear picture of blood on Wyatt's shirt. So how had he walked away unharmed? My hands shook. Was I remembering things that hadn't happened during my own life now? I swallowed as my throat started to squeeze. What was wrong with me?

Ajax nuzzled into me, sniffing like I was his lifeline to information. I wandered into the Fieldses' stainless-steel-everything kitchen and grabbed a half-empty gallon of milk from the fridge. Ajax's nose seemed glued to me.

I pushed his huge head away, more focused on my own thoughts than anything else. "I get it. I smell like blood. Okay. I'll shower. Just let me have a drink of something." I set a glass on the counter, and he whined. "I'm sorry, boy. I just—" What I'd seen had to be explainable. Right? I climbed onto the counter to get myself a tall glass from the top shelf. "Ouch." Sharp pain stabbed my knee.

I jumped down, glass in hand. It banged against the granite countertop and shattered. Ears laid back, Ajax raced out of the room. My hands shook as I stared at broken glass on the floor. Light reflected in every piece, magnifying the mess. The shards had boxed me against the cabinets, except I'd broken a house rule and still wore my shoes.

I stared at the mess and rubbed trembling hands over my face. Could nothing go right? I just needed sleep. And for Dave to come home. When Jean found out he'd skidded because of my running into the street, she hadn't even been mad at me. She'd comforted me. Told me it wasn't my fault. That I couldn't control wild animals. That it was an accident.

I sank into a crouch, absently picking up the big pieces, and my knee hurt again. Surprised at the amount of pain, I planted my palm on a glass shard as I tried to stop myself from falling. Seriously?

I pried the glass out of my hand and grabbed a paper towel for the blood that gushed out. Then I checked my knee. A shiny silver piece of metal had embedded in the cut. That needed to come out. I headed to the bathroom for tweezers.

Every touch sent a twinge though my knee, but I pulled. The metal slid free, and blood oozed, covering my exercise pants even worse—thank goodness for black. A drip of red rolled down my shin.

I dabbed the paper towel from my hand against my knee. It already felt better. Too bad I didn't. I pressed my back against the wall and sank to the floor, finally letting the buildup of trapped tears free. Ajax sat with his massive head on his paws, staring at me from the hallway. Who knew German shepherds could be so intuitive?

"Sorry I scared you, boy. It's just you and me tonight."

He whimpered and came closer, nudging me.

I cleared my eyes. "I bet you have to go out."

He spun in a tight circle.

"I'm sorry, bud." That's what I got for not taking care of the dog, like, ever. But to be fair, he didn't like me much when I first got there. Still holding the paper towel against my knee with my injured hand, I headed back to the kitchen where the mess on the floor stared me in the face.

This was going to be a long night.

I opened the side door, and Ajax shot out like a black-and-tan streak of lightning. I sighed. I'd just patch myself up first, then I'd take care of the glass.

Gingerly, I removed the reddened paper towel from my knee. It looked to have stopped bleeding at least. I threw it away on my way back to the half bath and glanced in the mirror. Holy crap. I looked awful. Bags under my eyes, tear streaks on my cheeks, and frizzy wisps of my hair had escaped my ponytail, the humidity molding them into a bizarre golden halo. Wyatt had certainly gotten a good dose of imperfect Ava tonight.

And still he'd stuck around. Made sure I was okay. Seemed to genuinely care.

I turned on the water and placed my blood-covered hand beneath the faucet. Gently, I washed the dried crimson patch away . . . and saw nothing. No cut. I blinked. There had been blood everywhere. Cuts like that didn't just disappear.

My veins froze. They had on Wyatt.

A shiver raced through me, starting with my scalp.

How could this be? I stared at my hand. Pressed against it. No pain. This wasn't real. This couldn't be happening. I could hardly breathe. Had . . . had Wyatt done something to me?

I checked through the tear in my black pants and stared at my reddened knee. Dried blood but no gash.

My breaths came shallow. My hands wouldn't stop shaking. What was going on?

Knuckles white, I gripped the bathroom counter as I fished my cell phone out of the front pocket of my hoodie. Wyatt's phone number stared back at me.

My knees grew weak, and I lowered to the cold tile floor. What if something weird had happened to both of us at the crash site? Maybe Wyatt didn't know what had happened to him, either. Maybe he felt just as confused.

I should call him.

No. He was in bed by now. Right?

Not if he was experiencing the same thing.

First, I needed to calm down. I put my phone back into my pocket and turned on the faucet, scrubbing my hands clear of blood for the second time tonight. Pink water rinsed down the drain.

Then everything shook.

With wet hands, I gripped the cold edges of the sink. It turned into a bucket—a wooden bucket filled with water. Not another memory that wasn't mine. Not now.

I tried pushing it away, but it seemed to be a fire in my mind that could not be quenched. And it overtook everything.

Dark water reflected the flickering light of a lantern. I plunged a reddened cloth below its surface, lukewarm on my hands, and scrubbed out the blood. Then I brought it out, squeezed excess wetness away, and laid it against a gaping wound on a man's chest.

He lay on the ground, moaning quietly. And I knelt in the grass, uneven clumps of dirt mounds pressing into my knees, my shins. It felt so real.

He shivered, and I touched his arm gently, trying to soothe him with a soft "shh, shh" as I dabbed the cloth against the man's gushing blood. It came out of a hole. Like something from a bullet. My stomach roiled. I didn't want to see the man's face. I didn't want to see any more of this memory. I crushed my eyes closed and prayed for it to pass.

All I saw was blackness behind my eyes.

Breathing in, I opened them. No more weird memory. But my blood still raced through me. My stomach still churned. That memory might not be real, but this was: I had self-healed. My knee and hand were injury-free. There was no walking away from that. Cold seeped into my veins and through my core. What was wrong with me?

My mind searched for answers. Maybe Wyatt sat freaking out at home, too—maybe he was experiencing other people's memories.

As if in slow motion, I pressed his number.

It rang.

My insides squeezed. What was I going to say to him? "Hey, I'm suddenly a self-healing freak, any ideas?" No way. I pulled the phone away from my ear, and my thumb went to press the end call button.

"Hello?"

Crap. Why was it so hard to breathe?

He sounded sleepy, groggy. Of course, I'd woken him. Now it would be rude to hang up. Right? Why did it matter so much? Why did I even care? Why—

"H-hello? Ava?"

I brought the phone near my ear. "S-sorry to wake you."

"No, don't be. You didn't. Are you okay?"

His voice calmed my shaking. Evened my breathing. Why did it feel like I'd talked to him a million times before? I sank to the floor, leaning my back against the door of the bathroom vanity, and settled onto the fluffy gray bathmat, not even caring that I sat in the bathroom.

"Ava, are you okay?" His voice held a slight edge of worry.

I nodded, my throat thick. I was not okay, but I didn't know how to say anything. "I . . . umm . . . I know we hardly know each other. I just . . . didn't know who else to call."

"You can always call me. Okay?"

Really? "Thanks." And for the first time during this horrid evening, I felt like everything might turn out okay.

"We can talk as long as you want. And if you need me to come over, just say the word."

"What word?" I giggled—I actually giggled. Chalked that up to the deluge of emotions I'd experienced tonight.

"Any word." He chuckled, and it brought a smile to my face.

Warmth coursed through me. It was like drinking hot cocoa after caroling in the snow. I wanted to say *the word*. But before tonight, I hadn't said anything to Wyatt Wilcox outside of handing him his books off the floor a bunch of times after someone had knocked them out of his arms. These strange feelings had to have more to do with the strangeness of tonight than anything else.

"Have you decided on a word yet?" His voice was soft again.

I pulled my knees up to my chin. "Like a code word?"

That chuckle. "Sure."

"And does it work anytime, or just tonight?"

"Anytime." He answered so fast, and his voice was so serious, I almost believed he'd drop everything for me. Almost.

A deep bark resounded outside. Ajax. Phone to my ear, I raced to the back door. But it wasn't Ajax's "let me in" bark. Way too deep for that, and he wouldn't stop. I opened the door. Cool air rushed in, slammed into my face, and whipped around my hair. Two figures—hooded men—raced away from the house.

"Ajax, here!" He chased after them, his tail up and ears forward, that booming bark in his throat.

One of them stopped and pulled something from his pocket.

"Ajax!" I yelled.

My phone clattered against the kitchen floor.

The guy looked at me, his face hidden under the black hood. Then he ran.

"Ajax," I called again, breathless this time. My throat raw.

He came running. Limping. What had they done to him?

"Come on, boy." I grabbed his collar and led him inside. Bloody paw prints scattered over the kitchen floor everywhere he stepped.

My heart thrummed in my chest. Great night to be home alone. Creeps in the yard. If Ajax hadn't been there—I hugged the big shepherd's neck.

"Good boy. Let's see that paw."

There was a tear in the pad. A pretty good one, too. Like he'd stepped on something sharp. I'd have to check outside in the morning, because no way was I going to look now.

Blood dripped out of his wound. He started licking it, and I wanted to puke. "Let me get the first-aid kit. No. Let me set the alarm, then I'll get the first-aid kit."

His brown eyes looked at me as if he understood what I was saying. I locked the side door, raced to the front, and set the alarm. Ajax followed me, leaving a trail of blood everywhere. Then it occurred to me, as I stared at the blood spots mingled with my shattered glass, that he'd likely been cut by a shard from the kitchen.

I sighed and grabbed Ajax a treat from the container on the counter. Then I sat with my back to the cupboard—away from the glass—trying to calm my nerves. Again.

"Let me stop the bleeding, boy." I retrieved the first-aid kit and pressed gauze against his paw.

He froze, attention swiveling away from me. A low growl rumbled in his chest, and he charged the front door.

My heart thumped wildly. They were back.

# 7

## CADE

"SEE HIM?" NICK BRACED HIS BACK against the vinyl siding of one of these cookie-cutter almost mansions in the strange suburbia he'd dragged me to after "catching the scent" of something he'd called a wraith.

Perfect green lawns. Five basic home patterns. Bells and whistles galore. I'd been in a place like this once. Didn't belong then. Certainly didn't belong now—dressed head to toe in all black, carrying weapons, sneaking through manicured backyards, practically begging the neighborhood watch to come out and play.

"I've heard beggars can't be choosers," I whispered, "but a life of crime wasn't what I had in mind upon exiting the foster system."

Nick's only response was a glare over his shoulder and finger to his lips.

Right. Quiet.

I pressed my back against the same house, standing on my brother's right, holding the unloaded crossbow. He lowered his 9mm, and I peered around the corner of the house. I looked over his shoulder. I saw it all right—the reason we'd left training at the cemetery.

The man—if you could call it a man—slunk with inhuman speed toward the house. It stopped. Sniffed the air in a way that showed off its grotesquely thin form, draped beneath a cloak of black that I'd guess came straight from the Grim Reaper's closet. Then it lowered its body to a hunched position, almost on all fours. Its arms seemed too long for its body. And the animalistic way it moved sent chills skittering over my skin.

It halted and looked up. Turned its head too far around, like an owl, and stopped with Nick and me in its line of sight. Hollow, black-as-night eyes, too big to be real, locked onto me from a ghost-white face.

Heart hammering, I pressed my back against the house. "It might have seen me."

"No. It heard your pulse change."

"My . . ." Maybe Nick was right. I shouldn't have come. The little he'd told me about wraiths suddenly didn't seem like a good enough crash course. Then again, I'd insisted. I gripped the crossbow tighter as if that could calm my shaking nerves. Might as well make myself useful.

Nick looked right at me. His steady gaze telling me to calm down. "Just remember what I said, and do what you're told."

Yeah. About that. Now probably wasn't a good time to tell him I didn't usually do as I was told. Then again, his instructions—don't look into a wraith's eyes, don't hesitate, and don't let it bite—seemed totally followable.

He holstered his weapon and pulled out a golden spike. "Don't hesitate. Stay in the shadows. When I tell you to shoot, aim for the throat or between the eyes. And don't let it bite or scratch you."

Okay. The amendments were fine, too. He stared at me until I nodded. Then he headed around the side of the house. I followed, hunkering low by the porch. My hands sweating.

"Stay here." Nick hopped the porch rail. "I lost sight."

Great. So had I. As Nick hurried down the porch steps and around the house, I decided higher ground was a better idea, so I hopped the porch rail, too, silently thanking the homeowner for such a nice view of the neighborhood. But I still didn't see the monster. Or my brother.

A slight creaking sound that seemed different than the normal wind made me look up. My stomach leapt into my throat, and I managed to hold in a shocked yelp. It was right above me, stretched to fit the porch's ceiling—one thin, stringy, bone-white limb in each corner, and a black cloak, tattered along the edges, magically sticking to the ceiling. My heart jolted, and I swore as I stumbled back, pressing into the side of the house. Its unnaturally long neck extended as the haunting face—if you could call it that—lowered, encroaching on my limited space.

Those black eyes were nothing more than gaping holes in a strangely pale countenance. The dark pits widened, narrowed, even gave the impression of a cocked eyebrow, as it drew closer to me.

I pointed the crossbow at it, then realized, golden arrows or not, I shouldn't shoot at a home.

In my moment of hesitation, the creature dropped onto the porch right in front of me. Slowly, it seemed to stretch to beat my height.

I had to get out of here. But I couldn't move. Shaking, I stared at the wraith. Willed myself to breathe. I should stab it. I should most definitely stab it, but my hands seemed frozen.

I'd broken two rules now. Idiot.

From here, its skin resembled a sort of rubber. If I didn't know better, I'd think it a pale, ill-fitting mask. But it was far too expressive for that.

Two tiny slits made its "nose"—no sign of a mouth.

That was good, right? How could it bite me with no mouth?

It tipped its head, as if curious, then a strange, jagged line formed where the mouth should be. It looked as if a child drew it. Then the zigzag split open, revealing needle-sharp teeth as long as my pinkie. My pulse sped into overdrive, trying to knock me out of my trance, but it wasn't working. The wraith lunged at me, maw gaping.

Oh no. Not rule number three.

Everything inside me begged for me to move.

Something slammed into it, pushing it over the porch railing and onto the ground near the neighbor's house. Nick. He was on top of it, but the wraith snaked its way out of Nick's hold. Fast. It bent its head at an awkward angle, and that black hole opened to reveal those needle fangs. It lunged for Nick.

A spike of adrenaline shot through my body, shattering my trance. I jumped over the porch railing, golden arrow in hand. The creature locked eyes with me. That gave Nick the time he needed to swing at it with his own golden weapon—a dagger. But the wraith ducked the blow and scurried away.

My brother scrambled to his feet and gave chase, motioning for me to go around the house the other way. I did, as fast as I could, and just as I turned the corner, I saw it.

I grabbed hold of its loose, cape-like clothes as it rounded the house. Its head turned to face me, and it hissed, an unbearable sound that pierced my ears. Before I realized it, I'd let go, covering my ears and bracing myself against the side of the house. It slashed at me with curved claws growing out of thin, bony fingers, but I ducked and tripped over some stupid bush, sprawling into the neighbor's backyard and falling onto my stomach.

Thick summer grass broke my fall but swallowed my golden arrow. I fumbled to get the crossbow, but the feel of something cold on my spine made me turn. The world seemed to spin as I tried to make my weak limbs support my weight.

Never had I ever felt the urge to run like I did now. The grotesque head lurched toward me, fangs exposed.

Nick jumped between us, and the beast slashed into his side with those freakishly long nails. Not my brother! Adrenaline surged through me. I rolled to standing and found the glint of gold in the grass.

Nick grappled with the creature on the ground. Pinned it.

He held his dagger, ready to stab, but the creature contorted its body around him and stabbed my brother in the shoulder with those retractable nails.

I had to get my fingers to work or I'd never get this crossbow loaded. "Now! Cade, now!"

I secured the arrow, aimed, and shot. The arrow lodged in its skull, and the creature turned into a pool of sizzling fog, which consumed every bit of the cloak along with it.

I sank to my knees, mouth open and staring at the empty space that used to be a monster. All my muscles turned to putty. "I can't believe I made that shot."

"I can." Nick fell on his back in the grass, and the booming bark of a dog alerted me to a huge German shepherd barreling our way.

Hot tingles shot through my bloodstream, igniting me into action again. I grabbed my brother's arm. "We have to get out of here." I towed him up, and he hunched over, blood trickling from his shoulder, his side.

He faced the dog and pulled a whistle from his utility vest. He held it to his lips and blew. Though I couldn't hear a thing, the dog paused, shook its head, and let out a whine. Its owner called. This time, Nick grabbed my arm, and we ran.

"What was that?"

"Annoying noise. It usually deters dogs from chasing. It didn't hurt him." He groaned and pulled his hand away from the gash in his side.

A boulder seemed to settle in my stomach. "You need a doctor."

"I do." He smiled weakly. "But I have you."

I rolled my eyes. "I have experience in this?"

He winced. "A little."

I stood still in my tracks. "Do you . . . sense that?" Something approached. It changed the wind in just a little way that made things seem sharper. A metallic taste drifted in the air. I recalled this sensation. The scent of a monster. I headed toward it. "I smell something."

Nick grabbed my sleeve. "No."

"Yeah. I'm sure of it."

"Not that one. Not tonight."

I looked down at my brother's gushing wound. "Doctor first?"

"I just have to get the wound clean. The healing will happen on its own." He handed me the keys.

"Really?"

He slapped his hand against my back. "It's nice to have you back, Cade."

We got into the car, and I started it up. The Challenger purred like a black panther. "Okay. Where to now?" We'd already dug up a treasure chest of weapons—at the cemetery of all places—and now I'd killed my first monster. Though I was far from being Boy Wonder, I had to think I was catching on quickly.

"Home. Or as close as we'll get to it for now."

I drove five blocks under Nick's direction, wondering the entire time if I should have disobeyed him and gone to the hospital. Finally, I pulled into the dark driveway of a fairly small house—something like a cottage on the outskirts of town. Homey perhaps. Nothing like the massive dream homes we'd just visited. This place was clearly a holdover from someone unwilling to sell to the new-build company that had swept through here. And so it sat, shrouded by trees, just off the road. An outcast to the perfect village it overlooked. Seemed fitting.

Nick got out of the car and headed up the weathered steps.

I followed him outside. "Have I been here before?"

He glanced at me over the Challenger's hood. "You died here once."

## AVA

L OUD BANGING ECHOED THROUGH THE foyer. Those strange men were trying to get in. A scream welled up inside of me, but I held it in, too afraid to make a sound. Ajax slammed his front paws against the door, his deep bark matching the bangs. I stood, frozen, hoping he'd deter whoever was there.

"Ava! Ava, open up!"

My heart stuttered. Wyatt? Heat coursed through my blood again as I raced to the living room and pulled aside the heavy taupe drapes in time to watch him ram his shoulder into the door. My shoes squeaked against the wood floor as I scrambled to let him in.

"Wyatt! I'm coming." My palm was sticky with Ajax's blood as I grabbed the brushed-nickel knob and turned. The door made a cracking sound and swung open, nearly crashing into me. The alarm went off.

Ajax jumped forward, teeth bared.

"Whoa, it's okay!" I lunged for his collar.

Wyatt tumbled over the threshold and sprawled across the floor. Ajax backed up, barking. The alarm blasted around us. I punched in the code. At last, silence. I turned back, half expecting to see Ajax cornering Wyatt. Instead, he sniffed Wyatt's shoes and lay down at his feet.

"I guess he likes you." I leaned against the door, closing it while my muscles seemed to melt against my bones.

Wyatt motioned to the blood on the floor. "Are you hurt?" His eyes widened, and he looked me over.

Funny he should ask that. "No. Ajax was bleeding. I—"

"Your phone connection just cut out. I worried something had happened." His chest heaved.

"I'm sorry. I dropped it when I saw the guys in my yard." I pointed down the hall to the kitchen.

"Guys?" Wyatt clenched his jaw, and the look in his eyes darkened. He stopped petting Ajax and raced into the kitchen. Ajax and I followed.

"They're gone. Ajax does a good job of scaring unwanted people away."

"I'm sure." The skepticism in his eyes remained. He picked up my phone, the dismantled case, and the battery. "You really need a better case."

"Apparently."

"You sure you're okay?" He handed the pieces back to me. "That's a lot of blood."

"I'm fine. Really."

Glass crunched under his shoe. "Looks like you need some help cleaning up. Do you have a broom?"

"Fresh out." I shrugged, putting my phone back together.

My comment sliced the tension clean through, and Wyatt let out a startled laugh. I joined him and grabbed a broom from the closet. He took it, smile still in his eyes and started collecting the glass shards with the rough bristles. I picked up the first-aid kit and called Ajax over to me. He limped.

Wyatt paused his sweeping. "What's wrong with him?"

"I think he stepped on glass."

"Rough night, huh?" He offered a contagious lopsided smile.

"You could say that." I reached for Ajax's paw, and he stepped back. I managed to get ahold of him. "It's okay, boy. This will sting, but—" Ajax pulled his paw from me and hunkered in the corner, head down and ears laid back.

"Can I try?" Wyatt held out his hand for the gauze and peroxide.

"Umm, he's not always the nicest to strangers."

He looked over at Ajax and smiled. "We go way back."

Wyatt crouched down, and Ajax walked over, all loose and wiggly. He sat and placed his paw in Wyatt's offered hand. The look he gave Wyatt, with a wrinkle in between his huge ears, pleaded for Wyatt not to hurt him.

Wyatt sort of frowned. "Sorry, buddy, this'll hurt a little. Ava, can you hand me a bowl?"

I complied and knelt close, on the other side of the finally corralled glass mess. Something about Wyatt's calm demeanor helped me, too. He poured peroxide into the bowl and then took Ajax's offered paw. Slowly, he held the bowl up to Ajax's paw, talking softly to him. Ajax sat still while the white foam bubbled around his cut. "So, tell me something about yourself."

"Umm, you are aware he's a dog, right?"

His return chuckle was soft and deep. "I mean you, Ava." He glanced up at me, smile in his eyes.

I really liked when he said my name. "Like what?"

"Anything. Sometimes it helps to talk. Ajax can't, but he's a good listener. Aren't you, boy?"

His tail swept back and forth across the floor as he looked up at Wyatt. He leaned forward and licked the tip of Wyatt's nose.

"Apparently he likes you."

"I'm a likeable guy." He lowered the bowl from Ajax's paw and inspected the cut. "Almost done." He glanced at me. "Hand me the gauze?"

I did. Wyatt's fingers grazed mine as he took it from me. He wasn't what he seemed. Not in the slightest. At school he always kept to himself in a way that made me write him off as some awkward guy. But here, helping the dog, he was confident. More like the guy who'd shielded me from wreckage, pulled a car door off its hinges, and tried to bust down my front door to come to my rescue. Not some weakling who couldn't stand up for himself.

"Why do you let the guys at school push your books out of your hands every day?"

He paused in wrapping the gauze around Ajax's paw and glanced at me over his shoulder, a smile lighting his eyes. "Not every day. Besides, who will they pick on if not me?" This close, I caught sight of the depth of color in his eyes. Layers of blue and green and a bit of gold.

"You can't possibly mean you let them pick on you so they don't hurt someone else."

He let go of Ajax's paw. "Good boy." He patted the dog's head, and Ajax granted him another kiss. Then Wyatt faced me. "I said tell me something about yourself, Ava."

Those layers of blue mesmerized me. I had to stop staring. I picked up the bowl and set it in the sink. Now that I wasn't so close, I faced him again. "I'm parentless."

He pulled his eyebrows together as he stood and grabbed the broom. "That's a strange label. Does it define you?"

Did it? "I don't think so. The fact that I had parents who died is a big part of who I am though."

"The fact that someone loved you?"

Whoa. Close to the mark, and I wasn't in a sharing mood. "My, my, this is some deep territory."

"Sorry."

I held the dustpan on the floor, and he swept glass shards onto it. If only a shattered life could be this easily fixed.

With the glass picked up, I got to work scrubbing blood from the floor. "It's okay. I suppose I opened that door. I just didn't expect you to be so intuitive." I offered a smile.

Wyatt tossed a bloody cleaning wipe into the trash. "Well, I know a little about being parentless."

"You do? Are . . . ?"

"Adopted? Yeah."

"I didn't know." Maybe I should have. It seemed like half the population in this tiny town was adopted. My only friend in town was.

"I was young. Eight. But I lost my parents when I was four."

Four. The same age they'd found me. I'd wandered up to the edge of town, still in the shadow of the woods, with nothing but tattered clothes on my back—singed on the edges as if I'd escaped a fire—and they'd taken me to the police. No one claimed me. No one knew me. They figured my parents had died in a fire when they'd found the explosion site.

I didn't recall a thing except my name. Ava Elderson. It didn't help them find information about me or my parents. I was no one. They let me keep my name.

And then something on the edge of my mind infiltrated the corner of my memory.

Like a loose string, I pulled it, and a picture filled my head. Barefoot, wearing a singed white nightgown, I walked through the woods. This I'd seen before. My earliest memory.

"Ava." A young voice, a child's voice, called after me. "Ava, where are you going?"

"Follow the light, Cade. Follow the light."

Cade.

My heart seemed to pause then rev, like a sputtering car. That last part was new. I'd heard that name before, in a vision. Not my memory. But this one was my memory, right? And the little boy, who was he? A neighbor? A brother? Why hadn't I recalled him before?

"Ava?" Another voice overlapped my memory, and I looked up to see Wyatt very close and very concerned.

"I'm sorry." I turned toward the fridge as my face heated. I didn't want Wyatt to think it had anything to do with him. Then again, explaining that I was having memories that weren't mine might actually be a worse excuse. Unless he was having a similar experience. "I've been a terrible hostess. Do you want something to drink?" I opened the door. The refrigerator expelled cold air, at least. "We have orange juice or apple juice or—"

"Water's fine."

"No problem." I pulled the pitcher out of the fridge with one hand and reached for the cupboard with the other. My fingertips grazed something soft and warm—Wyatt's hand.

He pulled back so fast I would have thought I burned him. "Sorry." Wyatt motioned to the cupboard. "Just trying to be helpful."

I smiled my most sincere smile, recalling how he flinched earlier at the hospital when I had intended to playfully push his arm. I tilted my head, taking in his guarded expression.

"You all right?" he asked.

"What? Yeah." I turned my attention to the water.

No. Not again.

A pulse of blood sped through my system as I stared at the water. It seemed to flicker for a moment. It was a plastic pitcher. Then it was a wooden bucket. I recognized that bucket.

My hands—they were bloody. Not now. The room started to spin as I fought the stupid vision. I squeezed my eyes closed.

A strong, gentle grip latched on to my arms, steadying me, and I opened my eyes—back in the kitchen. Wyatt's concerned expression met my gaze. "You sure you're okay?"

I pressed the back of my shaking hand to my forehead as I stared into those blue eyes. "I'm just a bit rattled, I think." My words came out soft and airy.

"Maybe we should sit down?" He grabbed two glasses from the cupboard and filled them both with water. "You had a really stressful night."

Understatement.

His gentle touch on my elbow shook me of my momentary trance. Something about his touch sent strange feelings through me. I looked up at him and he dropped his hand and sort of winced. "U-unless you want me to go."

"No." The speed at which I answered surprised me. I sounded almost desperate. I kind of was. I needed to know what was happening to me, and the only person right now who might have answers was standing in front of me.

"Okay. I'll stay." He smiled, and heat spread over my skin in a wave.

I looked at the cleaned-up kitchen. At least that was done. Then I turned away, heading to the living room and trying to get my skin to cool. I pulled my hood up in case it helped block the view of my burning cheeks. Whoa. Where was this coming from?

"Have a seat." I plopped on one side of the couch, trying to look casual. Probably failing. Everything inside of me felt on edge. Guarded. How was I supposed to coax this kind of information out of him without sounding crazy?

He sat on the other end of the couch.

Slipping off my shoes and curling my legs under me, I faced him. "So tell me something about yourself, Wyatt." I tried to make my tone challenging, while keeping an edge of humor to it. After all, I was playing his game now, turning the tables.

His chuckle was deep, lyrical almost. I bet he could sing.

"Not into sharing? That's kind of a double standard." I was sure to smirk playfully, so he knew I was teasing.

That just made him laugh more, though it sounded sort of uncomfortable. "No. I just don't know what to say."

"Come on. You've got to be a man of hidden talents. Just pick one to share." I set my glass on a coaster on the coffee table and pulled my knees up, folding my hands across the tops of them. How to get him to open up?

"Hidden talents, huh? What kind of hidden talents do you have, Ava?"

"You know, like double-jointed thumbs." I rolled my thumbs, and they jumped out of their sockets with a little pop. "Amazing singing voice?" I wiggled my eyebrows to let him know I suspected that as one of his—along with the ability to self-heal. "Or something about you that no one would guess."

He cocked an eyebrow. "And what would that be?"

I shrugged. Trying to make him feel at ease was harder than I thought. "That you can list all the members of the Justice League from memory, or maybe that you secretly hate school, or that you let people knock books out of your hands so no one else gets picked on." Something in my chest warmed as I said that, and I looked right into his eyes in time to watch them round a little. He swallowed, seeming a bit more uncomfortable. Not my goal. "Maybe you're a romantic. I know . . . you probably love stargazing."

He seemed to study me with his eyes. "You didn't tell me you were so good at reading people."

"I was right?" I sat up straighter. "About which thing?"

He shook his head. "All of them."

I stared at him with my mouth open. "You're a secret romantic?"

He laughed and ducked his head. For some reason, I wanted to move closer to him. "You're different than I thought you'd be."

His gaze met mine and seemed to hold as much curiosity as amusement. "How so?"

I shrugged, pulling my knees closer. "First of all, why do you hate school? Aren't you really smart?"

"Doesn't mean I like school." He leaned down and fondled the tips of Ajax's ears. "Bullies. Cliques. Fake people. Not really worth my time."

"I get that." That was the biggest thing about going to a new place. Wading through all the fake people. "But everyone wears masks." As soon as I said it, I wanted to take it back; it was too revealing. The intense look in Wyatt's eyes—the way he really paid attention to me when I talked to him—made it strangely easy for me to open up. That unnerved me. "It's like a defense mechanism. We can't just let everyone in all the time." My first foster home landed me in a new place because I'd been too much of myself, and I wasn't what they called "a good fit."

"Well, yeah. But revealing things as you get to know someone isn't the same as pretending to be someone you aren't."

"True. It takes a level of trust for that."

He nodded.

I lowered my knees and scooted closer to him. If I'd learned one thing about trust, it was that you have to give it to get it. I wasn't going to give it, but I was good at giving the impression I trusted someone. Then, once they gave me some trust, I could reciprocate. "I was lucky you were there today. Thank you for saving me."

Eye contact achieved. "I just did what anyone in my position would do."

"No. You—you're a good person, Wyatt. Better than your average *anyone*."

The momentary lift of his eyebrows told me he didn't exactly believe that. Interesting. "No, I just—"

"Give yourself some credit."

He shook his head in what looked like a blatant denial, but then he smiled. I was about to ask him another question about the accident site. My stomach clenched. I didn't know how to jump into this conversation without sounding crazy.

Headlights pulled into the driveway.

With a clatter of claws on wood, Ajax raced to the kitchen, likely waiting by the garage door, wagging his tail.

"I guess that's my cue." Wyatt stood up and headed to the front door.

I sighed. My questions remained unanswered. At least I could continue this conversation if I could get him to trust me. "Wyatt." I said his name at the same time as he said mine.

"You first." He motioned toward me.

I lowered my hood, wanting an uninhibited view of his face. "I—thank you so much. For—for everything."

"No problem, Ava. Any time. Really. You sound the alarm, I'll be here."

"Just say the word, huh?"

He smiled. "You got it."

"But we never picked one."

His eyes lit up. "What did you have in mind?"

A word seemed to whisper in the back of my mind like a soft reminder of something nostalgic. Something that made me think of the outdoors. Beautiful stars and warm, clear nights. I doubted it meant anything, but it made me feel safe, just like Wyatt seemed to. "How about *Andromeda*."

All traces of humor left his face, and his mouth opened slowly. "You remembered?"

My heart leapt off the starting block. "Remembered what?"

He shook his head and tried a laugh, but it sounded nervous. "Never mind. I—never mind."

"Tell me."

"It was just some report I did. On Andromeda. I thought— never mind."

He thought what? I stepped closer to him. I wanted to stop him from looking so embarrassed. But he kept backing away from me. The door from the garage into the kitchen opened, interrupting everything.

# 9

## CADE

NICK FUMBLED WITH THE KEYS, AND finally the huge, dusty oak door squealed open. He leaned into it and half stumbled into the house.

I reached for him, not exactly sure how to help. "Hey, dude. Do you need—"

"Yes. There's a metal lockbox in the trunk." He tossed the keys at me and hunched over as he stepped inside, flicking on a light switch that yielded nothing. "Bring it in. Please."

I headed out to the trunk and opened it. Apparently, organization was a skill he possessed. The lockbox sat behind a wooden chest that I really wanted to open, but since Nick was bleeding out in an abandoned house, I decided not to right now. But I brought it with me.

From the bright glow on the west side of the house, I gathered he must have found a working light. The screen door slammed behind me, and Nick yelled "ouch" from around the corner. I followed the sound through the living room and kitchen and to the bathroom off the side.

I set the wooden box on the kitchen island and took the lockbox to the entrance of the bathroom. "Found your tin can."

The huge gashes on his side and shoulder looked nasty. And infected. Already? My mouth seemed suddenly dry. This looked way worse than he'd made me believe. "Are you okay? What—?"

"Wraith saliva will do that to a phoenix. It stops our healing ability. They lick their claws before they fight us." He seemed so calm.

Gross. Wait. My jaw dropped. "We really do have healing abilities?"

"Yeah. Can you open it?" He motioned to the metal box.

I complied.

"There should be a bottle of blue liquid in there marked 'Wraith.'"

I handed it to him. He pulled out the stopper with his teeth and poured a few drops onto his shirt, which he'd set aside. Then he dabbed some onto the wound. A sizzling sound followed, and he sucked in air through clenched teeth.

Morbidly curious, I could not turn away. Slowly, the bubbling skin smoothed, redness abating, and the long gashes turned into thin cuts. Then nothing but healed skin. Not even a scar.

I dropped the keys. "Y-you just healed." My voice came out at a higher pitch than normal.

He chuckled. "Yeah. That saliva stings like a—"

"I can do that, too?"

"Well . . ." He replaced the liquid, locked the box, and pocketed the keys. "Technically you can. Your powers are a little spottier than mine."

I narrowed my eyes, not liking this direction. "Define *spotty.*"

"You heal, but sometimes it takes you longer, especially during the memory phase." He tossed his shirt over his shoulder and headed out of the bathroom, which meant nearly running into me as I stood rooted in the doorway.

I stared at his back. So, that was why he'd pushed me out of the way and let the monster stab him instead. Something inside my chest felt strangely full. I didn't exactly want to latch on to that feeling, but I didn't want to forget it, either. I followed after him as he headed into the kitchen and opened a rickety fridge. The light came on, revealing a few basics.

Willingness to keep me from getting hurt aside, Nick still hadn't answered my question. "Define *longer.*"

Nick peered into the fridge and drummed his fingers on the door.

Then he pulled out two drinks. A bottle and a can. As he shut the door, the kitchen light turned on with a flicker.

I nearly jumped. Nick just glanced up at the ceiling. "You're kinda like that."

"Like what? The light?"

He looked my way and shrugged. Then he tossed me the can. I caught it. Dr Pepper. Did he know my favorite pop? Lucky guess, probably. Or we had the same taste, though he twisted the cap off a beer. Perks of being twenty-five.

Nick took a long drink. Then he pointed at the ceiling light. "I turned it on when we walked in. It just took a while to make the connection."

A long while. "Great. I'm being compared to faulty electricity or a slow-moving current."

"Listen, Cade, I'm not sure what's wrong with your powers, but sometimes they short out."

*Fabulous.* I stared at the drink in my hand. Cold against my palm.

He arched an eyebrow. "You don't want caffeine this late? I thought it didn't affect you."

"It doesn't. But a night like this clearly deserves something stronger." I nodded toward his beer.

The challenging look in his eye sparked something in me that made me want to give him a hard time. "You're underage."

"Not if you add up all the years I lived before this." I wagged my eyebrows. "By my logic, I'm old enough for alcohol."

He pointed the beer bottle at me. "By my logic you're under my care. So, no dice. And you don't have all your memories back yet, so you're still only *nearly* seventeen."

"Your logic sucks."

He chuckled and took another swig. "For you, maybe."

I rolled my eyes, opened my pop, and took a drink, then I motioned to the wooden box. "So what's in here?"

Nick walked over and unlocked it. "This box is one of our most important assets." He lifted the lid, and it opened like a tackle box with layers of stacked compartments. I peered inside while Nick pointed to different bottles and pastes. "Antivenoms, monster-reversal potions. We're immune to a lot, but the humans we protect aren't. So we keep a lot of it on hand. Just in case."

I had a feeling I should be sitting down for this, but I was in it now. And I wanted answers. "What does that even mean?"

"Well, this one here." He pulled out a bottle full of a clear liquid that clung to the sides of the glass a little more than normal water would. "It's altered werewolf saliva. You put it on the wound if someone is bitten. But you have to do it within an hour or the bite sets."

"Sets?"

"The person will become a werewolf or die."

Everything in my brain wanted to blare warning bells that this reeked of crazy. But I knew too much now. Enough to know that these bump-in-the-night things were real. I shuddered. "How do you know all of this?"

He smiled and tapped his forehead. "Memories."

"You made all this?"

"I have to re-create what's lost. But phoenixes are pretty extensive in their research and willing to share. This has been a safe house for centuries. There was a lot still buried in the secret cellar."

I shook my head and supported myself against the kitchen island. "Safe house? Secret cellar?"

Nick touched my back. "You okay?"

He was really asking whether I was about to spiral into another memory. "I'm all right. I think." I sort of laughed.

That eased the concern in his eyes at least. He half smiled. "You have a lot to remember, little brother."

"Little?" I cocked an eyebrow—I had to be a couple inches taller than him. "I think you mean *younger.*"

He granted me a grin but didn't alter his statement.

I picked up a strange stone. Translucent. Pretty, with so many shades of blue. Not a normal sapphire, but it reminded me of one. Except for the strange darker part in the middle that seemed to follow me as I moved the stone, like an eye. "What does this do?"

Nick shrugged. "I'm not entirely certain."

I frowned. "How do you *not* know?"

"It didn't exactly come with a manual." He set his empty bottle on the counter next to the sink. "I'm going to turn in. There are three rooms upstairs—they have beds. Feel free to take one. I did get clean sheets for them. You're welcome."

He held out his hand. I locked the box and tossed him the keys, noticing the lack of furniture down here. So, my brother's priorities were beer and beds. Good to know.

Nick pocketed the keys. "Tomorrow evening, we'll make copies." He opened the cupboard below the island and revealed a safe. He put the boxes inside.

"Evening? So what's the plan for the morning?"

He closed the cupboard and started up the creaky stairs. His laugh resounded off the stairwell. "You'll be sitting at a desk surrounded by the rest of Haven Beach High School's finest."

"What?" I followed him upstairs. "You expect me to go to school? I just found out that I'm this amazing monster hunter and you're sending me to school?"

"Hey, I can't get in trouble with the state. Besides, it's a way for you to make a connection with Ava."

"Me?"

"She's a junior, like you." He turned in the doorway of what looked like the biggest room in the stuffy upstairs. "And let's remember, you might know you're supposed to hunt monsters, but you barely know what it means to be a phoenix."

"So enlighten me."

"That's the plan." He headed into his room. "Tomorrow." He shut the door, but his voice still bled through. "After you find Ava."

"What makes you so sure I'll find her?"

"You always do."

"What if—"

"Just remember, when phoenixes get their memories back, it's delicate. Don't push her."

"Let her remember?"

"Yeah."

"Are you sure that's best?"

"Good night, Caderyn. Sweet dreams."

Right. Silenced again. I peered into the other two rooms. One, closer to Nick's, was slightly smaller, but the bed looked really awesome. The other had the advantage of being slightly larger and didn't share a wall with the other two rooms. But the comforter was purple. Not really my thing. I took the middle room and fell onto the mattress, my head closest to our shared wall.

I stared up at the ceiling. "You better not snore."

"Earplugs in the top drawer," his wall-muffled voice answered.

I opened the desk drawer and found a new pack of earplugs. And a really old notepad. I flipped open the first page and saw a drawing. The dark made it fuzzy, so I turned on what seemed to be an ancient, ugly lamp.

Brown spots dotted the page, distorting some of the pencil marks. A drawing of Ava. I recognized her as soon as I saw the picture. Pounding pain throbbed behind my eyes, and her face changed to something real. Smiling. Laughing. Smacking my arm. Saying my name a dozen times, a dozen ways. Finally she screamed it, blood all over her hands. She knelt beside me, and I knew who the blood belonged to. Me.

I jerked out of the memory and stared at the pad of paper, willing myself not to vomit. Something dripped out of my nose, and I wiped it away. Red. That's when I realized the brown spots on the paper were old, dried blood.

My blood.

# 10

NICK

I TOOK OFF MY BOOTS AND FLOPPED onto the bed, staring up at the ceiling, aware that I still wore blood-spattered jeans. A huge sigh escaped me, and every muscle seemed weak. I just wanted to lie here and focus on the one good thing that had happened today: Cade had killed a wraith.

For a flicker of a moment, his speed had returned.

He might not be able to call them at will or control it yet—heck, he might not have even noticed that he'd used super-human speed tonight—but he'd used one of his powers. He still had them. Just knowing that sent relief pulsing through me. I hadn't failed him yet.

We still had time.

Not much. What little levity I'd just experienced waned as reality thudded into me like a medicine ball.

Gwen's voice echoed in my head, taunting: *"Careful, Nick. Cade doesn't have much time left. If you slip up again, you could lose him forever. Is that really the kind of gamble you want to make?"*

I closed my eyes to shut her words out. I had one purpose: protect the two phoenixes who would save our entire race. That kind of gamble wasn't okay, but I didn't have a lot of choice. Gwen had come out ahead every time so far.

And she was right. If I messed up this time, it could be Cade's last cycle as a phoenix. I rubbed my hand over my face. The ache in my heart pulsed. I wouldn't let that happen. I slammed my fist against the bed and sat up. As soon as we found Ava and reminded her of her purpose, I could begin training her to take out Gwen.

This time, we'd win. We had to.

I slid my hands over my thighs only to be reminded that the black, sticky blood on my jeans belonged to one of those nightmare-inducing monsters we'd fought tonight, and wraith blood tended to stain.

I groaned and stood, exchanging jeans for exercise shorts and a T-shirt. Better to clean up first. Besides, I'd given Cade a lot of information tonight. I should stay awake at least until he fell asleep, in case he lapsed into another memory seizure. My chest squeezed at the thought of him thrashing on the floor earlier.

He was getting worse.

Just like Gwen had said he would.

The only way to save Cade was to kill Gwen—for good.

And the only one of us with the power to do that was Ava.

If anyone else killed Gwen, she'd pop back up like a recurring nightmare.

I stopped by Cade's bedroom door in time to hear a human body drop to the floor. I raced into his room and kept his head safe while he thrashed on the carpet. "Cade?" He shook, his eyes open, not seeing anything but the memory.

"Leave him alone!" I screamed as if Gwen could hear me. As if it would make a difference. She wasn't here. Not yet. She wasn't strong enough to come after us, so she'd stay in hiding. Wait until the right full moon to call her monsters and hunt us down.

In the meantime, she was stealing Cade's life. His memories. His powers.

Cade's shaking slowed, and he started gulping breaths of air. His eyelids fluttered, and he looked at me. "Nick?"

He was still in that in-between phase. Not quite back yet. Not fully out of the clouds of his memories. I tried to swallow past the ache in my throat. I couldn't let him see my weakness. He wasn't ready to know the full scope of what was wrong with him.

"You're okay." My voice shook a little anyway.

He nodded. "I'm exhausted."

"I bet." I smiled to ease the worry that started to wrinkle his forehead. "If you puke on the floor, you clean it."

He pushed my shoulder. "I get it."

I helped him back onto the bed, and though it was clear he thought about telling me not to, he let me. He rolled over on the mattress, his words coming out slower than normal. "You could be a little nicer, though."

"Nicer?" I laughed and started to leave so he wouldn't see the shakiness in my arms. "It won't include cleaning up your messes."

"Jerk." He bit back. Then he sat up. "Nick?"

I faced him from the doorway.

His slightly squinted expression told me he'd remembered something important. It was always a delicate balance with Cade, never knowing how much to press in case he went back under. "Ava, she's my twin."

I nodded.

"Do I always remember her first?"

"Yes."

"And why shouldn't I push her memories?"

"Ava has trust issues. Call it a defense mechanism. If we push too fast or scare her away, she'll suppress the remembering. And we need her to remember as quickly as possible. And your memories . . . should stay buried as long as possible."

Cade's eyes narrowed. "And I'm supposed to just do your bidding and trust you?"

There was my brother. Always pushing back. Never one to do as he was told. I couldn't help but smile. "I'm protecting you. That's my job." I started to walk away. "Find Ava. Get her to trust you. That's yours."

"Good talk."

His words followed me out of the room and speared me. It wasn't like I wanted to keep things from him.

I had to act fast before he decided he didn't trust me and before he remembered that he never did what I asked.

I stepped into the bathroom and leaned over the sink while my thoughts spun. In a hundred lifetimes, I'd never seen my brother this bad. When the meaningful memories started hitting him, he'd be worse. How much more of this would he be able to take before she'd completely break him? I clutched the sides of the counter and gritted my teeth, willing those thoughts to leave me alone.

They wouldn't.

This whole thing was my fault, and if I didn't find Gwen and make sure she was dead for good, Cade would never be free.

I rubbed my hands over my face and washed blood out of my jeans. No matter how hard I scrubbed, they wouldn't come entirely clean. Water, ice-cold, ran over my hands, numbing my fingers. And a tiny tug in my brain—my thoughts—pulled me to a stop.

I stood rigid, feeling every thudding pulse.

Gwen.

She sensed me.

A shiver spread through my core.

How much time would he have? Two, three full moons at most. If Cade remembered things that quickly, would it break him? I needed Ava. We were running out of time.

# 11

AVA

I LAY AWAKE IN MY BED THAT NIGHT, not listening to the sounds of Dave snoring in the next room—because he was still at the hospital. At least it was just for one night. Of all the things that had happened tonight, I kept replaying Wyatt's short visit. The way he'd tended to Ajax reminded me of something strangely familiar. And his words echoed over and over in my ear: *"No problem, Ava. Any time. Really. You sound the alarm, I'll be here."* He'd sounded sincere, but it was never that easy. No one could keep a promise like that. Perhaps it was best to cut ties with him now, before I got attached.

My eyes started to close.

The room began to spin, and I stared into a memory again. Old and haunting. The same yellow glow from the light of a lantern cast moving shadows on my bloodied hands. This time, emotions raced into me as if they were my own. I wasn't just seeing the scene before me. I was reliving it, like some strange dream where I could feel the breeze and taste the tang of blood in the air. In the memory, my heart hammered, and my hands shook. An ache spread through my chest that made my eyes sting. I stared down at that same muscular chest again and pressed the wet cloth over it.

His hand touched mine. "You have to get the bullet out, Ava."

Ava.

Ava.

My name whispered over and over in my skull. In this strange otherworldly memory, the person's name was Ava. My name. My memory? No. It couldn't be. I looked at my hands. They looked like my hands. Only older. Rougher. They weren't my hands. A tingling sensation spread through my chest, pulling me out of the memory, but I squeezed my eyes shut and pressed my hand against my mouth. I had to know. I had to stay here, in the memory, for a moment longer.

I looked at the young man's face.

My eyes popped open, and I sat up, alone in my room. My heart galloped wildly. Booming in my chest, harder, faster. And I pressed both of my shaking hands over my mouth.

The memory had pushed to the back of my mind. But I'd seen his face. Wyatt. Wyatt Wilcox was the young man in this strange memory too? This couldn't be real. I stood. I paced. Bit my knuckle.

Why was this happening?

How was this happening?

"Ava, honey, are you all right?" Jean called from the hallway, her soft steps padding across the carpet toward my room.

I opened my door a crack, pressing my palms against the frame to still the trembling. "I-I'm okay. Just a little—I mean, it's so quiet."

She laughed kind of sadly and patted my shoulder. Something about that touch calmed me a little. "I know, but he's going to be just fine. They'll release him tomorrow as long as he's eating."

"Hospital food? It's like they want you to stay there forever." I made a gagging face, and she laughed.

"Get some rest." She left my door open as she left, giving me the option of whether or not to close it. I kept ajar just a little and climbed into bed.

Light out. Eyes closed. I tried desperately to even my breathing and not focus on the strange memory. But I failed. And the memory flooded back like a dream I couldn't control.

I gently pressed the cloth over the gaping wound in Wyatt's chest. My voice shook. My insides ached. And I was doing everything I could to remain calm. "The bleeding isn't stopping."

His labored breathing wasn't, either.

I pressed the wet cloth against the wound, and Wyatt made a sound between a groan and a muffled scream. His eyes flicked to me as if it would take too much energy for him to move his head. My nose burned, and I blinked back tears.

An eerie howl rose in the night, followed by others, and they seemed to be closing in. Wolves. I sucked in a breath, scanning the dark tree line. I had to get him back inside, fast. "I have to get the bullet out. We can't wait."

He swallowed. His neck wet with sweat and covered in dirt and grime. He grabbed my hand in his. Cold and slick. He squeezed. "Don't . . . waste . . . your time."

The ache in my chest ripped anew. I gripped his hand back and looked into his eyes. They still clung to life, but barely. If I let him give up, he wouldn't make it. I squeezed his hands tight, willing him to cling to life.

"Listen to me, Wyatt. You're stronger than this. I watched you save Tommy. I—"

"I'm not a hero . . . Ava."

"You are to me." I handed him a dry cloth. I wouldn't lose him. Not now. Not ever. "Bite down. I'm getting this bullet out." I pressed our joined hands against my heart. "I will not lose you." At this moment, something in my very being squeezed. I felt more for this Wyatt than I thought possible to feel for anyone, and it overwhelmed me.

I let his hand go. Trembling, I pulled out my tools: a knife, a bottle of myrrh, and a flask of whiskey. That, I gave to him first and helped him drink.

Then poured some on the wound. He bit down on the cloth, holding back a cry.

My stomach clutched. Tears blurred my vision, but I pushed my emotions aside as best I could and cut deep into the wound. His back arched, and he cried out into the cloth. But he tried to keep still. Warm blood wet my hands. There. I felt the bullet. My fingers worked from memory, and I pulled it free. Wyatt lay silent on the ground as I dropped the bullet, shiny and blood covered, into a cloth and put it in my pocket. I poured whiskey into his wound, and he flinched again, much weaker this time.

I grabbed his hand. "It's out. It's out."

He rolled over and threw up.

I cleaned his face. The sweat streaks through the dirt. He didn't open his eyes. The bleeding wouldn't stop. I breathed deep to combat the tightening in my chest. No falling apart yet. I had to get this stitched up. "Wyatt?"

"Thank you, Ava." He didn't even open his eyes.

The little boy Wyatt had saved limped over, giving me the clean cloths I'd asked for. Tears streaked his cheeks as he looked at Wyatt. "How is he?"

I wiped away my own tear. "He's . . ."

Wyatt opened one eye, and a half smile ghosted over his pale lips. "I'm fine, champ. How are you?"

The boy let out a shaky breath then smiled. "Fine. Thanks to you, sir."

"Good." He paused, taking a labored breath. "You better get inside, Tommy."

"You too, sir." The boy turned to leave but paused and looked over his shoulder. "Please."

Wyatt's mouth opened slightly, and then he seemed to force a smile, but it quickly turned real, if sad. "Of course."

The boy ran toward the house, and I grabbed Wyatt's hand. "Can you stand?"

His thumb brushed over the inside of my wrist, and the blue in his eyes shone brighter. "Just go."

I gasped, everything inside me freezing. He could not leave me now. Not after all this. No. Heat replaced the chill in my core, and I held his hand tighter. "I'm not leaving without you."

He cried out as I helped him sit up. I rubbed my hand over his back and then helped him stand. He seemed unsteady but found his balance as I supported him. "You ready?"

"I don't—"

My chin trembled even as I tried to keep my jaw firm. "There will be no arguing with me."

"Yes, ma'am."

I gasped as I pulled out of the memory.

It felt so real. The emotions. The way I knew what to do with the medical supplies. But it couldn't be. I pressed my head into my hands, trying to grasp some form of sanity. It couldn't be Wyatt. Couldn't be me.

Tonight he'd asked if I remembered. Remembered what? Pulling a bullet from his chest in the past?

But he'd asked. Every limb tingled as if I might faint. This was not possible. But it was happening.

When I'd looked at him like he was from another planet, he'd brushed it off as something else. Maybe he'd had a strange memory like this, too. And the fact that both of our wounds healed. My hand seemed to have a mind of its own as it grabbed my phone from the bedside table. I stared at the phone's bright light.

Wyatt's number sat at the top of my recent contacts.

My pulse sped as I stared at his name.

Heard my memory self say it. And with such strange affection. But why not? He seemed like a nice guy. Maybe we were friends. In what? A past life. I certainly did not believe in that. Afterlife, sure. Past lives, not really my thing.

Besides, Wyatt wasn't the same soul in a different form. He was the same exact person. He even had the same name. But there was no way he'd lived that long, right?

I'd officially read too many vampire novels.

And that would mean I'd lived that long, too. Not possible. I remembered my whole sorry life. Well, everything since I was four.

My phone's screen went dark, and I pressed it automatically. My actions taking charge over my thoughts again.

I typed: *You asked if I remembered. What exactly did you mean?*

I WOKE UP WITH MY PHONE SHOVED underneath my pillow. Apparently, I'd fallen asleep waiting on Wyatt to text me back that he'd remembered. I pulled it out fast and scrambled to look at the screen.

New text.

Adrenaline shot through my blood as I checked. It was from Wyatt: *Like I said. I thought you remembered my report on Andromeda.*

Really? I fell back against my pillow. He couldn't expect me to buy that, could he? Then I sat up fast; Wyatt Wilcox would be at school, and he might be able to hide behind a text, but if I got him talking, I'd know if he was hiding something. And I'd get it out of him.

After all, I'd seen the cuts on his back before they'd disappeared.

He was like me. He had to be.

And I didn't really want to go through this alone.

"Thanks for picking me up." I closed the door of Yuki's Volvo and leaned back against the passenger seat, expelling a huge breath.

Sunlight shone through the car window, giving her dark hair a pretty bronze glow as she turned to face me.

She touched my shoulder, and the look of concern on her face eased the butterflies in my stomach. "I can't believe you didn't call me to tell me about your foster dad. I would have come over. You know that, right?"

I knew.

I glanced her way, too lazy to lift my head from the back of the car seat. "It was a crazy night." And I didn't need to explain to my best friend how I'd miraculously healed.

Her eyebrows pulled together, and she shook her head like a comforting mother. She worried about me too much. "I just want you to know that you can count on me." She checked her rearview as she backed out of the driveway. "You shouldn't have to be alone for something like that."

"I—I wasn't alone." I drew out that last word with a slight wince.

Her eyes widened and her mouth opened. "Ava Elderson, what are you hiding from me?"

"Do you know Wyatt Wilcox?"

Her gaze latched on to me for a long second. "Yes! That cutie I sat next to in chemistry junior year? Are you dating him? How could you not tell me? He wouldn't even give me a second glance. Believe me, I tried to get his attention." She shook her head, and her dark waves cascaded over her shoulders, then she snickered.

Yuki was gorgeous, so that surprised me.

"Whoa." I laughed through the word. "Calm down. I didn't know you were interested."

She shrugged. "I'm not now."

"Okay. Good." Had I actually said that?

Her eyes grew wide. "How long has this been going on?" Her lips twisted into a scowl, and she gripped the steering wheel tighter, speed increasing. "I *can* handle this kind of stuff, you know."

"Yuki, I know you can handle it. I'm not dating him, okay." My face got really hot. "Don't worry. You will be the first person I talk to *if* I decide to date someone."

She glanced over at me, skepticism melting into a smirk. "I better be."

"You will be." I laughed.

She stared out the window again, speed back to normal, and chewed the inside of her lip. "I'm sorry. I shouldn't have assumed you'd—"

My turn to comfort her. "No worries. I can't imagine what it must be like to always think people are keeping things from you because . . ." Neither of us needed me to say why. "If anyone knows how strong you are, it's me."

That brightened her face. Her parents might attempt to soften the blow with every piece of news they gave her, but all it did was work her up. I couldn't blame her; no one wanted to be treated like an invalid. All that did was stress her out even more. And that certainly wasn't good for her heart condition.

"Thanks, Ava." She scrunched up her nose. "I know you're not like that. I'm sorry I assumed."

"Forgiven."

"By the way, when did you get the dark purple?" She touched my hair.

"Do you like it?" Mrs. Fields had let me get the purple streaks. They complemented my dark blonde hair perfectly.

"I love it. It's so you. "She pulled into the school parking lot, parked, and sighed as she looked out the windshield. "Here's to surviving another year."

I laughed. But it felt good—being at the same school two years in a row. The normal first-day-of-school jitters I got had been replaced by a small smattering of butterflies. We got out of the car and walked together toward the building. Yuki nudged me with her shoulder. "Hey, speak of the cutie."

I followed her gaze. Wyatt. He walked into the building ahead of us. I picked up my pace.

"Whoa." She laughed, catching up with me. "Looks like you have more to spill than I first expected."

She had no idea.

I held up my hand to shield my eyes from the sun. I'd lost track of Wyatt. At least I knew approximately where he'd be all day. The building blocked the sun finally, and I scanned the students littering the steps. No sign of him.

Yuki bumped into me as if someone had pushed her hard. She let out a "Hey!"

And I turned to stop her from pummeling the culprit, half expecting her to have her fists ready in a fighter's stance; instead, she just stared.

"I'm sorry." A guy with perfectly messy dark-blond hair steadied Yuki and scooped up her dropped schedule. Then he straightened his leather jacket and flashed a crooked smile, and all the air rushed out of my lungs. His gray-green eyes locked onto Yuki, but I couldn't tear my gaze away.

I knew that face.

Only I didn't.

Those fake memories that played in my skull—they knew this face. He had the same mole on the left side of his jawbone, the same gray-green eyes as me. It was him. In the memory, my voice had called him Cade.

Cade.

The pancakes I'd had for breakfast turned to stone in my stomach. This was not possible.

He walked away, right into the building, leaving Yuki and me standing there frozen to the sidewalk.

She turned to me and practically squealed. "Who was that?"

I shook my head, dazed. "I—I don't know." Which was true, technically. After all, there was no way his name was actually Cade.

"That smile." Yuki walked forward.

In my memory, he wasn't smiling. He was staring up at me, blood gushing out of his stomach while I cried. Something in my chest clutched, and I hugged my arms around my middle.

"Ava? You coming?"

I shook the thoughts clear and followed Yuki inside. My class and hers were on opposite sides of the universe, basically, so I managed the long walk to the science lab alone.

I stepped into the classroom just as the bell rang. The scent of formaldehyde was enough to wake me up. No one should be allowed to have biology this close to breakfast.

Mr. Cummins greeted me in monotone. "Ms. Elderson, nice of you to join us. There's an empty seat next to Mr. Wilcox."

Wilcox? I whirled around in time to see Wyatt slowly duck his head. Whoa. Wait. Was he avoiding me now? All because of that stupid text? How could he go from Mr. I'll-Drop-Anything-for-You to avoiding me? A speck of heat in the center of my chest fanned.

Figured.

A little more than miffed, I turned back to Mr. Cummins to ask for a different partner, when I noticed the guy who looked like strange-memory Cade in the doorway. He walked in and stood beside me.

I stared at him.

After realizing my mouth was hanging open and my eyes were glued to him, I closed it and gave him my best smile. His smile turned crooked and sideways, and he nodded once. Was he checking me out? I mentally slapped him. His face scrunched up in a wince.

Weird. "Are you okay?" I whispered.

He nodded, the skin around his left eye still crinkled.

"Too much to drink last night?"

He laughed, genuine. "Something like that."

I faced Cummins and pointed over my shoulder at Cade—or whatever his real name was. "I'll sit with him. Hospitality to new students and all."

"You're not part of the hospitality committee." Mr. Cummins looked down at me over the rim of his glasses.

They actually had a committee?

"It's a nice gesture." Cade looked flattered, but also like he expected any girl to flatter him. Gag me.

Why was everyone from those strange memories showing up in my biology class?

"Your seat has been assigned, Ms. Elderson." Mr. Cummins sounded annoyed, which was a lot of emotion for him.

"That's *Mr.* Elderson." Cade placed his student slip on Cummins's desk and nodded like Cummins was a little slow to the punch.

Not a great idea. Seriously, cocky much? Wait. Did he say *Mr.* Elderson? My heart took off like Yuki's car.

"Isn't that something? Two Eldersons." Cummins's mouth curved in what was supposed to be a smile, but it hadn't touched any other part of his face. Then he looked pointedly at me as though my being at his desk was as welcome as a tarantula at an exterminator convention. "Doesn't change your seat assignment."

"Elderson?" Cade faced me and leaned against Cummins's desk. He seemed intrigued. "That's your last name, too?"

My heart caught in my throat, and I nearly choked on it.

"Do you speak English?" Cade's question registered.

So did the fact that I was still standing at Cummins's desk, gaping at Cade. Again.

"It's not like it's the world's rarest name." I rolled my eyes and turned my back on him. Then winced. Why did I do that? Cade could have answers, and I'd really started off on the wrong note. I sat in the chair next to Wyatt, who was definitely avoiding me now. I crossed my arms and slumped in my seat.

He looked down at his book. Glasses on this morning. Yuki was right, though. Did he have to be so cute?

"I didn't expect friendship bracelets, but you're being awfully cold this morning," I grumbled.

Now I had his full attention. "What?"

"Hiding when he told me to sit with you?"

He shook his head and sat up straight. "What? No. I was—" He stopped and squared his shoulders as Cade walked up to the empty lab table across the aisle.

He shot Wyatt a wide smile. Then he sat down and looked at me. "Looks like I'll be sitting next to you anyway, Ms. Elderson."

"It's Ava."

He nodded. Almost as if he expected me to say that. "I'm Cade."

My pulse revved, and every inch of my skin tingled. Of course that was his real name. Could he possibly be someone related to me? Like a twin separated at birth or something. We both had dark-blond hair and gray-green eyes. Suddenly, I wanted nothing more than to talk to him. "Nice to meet you, Cade." My voice sounded so strange to my ears. Rehearsed and foreign.

"Likewise." His gaze wandered to Wyatt, and the smile turned smug. "You have a name?"

He didn't say anything, so I decided to squelch the rising awkwardness. "This is Wyatt."

Wyatt nodded a hello, then turned back to his book.

"Friendly guy." Cade half laughed. Then he winced again and pressed his left hand against the side of his head.

I leaned toward him. "Are you okay?"

"He needs dark chocolate," Wyatt mumbled.

I glanced over at him. "Are you a headache expert?"

"Just trust me."

No thanks.

Lisa Welch slid into the seat beside Cade and stole his attention in the way only a leggy blonde with a summer tan can.

I rolled my eyes and settled in my chair beside Wyatt.

He leaned closer to me, and he smelled amazing. "I wasn't avoiding you."

My eyebrows rose, and I waited for an explanation. Because it would have to be a good one. Unfortunately, Cummins stopped pacing in front of our desks and stood staring at us. We both straightened, and I folded my hands over my biology book. As soon as he turned his back and walked away, Wyatt looked at me as if he were trying to see into my thoughts. Like he thought something might have changed.

He wiped his hand over his face. "I wasn't avoiding you. I promise."

The way he said it, with such sincerity, had me staring at him like he was a little weird, which I felt bad for and amended my expression.

He sort of laughed. "Look, I just don't really know you, and I wasn't sure how you would react to me here—at school."

I expelled a deep breath. This I could understand. "You thought I'd treat you differently with others around?"

"I wasn't sure. It's not like we were friends last year. And this morning, when I waved at you, you turned around, so . . . I thought maybe you didn't want people to think we knew each other. Or something." The confident Wyatt I'd met last night had been replaced. This one mumbled through his words, not making solid eye contact.

My mouth fell open. "I-I didn't see you. I was actually looking for you." Now I felt bad.

"You were?" Those baby blues latched onto my gaze.

"Yeah." I offered a smile. "And I'm sorry I didn't remember your report on Andromeda."

"Do you now?" He tilted his head ever so slightly, and my breathing quickened, because for a moment I wasn't exactly sure he was talking about the report.

"Remember?" I ventured tentatively.

He nodded, barely perceptible.

"Did it have to do with the history of bullet extraction?"

The widening of his eyes told me he knew more than he'd said. He had the memories, too. My mouth seemed dry, and my breathing quickened. I opened my palm and showed him my empty hand. "I cut my hand last night. Before you got there."

He glanced at my palm. No cut. No scar. No trace of wound. But confusion didn't overcome his features. He looked back up at me.

Nothing in his intense gaze changed. But he didn't offer any words. He just waited for me to continue. Almost as if he could lure words out of me.

"You got hurt at the crash site. Didn't you? Like I did." I kept my voice low. "You can tell me. Did something happen to you last night?"

Slowly, his eyes narrowed. "At the crash site?" He seemed tentative. Like I was a poisonous snake flicking the air with my tongue and he didn't want me to catch the scent. "I told you I was fine. Are you sure you're okay?"

And my heart sank. I buried my hand under my desk, and my face heated. Maybe I was the only crazy one.

"Sometimes when we see something tragic like that, our minds—"

"You don't need to tell me about what the mind does when we witness tragedy, Wyatt," I snapped and added a glare.

He moved back.

Flushed, I looked away to calm down and caught Cade staring at me, and something about it seemed oddly protective.

He leaned closer to me. "He bothering you? Because I can have a talk with him."

The patronizing glance he sent to Wyatt made my stomach tighten. Half because I wanted to shoot another wedge between Wyatt and myself, half because I knew I shouldn't have snapped at him. And why did I want to put a wedge between us? He was only trying to help.

"I can take care of myself."

Cade held up his hands in surrender. "I didn't mean to insinuate I doubted your ability. I just thought our awkward friend here might need help taking social cues."

I looked at Wyatt. He didn't say a thing. Just sank deeper in his chair and crossed his arms.

Cade didn't exactly know when to quit. He leaned over his desk so Wyatt could see him. "She's not into you. Sorry, man."

The ghost of a smirk lifted the corner of Wyatt's mouth. "Relationship advice from you? That's rich."

Cade's eyes widened for a millisecond. He regarded Wyatt for three heartbeats before his charming smile returned. "Just trying to save you some heartache."

He turned to Lisa. "Hey, gorgeous."

Her sparkling eyes drank in the compliment and his smile.

I rolled my eyes, glanced back at Wyatt, and whispered, "What a jerk."

"You have no idea."

A shard of ice seemed to form in my gut. "You know him?"

"I know the type."

"Oh? So quick to judge?" Why couldn't I control my tongue?

He took a deep breath and faced forward.

And just like that, I'd accidentally closed conversation for the rest of class. Every time I looked at Cade, he was talking to Lisa. And she couldn't stop laughing at whatever he said. He clearly enjoyed it, too. I shook my head. Still, I couldn't help but see both Wyatt and Cade bloody in front of me. And it all felt so real.

If I wanted answers, I was going to have to do something I rarely did—get close to another person. A heaviness filled my stomach, and

I slumped forward. Making friends was not my strength. But nothing said I'd have to stay friends with them. After all, I excelled at pushing people away.

After class, Cade seemed to be in a hurry. Wyatt headed straight to talk to Cummins, so I raced to catch up to Cade. I found him hunched over, leaning against the wall just outside the classroom. "Cade? Are you okay?"

He stood up and rested his head against the wall. "I wish I were hungover."

I chuckled, then thought maybe I shouldn't have because he seemed to be in pain. "I, um. I'm . . . Have you ever met another Elderson?"

"Sure. My brother."

"Your—you have a brother?"

He cocked his head sideways, and I realized I sounded crazy. But he nodded.

"That's cool." I clutched my books close to my chest and stepped back from him.

Cade tore his eyes from me and nodded with that charming smile as Holly Eaves walked by. I rolled my eyes. How could I be so stupid? I left him and his annoying smile. Even if Cade was a part of what was happening to me, he didn't seem to be aware. And he was exactly the type of guy I stayed away from.

"Ava." He called after me, but I kept walking. Maybe the best way out of this was to pretend it didn't exist. Neither of the guys from my strange memories seemed to want to help me anyway. Fine with me. Who needed their help? I'd figure it out. Alone.

# 13

## CADE

S CHOOL WAS SCHOOL NO MATTER which way you sliced it. Just as bad here as anywhere. I closed my locker and headed out the front door. I'd pretty much botched my first meeting with Ava when I'd sent her friend flying into her. And then my second meeting by playing it so cool she may have thought I was hitting on her. My attempt at remedying that had completely backfired.

This "you don't know me, but you want to get to know me because you'll remember me" stuff was way more complicated and a whole lot creepier than Nick had made it sound during this morning's training session.

I twirled my keychain, wishing Nick had let me borrow one of the bikes this morning, not that I was complaining about the Challenger, but apparently he got first pick for work. Brothers.

I headed out and leaned against the hood. With a perfect view of the front door, I waited to see if I could catch a glimpse of Ava.

Our first meeting may not have gone as planned, but at least I had her in my sights. That guy she'd been talking to in bio—couldn't remember his name for the life of me—looked familiar. That wasn't possible, right?

Unless there were other phoenixes running around.

And why shouldn't there be? I mean, we couldn't be the only ones fighting the forces of evil to save humanity, or however Nick put it over oatmeal last week.

I should really make a list of questions for him. Too many swam in my head daily, and he was reluctant to speak, let alone offer information.

A petite Asian girl exited the building, nose in a book. Now her I remembered. I'd bumped into her this morning to get to Ava, then I'd spotted her in my AP English class. If the two of them were friends, she was a good place to start.

She walked right toward two guys tossing a football. I pushed off the Challenger and headed over to reintroduce myself. I intercepted the ball right before it was about to sail over Ms. Oblivious's head.

My backpack brushed against her arm as I snagged the ball. "Watch where you're throwing." I chucked it back at the kid who'd shot me a dirty look.

Then I turned just in time to steady Ava's friend. "Might want to watch where you're going."

The look she gave me—slightly enraged and slightly grateful—mingled in one bewildered expression I found kinda cute.

"Sometimes life is too short to watch where you're going."

I chuckled without meaning to. "I would be inclined to disagree. If you don't watch where you're going, you might miss out on life." I caught sight of the slightly purple tint to her glasses frames. This morning I had assumed they were black.

Her eyes narrowed, and she straightened her spine. "Cade, is it?"

I smiled. "You remembered."

She nodded once, and there it was. That judgy expression I'd come to expect from a certain type of girl. Generally they were brainy, modest, and a little uppity for my taste. But they only saw me as one thing. I had to admit it was a part I played rather well, but if she wasn't going to get to know the real me, I could give her what she expected. And then some.

"I'm sorry; I forgot your name."

She looked right at me, a deep kind of look. Almost like she wanted to say something witty but was biting her tongue, but also like she didn't really want to be angry with me. "Yuki."

"Pretty name."

"Thanks." Now she smiled. Real and uninhibited. But still slightly suspicious. This girl had the innocent yet wary thing down in a way I had never seen before. Intriguing.

"What are you reading?" I tugged at her book and pulled it out of her hands.

"Hey!"

"Are you serious? *The Iliad?*"

She snatched it back from me. "Yes. Thank you very much." She placed a bookmark in the pages and halted to put the tome into her backpack.

I stopped with her. After she replaced the book, she swung the backpack over her shoulder and then held her head high and walked right past me.

I caught up. "I'm sorry, did I offend you?"

She stopped and glanced over her shoulder. That look. A half sort of smile and the smallest amount of pity. She stood there, glasses perched on her nose, hair pulled back in a barrette. Decked out in a white blouse and gray skirt with black knee-high socks. She looked like she was wearing a uniform to a school where we didn't have uniforms.

Her glasses flickered away. She seemed to be wearing a kimono for a moment. Only it wasn't her. It was a memory. And this girl had a white-painted face.

Blood dripped down her forehead.

A wave of nausea overtook me, and the migraine slammed into me all at once. I pressed my hands to my head and tried to take a knee.

It landed rather hard, thankfully on grass and not sidewalk. But I followed fast. Like a sack of rocks. I heard swords clashing. Hooves hitting the street. And a language I didn't understand, but I knew what she was saying, *"The kasa-obake is here. You brought it. You brought the monster!"*

I cupped my head in my hands, willing the pain to go away. It persisted. I watched what looked like samurai fighting. Rain. Flower petals. The scent of cherry blossoms. I didn't even know how I knew they were cherry blossoms.

And then it was gone.

This reality came back, but I felt as though I was underwater, staring up at a bright light distorted by ripples. Sound muffled by the barrier. My head throbbed. If I moved too fast, I might throw up.

"Cade?"

That was Yuki's voice. I tried to stand up and thought better of it.

"Can you hear me?" she asked.

I tried to nod, my ears feeling impossibly hot. I just had to make a fool out of myself now, huh?

"What happened?"

I knew that voice. Ava was with her. Seriously, I had to get this under control. This time, I made it to standing but nearly fell over. They both tried to steady me. My stomach churned. I'd be mortified if I puked on their shoes.

"Whoa. Not too fast."

Another new voice joined the mix, and as my vision returned from the nebulous, I recalled that guy from bio. The one Ava hung out with. He steadied me as the world rushed back like the end of a coaster ride.

"Here." He pressed a bottle of water into my hands, and I recalled how Nick said it helped. I drank some.

And my mind cleared. But it tasted different. Familiar.

I handed it back. "Thanks."

"Keep it." He pushed my hands back.

"Thanks," I muttered again.

Yuki touched my shoulder. "Are you all right?" she asked. "Should we call the nurse?"

"I'm fine." I took another swig of water. Then I looked at the bottle. "What's in this?"

"Just some ginger and mint leaves," that guy said. "Here's a piece of dark chocolate." He shrugged. "It helps with headaches."

He offered the chocolate and a hand to help me stand. I took both. And as soon as I touched him, his face flashed into my vision.

Something similar. Me grabbing his hand. Him helping me up. Unlike the memory with Yuki, this one clearly shared the same face. He handed me a flask. A gun. And he said, *"Do what you have to do."*

Wyatt . . . I'd called him Wyatt. Was that his name?

I staggered back as reality flushed through me. And I stared at him. All three of them hovered as if trying to help me. I looked at the guy. "Wyatt?"

"Are you okay?" He leaned closer.

I looked at the water bottle. "I think this stuff really works."

Yuki was the one to fill my vision, standing in front of me as if criticizing artwork at a museum. "Do you have a doctor we need to call?"

"What? No, no. This was just a migraine."

She tipped her head to the side and nodded slowly. "That really knocked you out."

*Don't remind me.* I offered her my most winning smile and stood. "Nah. I've been knocked out. This was a different experience altogether." Then I twirled my keys again. "Thanks for the water." I held up the bottle and turned on my heel.

"Cade?"

Bingo. Ava's voice. Maybe Nick was wrong. Maybe it wouldn't take her as long to trust me as he thought. Maybe she got migraines, too. I turned to face her.

"Are you sure you should be driving?"

"Absolutely. I don't plan to walk that far."

The three of them stood there, staring. Yuki all worried, Ava all perplexed, and Wyatt . . . He looked a little guarded. As if he knew I'd remembered him. And he probably remembered me. Problem was, I didn't remember anything else about him.

# 14



I LAY BACK ON THE CREEPER AND PUSHED myself underneath the car. The sound of Mick's radio blasted country music through the garage. Country. Again. I guess if the guy owned the garage, he could listen to whatever he wanted, even if the rest of us were grumbling about it. I guided myself into the position beneath the vehicle. Oil changes would be so much easier if Mick let me use the bay, but it was occupied. C'est la vie. Someone had screwed this oil filter on tight. Nothing a dash of super strength couldn't handle.

I'd just yanked it free when a slightly familiar voice caught my attention.

Casually, I rolled the creeper out from under the vehicle to see Mick talking to that girl who worked at the bookstore in town—Kelsey. My heart tugged in a weird way. Long, dark hair that reddened as the sunlight hit it. Sparkling, brown eyes. The tug in my chest turned to an ache. She reminded me of Dinah.

I swallowed, hard, and turned away.

"Hey, Nick." Mick's voice caused my pulse to race, and out of the corner of my eye, I watched his scuffed steel-toed boots move closer to me. "This young lady says her car's got a 'weird clunking noise.' Think you can take a look at it?"

I glanced up at him and his eye roll. A *clunk* could mean anything.

"Nick?" Her face came into clear view, pulling more memories of

Dinah. Only she clearly wasn't Dinah. Her lack of a dimple, smaller nose, and slightly rounder face proved that. In fact, the more I stared at her, the more differences I spotted. Good, because it looked like Mick was pawning her car problems off on me. Bad, because I was openly staring.

She shrugged, hands buried in her leather jacket pockets. "Kelsey." She pointed to herself as if I'd forgotten her name. "I work at Crane's Bargain Books. This morning you—well—you probably don't remember me."

Oh, yes, I did. I nodded and picked up a rag, wiping grease off my hands as I stood. "Of course I do." I tried a smile and she practically beamed but ducked her head to hide it. "Let's take a look. Shall we?" I motioned to her car.

Yeah, she was too sweet and meek to be anything like Dinah. It didn't ease the ache in my chest as I followed her to her car. I stared at the Volkswagen Golf and scratched the back of my head.

"That guy said you knew your way around a Volkswagen." She bit her lip and stared up at me with big, brown eyes.

Eyes that sparkled with so much vibrancy.

I turned my attention away from her. That cultivated the reminder of Dinah. The glow in the depths of that brown held the same spark for life.

I cleared my throat. "Yeah." I motioned to the vehicle. I hated working on them. No hand space, for one thing. But her pleading eyes softened my resolve. "Let's see what I can find."

"Thank you!" She practically beamed, and immediately I regretted my decision.

I took the keys and slid into the front seat, pushing the chair back. And there, pasted to the dashboard, sat a collection of photos. I zeroed in on the one of her hugging a guy I knew. I pointed it out to her. "You know this kid?"

She peered in, close to me in this enclosed space. "That's my brother, Wyatt. You know him?"

"Yeah. He's a good kid." I managed to keep my voice steady.

Avoiding Kelsey just got harder if Wyatt continued to hang around.

And why wouldn't he? If Ava was a flame, Wyatt Wilcox was a moth—except that moths weren't typically considered dangerous.

I had to hope Wyatt would hightail it out of town once he got wind that Cade and I were here. If he didn't, I'd have that chat with him.

As I revved the Golf's engine, something in the air felt strange. The wind seemed to shift. I glanced out the window, now aware that Kelsey was trying to explain the clunking noise to me.

I tuned out everything except the scent of death and decay. A shadow puppet walked in daylight. A chill in my bones raised the hair on the back of my neck. I knew I wouldn't be able to see the monster if I looked straight at it. I scanned the world right outside the garage door, waiting to see movement in the shadow of the building. They hid there, in the shadows, undetected.

They followed their prey, feeding on fears and paranoia. Creating more with their ability to manipulate sound and ghost out of view as long as shadows were present.

There.

Movement. Since I knew what I was looking for, I could see it.

Its beady black eyes rounded, and it skittered back, rubbing gnarled fingers and lowering its horned head submissively. A grotesque, oversized lizard-looking creature with toad-like skin and a shifting form. A shadow puppet wouldn't hunt a phoenix, which meant one of two things: either it was after Kelsey, or it was one of Gwen's scouts. I couldn't let this one get away.

I held up one finger, silently asking Kelsey to stop talking. "Give me one second." I got out of the car, trying to stay cool, and headed around the side of the building, grabbing a wrench off the tool bench as I went.

"What's wrong?" Her voice followed me.

I picked up my pace and caught it by the slimy tail, which started to squish like putty in my hands. I wrapped it around my fist, securing my grip. The creature shrank away from me, then lunged at me, hissing. I ducked and swung at its exposed chest with the wrench.

It crouched away, writhing in my grip.

"What are you doing in broad daylight?" I demanded.

"She won't ressssst until she findssss you."

Gwen. A tremor rocked my core. If this creature got away, she'd know my location, and we weren't ready. I smashed the wrench into its head, and it slumped, first collapsing like a deflating balloon, then dissipating into a shadow. Gone. That was the thing about shadow puppets—they were easy to kill if you could catch one.

Typically they hunted in packs.

Thankfully, this one seemed to have been alone.

"Nick?" Kelsey's shaky voice sent a shot of ice through my veins. I spun to face her. "A-are you okay?" Her eyes were huge. She pointed down the alley. "I came that way. I-I thought I saw something. Did you?"

I walked back toward Kelsey. "I thought I saw something, too. Weird." I searched her expression. Was she simply scared because the shadow puppet had frightened her or because she'd seen me with it?

"You didn't see anything?" She kept looking past me. I turned and followed her gaze.

"Nothing." I shrugged.

She breathed deep, seeming relieved. Good sign. I held out my arm to guide her back toward the garage.

She bit her lip.

The thing likely hadn't been after her, but it had been scaring her since she'd gotten here. It needed to feed in order to keep its powers in tip-top shape. Her current fear a side effect of its leaching. Once a shadow puppet got ahold of a person, other shadow puppets could smell them for miles, until the wound in that person's aura healed. Not that I could see it, but hers had to be a gaping hole right now.

I couldn't leave her alone in that vulnerable state. "Listen, my shift is almost over. If you want, I can finish taking a look at your car and then give you a ride home."

She looked up at me and the look in her eyes said I'd rescued her. "Really? I mean, I can walk. It's not that far."

I nodded, not wanting her to feel pushed or unsafe. "All right. But if you change your mind. Let me know."

One shadow puppet feeding on people meant a nest around here somewhere. Looked like a hunt occupied tonight's to-do list.

# 15

## CADE

W EEK TWO AT H AVEN B EACH H IGH School wasn't off to a better start than last week's fiasco. Ava had turned out to be hard to read and even harder to gain trust from. But I really didn't want to admit Nick was right. Determination propelled me.

Just as I headed out to find a lunch table, opportunity knocked. Yuki sat alone in the sunshine. Warm rays cast a pretty reddish light on her dark hair. She pushed some behind her ear and then turned the page of her book. If the surefire way to a man's heart was through his stomach, the way to a woman's had to be through her friends. Like it or not, Ava wanted nothing to do with me. So time to turn on the old Elderson charm with her beautiful friend.

Stupid Nick and his "I told you so" frown flashed into my mind along with his words from yesterday, after I'd informed him that all Ava did now was roll her eyes and walk away when I tried to talk to her: *I warned you. Ava needs to see she can trust you. She's worse than a skittish wolf.*

I'd basically bit back at him that maybe he should try and make friends with her since he knew so much.

*I will. The thing is, she always trusts you first.*

Me, huh? I willed my feet to move closer to Ava's best friend. The mysterious Yuki. After all, I did have several classes with her, two already this morning—and I only just now realized that Mr. Thompson had done me an unexpected favor. Good thing, because getting Yuki to voluntarily hang out with me would likely be a challenge.

In short, she befuddled me. Maybe because my attempts to flirt were met with plain disinterest, but her eyes lit with excitement when I brought up whatever book she was reading. Maybe it was the complex emotions that whirled in her expression when she regarded me—like I was more than a bad boy with an attitude problem. Or maybe that she could scoff at my idiotic comments but seem genuinely interested when I had something intelligent to say in class—even if I disagreed with her.

Whatever the reason, when Yuki was around, none of the other girls vying for my attention mattered.

That thought scared me.

So did the fact that I'd finally reached her table, and in my stupid musings, I'd forgotten to plan what to say to her.

She looked up from her book, and as soon as she spotted me, her eyes narrowed. "What do *you* want?"

I slid onto the bench seat next to her, elbow on the table, ankle crossed over my knee, hoping to look very casual. "Did you see the list outside Thompson's classroom?"

"It doesn't matter who my lit partner is. I'll end up doing the entire assignment alone anyway, so I didn't see the point of looking." She turned her attention back to the book.

"Oh." I leaned closer. "You're one of *those* girls. I didn't know they existed."

"Smart ones?"

"No." I hoped my disgusted look showed my sincerity. "Ones who don't let their partners help with the assignment. As if our opinion doesn't matter. Let me guess, we don't help correctly."

"No, you don't."

"Well, I do help. And I expect equal say in this report."

Her eyes narrowed further, and her jaw came loose. "You're my partner? Could this get any worse?"

"Worse?" I acted mock-offended. Not hard, because I actually was offended.

Her eyes scanned my entire body as if my very presence displeased her. "No offense, but you're not exactly the type of guy I can count on. So do your own report."

"What?" I shook my head, trying to wrap my mind around what she'd just said. "You don't even know me. How can you be sure I won't be accountable?"

Her eyebrow arched the same way it did in class when she was about to prove a point with so much logical information to back her up that only a fool would consider a rebuttal. And a ghost of a satisfied smile appeared. "You've been here for two weeks, and you've already missed four days of school—that's forty percent."

"Yeah, that's—"

"I've never seen you cut lit class, but I have sources that tell me you've cut a few other classes, so when you actually do show up, you still miss school."

"The thing is—"

"You might be smart, but that's only going to get you so far before the lack of hard work catches up with you."

"I underst—"

"You are a grasshopper. I am an ant. We just don't work well together." She closed her book, picked up her backpack, and stood before I even had a chance to form an excuse.

"Yuki." I got up to follow her.

She paused, huge sigh totally audible, and looked over her shoulder. And that did it.

That . . . look. Oh no. She started to flicker. One moment she stood under the tree, late-summer wind tugging leaves free. The next moment, she—or someone who could pass for her older sister, face painted white and marked with pretty red makeup—stood beneath a cherry tree. Petals whirled in the wind.

In reality, I tried to lean back and catch myself on the table, but I missed, and my hand slammed into the bench seat. I tumbled to the ground. The vision winked out, and all I saw was a blur.

"Cade?" My name seemed to echo from two places at once: reality and memory.

"Cade?" This time it came from just Yuki. She shook my shoulders.

Her beautiful, worried face filled my line of vision, but I didn't want to lose my lunch on her, so I pushed her to the side as gently as I could and heaved. At least nothing came out. But seriously, did this have to happen now of all times? It was impossible to impress a girl while emptying your stomach on the ground next to her shoes.

A soft touch rubbed my back.

My stomach stopped roiling.

My heart jumped in surprise, and I looked at her over my shoulder. There had to be something about her. Her coppery-brown eyes. The beauty mark just above the right corner of her lip. Why was she triggering that memory? I tried to blink away her glasses. She looked so much like that older woman. A crease formed between her eyebrows, and I realized I was gawking.

"Sorry." I stood and offered her my hand to help her up.

She stared at it as though that was some strange gesture. Then she took it, and I pulled her to standing. She pushed her hair behind her ear and turned her attention to the ground, dragging the toe of her shoe through the grass. "Is that why you miss class all the time?" Those coppery eyes latched onto me.

I breathed deep. There went my "in" with Yuki. All that showing off in lit class so Thompson would make us partners flushed down the drain. She'd never cooperate on the project with me if she knew how often I nearly passed out. I clenched my hands reflexively and then gave her my most winning smile. "You caught me."

"I'll give you a chance."

What? I tried not to let the surprise show on my face, but I was certain I'd failed when a grin overtook her features.

She pointed a finger at me. "Don't blow it."

I motioned to myself with both hands. "How would I blow it?"

Her finger made circles at my face as if to emphasize her point, and she started walking backward toward the school, smiling at me with that satisfied smirk. "One idiotic comment about anything other than the project, and you're on your own."

I followed, grinning like an idiot. I sort of didn't care. The playful gleam in her eye had sent an arrow straight into my chest—one of Cupid's, I'd wager. I was in trouble. "What idiotic comment?"

"Oh, I don't know." The sarcasm leaked into her body language. "That one about how perhaps Hermia shouldn't have defied her father's wishes in the first place."

Okay, that *Midsummer Night's Dream* reference might have been for the sole purpose of riling her up. "I wasn't being serious. I was—"

"Trying to ruffle my feathers?" Her smug smile said she didn't need an answer.

I caught up to her and extended my arm behind her to prevent her from running into someone. "Careful there. Might want to watch where you're going."

"Oh, I'm watching *you*, Puck." She turned to face the direction she was walking, but now she walked close to me, her shoulder bumping my arm as more students returning to class walked around us.

"Puck?" I chuckled. "You think I'm clever and mischievous. I'll take it. But with Lysander's amazing looks, right?"

She rolled her eyes. "That's exactly the kind of idiotic comment—"

"That's hardly fair. You can't tell a guy he's like Puck and then expect him to act as serious as Macduff."

"Different play."

"I'm aware."

That got me two heartbeats of eye contact as she studied my face. I did a really stupid thing, and for that small moment, I dropped my mask.

Her eyes seemed to flicker with an understanding that made me regret that move. But we'd entered the school, so the mask slipped back into place reflexively. Other students mingling in the halls and heading to class caused my proximity to Yuki to close even further. She stopped at her locker and faced me. "Meet me Saturday. Student library. Bring good ideas."

"Is this like a job interview?"

She wore the same knowing smirk as that woman in the vision, and my heart skipped a beat. "Like I said, don't blow it."

I walked away from her, backward, so I could keep eye contact as long as possible. "I don't plan to." And as soon as I turned around, I remembered that I was supposed to be getting close to Yuki because of Ava. This was going to be harder than I'd thought.

# 16

## AVA

SUN-SATURATED SUBURBIA LAZILY scrolled by as I stared aimlessly out the passenger window. Two weeks of school had passed with no more weird visions. Maybe everything would go back to normal. I desperately needed normalcy. Even the typical "you belong nowhere and with no one, Ava Elderson" I'd spent my entire existence trying to change seemed better than this odd nightmare mess.

"Earth to Ava." Yuki's voice wrecking-balled my internal crisis for the moment.

I turned in my seat, realizing I'd been quiet for most of the ride home from school, and faced Yuki. "Sorry! I zoned out."

She smirked. "I noticed. Still thinking about Wyatt?"

Not if I could help it. Anything else. I needed to talk about anything else. What else had happened today at sch—oh! When the great topic change presented itself, I jumped on it. "Please tell me you're coming tonight?"

Yuki pulled into the Fieldses' driveway. "I don't know." Her shoulders slumped.

"What?" Definitely not a typical Yuki reaction. "Lisa Welch invited us—*us*—to her back-to-school bonfire party! Last year, her midterms bash was all you could talk about for weeks. Now you're not willing to go?"

Car in park, she clutched the steering wheel tight and fingered the rosary beads dangling from her keychain. "It's not that, Ava. I want to go." When she looked up, the pleading expression in her eyes sliced my soul.

"You just don't want to sneak out?"

She laughed, but it was halfhearted, and she stared at her lap. "I do. I just . . . I'm tired today. We'll see how I feel tonight. Okay?" Now she glanced up at me, begging me to understand and to refrain from asking questions like "are you going to be okay?" or "how much time do you have left really?"

The reality of my best friend's heart defect suddenly crushed me. Even when I stayed in one place for longer than six months, cruel fate ripped my relationships from me. But this wasn't the line of thinking I'd promised her. And I still had her right now. And honestly, no one really knew their time, right?

I swallowed the ache in my throat and focused on how much I loved my friend. I grabbed her hand and gave it a squeeze before letting go. "Of course. I get it. No pressure." That got me a soft smile.

"Thanks. You're the best." Then she leaned her head back against the car seat. "Tell me I'm crazy."

"What? Why?" I couldn't stop my surprised laugh.

"That guy. Cade. How can he be so perfectly handsome?"

That thought made me want to burst out laughing, and I had no idea why. I let a small giggle sneak out. "Tell me you're not crushing already!"

"I know! It's against my code! Every fiber of my being is angry that his smile keeps playing through my head on repeat." She looked over at me. "What are you grinning about?"

"Oh nothing. Just thinking he'll likely be there."

She laughed. "You're my friend. You're supposed to talk me *out* of this."

"Out of crushing over a guy while in high school? No way. I'm gonna let that linger for a bit and see what happens."

She fake glared.

I raised my eyebrows a couple times in quick succession. "So?"

She tapped her fingers on the steering wheel, considering. "I have a doctor's appointment in an hour. We'll see how I feel after."

"Okay. Text me." I grabbed my stuff and got out of her car. "It'll be fun!"

"I know, I know." She waved me away and pulled out of the driveway.

And I couldn't help but wonder if Yuki's parents knew about her condition before they adopted her. If they thought they could better her odds and save her, or if they just fell in love with her in a way no one ever fell for me.

Because no matter what happened to Yuki, she'd die loved.

Me? Unless she outlived me, no one would even notice I was gone.

Maybe it was time to change that. Maybe Ava Elderson would do what she'd never done before. Maybe it was time to start putting down roots.

I checked myself in the mirror again. The pretty dark-green tank top and perfectly fitted gray hoodie went amazing with my ripped jeans. Time to shine. Alone.

Because Yuki wasn't coming.

That meant tonight I faced my future as a new me. It could be a clean-slate night. I didn't have to worry about those troublesome visions, nor did I have to focus on the past at all. I could just put it all by the wayside and be normal. Maybe make some new friends.

I breathed in and out. Then I closed my closet door and turned off the light. The full moon shone big and bright through my bedroom window, and the room started to spin.

I fell to my knees against the door. Pinning it closed. Pinning myself in someone else's memory.

Not again.

The memory person—me—opened a door to a stable. The strong

scents of hay and horse met me—much better than the dank, dirty urine smell in the city—and I didn't mind. Something about living closer to the border, out in the country air, made everything freer.

I wiped my hands over my dress and its huge, floor-touching skirt. I wore an apron of sorts over the ugly, itchy ensemble. It almost looked like it belonged on a wax figure in a museum of history. Great, so a memory from a long time ago. Like chamber-pot-and-no-electricity long time ago.

I stepped inside the stable and caught sight of a tall young man I didn't expect to see. He stood, back to me, brushing the marchioness's bay mare. He gave her a handful of what I presumed to be oats. Then she pressed her head into his hand and pushed. He chuckled. "That's enough for you."

I cleared my throat, and he turned to face me. "Hello." My greeting hung between us as I granted my attention to his piercing blue eyes, and they stole my breath.

It was clear memory-me had never met him, but real-me recognized him: Wyatt.

He stared at me for more than a moment, and then his lips curved up, and his eyes lit in a smile. "What can I do for you, ma'am?"

Southern English accent. Warm and welcoming, but completely surprising. Something in my stomach fluttered, and I bowed my head in a quick curtsey, sure my cheeks were heating. "The marchioness wishes for you to ready her horse, Mr. . . . ?"

"Wilcox." He dipped his head low in a bow and looked up at me with that lopsided smile. "I will have the horse ready for her shortly."

"Thank you."

"My pleasure, Miss . . . ?"

"Elderson." I smiled politely at Mr. Wilcox, but his return eye contact pulled a real grin free, and it surprised me how easily it came. "You're new here?"

"The marquis hired me recently."

I approached the mare he'd been petting and ran my hand over her silky nose, aware of Mr. Wilcox's eyes on me. Heat flushed up my neck, and I glanced at him askance.

His tunic was tattered along the edges, and small tears near his knees revealed that his breeches were threadbare. Even his left shoe had a hole in the top. He seemed to notice me looking, for he rubbed the back of his neck and stepped away from me. "I should probably—" He motioned over his shoulder with his thumb and didn't finish the sentence as he walked away.

"Mr. Wilcox?"

"Yes?" He turned to face me, eyes expectant.

"As you know, the marquis and marchioness will be away for a few weeks. Tonight, many of us will gather in the ballroom for dancing and music. I hope you will join us. But it's a secret. No one wants to get in trouble while the cats are away."

The smallest smile lit his eyes. "Thank you, Miss Elderson. I will most definitely be there."

I curtsied as I left, nearly tripping over my own skirt and entirely too pleased that his grin deepened when I looked over my shoulder to wave again.

The memory swirled, but I didn't want to pull out of it—I craved answers—so I allowed it to take me further into the night. The sounds of music played beneath the setting sun, and faces of people I'd never seen, but apparently knew, laughed and danced as the light of day lingered for a little while longer.

I had yet to see Mr. Wilcox but wondered how late his chores would have kept him. A bit of disappointment sank like a stone in my chest. He might need all the daylight he had left.

"Miss Elderson?"

I turned at the sound of my name to see a truly handsome man with dark hair and deep, blue eyes. My hope rose, light and buoyant. And my face flushed. The fact that he caused this much fluttering in my chest made me quite embarrassed. I could barely look at him as I spoke. "Mr. Wilcox."

His eyes softened, tinged with what looked like joy, and he held out his hand as if asking for mine. "May I?"

I grasped it. His rough fingers touching mine sent a shock of warmth through me. He smiled shyly, and I took him in. He wore a jerkin and doublet, and it showed off his broad shoulders and muscular chest nicely. The sleeves and edges were tattered, and he was missing at least one button, hidden except when he extended his arm.

His fingers were strong. Calloused. Rough. Hands of a man who worked hard. He lowered his head, a small crinkle in the corner of his eye made me think him quite self-conscious.

Even his confidence seemed to wane as the arm he'd linked with mine lowered. Briefly his eyes flicked to mine. "I-I realize I'm not—"

I squeezed my arm against his. "Are you about to apologize for your wardrobe, Mr. Wilcox?"

He sort of laughed, more self-deprecating than anything, and glanced shyly at me. "More my lack of money." He looked around the ballroom at the other men all in their Sunday best—which didn't compare remotely to the wealthy people but did show their status as servants of the rich. "This is my only doublet, so I fear that while it's my best doublet, it's also most definitely my worst."

I laughed outright, and it felt amazing, as if some deep-seated worry that this vision didn't disclose to me melted, like butter over a stove. "Whether your best or worst, I think you're quite handsome."

His eyebrows rose, and those blue eyes widened magnificently in a way that revealed his true youth, not only in age, but also in the naïveté of these formal customs—clearly he wasn't a servant of nobility before coming here. He'd be someone who wouldn't be afraid to take me from the restricting structure in this room and out into the brisk, summer air. Under the moon. The stars. Something my brothers would never approve of.

Brothers?

That thought tried hard to drag me out of this memory, but I didn't want to go just yet. I pushed myself back in.

Wyatt, er, Mr. Wilcox led me toward the dancers. "You are too kind, Miss Elderson. For your beauty surely outshines everything in this room."

"Outshines? Really, Mr. Wilcox. It is you who is much too kind."

Then a true smile lit his eyes.

"Wyatt, what do you have here?" A saucy young man approached us, a mug of beer in one hand. Clearly another new hire since I'd never seen him before. "A beautiful jewel if I ever laid eyes on one." He extended his hand and kissed the back of mine. He glanced at Wyatt. "Do you mind?"

Did *he* mind? What if I minded? I stiffened. I'd seen his kind before, but I could care for myself. I touched this man's hand. "Are you offering a dance before introductions, Mr. . . . ?

"Denton. Why yes, I am. My apologies, lovely lady."

"It's Miss Elderson. And I hope you can keep up."

"Keep up?" He reached for my hand as I slipped it from his grasp. "Where I'm from, a man leads."

"Where you're from, the men must get lost often."

Denton stood there dumbfounded for a breath, but Mr. Wilcox bowed his head and hid a chuckle. In that moment, I caught his gaze. He stepped in and offered his hand. I took it. I didn't look away from his eyes as he led me to the dance floor.

Cade might have teased me relentlessly about never letting another man bridle my heart, and Nick would have scrutinized any man who attempted to rein me in.

I breathed deep as the memory blacked out.

My whole body shook. Cade.

Cade I knew.

But Nick? Who the heck was Nick?

And what were Wyatt and I doing in sixteenth-century England? Holy heavens. I pressed my hands over my ears as my blood raced through my veins. I needed to make this stop. I checked my phone. It had only been two minutes? How had all that happened in two minutes?

I leaned my back against the closet door to catch my breath and slow my pulse. Whose memories were these, and why were they replacing things with people I already knew?

Except Denton. I'd never seen his face before. And yet he'd been in my memory.

And Cade. I'd spoken of Cade as if he was my brother. We had the same last name. That made sense. I could easily put him in that memory because of the name similarity. Except why had he appeared in these memories before I'd met him? And brothers plural? Wait. At school, Cade had mentioned a brother. But he hadn't named him that I could remember.

If his name was Nick . . . maybe I wouldn't be able to put the past behind me at this bonfire tonight. Maybe I'd be marching right up to Cade and Wyatt and demanding answers.

If only I knew what questions to ask.

I had to get answers out of them. Because it all felt so real. Wyatt's hand on my waist. The way I wanted to stare in his eyes. I pulled out my phone and texted him. *You going to the bonfire?*

I thought I'd have to wait forever for a response, but it came in quickly: *No.*

What was I supposed to do with that? Ask him why not? I mean, I wanted to, but I really didn't want to put myself out there. Except he told me I could call him whenever. And I wanted him to come, so I needed a reason for him to not show. A reason that wasn't something awful like "I'm making out with my girlfriend. She likes comics and doesn't have weird visions of past events that never occurred. Stop texting me."

But another text came through from him: *I'm sick.*

I guess that was actually pretty awful. *I'm sorry. I hope you feel better soon.*

*Thanks.*

Poor thing. I stood. I wouldn't get answers from Wyatt tonight, but maybe Cade would be there. That one seemed the type to show up at a non-school party ready to claim popular status.

It was decided, then. The best thing to do was to make friends with him. Then I could get close enough for answers.

Another text vibrated. I checked it. From Wyatt.

*Call it a gut reaction, but I think you should stay away from Cade tonight.*

My blood frosted. What else had he remembered? And which one of them was I supposed to listen to?

# 17



## THE BONFIRE BLAZED, TALL AND HOT.

I headed toward a crowd of kids near the fire, hoping to catch a glimpse of Cade. No sign yet. Unwitting little toads jumped toward the heat. I stopped and turned one of them around. "At a distance, little guy."

"Wow. You're beautiful *and* you save animals."

I rolled my eyes and turned to face the jock standing with two red disposable cups as he nonchalantly offered one to me.

"Keep it. I pour my own drinks."

"Don't mind if I do." He took a sip. I cocked my eyebrow. He drank another—this one long and draining.

"In that case." I held out my hand for the now half-empty drink.

He relinquished it and started in on the other. "You're not very trusting, are you?"

"Does that scare you off?"

He shook his head.

Darn.

Now that I'd freed up his hand, he extended it. "Patrick."

"Ava."

"Pretty name, too."

I laughed. Wyatt's old-fashioned flirting had been so much better. Then I mentally shook that thought. Because was that even real?

"You looking for someone?" Patrick asked, and I realized I'd been scanning the other partygoers again.

"No," I lied.

He scrutinized me with a very judgmental cocked eyebrow. Wait. I'd seen this guy before. He was on the lacrosse team. Maybe he knew Cade. He seemed the type to try out for sports. What could it hurt to ask?

I reneged my lie, "Just some friends."

"Maybe I can help?"

"You don't happen to know Cade Elderson?"

"Uh, new guy? Yeah. But I haven't seen him." He seemed to be waiting for me to continue.

Oh. Right. I'd said *friends* plural. "Umm or Wyatt Wil—"

"Wyatt Wilcox?" He moved closer to me, shaking his head. "No, you don't want anything to do with him. Trust me."

My chest clutched. "W-why not?"

"Well . . . he has . . . a temper."

I hugged myself and waited for Patrick to explain.

He chuckled nervously. "I play lacrosse. He used to be on the team, but he got kicked off."

"For what?" Warning bells went off in my skull.

"About two years ago, one of the seniors on the team threw a party. The whole team was there. Wyatt, being the only freshman—well they hazed him pretty good."

"They?"

There was that nervous chuckle again. "Look, I was a sophomore, and it was my first year on the team, too, so I wasn't gonna do anything to attract unwanted attention, you know?"

I waved my hand to get him to continue, then I wrapped my arms around myself to try and look casual, but really I hoped it hid my worry.

"Wyatt got drunk. His older sister showed up to get him, and Scott intercepted her. When Wyatt found out Scott was trying to put the moves on his sister, he went off. Bashed Scott's face in—I'm not saying it was unprovoked. I'm just saying Scott ended up in the emergency room. So tread carefully."

My mouth went dry. "Wyatt beat him up? You sure Scott didn't start it?" I kept my arms tightly crossed.

"He did. But . . . Wyatt kept going long after it should have been finished."

I bit my lip. No way. That image didn't fit the Wyatt from my weird visions. Then again, they were weird visions. "He just seems so nice."

"You really liked him, huh? Sorry." Patrick seemed suddenly unsure. "I just never know how much to share on a first date—meeting! Did I say date?" He winced, and even in the firelight it looked like his neck might be getting a bit blotchy.

In fact, it seemed like my eyesight adjusted well in the dark. Better than ever before. Weird.

He kept mumbling about something, and I decided that in the spirit of New-Leaf Ava, I'd test the waters of friend making with Patrick. I mean, why not? I let him flirt with me for a while longer. His nervousness became kind of endearing. He was pretty easy to talk to, and before I knew it, we'd headed on a walk toward the wooded area beyond Lisa's backyard.

A huge boulder rested at the end of the game trail, down by the lake. Maybe I'd make out with him when we got there. Maybe not. But this guy hadn't appeared in any weird visions, and he made me feel slightly normal, so perhaps not finding Cade here tonight and learning about Wyatt's dark past was for the best. Maybe I could just walk away from the strangeness.

"So, you think these woods are haunted?" he asked as we walked along with nothing but phone flashlights and red Solo cups.

"What?"

"That's the whole thing about the property. They say the woods are haunted. Everyone says they don't believe it, but no one comes in here."

If he thought I was going to get scared and cuddle up to him, he was the crazy one.

Someone screamed. Like, a real terror-laced scream. I halted to figure out where in the woods it was coming from, and my blood chilled.

Patrick looked at me. "What was that?"

I dropped my cup, pocketed my phone, and reached for my belt. My stance defensive, grounded, something ingrained by muscle memory. Muscle memory from what? But I knew. Because when my hand didn't find a weapon at my side, a new wave of worry streaked through me. Okay. Weird. More screaming, crying, shouting, and . . . growling? I headed toward the sound.

Patrick stopped in his tracks. "You—you're going toward it?"

"What if she needs help?"

There was another cry, closer, and someone raced out of the trees. Patrick shined his flashlight, and she blocked her eyes, but it was clearly Lisa. True horror bled into her features, and she grabbed hold of me. Her fingers clung to my arm. And she was shaking. My blood pulsed faster through my veins.

"Something attacked Holly!" Tears streaked her mascara.

"What?" I steadied her. My eyesight revealed specks of blood all over her clothes and her hands. What on earth had happened? Part of me wanted to run, the other part urged me to . . . protect? "Are you hurt?"

"No." She tugged my sleeve and glanced over her shoulder. "We have to run."

I tried to steady her. To breathe. "Tell me what happened."

"He's still back there!" She shook me, hysterical.

"Lisa, calm down. Who?" I breathed in to steady my heartbeat, looked straight into her eyes, and willed her to be able to focus.

Her grip on my sleeves lessened, but she spoke through sobs. "Cade."

My lungs stilled.

"The new guy killed Holly?" Patrick toed the border of hysteria, too.

"No! Holly followed us back there. Cade and I were at the rock. Holly was jealous. This monster came from nowhere and attacked." Her voice came out between squeaks as she tried to breathe. "Cade was fighting it. I left. I left him." She shook me again, frantically tugging me to follow her.

"Calm down. I need you to call the police." I looked at Patrick.

"Get her home." I pried her arms off me and headed toward the trees on shaky legs.

"You can't go in there!" Panic rounded her eyes. She practically collapsed into Patrick. He stood ready to run, but indecision rooted him to the spot as he watched me head *toward* this mysterious monster. Truthfully, my worry stemmed less from that and more for Cade's safety.

A figure stumbled onto the game path from the woods and hunched over, hands on his knees. My stomach squeezed.

"Cade?" I marched right up to him. "What are you doing?"

Blood trickled from his hairline, and the right side of his leather jacket was shredded. He staggered forward and tried to stand. "Ava?" A wildness widened his eyes. "You have to get out of here."

I steadied him, and a spike of ice chilled me to the core. "What's going on?"

Patrick pointed behind us and stared, trembling.

Lisa screamed. "The monster!"

I didn't see anything, but the crunching of leaves told me something headed this way from the woods. I spun around, scanning. Shaking. Praying this wasn't real. It reminded me too much of the night of Mr. Fields's accident.

Cade looked right into my eyes. His grip on my arm told me he was scared, too. "I need you to trust me. Get them out of here."

He winced and leaned forward. I touched his chest to catch him, about to ask if it was another migraine, but my hand felt something warm and wet beneath his unzipped jacket. I pulled the shredded section aside and gasped.

So did Patrick. "Dude. Y-you're bleeding. Like, bad!"

Blood seeped through his shirt, wet and shiny, and very, very real.

Lisa started sobbing. "It got him. He's going to die. Where's Holly? Is she—d-don't tell me she's—"

Cade held out his hand, as if begging Lisa and Patrick to focus. "There's a maniac in the woods. Everyone needs to get out of here."

"Th-this is a prank, right?" Patrick clutched Lisa close.

I motioned to Cade's growing bloodstain, and my chest tightened.

"This is not a prank, Patrick. Please listen to my brother. Get everyone out of h-here." My voice started to break.

"O-okay." He pushed Lisa back up the trail toward the house, but she balked, sobbing about Holly. Getting her to comply was not going to be easy.

I draped Cade's arm over my shoulder and pressed my hand against the wound to stop the bleeding, and he breathed in through his teeth. "Can you walk?"

He handed me a knife. "Ava, did you—"

Lisa screamed again. The kind that curdled blood. And a shot of adrenaline seared my insides as a strange-looking creature leapt out of the woods. A man? Not quite. As my eyes adjusted, I could tell very clearly that it wasn't a man. Its muscles bulged, hair covered its entire body, and its limbs were long, grotesque, almost contorted. It had pointed ears on the top of its head. An animal? A wolf on some weird science-experiment steroids? What the actual heck!

It turned and sniffed the wind, revealing an elongated snout. Almost lupine. I held in my own startled cry. It burned in my chest like a fire that wanted to come out, but I knew instinctively I had to remain quiet. Calm. Still.

I trembled. Clutched the knife tighter.

Cade stood next to me, another knife in hand. "It's silver. Slit its throat or stab its heart. Anything to get the poison in its bloodstream fast. If we work together, we can get him. Remember: no fast movements."

Remember? Why would he use that word? Also, how was I so suddenly calm right now? It wasn't like I'd ever done this before. Right? But even as I thought it, I knew I had. Just like I knew in my gut how to kill this thing. It hissed through serrated teeth from its unnatural snout.

Lisa ran.

No!

Its head swiveled in her direction. Like a bolt, it tore off after her. I raced toward it, trying to head it off, but it was faster than me. A long, clawed arm reached forward. Nails grabbed Lisa's skin as she screamed. And it ripped into her neck. She dropped.

I stopped running, covered my mouth with a trembling hand, and my knees turned to water.

Patrick shrieked and wouldn't stop.

The beast turned toward him.

I had to do something.

With all my speed, I raced in front of him and stood between Patrick and the monster. "Don't move," I whispered.

He wouldn't stop whimpering. Was Lisa moving? No. I started to lose feeling in my legs. No, Ava. Stay calm. With that, my emotions transformed to sharp focus.

"Call an ambulance, Patrick!" Cade's voice snapped him out of his stupor.

The beast leaned forward, bloody saliva dripping from its jaws.

And Patrick lost it. "No way!" He scrambled out of there.

Why would no one listen? The monster tracked Patrick's movements, muscles quivering. I knew it would chase him. Cade swore and darted the other way—faster than Patrick—to get the monster to chase him instead. Deeper into the woods he lured it. How would he fight it alone?

My heart jumped into my throat. Not my brother! I sprang into action, legs pumping faster than ever before, dodging trees and sailing over brush like they were no obstacle. There, I had a clear shot. And suddenly, at this moment, I knew what to do. Without thinking, I threw the knife. It sank into the creature's back, between its shoulder blades. Perfect shot.

Slowly, it faced me. Golden eyes narrowing. Saliva dripping from sharp fangs. And it let out the most ear-shattering cry I'd ever heard.

It stepped toward me. Stalking. Willing me to run so it could chase.

I got that feeling I used to get when I was a kid. Right after I turned off the bedroom light but still had to make it to my bed. I could picture my room exactly how it was, after the light snuffed, bathing everything in darkness. During that moment, the monsters under my bed became a possibility. Things that existed in the dark. Alive like Schrodinger's cat. And I had to get off the floor before they could reach me and pull me under my bed.

That was this moment. I had to make to the bed—or in this case, slay the monster.

A strange sniffing noise seemed to echo on the wind. Then it broke apart from the breeze like a dissonance with nature.

Golden eyes gleamed in the full moon's light, but I could still see. And this thing was going in for the kill.

I didn't have a weapon.

My heart hammered.

If I moved, it would move. And it was a lot faster than me.

In a blink, it lunged for me.

I darted back but tripped. In the second it took me to hit the ground, the monster towered over me.

Cade raced up behind it and grabbed the creature's arm. Yanked, forcing the animal's arm behind its back. It tried to turn on Cade, and I heard a terrible crack. That didn't stop it. It snapped at Cade's face, and he slashed his knife across the creature's throat with speed that rivaled the monster's. And it fell, clutching its neck, blood spurting out from between its long, clawed, hairy fingers.

The form dissipated, turning into something more like a wolf. And limping, it ran away from us. Gone like a laugh in the wind.

I picked myself off the ground and caught Cade as he started to fall over. "You just saved my life."

He smiled. "Does this mean you hate me less?"

I released all the tension and adrenaline building inside me with a laugh. Cade joined me but pressed his hand against his side. "We should go after it." He handed me back the knife I'd thrown at the creature. Apparently he'd pulled it out of the monster's back.

I took it. "You're not going anywhere like that."

"I'll be fine soon. Just give me a minute." He pulled up his shirt; the wound seemed to be turning black.

My throat squeezed. "What . . . what's happening to you? You need a doctor. Now."

He grabbed my arm as I groped for my cell phone. "No." His voice came out strangled. "So, you don't remember everything?"

I stared at Cade, pulse pounding. "Remember? What am I supposed to remember?"

"You called me your brother."

I breathed out, my chest tightening. I had. And I'd believed it. "Do you . . . remember me?"

"Yeah." He groaned and fell forward.

"Cade, you need an ambulance."

"No, but Lisa and Holly . . ."

"Are they alive?" Panic rushed back into me, unwelcome and overpowering.

"I-I don't know."

"Well you are. So let me—"

His bloody hand stopped me from dialing. "I'll heal eventually, just find Nick."

Nick. Of course. My breathing stalled. The other name in my memories. My other supposed brother.

Breath left my lungs, and I wanted to sink to my knees. Cade grabbed the phone from my hand. Sirens wailed in the distance. Patrick must have called them.

I turned my attention back to Cade, my mouth suddenly dry. "What do you mean, heal?" Was he like me? Was I like him?

"Nick has all the antidotes in his stupid vest." Then his head lolled against my arm.

"Cade?" I tapped his cheek. "Cade!" I shouted.

More snapping in the brush made me clutch his knife tight and turn. I eased Cade's head to the ground and stood, scanning the trees. Quivering. A guy carrying a freaking bow and arrows stepped onto the path. He lowered his weapon and put out his free hand as if to calm me down.

Then he rushed up to Cade, dropped to his knees next to him, and ripped his bloody shirt apart. "He's not healing at all? It bit him." He looked up at me, eyes wide. "How long ago?"

"I-I don't know." I stared at my hands. Bloody. Shaking. Hands. The guy poured some clear liquid onto Cade's wound. In a few moments, Cade's breathing evened, and the wound started to slowly close.

Holy crap. I stepped away from him. "H-how did you—"

"Ava?" He glanced at me, and I knew those eyes. Gray-green eyes. Like mine. Like Cade's. Familiar eyes. Tears threatened. I did not want to believe any of this. It could not be real. Should not be real.

Tiny pinpricks seemed to skitter over my skin. "H-how do you know me?"

He nodded toward the bloody knife in my hand. "You remembered how to take care of the monster?"

I took another step away. "I might have."

The guy moved toward me.

I held up Cade's knife. "Get away from me."

He put up his hands in surrender. "It's me. Nick."

Breathing hurt. I didn't want any of this. "That supposed to mean something?"

I looked down at Cade.

A different Cade flashed in my head—a different memory.

Bloody Cade.

Dying Cade.

*"Cade! Don't you die, Cade. Caderyn, I'll never forgive you if you leave me,"* I'd said.

I shook the memory and stared at Nick.

And a different memory consumed me.

A warm chuckle behind me. Someone gently tugged my hair, braiding it. "You're pulling, Nick."

"Well, hold still."

"Why do I have to have braids anyway?"

"You get two because you're too young to kiss boys."

"Who would want to kiss her?" Another boy entered. Younger than the last memory, but still Cade.

I faced Nick. He looked so old, but real-me placed him at about sixteen. "How do I look?" my tiny memory-me voice asked.

"Beautiful, Sister." He smiled.

His expression sent a pang into my chest, almost as if I deeply missed his smile. Little girl me threw my arms around him and hugged him close. And my heart warmed. It felt so amazingly full. Like nothing I'd ever experienced in this lifetime. I felt loved.

The emotion knocked me out of the memory and to this very surreal reality.

"Are you okay?" Nick held out a hand for me, and the look of concern in his eyes made me avert my gaze. I didn't want him to see my tears. I covered my face and hid.

"Ava?"

"I'm fine. My head hurts."

"Y-your head?" The way the words came out surrounded by so much air made me snap my gaze to meet his. His eyes were wide. "How bad?"

I glanced at the still-sleeping Cade and recalled his migraines.

"Are your memories giving you headaches?" He spoke slowly.

"No. I didn't mean that. I'm confused."

His shoulders visibly relaxed, and he expelled a breath. "Confusion I can deal with."

I swallowed as my throat started to tighten and ache. "How do you know me?"

His Adam's apple bobbed. "Because I'm your brother."

The word sent a chill through me. Brother. Family. I wanted to cry, but I sucked it in and straightened my spine. Brother? And where had he been? Fire filled my gut. "Really? And how long have you known? Because I've been sitting in a variety of foster homes thinking I had no one. And now I'm supposed to just accept that I have a couple of brothers?"

"Whoa. No, I had to remember, too, like you're remembering. I've been searching for you."

I tried to infuse as much venom as possible, but inside, the bars around the cage in which I'd placed my hope started to flex. "And this is how you decide to break it to me?"

"Normally, I wait for you to remember."

"Normally?" I didn't even know how to begin to understand

that. I staggered back another step and dropped the knife. "Normally? As in—"

"As in you've been born before. Aren't you starting to remember your past cycles?"

"I'm sorry, cycles?"

"You're a phoenix, Ava. After phoenixes die, they are reborn in a different place in time."

"Like reincarnated."

"No. You're still you. No different body or anything. Just . . . you're here again."

Relief fought with sanity in my brain. "I'm supposed to buy this?"

"Give it time. You'll remember."

I looked down at Cade, still knocked out. "Does he? Is he even okay?"

"He'll be all right as soon as he comes to. It takes him a while to heal sometimes."

I backed away from Nick. Part of me didn't want to leave Cade. But then Nick picked up his crossbow and aimed it at the trees, away from me.

He looked over his shoulder at me. "She's looking for you. She can't know you're here."

Blood rushed through my body twice as fast and twice as hot. "Sh-she?"

Nick's eyes met mine, wide and wild. "Run, Ava. And don't look back. No matter what."

He didn't need to tell me again. Right now these trees were the only thing keeping Schrodinger's second monster from becoming a reality. So I ran like my life depended on it. Because I had a feeling that the box had been irreversibly opened.

So long, normalcy.

# 18



THE RUSTLING IN THE TREES HAD TOLD me another monster lurked close. Cade still hadn't come to, but the bite on his side was healing.

I picked up my crossbow, silver-tipped arrow already loaded, and stepped in between Cade and the trees. "Come out. I dare you."

Branches snapped to the left, and I pivoted to face it as it clawed its way into view. My heart revved, and my breathing quickened as the beast towered above me. I knew it. Well, I knew what it was. The lupine-like stretch of its face resembled a werewolf, but this beast didn't have a lithe, lanky body made for sneaking after prey. This creature was massive. Its muscular chest that rivaled King Kong's and red eyes—characteristic of vampires—told me what it was. A mutt of sorts. Gwen's creation.

I'd been right to tell Ava to run. Gwen couldn't know I'd already found her.

I needed as much time as possible. Gwen would wait until she was at full strength before she came hunting, but she'd sent her creations to scout us out. To get rid of me and Cade. To take Ava.

Over. My. Dead. Body.

Saliva stretched between its upper and lower canines as the monster opened its massive jaws and roared.

"Where is she?" I yelled.

It laughed, deep and throaty. "She knows where you are."

Panic jolted in my chest, but I held my weapon steady. "Then she wouldn't have sent you." I shot the arrow. It stuck right where the monster's heart would be, but this beast ripped the bolt out and snapped it in half. My pulse thundered. I had to think fast. I couldn't move away from my protective spot in front of my brother in case it wouldn't target me and went after Cade instead.

And since when were Gwen's creations strong enough to withstand a shot to the heart? How much stronger had she gotten?

How much longer did Cade have?

My throat felt thick, but I didn't have time to think about this. I had to figure out how to put this beast down. Now. Piercing the brain ought to do it. I pulled out my gun, silencer equipped, and prayed the police weren't out of their vehicles yet. Then I unloaded.

A shot to the head.

It staggered forward, losing momentum.

I shot again.

Again.

Red trickled down its fur, and it fell.

Turned to white dust and whisked away in the wind.

Silver alone might not be enough to take those things out anymore.

I dropped to my knees beside my brother, and Gwen's words about Cade, from the last time I'd seen her, rang crystal clear in my brain: *"He doesn't have long now. And all of his secret, buried powers are coming alive in me. I'll take Ava's powers, too. I'll be stronger than you soon. You'll never stop me."*

If she was truly taking Cade's powers, no wonder her creations were getting stronger. I needed Ava. I needed her to take Gwen out for good. And the only chance I had was if I could get Ava to access her fire. If she didn't have that, Gwen and her monsters would take us all out again.

I breathed deep, letting myself feel for her presence. She wasn't that close yet. If she were moving in, she'd choose a full moon night. There weren't enough of her creations in the area for it to be this night. If it were, I'd know. I'd feel her.

Unfortunately, she'd feel where I was, too. I turned to my brother. "Cade?" My heart clutched as I shook his shoulder. "Cade!"

He gasped in a breath and opened his eyes. "Nick?" He tried to sit up and pressed his hand against his head.

"Can you walk? We need to get out of here."

# 19

AVA

Last night, when I'd returned home, I hardly said anything to Jean or Dave aside from smiling like I'd had fun and making up an excuse about being tired.

Thankfully Holly and Lisa had made it onto ambulances, and Patrick's ramblings had led to a "wild-animal attack" conclusion.

But none of that helped me. So, this morning I sat on my bedroom floor, leaning against my bed, Ajax next to me with his massive head in my lap. The soft sound of Dave laughing in the other room at something on TV made things even more surreal.

I'd fought a monster.

A real monster.

I'd thrown a knife into its back, and I'd felt nothing.

Well, I felt plenty, but all of that had crashed into me later. I'd hidden up here in my room, shaking. Pacing. Disbelieving. Even now, I couldn't believe this was real. I pressed my face into my hands. What the heck was a phoenix? Nick with those scared eyes. And Cade—his wound had closed. I'd watched it close!

Holly and Lisa were in the hospital.

And Nick had said *she* was after me. She who?

How much trouble was I in?

I was a phoenix—whatever that meant. Nick had said something about being reborn. Like a flower that came back every season? It obviously gave me healing powers.

And that explained the memories. *If* all of this was true. I buried my fingers in Ajax's fur. Something deep in my mind agreed that this made sense, even as the rest of me tried hard to reject it.

It explained my . . . existence.

I couldn't remember anything before the forest, but every police report had called me the girl with no past. I'd come from nowhere. It was like I'd been born there. Soot stained my clothes. I saw a huge bright light and Cade holding my hand.

Why it had taken me so long to remember he was there, I didn't know. Maybe because they never told me I was with someone.

But when I tried to look back now, all I remembered was a bright light surrounding me, engulfing me. Like fire. Then I just emerged into the woods. My white nightgown, skin, and hair all stained with soot.

I'd wandered into town, apparently.

I stroked Ajax's head. If Nick and Cade were my brothers, who was Wyatt? Just another phoenix? And why did I remember him first? Why would he tell me to stay away from Cade? And how seriously should I take that story Patrick had woven about him?

None of this made sense. More than ever, I needed answers. Cade had them. Nick had them.

Did Wyatt? He had to be going through this, too. Alone maybe.

I'd been sitting in here for hours, trying to trigger a memory from a past cycle, or whatever Nick had called it. I just didn't exactly know how.

Opening up to the possibility that these two guys were actually my brothers was scary territory. Ajax tilted his head to the side as if trying to discern my thoughts. Something in my chest tightened. Maybe I'd called Cade *brother* because deep inside, I believed it. Deep inside, I wanted to trust him.

And that terrified me.

It didn't make sense. I hardly knew him. But he'd done nothing to mislead me. In fact, he'd been actively trying to talk to me. And I'd been brushing him off.

Oh no. Here it came. The memory I'd been prodding all morning.

"It's okay, Ava."

I leaned over Cade's body on the ground. Blood poured out of his mouth. His chest, from a hole. I ripped his shirt. My insides ached, and I held in a sob. "Sh-she stabbed you?"

"She took my powers."

Something inside me seemed to break, painfully. "How did she—"

"Sh-she's n-not who you think. Sh-she's Guinevere."

He grabbed my sleeve with his blood-covered hand. How had everything spiraled into this?

"Ava?" He coughed and choked on blood.

No. Not like this. Tears blurred my vision. I pressed my hand against the wound in his chest and tried to call my powers. They didn't come. Why wouldn't they come? It was as though they were trapped behind a door I couldn't open. A sob tore through me. "Cade! Don't you die, Cade."

His head fell limp, and his grip on my arm loosened.

I cried out, from the bottom of my soul. "Caderyn, I'll never forgive you if you leave me!"

"Move." Nick pushed me aside and pressed his hands into Cade's wound. "Cade!" He let out a shaky breath and closed his eyes.

Bright, white light emanated from his hands. Grew bigger. Stronger. Until it enveloped Cade's whole body in pure white. Then it slowly faded.

Nick sat back, eyes wide and scared. "Cade?" he said softly.

Nothing. I held my breath and stared at Cade, at once very much aware that Guinevere didn't have the ability to kill Cade for good. That fueled a fire inside me, but no power latched on to it. I'd lost my fire. Another ache ripped my insides. She'd somehow stopped me from using my powers. How?

Cade sucked in a breath and sat up. He looked down at his bloodstained chest, but no more wounds marred his skin. His eyes met mine. "You healed me? I thought she—"

I hugged him, burying my tears in his shirt. "Nick healed you."

His voice was weak. "Thank you."

"I wasn't going to lose you both." Nick's voice came out strong.

I grabbed Nick's shirt. "M-my powers. I don't have—"

"They'll come back, Ava." He wrapped his arm around me and pulled me close. "That weapon only works temporarily." And I cried into his shirt while he tried to soothe me. "And we have to make sure she can't do that again."

The memory kicked me out, and I was back on the bedroom floor with Ajax's head in my lap. The remnants of anguish still pinched my throat closed. And I had so many questions. Who was Gwen—Gwen something? What had they called her? Was she the person Nick had warned me about tonight? Why had she tried to kill Cade? Why did Nick think he would lose both of us? And did I seriously have powers?

Ajax licked my face, and I realized a tear had trailed down my cheek. I pulled my knees to my chest. Residue from the brokenness I'd just experienced through that nightmare of a memory settled inside me. Cade and Nick, I'd loved them so much. I couldn't imagine them doing something to harm me, but Wyatt had told me to stay away.

I didn't understand. Who could I trust?

Despite what Patrick had said, Wyatt had been there for me. This whole time. I sighed, deciding maybe it was time to just ask them. To trust that my questions wouldn't make them run screaming. Otherwise, this mysterious *she* would find me. And I'd be alone.

As if that thought had turned the key far enough to unlock the door, another memory shook me like an incoming avalanche.

The world outside swirled, and the stars seemed brighter. Thousands flooded the sky. No city lights. Just stars. Out here, in the cover of the garden trees, nothing inhibited their glow.

"Miss Elderson?"

My pulse sped, and I turned toward the familiar whisper. "Mr. Wilcox."

Wyatt walked toward me down the cobblestone garden path, hands in his pockets.

I stopped by the white roses, pretending they'd taken my attention. "It's a beautiful evening."

"It is." He stopped a few meters from where I stood, rosebush between us.

I tilted my head, challenge in my grin. "Are you going to chastise me for being out here by myself?"

Humor lit his expression, and he reached to lift one of the flowers to his nose. "I find you a perfectly capable woman, and I find *chastise* to be a strong word; however, I do wonder if you would prefer company." Now those blue eyes met mine, practically glittering in the waning moon's light.

My cheeks flushed, and I hoped the darkness hid it. "I would love for you to join me, Mr. Wilcox."

He held out his arm for me to thread my hand through, and I rounded the bush and complied. His body heat warmed me, and his hold on my arm felt so comfortingly strong. "Please, call me Wyatt."

"Only if you'll call me Ava."

"Ava." In the dark, I could detect the smile in his voice, but his face became unreadable for a moment. My eyes had adjusted to the lack of light, but I wondered how much he could see.

I smiled at him, and he looked away all too quickly, seeming slightly bashful.

"Don't you love the stars?" I looked up.

"I do. Especially constellations." He stopped walking. "You?"

"I can't say I know much about them."

That sparked a fervor in his voice. He pointed at the sky. "Look. This one here is Ursa Major. Do you see?" His fingers traced the outline of the stars, and I glanced at him. In the moonlight, I could clearly see his grin and the excited glitter in his eyes. He pointed to a few other constellations. "And this one was said to be a woman of unparalleled beauty. Cassiopeia." He motioned to a zigzag of bright stars. "But she was quite full of herself. Her daughter, Andromeda, however, was equally beautiful." He motioned to a cluster near Cassiopeia.

"How do you know?" I smiled in wonder at his knowledge. Had someone somewhere taken the time to educate him?

He could see me. The way his gaze locked onto mine proved that much. And that surprised me. "Don't tell anyone. I can read, too."

I stared with my mouth open. "Tell me about this Andromeda?"

"Well, the hero, Perseus, rescued her and eventually married her."

"Because of her beauty?"

His soft eye contact stole my breath. "No. Because of her heart."

And the memory swirled.

I recalled dozens of times when Wyatt and I would pass by one another while doing our chores, and one of us would mention Andromeda, and later, once everyone was asleep, we stole away and met one another in the garden.

Our stolen moments.

Our secret word.

Andromeda.

And the memories ceased, leaving me back in my bedroom. My pulse thrummed through my entire body, spreading fire through every part of me. He'd lied to me? It wasn't a stupid report after all. Why wouldn't he just tell me?

I needed answers. Now. Whoever I ran into first at school would give them to me. I didn't really have an "or else" to go with that, but the motivation to get to school carried ferocity at least.

# 20

## CADE

I WOKE TO NICK SHAKING MY SHOULDER and standing over me with a glass of water. I wasn't sure whether he meant to splash it in my face.

"How are you feeling?" He handed me the water.

I sat up, rubbed my eyes, and took the glass. Then I managed a teasing smile. "Honey, you're home! How was work?"

"It sucked. How's your head?"

How long had I been out? That memory this morning had flattened me. I noticed blood on my pillowcase. I'd missed school again, which I knew Yuki wouldn't be thrilled about, but I still had this weekend to make it up to her. I would win her over. I had to.

Nick headed toward my bedroom door. "The U-Haul is here, so if you're feeling up to it, I could use some help unloading."

"As in, actual furniture." I got up and followed him downstairs. "As in, we can have company over, and they won't wonder if this house is a front for something else."

He chuckled. "Don't get too excited." He opened the screen door and slid the little metal piece of hardware to keep the door open.

There sat the truck. Yeah. I wasn't getting too excited at all; it had to be the smallest rental U-Haul offered. "Please tell me there's at least a couch and TV in there."

He opened the back, and the truck's door slid up with a rumble. "Wish granted."

I peered in. Real furniture all right. Just the basics. But it all looked heavy.

He hopped into the truck and picked up one side of a bulky recliner chair. "We have a few hours before dark."

I dropped the ramp, then turned to help him. "We're going to hunt?"

"I am. You aren't."

"What? You can't go alone. You said it could be just as bad as a full moon the night after."

He raised his eyebrows and stared at me. "Your concern is touching, but I've been hunting alone for almost three years."

Right. I swallowed. Last full moon night he'd made me stay home—then again, we'd just met. Then last night, I'd pretty much failed, epically. "I have to get back out there."

Nick paused, clenched his jaw. Did that mean yes or no? "You're fast, Cade. You've remembered a lot over the last month of training. But last night . . . I'm not sure you're ready."

Well that stung. I wanted to toss the chair, not that I could. Instead I helped carry it like a good brother. "I thought our job was to protect people. Why are you bent on protecting me?"

"That's my job." He nearly growled the words, glowering at me as we carried the chair off the truck.

"I'm gonna need a lot more than that."

His exasperated sigh told me he'd give in, and I might hear two complete sentences from my brother. "What if something triggers another knock-out migraine, leaving you mincemeat in front of some bloodthirsty beast?"

Wow. I had not expected . . . concern. The recliner jerked forward, and I realized I'd slowed my pace for a beat. "Okay, valid point." I struggled to regain cocky, confident Cade, but I found him. "Stop worrying. You said before, I don't get memories until after the adrenaline wears off, remember? I'm not gonna leave you hanging."

He looked at me like he regretted telling me that earlier. Ha. Served him right. What was his deal anyway? Didn't he want my help?

Or . . . he clearly didn't need it. My chest burned. Apparently, I was good for one thing: getting Ava. I glared at him over the chair back and wasn't even sure why, so I shook that away before he could see it.

We reached the door, but the piece that should have propped it open had slid, so it sat closed. I set down my end of the chair and opened the door. "I won't learn if you keep holding me back."

Jaw tight, he pushed the chair through, over the threshold.

"Nick, you have to stop trying to protect me from being who I am."

He paused, just inside the doorway, then glanced at me over his shoulder with a look that failed to mask his annoyance. He breathed in—slow and deep—then, squatted low, slid his arm under the recliner, and stood, lifting the whole thing with one arm.

Whoa. "We can do that?"

He held his arm out straight to the side, and slowly lowered the furniture to the middle of the living room floor. "Well, I can."

"Am I supposed to clap?" I crossed my arms, but really that was impressive—which I hated to admit.

"When you can call your strength at will, and control it, you can hunt with me."

"That's hardly fair! You said my powers short out. How am I supposed—"

"It's one night, Cade. I almost watched you die last night, so let it go for this one night."

The finality in his tone told me to drop it. Who knew a brother could be so moody? He breezed past me without a word.

I paused a beat, then hurried to catch up. "This means you got the rest of the furniture by yourself, right?"

He stopped, head hung, then walked back to where I stood in the doorway. "Obviously I can't let the neighbors see me toss a couch over my back and jog up the porch steps with it."

"Obviously." Dang it. I really wished I wore jealousy well.

He headed toward the truck again, apparently expecting me to follow.

"Nick, what are you so worried about?"

"Drop it." He didn't stop.

"What aren't you telling me?" I jogged after him, but he didn't respond. "I'm just going to remember."

"I know." He whirled around.

"So why not just tell me?"

He wiped his hand over his face. "Monsters are just part of it. There's also an order of dark phoenixes. One of them in particular is after us."

"Us. As in, Ava too?"

"Most definitely." He jumped into the truck, and I hopped into the back to help him with the next piece of furniture. He'd grabbed a box, though, and headed toward the house without my help. I was starting to sense a trend.

I picked up a box and followed. "Why is she after us?" The front door slammed shut behind me.

"She wants to kill the light phoenixes. She . . . creates monsters like the ones we're hunting."

"We are light phoenixes?"

"Yes. We exist to protect humans from all the evil creatures of the underworld. Dark phoenixes don't care about man. They would rather humans didn't exist. Only phoenixes. So they use the monsters to hunt and destroy."

"Wow. Why?"

Nick shrugged. "Long story. Let's just say once a phoenix fell for a human and turned him into a phoenix."

"We can do that?"

Nick seemed unsure how to answer. "Not anymore. Anyway, that human-turned-phoenix wanted revenge. He didn't actually love the phoenix who turned him. Decisions were made to take away certain powers and, voila, dark phoenixes were born."

"You're saying one human bent on revenge ruined everything?"

"Basically."

"Okay. But who cares if this evil phoenix kills us? We just come back again."

Nick sighed and leaned against the kitchen island. "Here's the thing, we don't get unlimited chances to destroy her."

Whoa. Okay. I held out up my finger for him to stop right there, then I pressed my hands on the counter as I processed.

"You okay?" Nick leaned close to me, his eyebrows pulling together.

This idea that someone actually cared—that *he* actually cared about me kept trying to become my focus, and I could not deal with that kind of revelation right now. I pushed it away and cleared my throat. "The headaches. The bloody noses. You said you don't get sick when you remember?"

He shook his head and swallowed hard. "I think you're almost to your last cycle." His voice cracked. "You've been getting steadily worse these last few times you've come back."

My pulse quickened. "H-how many cycles do I have left?"

His shoulders drooped, and the look on his face was so dejected. "If we can kill this dark phoenix who's hunting us, you'll keep coming back, forever. If she kills you again—"

"Again?" That knocked the air out of my lungs, and they ached. I braced myself against the counter, trying to breathe. Trying to think. To wrap my head around what that meant.

Nick winced and pressed his face into his hand. "Yeah. She—she kills us every time."

I gasped, surprised at how shaky my breaths had become. My knees weakened.

"Cade, are you—"

I held up my hand. "Are the memories killing me?"

"In a previous cycle, she tricked you. And now, when your memories come back, she gets them, too. It—it's sucking your life away. Your powers—I think it affects your powers."

I needed to sit down. This could not be real. Every breath hurt. "How do we—"

"Ava can kill her, for good."

My eyes snapped up to meet my brother's. "Only Ava?"

"That's right." He flipped on the kitchen light, and it flickered, trying to do its job. He handed me a glass of water.

I drained it. "Why does it affect my powers?"

He didn't answer right away, nor would he make eye contact. "Let's just say you made a mistake."

"What the heck kind of mistake causes someone to drain my powers from me lifetime by lifetime?"

Nick just stared at me.

"You going to answer me?" I couldn't believe I was yelling at him over *my* past mistakes. The thing was, he knew what they were and wouldn't tell me. I clenched my jaw. Not remembering anything was starting to get very frustrating. "Does this woman have a name?"

"Yes. But she changes it. Maybe she thinks it makes her more elusive." He offered a slight smile. "It's usually some variation of Gwen. Not always."

I chuckled. "Okay, so Gwen the Psycho Chick. Great."

"Psycho Chick?"

I set down the glass. "Well, until you come up with something better, that's what I'm gonna call her."

Nick pulled out a beer and popped the lid.

"So if you kill her, she comes back?" I swallowed. "If I kill her?"

"Same."

"Are my powers too weak for that?"

Nick set the bottle on the kitchen island and leaned his back against the counter behind him. "You have a different kind of power."

"So I'm totally useless?"

Nick's lips pressed together, and he scowled.

"What? It's obviously true." I crossed my arms.

"No. It isn't." His voice was hard.

The room seemed to spin, and I gripped the edges of the counter, tight. "H-how long until she finds us?"

He winced. "When she gets her memories back and gains enough strength. So . . . not long." He nodded toward the front door. "Come on. Daylight's burning."

I tried to even my breathing and followed him toward the door. Leave it to my jerk of a brother to drop an important conversation because he thought I was too fragile to handle the stupid memories.

I gripped my head as a faint throb pulsed behind my eyes. Actually, remembering right now might be a terrible idea.

Maybe Nick had become well-versed in when to stop sharing information with me. I wasn't going to press it, then. Not when these thoughts seemed to tug at hidden memories. Memories that were possibly killing me. Possibly giving Psycho Chick access to my past. Not to mention, I was pretty sure the memory that tapped on my brain was the memory of the biggest mistake of my lives.

I followed Nick back out to the truck with one burning question on my mind: if we'd never succeeded in killing Psycho Chick before, how would we now?

I found him pulling out a huge tabletop. Wow. No more eating while leaning against the counter? I helped him unload it, and we headed back to the house, but the door had closed again. There was no way I could hang on to this with one hand.

He could, I thought bitterly. And honestly, who would be around to see?

"Do you need help?" A distinctly feminine voice caused me to look up. A girl with long brown hair and dark brown eyes raced up our porch steps. She'd apparently been out for a run. "Hey, Nick." She smiled at my brother.

Nick offered zero social cues, and I grimaced inwardly.

She pointed at herself, seeming unsure suddenly. "I'm Kelsey. M-my car was—"

He chuckled. "I know who you are, Kelsey."

"Oh. Good." She settled comfortably into that smile again, and Nick made no move to say anything more. He just stared at her, eyes narrowing.

I suppose I had to jump in before he scared her away. "Would you mind getting the door for us?"

"Sure." She blushed slightly as she passed by my brother and opened the door. Even sweaty and gross, this girl was gorgeous. Nick was an idiot.

"Thanks," Nick said as he walked through the doorway past her.

I made meaningful eye contact with my brother and mouthed, "Why haven't you mentioned Kelsey?"

He just glared at me. "We don't have time for friends."

"That's the most absurd thing I've heard you say. And I've heard a lot of crazy talk from you."

Nick rolled his eyes.

We brought the tabletop in and headed out for the next item. Kelsey was still holding the door open. Standing there, unsure, and staring at Nick.

He stopped and looked at her. "You're still here."

She laughed nervously. "Yeah."

This was painful to watch. "My brother means, thank you for holding the door." I put my hand on Nick's shoulder. "You know, we should just remove the door."

"You could just prop it open with this little thingy here." She bent over and moved that little sliding latch.

"Thingy?" At least Nick smiled.

I rubbed my hand over my face. In a hundred lifetimes, had he never flirted with anyone?

"Yeah." She faced my brother, and the two of them locked gazes. I became invisible. "See. It's the technical terms I'm not good with. Visuals. I can deal with visuals." The way she stared at him had me ready to just sink right off the porch.

He leaned toward her and caught the screen door before it slammed into her back. "The thingy appears to be broken."

Yep. Time to leave the two of them alone. I clomped down the porch steps.

Nick followed me. Idiot.

"What's next? Couch?" He glanced at me.

"You seriously going to keep her on door duty? We should just remove it. And you should actually speak words to her."

"Like I said, we don't—"

"Do you like girls?"

"Yes. I—"

"Okay. Do you like that particular girl? Because she is clearly into you." I looked over Nick's shoulder at Kelsey, who stood there manning the door and biting her lip, trying to act like she hadn't been caught staring.

Nick glanced at her, too. "Wha—I—Cade, we can't do this."

"Do what?" I brushed past Nick, walked back up to Kelsey, and extended my hand. "Cade. The younger brother."

She shook it. "Nice to meet you."

Maybe a friend, especially one that basically made my brother's eyes pop out of his head, would be good for his sour mood. I nodded toward the inside of the house. "Can I get you some water? Or . . . actually . . . I don't even know if we have clean glasses unpacked."

"No, thanks. I'm out for a run." She motioned to Nick. "Just saw a fr—um . . . someone I know in trouble."

Nick reappeared with a box. "Did you invite her in?" His tone was a little incredulous.

"Relax, Nick. You'll make your own friends."

Nick seemed to growl something as he passed between us.

Kelsey motioned toward the sidewalk. "I should go."

"He's just hangry." I waved dismissively at Nick. "I should feed him before he bites my head off. Do you know of any good pizza places around here?"

Nick appeared in the doorway again. "Are you making dinner plans in the middle of moving?"

"Nick, the guest you're being very rude to is standing in front of you."

"No, no, no, no." She waved her hands. "I'm leaving right now. I—"

"But seriously, you know the number of a good local pizza place?"

Nick brushed past us. "Preferably with delivery."

"See." I put my hand up to my mouth as if telling her a secret. "Hangry."

She laughed. "Fricano's has really great pizza. I know their number by heart." She rattled it off, and I dialed. Nick would thank me later. I handed Kelsey the phone because my idiot brother was lifting the couch. "Bacon and whatever else you like."

"What?" She grabbed the ringing phone.

"You idiot," I called after Nick and raced out to the truck.

"What are you doing?" He glared at me.

"Making friends." I lifted one end of the couch.

He rolled his eyes, and we carried the couch to the door that Kelsey still held open for us. At least Nick had the decency to tell her thank you.

I backed into the house and the couch stuck in the doorway. Everything jolted to a halt. "I told you we should have removed the door first."

Nick let out a frustrated sigh. "We're going to have to turn it. Push it back out."

I placed my shoulder against the arm and pushed. Then I looked at Nick over the couch. "I did." It hadn't budged.

"All right. Set it down."

The glare he gave me—which thankfully Kelsey didn't see, since she was ordering our dinner—said plainly *If this human wasn't standing on the porch, I could just manhandle the sofa into the house. Look at the mess you've created.*

The look I returned hopefully said *Deal with it.*

Thirty minutes later, the door was off, the couch moved in, Kelsey had gotten Nick to smile several times, and the pizza had arrived. Nick glanced at Kelsey and motioned to the pizza box. "You earned some of this."

"Now who's inviting in strangers?" I laughed at Nick and took the pizza from him.

"Make your own friends, Cade."

I smiled to myself. Maybe my brother did have game after all. Nah, probably not. I ventured into the kitchen, set the pizza box on the island, and grabbed a slice. One look at it and I rolled my eyes at Kelsey. "Mushrooms? Come on."

Kelsey shrugged. Her phone rang, and she dug it out of her pocket. The screen showed a picture of who was calling. And something in my stomach squeezed. Wyatt.

I looked up at Nick and his tight expression. I was right. I knew it.

Wyatt was someone I was supposed to have remembered. I turned to Kelsey. "Wyatt's a friend of yours?"

"He's my brother." She smiled.

Brother. Right. Oh crap. My stomach roiled. Everything in the room seemed to tip, and I might have pitched forward. I wasn't sure. All I heard was Nick yelling my name. My head felt like it was splitting open.

And then the memory consumed me.

Wyatt leaned over me as I lay flat on the ground. Only this Wyatt wasn't wearing blue jeans. I clearly knew him from the past. He extended his hand as though to help me up. "Loyalty doesn't suit you, Cade. You're too trusting."

# 21

## CADE

WHOA. MY STOMACH GOT REALLY queasy. I curled over, and a spike of pain seemed to want to split my skull open.

I screamed. I think I screamed.

Because suddenly I wasn't screaming.

I was standing in front of Wyatt. His eyes flashed a golden hue, and he turned to look at me. Then a devious smile overtook his face. "Loyalty doesn't suit you, Cade. You're too trusting."

A woman's laugh sounded from behind me, but I couldn't turn. Then I felt pain. So much pain. She was torturing me.

One memory flashed into another, and I stood in a room with Nick. He placed an arrow into a crossbow and put a loaded gun in his belt. Tonight we'd defeat the one woman who was out to eradicate the race of light phoenixes.

Nick glanced up at me. "Remember, only Ava can kill her for good."

He didn't have to remind me of my uselessness. I got that clearly.

Finally, I pulled out of the memory, sweating and trembling on the couch. My throat raw. I needed water.

When I came to, Kelsey seemed relieved, which meant I had to go along with whatever Nick had told her. But she seemed satisfied enough that I was okay, after checking me like some nurse might. She headed out, Nick walking her to the door.

And the moment Nick came back in sight—moody as Hades—I planned to confront him, because I needed answers.

He sat back in the armchair across from where I camped out on the couch, obvious relief on his face. "You couldn't leave it alone, could you?"

"You recognized the photo of her brother, right?"

He took his time answering. "I know Wyatt." His voice gave nothing away, but the look on his face said that he very much disapproved. Angrily so. More angry than normal Nick.

I paused and swallowed hard. How many phoenixes were there? "He's related?"

"No."

"Is Ava in danger with him?"

He glanced at me, eyes narrowed. "What do you remember about him?"

I tried to recall the memory without going deep enough to get a headache. Then again, why prolong it? "I think he betrayed us. Her."

"That's one way to put it." His nonchalance was about to earn him a punch in the face.

"Sometimes you can be a real jerk, you know that?" I sat up, slowly.

He sighed and drummed his fingers against the armchair. "There's a lot of history. I can start to tell you, but your memories will be triggered most likely."

"If it's going to happen to me anyway, why not just help me remember?"

"I have in the past. And . . ." He shook his head and leaned forward, elbows on his knees.

The sympathy in his gaze was totally unexpected. "It's worse?" My voice came out dry.

He rubbed his hand over his face. "I want you to remember, Cade. It's easier when you remember. Until then—"

"Just tell me. Seriously, what will it do, kill me?"

He stood up and headed to the kitchen.

Fine. Real mature, older brother. "Jerk."

"Yes, Cade," he practically yelled. "It almost killed you."

I slumped in my seat. A shiver throbbed in my core, and I whispered, "Why didn't you just tell me that?"

"I can't—Cade, when I tell you things, Gwen remembers them, too."

I closed my eyes. "I need my memories if I'm going to help you fight her, Nick."

"What did you remember?" he asked quietly.

Did this mean he'd entertain questions? "What did I do that made her take my powers?"

"I really don't want to trigger any more of your memories right now." One corner of his mouth darted up, but it didn't mask his sadness. "You look like you're ready to fall over."

I felt like I'd dragged myself out of a trash compactor. "The plan is using Ava to get to this supervillain?"

"You mean Psycho Chick?" He chuckled and brought me a glass of water. "Something like that."

"Why Ava?"

He breathed in as if he might tell me, then he stopped. Finally he conceded. "I think you might want to slow down with the memories. Let's just say her powers are strong enough to take out Psycho Chick." Another weak smile.

I sat up straighter. "Wyatt. He was there. In the memory. He—he did betray us."

"That one. I'm sorry man, I should have known."

"So you know? He's on her side. The phoenix gone bad. He's—we have to kill him."

"We can't."

"Why not?"

"Wyatt is not my most urgent concern. But only Ava can kill him, too."

I balled up my hands and shook them. "Of course she can. Ava, Warrior Princess. Able to save all the weaker Eldersons in one single blow." I sort of regretted yelling because my throat burned. But seriously, what was I good for?

Nick cocked an eyebrow. "Did you just make a nineties reference?"

I half growled a sigh. "Is that a problem?"

He actually laughed.

Weird that he was in a laughing mood when I wasn't. "So what do we do about Wyatt?" I asked.

"We warn him to stay away from Ava."

"You mean threaten?" That I could do.

"I'll handle Wyatt if I need to." He started to walk toward the stairs, and I called after him.

"Tell me how to handle him."

Nick paused. "Just remind him that he betrayed us before. The guilt should take care of him."

"What guilt? I didn't exactly remember what he did."

"Good talk, Cade."

Really? He was just going to leave it at that? What was my memory hiding that was so important to this Psycho Chick? And what could I do to pull my weight around here. I'd already missed half the fight last night because I'd gotten injured and then passed out. No wonder Nick always seemed annoyed with me. I leaned over and pressed my hands against the back of my neck. "Hey, Nick?" I wasn't sure he'd hear my muffled words.

"Yeah?"

I swallowed past the lump in my throat. "Is Wyatt dangerous to Ava?"

He took his time answering. "He definitely could be."

"Does he not remember?"

"He knows. He remembers early, like me."

If Ava was supposed to save me from Gwen, then maybe the least I could do was protect my sister from Wyatt.

WYATT WASN'T AT SCHOOL TODAY.
Neither was Cade. So I had zero answers. Which meant I had to find them myself.

By the time I finished baking a batch of chocolate-chip cookies, Wyatt still hadn't responded to my texts, so I put two dozen homemade reasons for him to give me answers into a disposable plastic container and headed over to his house.

Way more nervous than anticipated, I knocked on the front door. A woman answered, and I presumed she was his mom. She seemed very unhappy that I'd showed up unannounced, and at her "explain yourself" look, I stuttered. "I'm—is—I'm a friend of Wyatt?"

I didn't mean for it to be a question.

"If his car is here, he's in the shed out back." She motioned to the driveway where his dull red Toyota with the retractable headlights sat. She didn't even invite me in, so I assumed I should head out to the back shed. I made my way down the walkway to the driveway and past the ancient Toyota. One of the headlights remained visible while the other hid in its compartment. The driveway led to a well-worn path with a couple of half-buried stepping-stones. I followed that to the little shed. It had to be the size of an old carriage house in need of a serious paint job. The door was warped, but the knob and lock looked newer. I breathed deep to calm my jitters, raised my fist, and knocked.

"Yeah?" Wyatt's voice all right, but he sounded terrible. At least I knew he wasn't lying about being sick.

I waited for him to open the door, but no one did. What did "yeah" mean? Was I supposed to go in? Or just wait out here? "I missed you in school, and you're not answering your texts."

"Ava?" A bit of shuffling and fifteen seconds later he opened the door a crack and looked down at me with one eye squinted closed.

"Rough night?" I smiled and held up the container. "I made cookies."

His squinted eye opened slowly, and he stared at me for a beat too long to be considered normal surprise.

I rattled the container, hoping they'd at least earn me an invite inside. "Does the word *phoenix* mean anything to you?"

He expelled a breath, then said quietly, "You remembered."

Those two words hung in the space between us like a mist I could almost see but most definitely feel. And the relief on his face sent a shiver through my core. Hope rose inside me, but so did a spike of ice in my blood. All this was real. And Wyatt would finally give me answers.

"Can I come in?"

"Of course." He opened the door, and I stepped inside the room. That's all it was. One room with two windows each on two of the walls—all covered with thick shades to keep it dark inside. A drawing table sat near the door. A coffee table near the tattered couch where a tossed-aside blanket told me he'd likely been sleeping.

And shelves and a work bench lined the back wall. Books, test tubes containing who-knew-what, and papers filled the shelves.

"Nice place." I turned around to face him, and that's when I saw massive bruises all over his left arm, which he cradled protectively. "What happened?"

"I broke it."

My pulse thrummed. "What?" I reached for it, then wasn't sure I should touch him. His arm was definitely swollen, but there weren't any hospital bandages. Then again, if he was also a phoenix, he'd be healing, right? "Are you okay?"

"I will be."

Cade had said that too.

Wyatt led me to the couch with the ripped seat cushion. He moved the cream-colored blanket and offered me a seat. I took it.

Gingerly, he sat down. "It takes me longer to heal after—" His elbow bumped the couch's armrest, and he winced, breathing in through his teeth.

"Oh, Wyatt, can I do anything for you?"

He shook his head and leaned toward a bag of ice on the table beside the couch.

"Let me help you, please." I reached it for him. "Maybe you should take it easy."

"Thanks."

He breathed deep and positioned himself on the couch. I didn't really understand all of this, but I did know my . . . brothers . . . had been hunting monsters last night. Apparently Wyatt had, too. And after what I'd seen from Cade, I understood it could take time to heal. For Wyatt's sake, I hoped it wouldn't take too long.

"What do you need?"

"I'm okay for now." He smiled ruefully. "All things considered."

I looked into his expectant eyes. It was time for me to let him closer, wasn't it? To stop keeping him at arm's length? If I were to trust him, I'd have to let him past a wall or two, so he'd open up. "Why didn't you tell me?"

He chuckled, and the sound brought me an inexplicable joy. "I always remember before you."

"Really?"

He nodded. "I know by now not to rush your memories. You always find me when it's time."

"I do?"

His smiled and lifted the cookie container. "Yeah. And you typically bring me some kind of bribe."

Something in my chest warmed. "Is that so?"

He nodded. "Something about your eternal optimism that I'll reveal everything over a plate of sweets."

Eternal—it hit me like bricks. Each time I'd met him, were we always the same? No wonder I'd felt so comfortable with him. "And does it work?"

"You don't remember?"

"Apparently not everything." I stared at him. The uncertainty in his eyes. Something in my stomach fluttered, and my hands started shaking. I was about to get answers. "How many times—"

"I've been on your cycle five times now."

I breathed the sentence out, light and airy. "We've had five lifetimes together?"

"How many do you remember?"

"So far, one. Long-time-ago England."

His lopsided smile melted my insides. "That first one is rough. But I have a lot of fond memories from then."

I rubbed my hand across my face. "How are we . . . born?"

His eyes narrowed for a moment, as if he was trying to recall the best way to answer my question. "There's a fire. It's a contained fire. It burns, but not the way you'd expect. First it scorches the earth, and then it seems to make the area more . . . lush. It causes vegetation to grow, dead trees to thrive. And then you emerge. Usually you and Cade are together, because you're twins. But you rarely remember being with one another, because young phoenixes are dependent on other phoenixes or humans to survive. So you search for population much like a newborn pup searches for a heat source."

I stared at him with my mouth hanging open. He chuckled, and I clamped my mouth shut, looking away while my cheeks heated. "This is a lot to process."

"I know." He touched my hand, sending a jolt through my core. "But you're not alone."

That touch. That small, infinite moment brought back a rush of feelings from the memories. Those stolen nights under the stars.

"I remember Andromeda." The words tumbled out in a whisper.

He didn't say anything, so I looked up into his eyes. They were the same kind eyes from the memories. Trusting eyes. I was not ready to feel these things. In this reality I hardly knew Wyatt. My skin heated. I slipped my arm away from him.

Wyatt pulled back, putting his hand up to show he hadn't meant to make me feel uncomfortable. "I'm sorry. I—"

"It's okay." I breathed deep and then forced myself to look at him. "Your eyes are the same. You—you are the same."

"So are you."

"Do you remember . . . anyone else?"

"You mean Cade?"

I nodded, and something inside cracked, like the dam breaking. Was I really ready to let the waters run free? Was I really ready to trust? And be trusted?

If not, I'd remain alone.

Was I ready for that reality?

"I remember him." He looked down at my hand. It rested against the couch cushion millimeters from his. Slowly, I let my pinkie finger brush up against his, the electric feeling humming through my body. He didn't move.

The touch. I recalled this touch. I closed my eyes. It felt so familiar. Exciting. Forbidden.

I shook my head as a memory started swimming in my mind.

I sat beneath the willow, a brush of wind on my face. The sky growing darker in hints of red and indigo and purple. A rush of shivers shot through my core as Wyatt's hand stroked mine.

I turned to look at him. He lay next to me, his left hand propped under his head and his right grazing against my skin. I linked my fingers between his. "My brother would not approve."

He chuckled. "So I hear. But he trusts me, Ava. Both of them."

"Nick doesn't trust anyone. But Cade speaks of you often." I rolled to my left side so I could look into his impossibly blue eyes. "I think he knows," I whispered with a slight giggle.

"Really? It's not from my part. I've been nothing but secretive."

I sighed, and tingles danced over my skin as his fingers trailed my forearm. "Cade sees the way I look at you when you're not paying attention."

His gaze pulled me in. "I'm always paying attention."

His gentle touch sent a buzzing through my core. And he tugged me closer.

I closed my eyes.

And shook free of the memory. My heart pounded.

But the memory tried to slip back. I didn't want to see it. I wasn't ready for that kind of—for that emotion.

"Ava?" I thought I heard Wyatt talking to me, but I didn't. It was the memory again. Only I was no longer under the willow tree. This time, I found Wyatt in the stables getting his horse ready.

"What are you doing?" A pit formed in my stomach, huge and hollow.

He looked away.

"Wyatt? Look at me."

"I have to go."

I tried to get in his line of sight and failed. "You were just going to leave in the middle of the night without telling me?" My voice wavered.

He took his time answering. "I think it's for the best."

"Whose best?" My pulse thundered, and I tried to speak past the ache in my throat. "Nick's? He doesn't understand now, but—"

"Ava." He touched my hand. "He said you're forbidden to fall in love with me."

My blood raced faster. "Nick's words. Nick's rules. If he wants to live alone, so be it. But he should know better than to make me live without you."

He turned away from me. Wouldn't stop fixing the saddle.

"Wyatt? Say something."

He paused. "It's not just that." He looked at me now, the blue in his eyes shrouded by the overcoming darkness. "I'm not good for you." He shook his head. "I'm not even good."

I grabbed his hands, and the love in my chest swelled. I didn't know person could feel so much for one person. "You *are* good."

He breathed deep, shook his head. "We're all full of darkness, Ava. Some of us embrace the light, even when it shines bright on the darkness inside us. Sometimes we have to do what little good we can. I have to hope it builds over time. Like a snowball. And then maybe it shows who we really are, despite the times we lose control and act in evil."

"Is that why you saved Tommy from punishment? Is that why you saved the boys from drowning and told little Ella her mud pies are wonderful? To counteract the evil things you've done?"

"I do those things because it's right. I can only hope it counteracts the evil things I've done."

"You don't seem evil, Wyatt."

He swallowed. Closed his eyes. "You are a light in the dark, Ava. You see things in me that no one else can. That I-I didn't even know were possible."

I ached for him to touch me. To see the truth of my words. "I see your heart."

His eyes opened. So close now. The air between us alive with hope and desire. "Then see all of it. The good. The bad."

"I have, and I do." I touched his cheek as he started to turn away from me again. "And you don't need to hide from me. I can take care of myself."

The heat in his eyes drew me in. Captivated me. His hand cupped the back of my neck. Warmth spread through me. And that much passion seemed too large for what I knew of Wyatt now.

Not ready to experience this, I jolted free of the memory.

That felt like a stolen moment between two people. Two separate people. Like characters in a story. I was experiencing their feelings, but they weren't mine.

Only supposedly they were.

And I didn't feel that strongly for this Wyatt. My throat felt thick. I had so many questions. When had I fallen in love with him? Did Wyatt remember loving me? Would I fall for him again?

I glanced over at him, and he made similar, tentative eye contact—like the Wyatt I'd just seen in the memory.

Slowly, his eyebrows rose as if asking me if I'd just remembered something.

I cleared my throat, afraid my voice might warble. "My brothers didn't approve."

He laughed—a welcome break in the tension. "Understatement. But can you blame them?" That rueful look I'd started recalling looked so natural on his face. "Phoenixes aren't supposed to fall in love."

"What? Who is Nick to make that choice? And why aren't phoenixes supposed to fall in love?"

He hesitated.

"I'm just going to remember if you don't tell me."

He nodded. "All right. When a phoenix uses love to heal someone from death—"

"Death? We can—that's something we do?"

Wyatt licked his lips. "Only once."

My heart thundered inside its cage. "Once," I whispered, trying to force it to make sense.

"The person a phoenix brings back," Wyatt continued, "is forever placed on their life cycle." He shook his head. "I think it might drain your powers. Put a strain on you."

"So, wait, the . . . resurrected person will become a phoenix?"

"No. Not exactly. They just . . . they're reborn with you. That's why phoenixes mate for life, if you will."

"For life." That was too much to handle right now. I couldn't breathe. "I can only heal so many?"

"Well, you can only bring back one. You can heal many. And you have. You can bring back other phoenixes. But only one . . . human. Although it's basically illegal."

Why did I suddenly feel so weightless? Dizzy? I tried to breath deep. "Only one?" Tears threatened as confusion turned to flame in my chest. My gaze snapped to meet Wyatt's, and I balled my hands into fists. "So why shouldn't I fall in love?"

"That's a question for Nick." Wyatt shifted his weight and winced.

I touched his good shoulder. "How's your arm?"

"I think by tonight I should be good as new."

Because he'd heal. Because he . . . was a phoenix. "What if two phoenixes fall for each other. You said they can heal one another. Does that mean . . . Can they be together?"

He stared back at me, eyes squinting. "How much, exactly, do you remember?"

I thought I was just finding normalcy, but who was I kidding? This was too weird for words.

"Not enough."

"Phoenixes aren't supposed to fall in love, Ava. Not since the great curse. I know it's a lot to process. So take your time." He lowered his eyes, shyly. "I meant what I said. You can call me any time. Cookies are good too." He smiled then, lopsided and unsure, as though he was offering me something he wasn't certain I'd take. Something intangible but no less real. Trust?

I chewed the inside of my lip, suddenly unable to look at him. "I'm going for a run tonight, but I don't really want to go alone." My eyes wandered up to meet his.

That intense stare with a hint of concern speared me. "I could go with you, if you want."

"Really?" I placed my hand on his good arm, then I remembered how sensitive he'd been the other times I'd moved to touch him.

This time he didn't pull away. Instead, he glanced at my hand and then looked up at me, tenderness in his expression. "Just tell me when and where."

It couldn't be that easy. I slid my hand off his skin, still feeling his warmth on my palm and the warmth of his offer in my chest. Just who was Wyatt Wilcox? And why was he so willing to chase away my monsters?

"You think you'll be healed enough by tonight?"

"Absolutely. Look." He lifted the limb, and I gasped. Much of the bruising had faded. And the swelling abated. It looked otherwise normal.

"Wow."

"I'll pick you up at nine?"

I nodded my agreement.

Now to pay my brothers a visit.

# 23

NICK

I SAT AT THE TABLE IN THE COFFEE SHOP, turning Kelsey's ID over and over in my fingers. She'd accidentally lost it at my house while helping us move earlier.

She didn't live far from me at all. I had her address right here, but something about showing up on Wyatt's doorstep seemed like a bad idea right now since I'd seen Ava's car there.

That meant I needed to tell Wyatt to stay away from my sister. A conversation I'd have later; I didn't want Kelsey around for that. Having her as an ally right now seemed like a good move, knowing Wyatt's past.

So, I'd texted Kelsey and asked her to meet me here.

I stared out the window as rain droplets splashed against the glass. I hoped the book I'd found at the library proved useful. If it didn't, I might be out of time to fix that situation. My past sins knocked on the door of my memories. They blurred as the memory raced back to me. As I remembered why my father used the memory stone on Ava and Cade.

Trembling, covered in blood, I stood outside the council room where my father was conducting a meeting with the other six heads of the phoenix families.

My knees shook, and my heart wouldn't stop racing.

"I can hear your armor rattling through the whole building."

Dinah's teasing voice made me close my eyes and breathe in calming air.

I turned toward her, and her smirk faded. Her eyes widened, and she touched the red sash I wore. Her gaze traced my face, and softly she pressed her palm against my cheek. Her jaw tightened. "How many?"

A heavy weight sank into my gut, and I turned away from her.

"Don't look away from me, Nick. Please?" She coaxed me to turn back to face her. To look into those dark pools of eyes. "You have no reason to be ashamed with me. Do you understand?"

I looked at her, touched her face. "How do you know?"

She smiled sadly. "Because I can see it in your eyes."

She could see it in my eyes. I knew that's what she'd say. She always said that. My eyes told her my secrets. My fears. I could keep nothing from her. "Three." My voice broke like sandals sliding over crushed stone. I'd killed three dark phoenixes tonight. Two women and a man. People I'd known once. They'd become so different. Animalistic. Wild in a way that didn't seem free and untamed but rather desperate and hunted.

The darkness they'd embraced was tarnishing them.

"I'm sorry." She linked her hands around my neck and pulled me in. Kissed me with fervor and support and desire. Everything inside of me broke away from the walls I tried so desperately to raise. To keep the hurt inside. And she pulled it away from me with a kiss. Filled me with strength.

She smiled, sadly. "Thank you for protecting us. I am sorry you must bear the burden of killing friends."

Born a Taker, I had the ability to kill other phoenixes permanently. No more cycles. Their ashes blew away in the wind. Specks of a forgotten hope. Gone. It was my burden.

Ava's burden if I failed.

Which was why, no matter who my father and his council sent me to kill, I would do it and save Ava the heartache.

Dinah grabbed my hands, and her eyes drank in every part of me. "I'm sorry I cannot carry this burden with you."

I squeezed her fingers. "But you do. Every time I come to this door to report to my father what I've done, you carry what I can't take in there." My sorrow. My shame.

Her fingers slipped from my hands, and she pressed them against the back of my neck. Her eyes smiled as she looked at me. "If I could do more, I would."

"I love you."

A sultry smile stretched her lips. "Do you want to know what I learned?"

My glance darted to the door. "You were listening in?"

"Of course I was." Her gaze drifted away.

I touched her chin to try and bring it back to my eyes. "What is it?"

"Guinevere. She's fallen in love." Now she looked at me, and her brown eyes were wide. "With a human."

My heart sputtered. "No," I whispered. "She didn't go before my father, did she?"

"She told the whole council, in no uncertain terms, that their ashes could blow in the wind for all she cared. No one would stop her from healing the human."

I pressed my hand against my forehead, feeling the dried blood spots from my victims tonight. Dark phoenixes. Those who defied the council's rules and chose to stand up against us.

I hadn't agreed with this name we'd given them at first. Not until I saw their true motives. Not until I witnessed how they cared nothing for the good of humanity. That they wanted to destroy it.

Guinevere used to be a phoenix who could create new phoenixes—a Giver. Her powers had been stripped of her when the Elder Phoenix took that power from everyone. Only Cade had that power now—dormant—not that anyone knew besides my parents, Dinah, and me—and Guinevere.

If she still had her power, she'd be able to turn the human she'd fallen in love with into a phoenix. "Did she ask for her powers back?"

Dinah nodded. "It didn't go well for her."

"I need to talk to her. Will you please give my father my report?"

"I will."

I headed down the hall, and Dinah stayed rooted. She held my hand for as long as possible as distance tore it away from her.

When I made it to Guinevere's room, I spotted candlelight beneath the door.

"Gwen?"

"Go away."

"Please, let me talk to you."

"You just want to tell me what I must do." She sighed.

I stepped into her room. She sat in the corner on a pile of pillows. Candlelight flickered over the walls, making it possible to discern her puffy eyes. "Have you been crying?"

She stared at me, mouth agape. "I told you to go away."

"Only you can tell others what they must and mustn't do?" I cocked an eyebrow. She stared at me, eyes growing wider, and I realized my mistake. I'd forgotten to wash the blood off my face.

"You killed more," she whispered.

I leaned my back against the wall, removed my sword, and sank to the floor.

"Why do you do what Father tells you?" Her eyes hardened.

"He is the leader of phoenixes."

"Of light phoenixes."

A strange weight settled in my stomach and I leaned forward. "That includes you, right?"

"Cade still has his powers." She looked at her hands.

I ran my fingers along the sheath of my weapon. "So do I."

"Because you're a Taker. Since when did ending life become more important than giving it?"

"Gwen, this isn't about—"

"Yes, it is. You're too blind to see it. What if the dark phoenixes kill Cade? Shouldn't there be another who wasn't stripped of their Giver powers?"

"It was all or nothing, you know that."

"Except Cade and Ava."

"They were in Mother's womb."

"You think Grandfather didn't know that? Now Cade has his

power, and they have their phoenix fire." She looked at her hands. "Father won't even let them fight, and they have our kind's most effective weapon." When her eyes met mine, a strange hatred seemed to fill them. "The dark phoenixes will figure out how to get their fire back, and you will be left with nothing."

I swallowed, aware that nothing right now would be good enough to appease her. "When the dark phoenixes are gone, Cade will make more. Someone needs to fight the monsters and protect humankind."

Her eyes darkened. "Yes. We are to protect them, but what of loving them?" Tears sprang into her eyes. "I love him, Nick." Her voice was but a whisper. She clutched a pillow and squeezed it. "If I had my powers, I could put him on my cycle as a phoenix. He wouldn't be a human. They wouldn't have to worry about the corruption. About my powers being drained."

"But the rules—"

"To the wind with the rules! One man corrupted a few phoenixes long ago. That's not my Jon, and that's not now!"

"Gwen, I—"

"Don't tell me you understand." Her voice grew dark. "Dinah is a phoenix. You are allowed to love her."

"You are allowed to love a human as well. You just can't bring them back from death."

"I can if I become a dark phoenix."

My lungs emptied. "Gwen!" I leaned forward and held out my hands, signaling her to quiet down. "Their powers have been stolen, too. They created an image of their old powers through a deal with evil monsters. You can't trust that kind of magic. It taints you." I recalled today stabbing my sword through an old man who twitched and writhed in his own body because the dark magic had finally gotten to his brain.

Tears streamed down her face, and she glared at me as if I'd hurt her. "Phoenixes are supposed to be allowed to fall in love with other humans. It was the original design." Her voice broke. "We're supposed to be able to heal them so that other phoenixes with powers like Cade's"—she thumped her finger into her chest—"with powers like the ones Grandfather stole from *me*, could then make them phoenixes if they were deemed worthy. Don't you see?" She pressed her head in her hands and grabbed fistfuls of hair. Then she added quietly, "Everything is ruined."

I took her hand in mine. "Gwen, you know that the dark phoenixes arose because humans are susceptible to a darkness we do not possess. Because the wrong humans were turned into phoenixes. That is why we are forbidden to turn—"

Her tearful eyes narrowed as if she was disgusted with my answer. "What do you know of love, Nick? And what of death?" She motioned to my sword. "You are sent to eradicate them."

The heaviness in my chest dropped. Everything inside me squeezed painfully. "They're monsters, Gwen. They try to kill me. Kill all of us."

"Us." She said the word quietly as she nodded. The way it hung in the air—hard, yet almost a question, almost like that one word opened a forbidden door—chilled my very soul.

She chewed the inside of her cheek while she stared at me. "And love?"

"I know how real it is. I know that when a phoenix falls in love—"

"It's forever, Nick." She used that same quiet, soul-chilling voice. Then she stood. Elegance in her steps as she walked past me and to the door, where she paused. "I'm sorry, Brother. I thought you of all phoenixes would see my side. But now I know you are as blinded by the love of law over the love of what is right."

I scrambled to my feet, and my chest pounded. "Gwen, what do you mean? Why are you sorry?"

A delicate smile touched her lips, ruefully. "Because I want what I can't have."

I pulled out of the memory there. No reason to relive the carnage of that day.

I realized I held Kelsey's ID so tightly that my hand trembled. I glanced around the coffee shop, and no one else was looking my direction. I rubbed my finger over my cheek, desperately trying to calm my shaking nerves and loosen the tightening in my throat.

I thumbed through the library book while I waited. The only result the library had yielded on my search for the Phoenix Blade. The book spoke of a legendary knife that could be used to shear a phoenix's feathers off and make it so the mythical bird could no longer fly. That was the thing about these interpretations. When a race of beings meant to keep humans safe from evil creatures is formed, there's no telling the people about them; otherwise, the people have to know about the vampires, werewolves, wraiths, shadow puppets, redcaps, shifters, and—well, the list went on.

It basically made my search of a way to separate my connection with Gwen impossible. Even if this blade was a literal blade—like the woman whose family I'd met in Japan seemed to think—this book didn't know any more than I did about how to find it.

I closed the book and tapped Kelsey's ID against the cover.

I was no closer to my goal.

Someone walked in, and I glanced at the door. Kelsey stood there, sunshine illuminating her crown like a halo. She spotted me and smiled. Her tiny wave sent the lump right back to choke me.

Why was I doing this?

I waved back, showing her the plastic card between my fingers.

She walked up to the table I'd snagged and pulled her purse off her shoulder as she sat down. Her eyes beaming. The scarf around her neck—red—reminded me of the crimson sash we wore when fighting. I crushed my eyes closed and fought the urge to stand up right then and leave her.

But I'd invited her.

I had reached out to a human. For what?

"Hey." She sighed and placed her elbow on the table, leaning forward with her chin in her hand and her eyes so full of life. "I never expected you to text me. Not in a thousand lifetimes."

I passed her the ID across the smooth Formica tabletop as her choice of words slayed me. "Yeah?" My voice broke and I cleared my throat. This was a mistake. "You left this at my house."

Her fingers touched mine, and warmth shot into me. I swallowed and looked up at her. "Thank you! I was looking all over for this. I hoped I hadn't dropped it on my run, and then I saw your text. You saved me a lot of worry." She put the ID in her purse as she prattled on, and I realized how different she was from Dinah. She motioned over her shoulder. "I think I'm going to order something." She looked at my cup. "Do you want anything else?"

I shouldn't do this. It would be so much easier to let go if I didn't foster a relationship with her now. "You know what, I think I should go."

"Oh." Her eyes widened and her lips remained in the little circle, as if she were frozen in the moment. Then she blinked rapidly. "Yeah." She picked up her purse and stood. "You know, that's good because . . . I wanted to head to the—" She paused and looked at my book. "You really have an interest in ancient artifacts."

"Yeah."

Her sparkling eyes appraised me again. "Once upon a time I wanted to be an archeologist."

"Really?"

She nodded. "I've actually seen this book before. My brother checked it out once. It's fascinating. Do you think any of those things actually exist? I mean, I have my own theories, but it's very rare to find someone else interested in this stuff."

Wyatt had looked at this book? That caused my stomach to tighten. What could he possibly want with it? My breath stalled. Something for Gwen. Of course she'd be looking for it, too. Maybe getting close to Wyatt's sister wasn't such a bad idea after all. I glanced at my watch. "You know, I have a few minutes. I wouldn't mind spending some time with you before I have to leave."

"You wouldn't? I mean, of course. Do you mind if I get some coffee?"

"Please."

That smile found its way back to her face, and she walked up to the counter. How was I going to describe to her that I wasn't a regular twenty-five-year-old guy? That I had lived through things—experienced more things—than anyone my current age? That relationships were not on the table for me, no matter the attraction I felt to her? I couldn't.

A strange tug inside my chest pulled, and I looked out the coffee shop window, scanning the parking lot. Gwen. She had to be close. I didn't see her. Didn't see anything but cars and red, orange, and yellow leaves skittering across the pavement in the streetlights.

But I'd felt her.

This next full moon could be hers. I needed to be ready.

Kelsey returned to the table, coffee in hand. "It's really getting cold out there." She smiled and sat down. Then she frowned. "Is something wrong?"

I shook my head and shrugged. Aside from the fact that I'd just recalled how my conversation with Gwen, my twin sister, had resulted in her betraying our entire family and all the light phoenixes, nothing was wrong. And yet I felt like I'd just slaughtered someone all over again. Like I stood outside of my father's council room door again, waiting to give him the bad news. That I'd killed three of the four he'd asked me to go after.

That I'd failed.

Kelsey tilted her head to the side. "You don't have to tell me." Her big, brown eyes rounded. Soft and comforting. She reached across the table and touched my hand. "I know something's wrong, though."

For a moment that seemed to stall time, I stared into her eyes. My heart blazed because I wanted this. I wanted something. Companionship. A deeper connection. Something more than fighting and protecting without ever feeling loved in return. These were the hardest days, when Cade and Ava didn't remember. When they would start to recall all the ways I'd failed them. All the things I'd done to betray their trust.

All in the name of protection.

So I stared deep into Kelsey's eyes because I wanted the comfort I'd received so long ago. But she couldn't give it to me. She'd never understand. She was human. I was a phoenix. I could never have this. Not anymore. It was forbidden.

The tightness in my chest pulled so hard it hurt. And I tugged my hand free of her grasp. "Kelsey, you're a nice girl."

"I know." She sighed, and her lips twisted as if fighting a frown. "You lost someone. I can see it in your eyes. I'm sorry."

"S-sorry?" The air left my lungs as if someone punched me in the gut. She could see it in my eyes? Why did she have to say that? Why couldn't she have said a million other phrases? A sharp heat seemed to flood my skin. She had to say the same thing Dinah always said to me. I could hardly breathe.

She looked up at me tentatively. "Do you want to talk about her?"

"No." My voice sounded husky.

"Okay." She sighed and leaned back. "My fiancé died ten months ago."

"What?" I looked into her eyes.

She smiled sadly, but tears had started to form. A drop slipped out, and she wiped it away. "Yeah. He was a cop and—well—" She paused and fought more tears. Then that sad smile returned. "I understand that kind of loss. I'm not going to push you, Nick. But if you need a friend." She shrugged. "I'm here."

"Kelsey, you're—"

"A nice girl. I know. And I know what that means." She picked up her coffee and headed out. I wanted to stop her, but there was no way now. I couldn't drag her into more heartache.

Because that was all I left in my wake.

# 24



I GAVE KELSEY TIME TO LEAVE, AND THEN tossed my cup into the trash and exited the coffee shop. The scent of something evil rode on the wind, and I turned. Sniffing. Feeling. Watching. There. In the shadows. Another puppet. As soon as I made eye contact with it, the creature ran. I caught up with it behind the building. No one else in sight. I pulled out my knife, ready to throw it. "What do you want?"

It slithered closer, its translucent gray body twisting in and out of the shadows. Its snakelike tongue flicking in and out of its wide, scaled face. "She knowssssss where you are. She knowssssss who's important to you."

Important? Kelsey. The air left my lungs. They'd seen her with me. I lunged forward and grabbed the creature by the throat. "What did you do to her?"

"Nothing." It hissed out a laugh, tearing at my hands with its lizard-like claws. I squeezed harder, and it sputtered, coughing. "Gwen is sssssstrong enough. But now you have given her the bessssst puzzle piece of all."

"I am not in love with that girl."

"No? Gwen herself sssssaid you'd never fall in love again. Imagine her sssssssurprise when I tell her."

My blood boiled. "Tell me what you came to tell me."

"I only came to observe."

She didn't know. Or maybe she did.

"You can run." The puppet choked on its hiss. "But you won't essssssscape her. She sssssent monsters here to feed on this town. Who will protect them if—"

I snapped its neck and dropped it. The creature didn't even hit the ground before it turned to smoke and dissipated.

With trembling hands, I called Kelsey.

"Hello?"

"Hey, I . . ." Wasn't sure what to say. "Are—are you okay? The way we left things . . . I just want to make sure you're all right."

"I'll be fine, Nick."

"Yeah? Good. I—I'd like to see you again." I was weak.

She paused for an eternity. "I'm going out with some friends later this week. I can text you details if you still want to meet."

"That . . . sounds great." I ended the call and leaned against the brick building. If the monster hadn't taken her, what was Gwen's plan? And where was she? I turned around and slammed my fist into the wall. Blinding white shot through my vision, and the pain steadily grew in my hand with each pulse. Then it started to recede as the healing overtook it. Mending. Fixing.

If only everything I'd done could be fixed so easily.

I stared at the blood on my hands. This time it was mine.

But I couldn't shake the memory now, so I might as well let it swallow me.

I stood ready in the courtyard. The dark phoenixes had infiltrated our home, and Father had sent me here, yelling that it was Dinah's and my job to protect Ava and Cade at all costs. They were the only ones who could save us now.

"This way." Dinah led the twins to the tunnel we'd been forced to dig after Gwen betrayed us and left. Ava followed, but Cade wanted to stay and fight. "I'm trained, Nick."

I pushed his shoulder. "When tonight is done, you will rebuild the phoenixes."

"I can help you. I'm faster. I'm—"

"Cade, go."

His eyes widened, and a scream echoed from inside the tunnel.

Ava ran out followed by Mother and Dinah. "There's no way out. Someone blocked the escape. We have to run."

"Too late for that." Gwen stood in front of us with seven other dark phoenixes I knew. At least one of them had my power. Whomever he killed would be gone forever.

My breath caught in my lungs. I stared at dull eyes. Then a fire lit behind them. Not a normal red or orange flame. No, this flame was the absence of light. Devoid of color. It was a shadow that danced like a fire. And the heat that poured out of her smoldered.

"I chose love. And no one will take him from me." She held out her hand, and the black-as-night flame danced in her eyes.

Fire.

She had fire again.

My blood simmered, and my voice escaped in a low whisper. "You brought them here?"

"I believe you are eradicating the wrong side, Brother."

"Those powers . . . that's not your fire, Gwen."

She laughed as if she pitied me. "It is now."

Cade stood behind me, and my heart stalled. If Gwen was a dark phoenix now, did that mean they would make Ava kill her?

My knees weakened.

If Ava killed her, she'd be killing the phoenix in me, too. I would become human.

Then I would die for good.

But as her twin, I couldn't eradicate her. The laws of balance forbade me from doing so. Either I died with Gwen or the dark phoenixes would hunt us until they were the only race of phoenixes left.

Gwen and her friends surrounded us, pushing us toward the entrance of the tunnel. It would increase my odds if I could limit the number of them that came at me at once. I glanced at Dinah. "Get them inside."

My mother swirled her hands together until a huge ball of fire filled her palms. She looked at me. "Your grandfather spared me from losing my fire. He could choose one. It was me—to make sure the twins in my womb were protected from losing theirs. Tell no one."

I nodded, trying to tear my eyes from the fire.

Mother herded Ava and Cade inside, and they ran.

Dinah stayed beside me, spear ready. "Don't give me that look, Elderson. I fight with you."

I nodded and hoped she'd be all right. Then I turned my attention to Gwen. She smiled, but there was no love in it. No affection. It seemed to brim with hatred. Was that how quickly the darkness had consumed her? Fed her selfishness?

"Kill them," Gwen said.

And her phoenixes raced forward. The tunnel mouth limited how many could come at Dinah and me at once, and we fought side by side, but we had no fire. They did. Gwen shot dark flames from her hands, and they pinned Dinah to the wall.

She cried out, and I launched myself at Gwen, only to have one of her phoenixes get in my way.

"Enough, Gwen!"

Her fire stopped, and Dinah slumped to the ground. Breathing. She was alive. I raced toward her, but before I could reach her, Gwen whirled around and stabbed Dinah. I yelled, my throat raw.

She jumped back and said to her Taker, "Kill her."

He shot the sickly greenish-black flame at Dinah's form. It exploded into her, knocking me backward. Flame enveloped her until she stopped screaming, and snakes of black veins covered her body. She seemed to crumble into a thousand pieces and explode into a puff of smoke and ash that blew away in the wind.

No.

My soul shattered. She was gone forever.

I rose to my knees; someone grabbed my shoulder. I didn't care. Cade, Ava, and Mother had made it through the tunnel. They didn't need me anymore.

"Nick!" Cade shook my arm. "Hurry. More dark phoenixes block the way out. Mother needs you." He gasped. "Dinah?"

I pushed my brother off me. "Get out of here! Run for your life."

"That's right, Cade. Run." Gwen's voice grated.

My body shook with rage. I pulled out my sword and faced her, growl burning in my chest. "How could you? I loved her!"

She glared. "Kill me then."

I clutched my sword tighter. "I would if I could." I raced after her, and she took my moment of weakness to rush past me while two more dark phoenixes ran into the tunnel. Cade. My heart jolted painfully.

I swung my sword, and it clashed with another. He shot dark fire in my direction. I ducked, rolled, and sliced him open. Then I headed after the person I'd once called sister.

As I rounded the bend in the tunnel, I caught sight of Gwen blasting fire at my mother. Ava whirled out from behind my mother and shot fire from her hands.

White. Hot. Pure.

I'd never seen anything like it.

And it headed right for Gwen.

This was it. My final lifetime.

I was okay with that. I'd lost Dinah.

"No!" my mother keened. She jumped in front of the flame, and she yelled, "Nick! No!"

No? No what? But her saying my name jolted me to action. How could I think of giving up right now? I raced toward my mother, but her body seemed to light up from the inside. Cracks broke out all over her skin, and she shattered into a thousand pieces.

She became ash, and the wind took her.

Gone.

Forever.

Dead.

I shook. Why had she jumped in front of Gwen?

Wasn't Ava supposed to kill Gwen?

"Retreat!" A voice sounded from the outside, and Gwen glanced at me for a moment before she ran. Something in her eyes expressed a longing—a piece of my sister. Could she still be turned back? I chased after her, not about to let her get away. If Mother willingly saved her, was there a reason? I rounded a corner, cautiously as possible while maintaining speed. And Gwen spun to face me.

She held out her hands. "Don't follow me, Nick."

"Gwen"—my voice broke unexpectedly on her name—"you still have a home here."

Her laugh bounced off the tunnel walls. "With a family who thinks we're expendable? They love Cade and Ava, not us, Nick." Her eyes expressed that longing again. "Come with me."

What? I forgot to breathe. How could she believe I'd consider becoming a traitor? I stared at her outstretched hand. Watched it tremble.

Her eyes started to fill with tears. "You always loved me. You were the only one. I thought you'd understand."

The sounds of other phoenixes coming to my aid rumbled through the tunnel. I shook my head and backed away from Gwen. From her outstretched hand. Her offer. "I don't understand."

She retracted her hand, and heat filled her eyes that spoke of hatred. "Then you are my enemy." She raised her palms, and dark, sick fire shot out at me.

I ducked around the bend in the tunnel as the stream of flame slammed into the wall I'd been standing in front of. When the fire stopped, I turned the corner, stilling the others from following. But she was gone.

I headed back and found Cade hunched over Ava's crumpled form on the ground. She was sobbing.

She'd killed our mother.

Father stood there, standing still over the charred spot on the floor where I'd last seen my mother. His red-rimmed eyes turned to me.

He placed his hand on my shoulder. "I don't blame her for what she's done." A heaviness filled his voice. "You and Ava are the only Takers left. Cade's power will remain dormant until every dark phoenix is dead. I cannot change that now, Nicodemus."

"She has to kill Gwen," I whispered.

My father closed his eyes and bowed his head. He held up a stone. "I'm going to make them forget."

"Forget what?"

"Who Gwen is. How your mother died."

"Ava won't remember her fire. She won't remember how to use it."

"That's why you will remember for her. I'll tell you how it's done, and you will share that with her when it's time. You are her only guardian left now." He started walking over to them.

"Father, I—she'll kill me. She won't do it if she knows."

He nodded. "I know, Son. Can you keep the secret from her?" He held up the phoenix stone. "Because this will be the last memory I will steal from my daughter."

I thought my heart would shatter in my chest, but it turned numb. Dinah. I pressed my hand against the tunnel wall so I wouldn't fall over. I had nothing to live for now except protecting Cade and Ava. "Do it."

I shook myself free of the memory that had the ability to crush me. The one I'd begged my father to take from me.

But he'd said I needed to know that when Ava killed Gwen, Cade would be okay, but I'd cease to be a phoenix. When I died, it would be for good.

This was either my last lifetime or Cade's. Unfortunately my father had perished in ash on the wind before telling me how to unlock my sister's fire. Soon after our mother's death.

He'd taken his secrets with him.

And I had to find out how to unlock Ava's fire. This cycle. For Cade. Even if he did survive one more cycle, which I didn't find likely, that was sure to be the final one. Not a chance I was willing to take. It had to be this time.

Gwen had to die.

Which meant I had to die.

An ache hollowed out a hole in my insides.

My purpose was clear. My father wouldn't have wanted me to fail. I'd already failed so many times.

# 25

AVA

WYATT HAD GIVEN ME CADE'S ADDRESS. I walked up to the out-of-place-looking cottage in perfectly manicured suburbia. It sat off a road, on its own little cul-de-sac made of gravel, like a forgotten son. I marched up the well-worn wooden steps, banged my fist against the front door, and waited for one of my brothers to answer. Brothers. I still didn't know how to process that.

Cade opened the door, hair sticking out in all directions in what seemed a purposeful chaos. He squinted as if the daylight bothered him.

"Ava?" He opened the door, and I walked right past him and his surprised face into the very sparsely decorated—if that term even applied to an old dining table with mismatched chairs and a floor lamp—front room.

I faced him as he closed the door. Darkness shrouded everything. No wonder he'd been squinting. "Avoiding the sun? What are you, vampires?"

"Ha. Ha."

"Where's Nick?" I breezed past him and into the kitchen, which was much bigger than expected and led right into the spacious family room. That's where the TV, couches, and gun safe sat. Good to know there were priorities. The view out the back sliding door led right to the woods. Pretty. Calming.

"He's not here." Cade's voice followed me, and he walked into the kitchen a moment later.

"Of course not." I looked around. The gun safe in the family room wasn't the only sign of weapons here. "You guys really should put some of this away. If someone were to come in—"

"We aren't exactly expecting guests."

"No. Just monsters."

Cade wandered over to the cupboard. "Not expecting them, just ready for them." He pulled out one of the five mismatched glasses on the shelf and turned around to set one on the kitchen island. "Do you want a drink?"

I crossed my arms. He really had no sense of why I was here, but that wouldn't stop me from being angry. "I'm not staying. I just need to talk to Nick."

"He's not here. Have a drink. Or we could get started without him."

My breath caught. "Get started with what?"

Cade did not use one of the fancy glasses. He drank orange juice right from the container. As he put the carton back, I was sure to make a grossed-out face at him, and all he did was laugh. Something deep in my core warmed. Another something in the pit of my stomach warned me not to get attached. I tried to ignore it. Because he was my brother—if all this craziness was true.

I followed him outside where a plethora of arrows and crossbows leaned against the aging brick house. No wonder they had an eight-foot privacy fence on either side of the yard. But the back was open, right to the forest. "I bet the neighbors love you."

He shot me a look that told me he thought my comment funny. "Birds and squirrels steer pretty clear." He nodded toward the armory. "But we can't exactly shoot guns out here in suburbia."

I picked up a knife.

Cade crossed his arms and gave me a cocky grin. Then he nodded toward the targets at the end of the yard. "Go for it."

My fingers curled around the handle, and confidence brewed inside me. Before I could think, my body started moving to a stance. I let myself go through the motions and tossed the knife. Bull's-eye.

"Whoa." Cade half laughed through the word, while I stared disbelieving. Then he scrambled for a crossbow. "Try this one."

I was going to ask how to use it, but my muscles knew what to do. Exactly how to hold it. Load it. Bull's-eye again.

Cade raked his fingers through his hair. "This is not fair."

"You're not a natural?" My turn to smirk.

"Shut up." He took the crossbow, smiling, and hit the target dead center.

A fire fueled inside me, ignited by adrenaline. "What else do you have?"

"I want to take you to the firing range. Or at least for a game of paintball."

"I played that once! I smoked everyone." My heart felt lighter. I had a past. An actual past. And a family. I just had to remember. But as I stared at him, his face kept flashing to that memory of him bleeding on the ground.

Cade's smile left. "What's wrong?"

"Nothing." But even as I said it, my throat was tight.

I wanted to tell him that I wished I remembered more than him almost dying and Nick braiding my hair. I wanted nothing more than to remember them. To belong somewhere.

"Do you want to see your room?" he asked, head tilting back toward the house.

My heart leaped. "I have a room here?"

His smile was warm. "Yeah. Come on. I'll show you."

I followed him up the rickety stairs, hand trailing the worn wooden banister. The room to the left caught my attention first. The front of the house. Most exposed with windows on two sides. The bed was made. Nothing on the walls. I bet if I opened the bedside drawer there would be a gun and a knife and maybe some brass knuckles inside. I ventured closer.

Cade followed me. "That's—"

"Nick's." I knew. Something pulled me to investigate. To remember.

"Yeah." He didn't stop me as I walked in. A gun behind the door. The table was full of weapons and an envelope I wasn't going to touch. I didn't want to pry, just learn. Absorb. Like a dog sniffing out its new home. Nothing here made this his. Nothing personal. Nothing to warm it or claim it or give it an illusion of permanence. Just like every room in every foster home I'd ever stayed in, which meant Nick was carrying the truth about who he was somewhere else.

I kept mine in my playlist and my sketchbook. Where did Nick keep his? "What's he like?"

"A jerk."

"Okay." I faced Cade.

He pinched the bridge of his nose. "Sorry, Ava. I know what it's like to want a family. I checked out your room too."

He had? They were remembering me like I was remembering them. We were in this together. For the first time I felt like I might not be alone in all of this. "Show me yours?"

He grinned and motioned for me to follow, but I took one last look at Nick's room. Then I headed straight in again and opened his second dresser drawer. A mysterious guy like Nick wouldn't hide his special belongings in the top drawer. He'd go for the second. Under his shirts. There. I pulled out an old, yellowed envelope. There was a photo inside. Me, Nick, and Cade. All of us smiling. We looked to be at an amusement park. And those clothes! Nick's arms circled both of us, and he hugged us close. Big grin on his face. I had a dandelion behind my ear.

I turned to Cade, who had wandered in after me. "If we can't take anything with us, how does he have this?"

"He remembers first. He told me of a few hiding places, but he said a lot have been destroyed over the years." He took the picture. "We look happy." Then he handed it back. "Nick is mostly business now."

I put the picture away and headed out into the hall, then beat Cade to his room. "Wow. You couldn't wait to showcase your differences, huh?"

"Shut up." He laughed.

A leather jacket hung on a chair, pictures of muscle cars decorated the walls in a fairly artistic way, and a stack of comics sat beside his bed. Electronics plugged in to every available outlet.

"You like cars?" I picked up a model, and he practically took it out of my hands like it was an egg I might crack.

"Careful with that. I'm going to own one someday."

"And Batman?" I reached for a comic.

"Sure. Yeah." He herded me away from the stack. "But I'm more of a Dick Grayson fan."

"What's this?" I wandered to his desk and picked up a book off the table. "Are you seriously reading Shakespeare?"

He plucked the book from my hand and shoved it into the second drawer. Before he could close it, I stopped him. "You like dark chocolate, too?"

"Yeah." He pulled out the package and offered me some. "It helps with headaches."

I took a piece.

He put the chocolate away, but I caught sight of another book. *Catcher in the Rye.* Cade, the secret literary lover. For some reason that made me smile. Maybe he and Yuki did have something in common. He tipped his head toward the hall, and I followed him to my room.

Tingles spread over my skin. Would it match my tastes? Was I the same person in every cycle?

I entered and sucked in a tight breath. My mouth opened as I stood there. Took it all in. The strange sense of familiarity. Of belonging. It tugged at the hole in my heart like stitches closing a wound. A strange burn settled in my chest and flooded me as if I wanted to cry but couldn't because I was too absorbed in the world around me. The room around me.

Almost everything was . . . perfect.

My eyes burned, and I blinked to refrain from shedding tears.

I stared at the ugly lamp. It had to be ancient. And it made me laugh. The dresser, though old, appealed to me with its sturdy, plain frame and pretty wood grain. I loved it. The bedspread looked new. Soft periwinkle with the white silhouette of a dandelion, its fluff being blown in the wind. I would have picked this myself.

And the line of three black-and-white photos on the wall stole my breath. The center photo boasted the silhouette of a huge oak tree with happy branches and a strong base. The tree sat in a field of dandelions, some still flowers and others fluff ready to blow in the wind. Rays of sun shone through the branches, and birds flew away from it, leaving nests for the day.

The left photo showcased a close-up of the birds—silhouetted in the sun. The right focused on a tall dandelion, perfectly fluffed, with a few seeds wandering off into the breeze.

Everything about this embodied my thoughts—my feelings—of belonging and family and freedom. I couldn't describe its beauty in words. And to think it was mine.

"Do you like it?" Cade asked.

I faced him. "Did you—"

"Nick picked out the bed and furniture. Except the lamp—that was me."

I bit my lip, but he burst out laughing. "I'm kidding about the lamp. It was in my room, but I hated it too." He motioned to the pictures on the wall. "I picked those for you." His gaze darted to the ground for a moment, suddenly seeming vulnerable. Strange for Cade.

"I love them. Where did you find them?"

He stared at them with his mouth open, as if he wanted to explain where he got them but suddenly wasn't sure.

Realization hit me. "You took the pictures?"

This time when he shrugged, he dipped his head low. Was Cade Elderson actually hiding his pride?

"They're beautiful, Cade."

"I don't know what it was, but before I even met you, I just had this feeling every time I looked at these photos, that they reminded me of someone—later I realized who."

I bowed my head and brushed my hair away from my neck to show him the tattoo on the back of my left shoulder. "Look familiar?"

A dandelion with roots like those of an ancient tree. The white seeds blew in the wind, turning into a flock of flying birds. The perfect blend of his photos.

"Whoa."

I faced him, a joy welling in my chest, filling a void. It scared me a little. But mostly, I relished the feeling. I suddenly wanted to hug him, but fear startled that thought away. But . . . maybe it was safe to show love to someone who had loved me back for lifetimes?

"I'm glad we found each other," he said quietly.

That jolted my heart to a faster beat.

I could accept his love, or I could push him away.

I stared at him for a moment, watching him take a step back, eyes rounding as if he thought maybe he shouldn't have said that. It was now or never. I touched his arm. "Me, too."

His smile warmed my insides.

I swallowed, and hope dared to rise. "So, phoenixes, huh? What exactly does that mean?"

He sat on the bed, and I joined him. "Some kind of person created to protect humans from monsters. We are reborn in different places in time."

"Bound by time?"

"I think so. We always move forward in time. But to different places. We fight the monsters. And Nick says we're stretched thin because of the dark phoenixes. One in particular, who is trying to kill us."

Could it be the woman from my memory? The one who'd stolen Cade's and my powers temporarily. I swallowed, and my pulse pounded as Cade relayed to me that she was indeed the dark phoenix trying to eradicate us. And that, for some reason, I alone could kill her—for good.

My mind reeled. I wanted to throw up.

"Ava? Are you okay?"

I put out my hand to stop Cade form talking. Why me? My throat constricted. Suddenly, I wanted nothing more than to go back outside and make sure my aim with those weapons hadn't been a fluke.

I looked at Cade, my pulse still thrumming in my ears. "Why am I the only one who can k-kill her?"

Cade half frowned. "Yeah, I asked that question, too. Something interrupted us, and Nick never answered."

The door downstairs squeaked open. "Cade? I'm home."

I stood, eyes wide. "Nick?"

Cade nodded, and I tore out of the room, headed downstairs to meet my other brother and ask him a thousand questions, starting with why I had to kill the princess of evil.

And how.

# 26

AVA

I RUSHED DOWN THE STAIRS. NICK stood in the kitchen, pouring a glass of water, his back to me. I wanted to say something—see how he would feel about my being here—but at the same time, the thought of finding out made my palms sweat.

Cade clomped down the steps after me, and Nick turned toward us. His eyes met mine and widened. "Ava?"

My throat tightened. I wanted to speak, but I wasn't sure sounds would make it out. Nick crossed the kitchen before I could even say a word. He opened his arms and wrapped me in a hug so tight I thought I'd burst. I sank in, and tears threatened all over again.

He stepped back, hands still gripping my upper arms. And he took in every inch of me. "What do you remember?"

He didn't give me a chance to answer. He just pulled me in for another hug and, surprisingly, he pulled Cade in too. "I'm so glad to have you both back."

My eyes stung and I squeezed them closed. No one had ever showed this much love to me.

Nick let us go and smiled, but sorrow tinged it.

I breathed in, loosening the tightening in my throat and making sure my voice wouldn't waver.

Then I pulled my typical cloak of defiance over me before I could even think about the consequences and crossed my arms. "Cade tells me I have to kill someone?" The defiance did not come through in my words. My voice sounded light, airy, and unsure.

He winced, shot Cade a frustrated glare, and backed away from us, heading to the fridge. "Her name was Guinevere. She's gone by Gwendolyn, Gwen, completely different names like Saki and Rosemary and Angelica of all things." He set two cans of pop on the island. One Vanilla Coke, which was my favorite, and one Dr Pepper, which Cade nabbed.

I wrapped my arms around myself, and my voice came out small. "Why me?"

Searing pain spread out across my stomach. I grabbed the edge of the kitchen island, buckled over, and let out a strangled cry. Then the pain left as suddenly as it had come, and I stood there, shaking with my eyes wide.

Nick and Cade both raced to my side. I pulled up the edge of my shirt and a very strange and brand-new scar showed itself on my stomach.

Not a new wound—an old scar, as if I'd had an injury there before.

"What's that?" I tried not to panic.

"That is the mark of your first death." Nick's tone turned grave.

"What?"

"A phoenix can be killed in every cycle. We keep the scars of our first death. Yours . . . the woman we're hunting down, she murdered you when you were sixteen."

Cade set his pop can down with a clack and pressed his hand to his side as Nick said this. Cade pulled up his shirt to reveal the same type of injury. "She was at least methodical, yeah?"

I stared at the similar scar. "Why would she—"

"You were both coming into your powers. You're twins, and therefore a special kind of phoenix." He nodded toward Cade. "You are what's known as a Giver." Then he looked at me. "You're a Taker."

"Meaning?" Cade waved his hand to get Nick to continue.

He looked at Cade as if concerned.

Cade shrugged. "I think if we're racing the clock, it's best Ava and I know what we're up against. Don't you?"

The clock? I glanced back and forth between the two of them, but Nick opened his mouth to answer at least some of my questions, so I wasn't going to interrupt.

"Cade, Givers like you used to be able to create phoenixes. That power was eradicated once the dark phoenixes came to be. They used to be light phoenixes, like us. Then there was a fight and a split. So the elders decided no one should be able to create more phoenixes. It would hopefully stop the dark ones from making more."

Cade's eyes widened, but a pit formed in my stomach as the word "Taker" resounded in my skull with every heartbeat.

Nick looked at me. "As a Taker, if you kill a phoenix, you end their life cycles permanently." His gaze flicked to Cade's. "The only one you can't kill is Cade, because he's your twin. Or—well, you can't kill yourself, either."

My soul whispered the words *kill* and *permanently*, and my chest tightened. "My powers are still active?"

Nick nodded. "They needed phoenix enders so the dark ones could be destroyed. Our Psycho Chick is the last of them."

"I'm sorry, Psycho Chick?"

"My idea." Cade stared at me with his lopsided grin.

I rolled my eyes, then the slight levity he'd created snuffed out as the weight of Nick's revelation hit me again. "Why is she trying to kill us?"

"Dark phoenixes declared war on light phoenixes because one of them fell in love with a human and healed him."

I stepped back from him. "How is healing someone wrong?"

"It's not." Nick's voice was quiet. He swallowed and looked down at his hands. "The problem was phoenixes used to be allowed to marry another phoenix or a human until one of those humans turned out to not have a very good heart. He didn't like that the light phoenix elders were the most powerful. He tricked the phoenix who loved him into falling for him. When she healed him . . . he became a phoenix. Then he started using his powers to harm the other humans who had caused him grief. A Taker was sent to stop him. Permanently."

I gasped and pressed my hand to my mouth.

Nick glanced at me, wincing. "It wasn't you, Ava."

"H-how many phoenixes have I—"

"Ava." He grabbed my shoulders and looked me in the eyes. "You protected your family once. That's all."

My knees gave away, and Nick supported me while I clutched the kitchen island for balance. "I—but I have to kill Psycho Chick?"

"Once you do, we'll be free. Our powers will come back."

"More powers?"

"Yes. We kept the ability to self-heal. To heal other phoenixes. We're fast enough and strong enough to fight the monsters. But we used to have fire. A flame we could control, specific to our personalities."

"How do I k-kill this . . ." Calling her *Gwen* made her sound more human than monster. "Psycho Chick."

"Access your fire. Yours is the strongest I've ever seen."

"And you can train me to do this?"

Cade groaned and buried his head in his arms. "Tell her the part about how Psycho Chick has basically beat us in every past life and we get killed first."

"Cade." Nick's voice was harsh. "Let her process this first."

"What?" I couldn't breathe. "Sh-she—it's a good thing we're reborn, then. Yeah?" Why was I shaking?

"I'm sorry, Ava," Cade said sheepishly, then he led me to the couch, and we both sat down.

"I thought you said Nick was the jerk." I half smiled.

"I guess it runs in the family."

"Why do you look so sad?" I turned my attention to Nick, who sat in the chair across from the couch. "Both of you. There's more bad news, isn't there?"

"Psycho Chick did something to Cade cycles ago. She may have found a way to take his dormant Giver powers."

"I thought you said—"

"I did. Cade and you were supposed to be our last hope. When all the dark phoenixes are gone, Cade's Giver powers are supposed to return. A way to create more light phoenixes."

My heart beat so fast I started to get dizzy. "But Psycho Chick has that power now? I don't understand."

"Not completely. Cade's powers are still dormant because dark phoenixes still live. But I think she's finding a way to use it. I know for sure she's taking his powers. And it's turning Cade into a human. If we don't end her this time, it could be Cade's last cycle. And if she kills him . . ." Nick's voice wavered, and he cleared his throat. "Twins are bound. Your life forces are connected. If Cade dies for good, when you die, it's for good, too."

I leaned back against the couch as his statement knocked the air out of me.

"That's most definitely worse news." Cade stared at Nick as though it was the first he'd heard that tidbit.

Nick stood. "We're going to get her this time. Trust me. I won't let anything happen to either of you." Then he motioned to the back door. "Who's ready for a little target practice?"

My stomach churned, and my breathing shook, but if saving these two—my brothers—was my destiny, then I didn't want to miss out it. On a family. "I'm in."

Nick's proud smile lightened the heaviness in my chest.

Cade stood too. "Are you going to tell her about Wyatt, the evil dark phoenix?"

Something inside my chest shuddered. It echoed no in a hollowness that grew and throbbed around the edges.

"What?" My word came out an airy whisper.

Nick held out his hand to calm me down. "Cade doesn't remember exactly what he's talking about. Wyatt—"

"Is not evil!" I was quivering.

"Ava." Nick's gaze held so much sympathy. "Wyatt has betrayed us in the past. Please be careful around him. Gwen has . . . a pull on him he can't always resist."

"But he wants to?" Hope exploded into that hollow space, and against reason, I latched onto that feeling. "Resist, I mean."

Nick sighed. "Please be careful around Wyatt."

I nodded, not sure who to trust. How to feel. What to believe. The only thing that would sort out this mess was my own memories.

"I'm sorry, Ava." Cade's words sounded clipped. I faced him, and he pressed his palm against his head and swayed. "I didn't mean to"—he closed one eye and hunched over as if in pain—"stir up trouble."

"Cade?" My heart revved. What was happening to him?

Nick raced toward him. "Ava. Get him a glass of water, please?" Nick caught Cade as he collapsed, gently guiding him the rest of the way to the carpet. Cade started convulsing, and Nick cradled his head so he wouldn't hurt himself any worse.

And I stood there, helpless. "This is how she takes his powers from him?"

The concern in Nick's eyes didn't douse my worry. "I've never seen him so bad."

"Hey." I touched Nick's arm. "How much time do we have?"

He shook his head. "A couple of months at most. Usually once you get your memories back, it means she's strong enough to fight the three of us. She waits for a full moon so she can bring her army."

I breathed in a shaky breath. Not much time for me to learn how to become the Taker I was born to be. "What makes her strong enough?"

"Remember I told you Cade is a Giver? Gwen was, too. Her dark phoenix powers are a perverted form of the powers she had. They give her the ability to create monsters." He sighed. "That beast in the woods the night I met you? Not the werewolf that got Cade, but the other monster. The one you ran from? It was one of hers."

"Th-that was a werewolf?" A chill swept through my bones. "And there are other m-monsters?" I just got my brothers back; I wasn't about to lose them. "I'm going to kill her. We'll free Cade. Okay? Tell me what I need to know."

His jaw clenched. "I'll train you."

# 27

AVA

I TEXTED WYATT TO MAKE SURE HE wasn't going to stand me up for tonight's run. Yuki could barely get over the fact that I'd asked him out, even though I explained that exercising was hardly a date. Her teasing had been relentless, so I missed Wyatt's first text.

The second came right as Jean glanced out the window, less-than-nonchalantly making sure I had a running buddy. She informed me of his arrival before he even turned up the walkway. "Looks like Wyatt is here. Do you want to invite him in for a—"

"No. He wants to get going." I practically jumped off the couch and texted Wyatt that I'd be right out.

"All right, well, if he wants to stop in after—"

"I'll let him know!" I called as I raced to the door.

Dave beat me to it. He must have been on his way to the living room from the kitchen.

Cool evening air wafted in, and Wyatt's eyebrows popped up when he saw Dave standing there.

"Hey, kid!" Dave held out his hand to shake Wyatt's, a huge smile on his face. "How've you been?"

"Great." Wyatt shook Dave's hand. "Feeling better, Coach?"

"Yeah. Thanks to you. Ava said you were there. I don't even remember."

"Probably not a bad thing." Wyatt smiled ruefully.

Dave nodded. "Just glad to be in one piece. And I'm really glad whatever ran out in front of my car didn't hurt Ava or you."

"Yeah. Close call."

"The team isn't the same without you. The offer for you to try out again still stands, you know—if you change your mind."

Wyatt bowed his head, gaze on the ground. "Thanks. For that."

"All right, well you kids stay out of trouble." Dave moved aside for me to step out the front door.

I joined Wyatt on the porch.

Dave nodded toward Wyatt. "You take care of her. Okay?"

"I know she can take care of herself," Wyatt's blue-eyed gaze settled on me, and his mouth curved up slightly, "but I'll watch out for her anyway."

I cocked my head and gave him a challenging grin. "What you're going to have to do is keep up with me."

That deepened his smile and sent a flurry of flutters into my stomach.

The two of us headed down the walkway and out to the sidewalk. "How's your arm?"

"Good as new." He rolled up his sleeve as evidence.

"Perfect. Then try to keep up." I picked up my pace and raced to the woods.

Wyatt hurried to catch up to me. "Whoa. Hey, I didn't realize this was going to be marathon training."

"Already complaining?"

"No." He glanced at me, and the streetlight illuminated his smile. His pace matched mine, and we headed toward the woods. When we reached the place of the crash site, I realized I hadn't been running this way since the accident. The memory of a few weeks ago slammed into me. All I could see was headlights, and all I could hear was metal screeching, that creature howling. And all I could feel was Wyatt's arms around me, pushing me to safety. I balked.

"You okay, Ava?"

I looked up at him, realizing that I'd slowed, staring at the corner. At the glitter of glass in the streetlight. The debris.

"I'm okay." I picked up the pace and crossed the empty dirt road, glass crunching beneath my shoes. Together, Wyatt and I entered the woods.

I thought of flicking on my light so we could see our path clearly, but I didn't need it. Wyatt hadn't slowed, either, so I assumed our phoenix night-vision must be kicking in. "So you played lacrosse?"

"Yeah."

"Mr. Fields said you were really good. Why'd you stop?"

"I . . . umm . . . got kicked off the team."

Stupid question. "I meant, why didn't you try out again?"

"Lost interest, I guess." He glanced my direction, and I could almost feel the heat in his next question. "Did someone tell you what happened?"

"W-well—" Oh great, I'd hesitated.

Wyatt's eyes narrowed slightly. "Who?"

"I've heard rumors that you beat up Scott Mitchell."

Wyatt's silence made me wonder if I'd offended him.

"If you want to give your version—"

"I'm sure the one you got was accurate." His voice sounded tight. Not the conversation tone I was going for.

"He probably deserved it," I said.

"I don't know."

I glanced over at him. "What did he do to your sister?"

Wyatt used the edge of his shirt to wipe his face, but I wondered if it was more to hide behind.

"I mean, you don't have to—"

"We were at a party. He drugged her drink and took her upstairs. As soon as I found out where they'd gone, I busted the door down." He paused. "I threw him against the wall. That was probably enough, but I didn't stop there."

"Whoa." I slowed to a halt, an ache spreading in my heart, and Wyatt did, too.

He faced me. "I-I'm not—"

"I'm sorry that happened. Was your sister okay?"

"Yeah. She is now. He hadn't really had a chance to touch her. She doesn't remember much, which is good for several reasons. But the thought of her watching me slam my fist into Scott's face over and over"—he crushed his eyes closed—"and over . . ." He stared at his knuckles as he slowly made a fist and spread out his fingers again. "It's hard to take that kind of justice into your own hands. In that moment, it's hard to know what's right, what's wrong. Everything's blurry."

"I couldn't imagine." I grabbed his hands and squeezed.

"I broke his jaw—dislocated it—and his nose. Fractured another bone in his face. He was lucky I didn't permanently damage his eye." He wouldn't look at me. "There was so much blood. I honestly don't know what came over me."

"You were protecting your sister."

He gave me eye contact now, and he frowned sadly.

Standing here, seeing the guilt he felt over something I couldn't even fault him for gave me all the information I needed. He might have a temper, but Wyatt wasn't some evil dark phoenix.

"It's not like you made a habit out of beating people up, right?" I offered a smile.

The way his gaze locked onto mine, suddenly easier to read, though the moonlight was blocked by branches here, made me think he might be staring deep into a memory, too.

"Wyatt?"

He sucked in a breath. "Right. I don't go around hurting people."

"No. You let them pick on you." I released his hands.

His small laugh seemed to drip bitterness. "Well, I can't exactly fight back—I'd be in so much trouble if I were to have another . . . incident—and they know it."

That ignited a fireball in my stomach. That's why they picked on him? "How can people be so cruel?"

"I deserve—"

"No. What Scott did to your sister was unthinkable. I'm glad you were there to stop it. *He* deserved punishment for that, and I don't fault you for protecting your sister."

He stared at me, unspeaking.

I motioned down the path ahead. "Can I show you something?"

"Of course."

Within a few minutes, we'd reached the part of the woods where sand mingled with dirt and coated the hillside between the trees—in daylight it looked like golden streams, like rays of sun from heaven itself. At night, they were silent gray fingers reaching into the trees. We climbed the sandy hill and arrived at my favorite place on the run. I stepped through the thinning dune grass and out onto a sandy cliff on top of a dune. From here we could see over Lake Michigan. But the sun had already set, leaving nothing but darkness in front of us. Here, at night, the best view was looking up.

"Will you sit with me?"

Wyatt's eyes widened.

I sat down anyway, motioning to the stars. "I looked up Andromeda after that first night you came over."

"Yeah?" His voice carried the hint of awe and surprise mingled together as he settled next to me.

"But I don't know which constellation it is."

He leaned close enough that his shoulder brushed against mine. "There." His finger traced an outline of stars. "It's been said that she's a beautiful princess."

"I read that, too." I chuckled. "But like all princesses, she got into trouble."

He laughed. "Yes. She got herself captured."

I made my voice mock-dreamy. "But her handsome prince—what was his name? Perseus!—saved her. I can only imagine they lived happily ever after."

He didn't respond, so I tore my eyes away from the night sky and found Wyatt already looking at me.

"Thank you," he said, turning his attention back to the stars as a breeze off the lake muffled his quiet words. "For not making me feel like a monster for what I did."

I wanted to touch him again, but I refrained. "You're hardly a monster, Wyatt."

The gratitude in his soft smile made my pulse race.

My brothers were wrong about him. And I'd prove it.

After all, wouldn't we need every ally we could get in this war against Psycho Chick and her minions of darkness?

# 28

## CADE

Homework on Saturdays was not my thing. But the thought of meeting with Yuki, even if it was in a library to discuss our lit project, got me out of bed.

Nick leaned his back against the kitchen sink and glanced at me over his bowl of cereal, even though we had a table now. I couldn't fault him; I still sat at the kitchen island.

His spoon stopped midway to his mouth, and he narrowed his eyes. "What's got you in such a good mood?"

"Maybe I don't wake up like I hate life every day like you do."

"Sorry. I was just trying to make conversation."

"No. You were trying to make an observation."

"And I completely failed. Apparently you're in a defensive mood this morning." His eyes searched my face again. "You remember something else?"

I cocked an eyebrow. "Why? Will I remember something that makes me . . . defensive?"

He set the bowl in the sink and ran the faucet to rinse it out. "Sorry I asked." Then he walked out of the room and grabbed his jacket.

I followed and leaned in the kitchen doorway. "Where are you going?"

He shrugged into the leather jacket. "Work."

Apparently he wasn't going to elaborate. "And you'll be home . . . ?"

"Eventually." He faced me. "I think I'm closer to finding something that will help us defeat Psycho Chick. I might stop at the library after. Or the bookstore—"

"Where Kelsey works?" I waggled my eyebrows.

"For that, tonight's training session will be brutal."

I didn't doubt it. "I'm headed to the library. You want me to check out something?"

He paused, seeming to consider it. "If it triggers a memory—"

Not this again. I wanted to punch something. "So be it. How do we stop her?"

"We have to find her and kill her. If you're not busy later, I'd suggest you start hanging around Ava—it'll help jog her memories. She's the one who needs to be reminded of her training."

"We'll see what happens. I have a school project I'm doing today."

His eyes narrowed. "With a girl?"

"Why would you ask that?"

"You're in a good mood about going to the library to do homework on a Saturday. Hardly rocket science."

I rolled my eyes. "Okay, you got me."

He sighed.

"What?"

"Be careful."

"Because an attractive girl in my high school class might be a monster?"

"No."

It was like pulling teeth. "Just spit it out."

"It would be good for you to remember that life as a phoenix is lonely, Cade. Falling in love isn't a good idea. In fact, it's forbidden." Then he put on the helmet and left.

I stared at the doorway and shook my head. My brother the conundrum.

And since when was love forbidden?

Since it was such an amazing day and I wanted my good mood back, I opted to take the other motorcycle that Nick had told me not to take without permission. Giving permission wasn't really in his wheelhouse, so I took it anyway. Best decision ever.

When I finally pulled into the library parking lot, I found myself checking my helmet hair in the rearview mirror. I'd known Yuki all of a few weeks, and I was already feeling self-conscious around her. Not good for my uber-confident self-image.

I spotted her sitting at the table through the huge windows in the side of the building. She leaned over a book on the table, her fingers gliding through her brown hair. Lighter when the sunshine touched it. Petals from a flowering tree right outside the window blew in the breeze, and I recalled the strange memory I'd had of the Japanese woman.

Yuki turned her head, and her eyes met mine through the glass. She waved tentatively. I waved back and headed up the steps. The face from my memory—painted white with bright red lipstick—could have passed for older Yuki.

The library door opened as a blonde woman walked out, nose in a book. She bumped shoulders with mine.

"Sorry!" She offered a smile and touched my arm briefly. I shrugged it off. Maybe Nick was right. Maybe I was in a good mood this morning.

I went inside and joined Yuki at the table. "Good morning."

She regarded me for a few moments. "I didn't think you'd actually show."

"What?" I slid into the chair across the table from her and gave her my best wounded look. "What do you take me for?"

A sweet but slightly venomous smile curved her eyes. "How about a slacker who floats by in his classes by tapping into his superior intelligence only enough to glide by as an average student without ever divulging that 'average' in his case merely means minimal effort."

"Someone's been taking notes on more than class material."

"Hardly. You're easier to figure out than you think."

Ouch. "Doubtful." I leaned over the table.

She sat back, completely unintimidated by my blatant staring, and crossed her arms. "Why did you come, really?"

"Nothing ventured, nothing gained."

Slowly, she uncrossed her arms but didn't release her eye contact. "All right, Elderson. This partnership might work out after all."

I couldn't stop my growing grin.

She held up her finger as if to stop me from getting any ideas. "Might. Just don't blow it. I'm going to Harvard, and a botched presentation my sophomore year is not in that plan."

"You have everything planned out?"

She shrugged, but for the first time that confident eye contact wavered. "Not everything." Again, she pinned me to my seat with those piercing eyes. "In fact, I like a bit of spontaneity. If it's done well, of course."

"I think that still falls under the term *planned*."

"You don't think I can be spontaneous?"

I couldn't hold in my chuckle. "Let's see. You walk to your car, which is parked in the same part of the lot, at the same time after school every day. You take the same route, always reading, and you always wait for Ava. You predictably use your blue pen in history, black in Spanish, and a pencil in math, and you take notes in specific colored notebooks for each class. For example, green, science. Purple, lit, which makes sense because lit is your favorite subject and purple your favorite color. So, no, I don't think spontaneity is your scene. But if you're willing to give it a shot, I can take you somewhere right now."

She stared at me, eyes wide—I couldn't tell whether the look read "slightly horrified," and I mentally kicked myself for saying too much. But then she cocked her eyebrow. "A challenge?"

I tilted my head, hoping to entice her to give in at least once. Also, I really wanted to know if I was right about purple being her favorite color.

She slammed the book in front of her closed. "Sure. Why not?"

"Really?"

"Nothing ventured, nothing gained."

My smile grew as I stood. "Then let's go." The thought of her behind me on the bike with her arms clinging to me sounded pretty good right about now, and I didn't want to mess this up. Not that it was love or anything, but it still felt forbidden, and that sent another thrill through me.

Yuki held me tight as I revved the engine. "You ready?"

"Like this?" She wrapped her arms around me.

"Exactly like that." I was grateful that she couldn't see my grin. "Have you never ridden a bike?"

"Never. My parents are kind of . . . protective."

"I don't want to get in trouble with Mom and Pop."

She laughed. "I'm certainly not going to tell them. But you don't really seem the type to care about that."

I looked over my shoulder at her. "How about for the next hour, you throw everything you think you know about me out the proverbial window."

"Everything?"

What was I doing? Getting close to someone wasn't part of my mantra, but something about her made me want to drop a wall or two.

She laughed. "Like the fact that I believe you're a cocky know-it-all with really good looks and a shallow personality?"

"Whoa, whoa, whoa. Not everything. That second-to-last one is completely true."

"And you're conceited."

"Give me chance, okay?"

Her eyelashes fluttered, and she looked utterly serious. "A chance to what?"

"To show you a different side of Cade Elderson." I released the brake. "Now, hang on tight."

I took her down along the beach drive, which she loved. She turned her face into the wind, letting my shoulders buffet her only once we pulled away from the water. Then I drove her through the quaint little downtown. Only when we reached the third red light did she say something. "This is pretty amazing."

"I'm glad you like it."

"How much longer?"

"How long do you want?"

She paused. The light was about to change. "Can you . . . go faster?"

I laughed. "I know just the place."

She squeezed tighter as I took off at the green light. I took her outside of town to a long stretch of road and shot out like a bullet. She squealed, delighted, and hugged me close.

When it was time to head back, I drove near the water again. Her hold on me grew much more comfortable. At one point, it almost seemed as though she forgot herself and actually snuggled into me.

Just as we pulled in front of a corner store next to the pizza place, nearly back to the library, Yuki's hold on my waist loosened, and she seemed to lean right into me, heavy. Was she falling asleep? I pulled over and found her on the verge of fainting. I parked and caught her.

"Yuki?" I didn't know what to do, so I pulled off her helmet and tapped her cheek—harder than intended. My heart ached. "Yuki!"

Her eyelids fluttered and she sucked in a breath. "Where am I? What—how long was I out?"

"How long—does this happen regularly to you?"

She shook her head and leaned back on the brick wall of the storefront. I realized people walking by had taken to gawking.

She offered a weak smile at a couple. "I'm fine." As she pushed off the wall and crossed her ankles into a stumble, it was clear she wasn't fine.

Thankfully, I caught her. "What happened?"

A few tears dripped down her cheeks, but she dashed them away quickly. A sign of vulnerability she didn't want to share. Wishes I could normally respect if it weren't for the fact that I couldn't let this go until I knew for certain she was okay.

She looked up at me, smiling.

It looked like a real smile, but it couldn't be. Not after what I'd just seen. Then I recalled how supportive she'd been about my headaches.

Like she understood what I'd been going through. I helped her gain her balance. "I think I should drive you to the hospital."

Her fingers gripped my sleeves tight, and a wild look broke through her composure. "No!"

"Why not?"

She looked away. "I . . ." She leaned against the wall again. "I don't want to go."

I removed my helmet and leaned next to her. "How often does this happen?"

"More now. I don't know. Once a month." Another tear spilled out of the corner of her eye as she stared up at the blue, blue sky.

I looked up, too. So bright. Vast. Like her planned-out future. "I take it you know what's wrong with you?"

"No one does."

A tight pang hit my chest. "What do you mean?"

She shook her head and smacked a loose fist into her thigh. "They can't figure it out. I get dizzy, faint. No one knows why."

"Is . . . is it serious?"

She sniffed and let out a frustrated laugh. "They just know something is wrong with my heart. Maybe a lot of somethings. I probably need a new one."

Whoa. Something in my chest dropped like a stone. I faced her, unsure what to say. But maybe this was one of those times to say nothing.

She pushed off the wall and gazed at me, smiling ruefully. "I don't have a lot of friends, but all of them know about my . . . condition. Everyone is always so careful with me, like I'm some sort of fragile porcelain doll. But you—you treated me like a regular girl. That hasn't happened to me in a while." Her hand rested on my upper arm and she smiled, slightly sad. "Thank you for today. It was the best day I've had in a long time." She paused, searching my face with those pretty brown eyes. "And you're not exactly the person I thought you were." Then she started walking away.

The library wasn't that far from here, but I'd been heading back that way. "Yuki, wait." Everything about this was wrong. She'd nearly fainted and could have been seriously hurt if I hadn't caught her and pulled over. What was she thinking? The heat in my chest died as I reheard her words. She wanted to live. Like a person who didn't have to worry about taking it easy.

And here I was getting so mad at Nick about the same types of things.

I raced after her and caught up. "Where are you going?"

"Library. Then home."

I tugged her shoulder until she stopped and faced me. "I can't not take you to the hospital, Yuki."

Her eyes grew harder, and she stared into me. For a moment, I thought she might actually be contemplating taking me down. And for a moment, I also felt she might be able to. Almost like I knew—no, no. Oh no. I gripped her arm as I doubled over, clutching my head in my other hand. Everything spun as the memory crashed into me.

This time, the woman standing before me, long dark hair pulled into a tight ponytail, was most definitely Yuki. An older version of her. No makeup. No mistaking. This woman had the very same birthmark on her cheek.

And she pressed a *naginata* against my throat—the blade was very sharp.

I held my hands up in surrender—far away from my weapons. The owner of the restaurant was certainly not going to let me back here if people kept making threats on my life, especially with swords. "I-I'm sorry. I didn't realize women could become samurai."

The sword's sharp side rested against my skin, and I was sure she'd get blood all over my clothes. Annoying, since I didn't really have another shirt.

Her glare intensified. "You don't realize much, *baka*."

If she wanted to call me a trickster, maybe she knew me better than I thought. "Hey, that's a little harsh."

One side of her mouth curved in a smile. A half smile was really my charming technique. And here she was stealing that. Not to mention my credibility. Actually, she'd make an excellent monster hunter.

I swallowed, causing the blade to drag against my skin. "What I mean to say is, I'm sorry. I never meant to insult you."

"No?"

"Just poke a little fun."

"You are *baka*."

"My name is Cade."

The *naginata* fell away from my neck as she lowered her arm, and her eyes widened. "You are Caderyn?"

I checked for a slice on my neck. No blood. "You've heard of me?"

That half smile lit her face again.

"I see. The bad stuff."

She shrugged. "Some good."

"A samurai with humor? I like it."

She glared again, but the ferocity she'd just shown was no longer in it. She sheathed her sword and ordered a *sake* as she sat across from me on the floor. Those eyes never left my face—a cat waiting to pounce. "I know why you are here, Caderyn. And I need your help."

I sucked in gasoline-tinged air, and the memory spit me out into the present.

Yuki gripped my shoulders, concern plain on her face.

I shifted to sit on the dirty sidewalk and breathed. "I'm okay."

"Clearly." Her voice carried the same no-nonsense tone as memory Yuki. A samurai. The girl in front of me—bookworm, straight-A student—didn't seem like a female samurai.

She tilted her head to the side, her compassion returning. "How often does that happen?"

Daily. "It really depends." Maybe her episodes were the start of returning memories, too. "Hey, do you like swords?"

She slugged my arm and started to stand. "Gross, Cade."

"No!" I grabbed her wrist before she could go. Her pulse tapped against my fingers, delicate and fragile, strong and wild. I let go. Who was this girl? "No." I repeated softer this time and stood, dusting off my pants. "Swords, like weapons."

"My father bought me an authentic katana for my eleventh birthday." Her eyes practically sparkled. "I took lessons until . . . until they found out about my condition." She bowed her head. "They said it was too strenuous." She glanced up at me. "I'm sure you can relate."

On a smaller scale. But if she was a phoenix, too, I might be able to tell her why she was getting sick. I just had to get her to trust me. "I'm guessing your parents won't like me if I drop you off at home on my bike?"

She laughed but then lost a bit of the smile. She tucked her hair behind her ear. "It's like they're trying to walk the line between keeping me alive and letting me live."

A hint of that half smile returned, only this time happier.

I took her hand in mine and towed her toward the bike. "Come on."

"Where are we going?"

"Just trust me."

# 29

AVA

REEDS SNAPPED AND CRACKED AS I headed deeper into the swampland, trailing Nick and Cade and holding the small dart shooter contraption Nick had said phoenixes invented for vampire hunting.

Nick turned and looked at me, even in the dark—with no light to aid us except the nearly full moon—I could read his rueful expression. "I really need you to focus on being quieter," he whispered.

My shoulders curled in. Even traipsing through reeds he expected quiet? Impossible.

But Cade's sudden appearance next to me, soundless, twisted my stomach. I bet his first hunt with Nick had been flawless.

A sharp hiss caught the wind and filled the air, whispering over the cattails as if it belonged there. Cade faced Nick, who held up his hand to tell us to freeze.

"Vamps." Nick raised his weapon. "Remember your training, and you'll be fine."

The three of us assumed position, standing back-to-back, lifting our weapons, trusting our night vision. I didn't think they were shaking like me, though.

After a few moments of silence, Nick turned to me. "Remember." He handed me a wooden stake. "Heart." He pointed to his chest. "You're strong enough to puncture, you just have to believe it."

I was ready. I had to be, whether he thought so or not.

A dozen forms ghosted though the trees so fast I saw only a blur. White like a pale fog and moving with joints way more flexible than my own. I tried to steady my weapon. Made sure the stake was secured on my belt.

One of them locked eyes with me. Red, glowing eyes. Such a strangely peaceful face. But when it smiled, razor fangs elongated. One sliced his bottom lip, leaving a trail of red.

"Don't stare, Ava!" Nick's voice broke the cloud of my thoughts, and I fired. My wooden arrow pierced that one in the heart. It shrieked and sunk beneath the reeds, but before I could react, another was already next to me.

I swung the stake like Nick had taught me. One of them jumped back, but they kept coming like curious ghosts. I shuddered. This was quite different from training, but I had done this before, whether or not I could recall, and I had to do it now.

My brothers were counting on me to save our race. I had to prove to them I was ready to take down the monster so I could start to prove Nick wrong about everything.

I stabbed but missed the heart.

Cold, dead fingers wrapped around my arm and pulled the stake from its flesh as I held the grip.

"You missed," it hissed.

I tried again, but it was too fast.

"Ava!" One of them fell as Nick raced in, vampire on his back, and stabbed the baddie in front of me.

Another grabbed my brother's arm and yanked it out of place. With a roar, I thrust the stake into it. That one fell dead.

"Look out!" Nick pushed me aside and stabbed again. Three vampires took hold of him and forced him to the ground. I pushed the stake into one, not in the heart. It turned its attention to me, and I stumbled back.

"Weakling!" it hissed.

Cade appeared, taking out a vampire before I even had a chance to adjust my grip on the stake.

I was strong enough. I was supposed to be strong enough. But I didn't remember.

I stabbed another, and a shot rang out, making one of the vampires stop and target Cade.

Not my brother!

A monster grabbed me by the hair. Fangs inches from my neck. I struggled to get away, but its hold remained secure.

A growl started up from behind me, and a weight knocked us both to the ground.

Huge jaws clamped around the vampire's neck and pressed until it ripped the beast's head off.

A huge, wolfish monster stood above me, golden eyes flashing a pale blue, blood dripping from its jaws. I stifled a scream. But it killed another vampire and chased a third deeper into the woods.

Werewolves fought them. I remembered Nick telling me that. But—how? It wasn't a full moon yet.

I got up, searching for my brother.

Nick was on the ground beneath another vampire. It was my fault so many had gotten to him. If I had just remembered my training, I wouldn't have put him in that position. I flung myself onto another vampire and stabbed with all my might. The wood punctured through the back, and I pushed deeper than I thought possible to reach the heart.

It turned to dust that fell on Nick, then so did I. He stood, towing me up with him, and wiped his clothes. "Nice shot. Thanks."

"You were right. I'm not ready."

He gripped my shoulders and pulled me into him. "It's okay. You will be."

I wasn't sure.

Nick turned around, no more vampires in sight. "Where's Cade?"

He sped out of the woods as fast as the vampires. "Just making sure the job's done."

Nick turned to him. "All right. I think that's enough for tonight."

"We just started." Cade held out his arms as if Nick couldn't be serious.

But Nick just picked up discarded weapons and headed for the car. "You know by now how you get after a battle. Until all your memories have returned, it's probably best if you head home before you cash out or throw up."

Cade sighed.

I turned to Nick. Replayed him almost getting killed because of my stupid mistake. "I—I can't possibly go after Gwen like—"

"Hey." He walked up to me and placed a hand on my shoulder. A sign that I was part of his family. I knew that deep in my heart. And I wanted to cry, but I couldn't yet. Because there was still a wedge between us. A wedge named Wyatt.

Nick might be right about a lot of things, but Wyatt's goodness wasn't one of them. Wyatt was good.

Nick's hand squeezed my shoulder. "You're more ready than I gave you credit for."

"Really?"

"Yeah." He chuckled and flashed that hint of a smile—almost like for a moment he was braiding my hair again. I couldn't help it. I wrapped my arms around him, not caring how much creature blood was on his shirt.

And I hugged him so tight. So close. "I'm sorry."

"Ava, all is forgiven." He stroked my hair. The feeling strangely foreign and yet natural. At this moment, it was all I wanted. Then he gently gripped my shoulders and pried me back a bit so he could look into my eyes. "Let's have another training session Sunday. We'll go over the mistakes you're afraid you made tonight. As for right now, get some rest."

On the way to the car, Cade hung back a bit.

I slowed to walk next to him. "You okay?" I asked quietly. "Did you have another memory out there?"

He paused, glanced ahead. "I'm fine."

I touched his shoulder. "Are you sure?"

"I appreciate your concern, Ava. But I can take care of myself. I've been doing it for a while now."

He started to walk away, and I realized my life—my being alone and not wanting to get attached wasn't unique to me. Cade—and likely even Nick—had grown up with the same thing.

"I will kill her, Cade. I won't let her hurt you."

He faced me, chest heaving. "You and Nick need to stop looking at me like some invalid who can't take care of himself. I took out more vamps than both of you combined. I'm faster. Stronger. I will help you get to Gwen. Please don't discount my ability to protect you, Ava." His eyes pled with me to hear him. See him.

I touched his arm. "Thank you."

He nodded once, then cracked a Cade grin. "I'll race you to the car."

I SETTLED INTO MY SEAT IN BIOLOGY and slumped. I'd had a wonderful time over the weekend. Hunting with my . . . brothers . . . gave me a rush I'd never experienced with anything else. Who knew ridding the world of monsters could be so satisfying.

And I'd gotten better. At least, I hoped. Nick had said I was improving.

But I'd hung out with Wyatt over the weekend, too. And the thought of seeing him in class today made me nervous—mostly because I was definitely falling for him. After learning how my brothers felt about him, I wasn't sure I should let on that I was hanging out with Wyatt. What had started as a mission to get answers had become less mission and more fun . . . and that was scary. Dangerous. Maybe Nick and Cade were right.

No. That was the Ava who tries to push everyone away talking.

Maybe being a phoenix had screwed me up. It seemed like the perks of being born again meant we never got to lay down roots. Story of my life. Lives? I didn't want to feel like any place could be permanent at all. It hurt too much when they pulled me out of the ground and shipped me off somewhere else.

Nick and Cade were entitled to their opinions, but did they really know *this* Wyatt? Maybe they were just being overprotective.

Cade walked through the door, and when he glanced my way a real smile filled his face. He took his seat right as the bell rang. I frowned at the door. No Wyatt today. Why did that make my joy wilt?

"Ava?"

I shook free of my thoughts and looked at Cade.

"Are you coming over after to school to train?"

"Yeah." What if I'd lost everything I knew how to do before? What if defeating Gwen was impossible? I looked at Cade and his sideways smile.

"Don't sound so enthused."

"Sorry. I'm just worried."

He leaned over the edge of the lab table and gave a "listen close" look. "You will not be another Nick. I can only take so much pessimism."

I wanted to roll my eyes, but his giddy expression dragged a grin out of me.

"I made a playlist. You're gonna love it."

I couldn't stop my laugh. "A playlist?"

"Yeah. Beating Nick up to the sounds of 'Eye of the Tiger' is epic."

"You're going to make me listen to—"

"Don't." His expression turned mock-serious. "It's a good song." He leaned closer. "And it's satisfying to throw punches while it's playing. You'll thank me later."

My laugh caught Mr. Cummins's attention. Both Cade and I straightened back into our seats, and Wyatt rushed through the door, still wearing his backpack.

"You're late, Mr. Wilcox." Cummins's voice barely registered as I watched Wyatt hurry to his seat next to me. A rush of cool, fresh air seeped off him.

"Sorry, sir."

Cummins seemed appeased and started handing out sheets of paper while he prattled on about microscope settings.

I was too preoccupied to hear because Wyatt took all of my attention. "I wasn't sure you'd make it today."

He hurried to get his textbook out and set it on the desk. "And miss seeing you? No way."

A stupid grin stretched my lips, and my cheeks practically caught fire. I let my hair fall in front of my face so he wouldn't see. Then I caught Cade's cautious glance out of the corner of my eye. I mouthed, "I know what I'm doing." But I didn't.

I so didn't.

Class wore on, and I peered into the microscope at some cells. Again. New cells, I guess. I mean, whatever.

Wyatt's fingers brushed against mine as he slid the device from me. "Are you—" He paused, his blue eyes met mine, unsure for a moment.

My heart beat faster.

He tapped his fingers nervously on the table.

I offered him my sweetest smile and touched his hand, stilling it. "What were you going to ask me?"

"Uh." He laughed shyly and ducked his head. "Never mind."

"You can ask me anything."

His eyebrows rose. "Okay. Can I take you out Friday night? Like on a date?"

A firework finale let loose in my chest. I wanted to squeeze his hand. I wanted to text Yuki. I wanted to squeal. So I tilted my head to the side, hiding my burning cheeks once again. Then I looked him in the eyes. When I was sure I'd have control over my voice, I said, "That would be amazing."

"Really?" He wore this huge and dorky smile in the most adorable way. "Great. That's great."

". . . and all your microscopes away," Cummins interrupted our awkward staring, and Wyatt started putting away slides and things.

I turned away, trying to cool the heat in my face. I almost hadn't realized how much I wanted this until now.

"Still know what you're doing?" Cade's voice pulled me out of my thoughts.

Nick might think he deserved my trust because he was my brother, but I remembered more about Wyatt. And . . . well, those memories were good. I had to make *my own* decisions about whom to trust and why. If I was going to get all the information I needed, I had to remember both my brothers and Wyatt. That meant keeping all of them close.

"Yes. I know what Nick thinks. But I also know what I remember." I wanted to trust Cade so badly my chest ached. But I needed him to trust me first. Right? I locked eyes with him, hoping he could sense my sincerity. "Trust me?"

His jaw clenched and he nodded once, tight. I wasn't sure if that meant he actually trusted me, but I knew he'd at least try. And that was something.

# 31

## AVA

Nick clasped my hand and pulled me up. "Amazing job again today, Ava." His eyes lit, like he was so proud of me, and that warmed my soul in a way I wasn't sure it had ever been warmed.

"You think?" Cade was right, punching Nick with "Eye of the Tiger" playing in the background was super satisfying.

"Yeah." Cade spoke around a mouthful of pizza. "You really picked up on that quickly."

"I unstrapped my fighting gloves." It feels like I've done it before.

"You have." Nick's proud smile deepened.

I just couldn't remember. What had our lives been like in the past? Were we happy? Always running for our lives? Because right now, watching my brothers push each other's shoulders and fight over the biggest slice of pizza made me feel like I'd missed something. Like there was a hole of buried memories I needed to uncover. I wrapped my arms around myself and watched them, smiling.

Our training had been going well, and I'd recalled a lot, but so had Cade, and his reactions to the memories had gotten worse. It was clear we didn't have much time left.

Nick said Gwen's return was close. The rueful look he gave me only made me train harder. I was just getting my family back. I wasn't going to lose them.

I pulled off my fighting gloves and grabbed a drink. The sun was setting and it was time to hunt soon. "I'm ready, Nick. Tell me where Psycho Chick is, and I'll kill her."

"Hold on." He chuckled. "You still haven't unlocked three very important things."

"Seriously." I wiped my face with a towel. "We've been over these moves all week. It's clear I'm remembering everything."

"Really? Then punch me."

"Again?"

He nodded, smug smile on his face.

Cade laughed. "This should be good." He followed us back outside, but leaned in the doorway, still not parting with his food.

A breeze trickled through the yard, but I was still warm from sparring, so the late-September air didn't bother me. Nick stood in front of me and squared his shoulders.

As soon as he nodded, I punched as hard as I could. And I wasn't sure what happened, but suddenly the world spun, and I ended up on my back in the grass with Nick bending over me, ready to strike.

My hands flew in front of my face before I realized he didn't intend to punch me. I peeked out from behind them. "How did you do that?"

He held out his hand to help me up.

"You have those reflexes too, Ava."

"Show me."

Cade winked. "We have superpowers." He wiped off his hands.

"Why do you look so smug?"

"I already unlocked my super-speed and uber-strength." He motioned over his shoulder. "You mind if I head upstairs and . . ." He didn't even pretend to finish that, and Nick eyed him.

Yuki's date. I put my hands on my hips. "If you break my friend's heart, Cade . . . Please be careful with her."

"Cade?" Nick frowned.

"Whoa." He held out his hands. "No one's falling in love."

Nick leveled his stare. "Good, because you know it's forbidden."

Cade put up his finger as if to stop Nick right there. "First, you know saying something is forbidden only makes it more tempting.

Second"—he glanced my way, and the look in his eyes softened—
"I'm not planning to hurt her. Ever." He turned back to Nick, eyes
narrowing. "And third, aren't you meeting up with Kelsey tonight?"

Kelsey. I knew that name.

Nick's glare could commit murder. "That's different. She's . . .
connecting to her is strategic."

"Listen to yourself. That's what she is to you? A pawn?" Cade
crossed his arms. "No, Nick. She's a person. With feelings."

I remembered where I'd heard the name. "She's Wyatt's sister!"

Nick sighed and rubbed his hands over his face. "She's a friend."
He looked at me. "And, yes, being friends with Wyatt's sister is a good
way to keep tabs on him."

"So is befriending Wyatt himself, which I can—"

"Ava, I've asked you to be careful around him."

"What does Gwen have over him? You know what? Never mind.
Maybe I'll ask him myself."

Nick stood there, mouth open as though he'd like to say something
but then realized this wasn't an argument he could win. Boy did he
know me well. "Maybe you should," he finally said.

And that stabbed a spike of fear through my heart. What had Wyatt
done? I steeled my resolve. "Do not hurt his sister. Please?"

"It's not my intention."

"Oh, well as long as we're clear on that." My sarcasm created
a puddle.

Nick hardened his gaze, then closed his eyes and shook his head,
all the fight leaving his expression. "I don't want to hurt anybody."

And that drained all the anger from me. Of course he didn't. He
was just as tied to these circumstances as I was. All the more reason
for me to help my brothers see that Wyatt was like us.

Sometime during our heated exchange, Cade had disappeared
upstairs. I shrugged and leaned against the counter. "Does this
mean we're done for the day?" I . . . had a date tonight with the very
person my brother would disapprove of most, so I thought I'd act
nonchalant instead.

"Give me a few more minutes please, Ava. You need to unlock your speed, your strength, and your fire."

"Fire? You meant that literally?"

Now he grinned.

A few more minutes turned into half an hour, and Nick showed no signs of letting me go. "Again."

I shot a kick toward his stomach, and he scooped up my leg. I twirled to get out of it and face him again, but he was ready with another kick to my leg this time. Footing off, I knew I couldn't dodge, but I could step in with a cross, so I punched. Buried it. Nick backed up. "Better."

"Better? That's all you have for me?"

"Relax. Loosen up. Remember how fast you are. You're faster than you think. Stronger than you realize. You're fiery, Ava. Put that into your fighting."

He kept saying things like that. *Faster than you think. Use your fire, Ava. Where's that fire? Tap into your speed. That's right. Now hit harder.* I wanted to punch him in the face. I swung, he dodged. Swung again. He blocked it. He punched. I ducked under his arm and buried a right hook to his body as I came out of my crouch. I aimed another hook to his face, but he blocked before I could land it. "I'm not going to get any faster."

"Then you won't defeat Psycho."

I fisted my hands and spun around, frustrated. They were all waiting on me, and here I was, world's slowest phoenix. I faced Nick, blood pumping hotter. How was I going to kill someone who *always* killed me first? "It's impossible, Nick!"

"It's not." He stood there, so stupidly calm.

"Then show me how!"

He swung for my face.

Idiot brother. Not today. Everything inside me felt alive. On fire. I latched on to that feeling. And I burst into motion, ducking his punch. His hand sailed over me in what looked like slow motion.

Whoa. I had time to deliver three body punches and move out of hitting range. I stared at my hands. They almost buzzed. They seemed to glow. Vibrate. They felt hot. Not uncomfortably hot. Just different hot. Like not normal. Something like heat fog seemed to emanate from them, blurring things behind them.

"Shoot it, Ava. Shoot the fire." He pointed at the target.

I lifted my hands, pointed them at the target, and pushed the imaginary heat with all my might. A tiny flame, like a blow torch, spurted out of my hands and died. My heart jumped, and I turned to Nick, beaming. "Did you see that!"

He surprised me with a crushing hug. "Your fire. You found it!"

"And you didn't think I could." I smirked.

He let go of me and pushed his finger into my shoulder. "Yes. I did." He backed up and took on that familiar fighting stance. "Again."

He kicked my leg and that brought me back to focus. I'd moved faster. Sharper. I breathed. Focused. He seemed to be moving slower. Sounds seemed less distracting. I moved in, faster than I thought possible and punched. Jab, cross, hook, uppercut. That fourth hit knocked my brother off his feet and sent him sprawling yards away. What the heck?

Nick cupped the side of his face. "Wow. I felt that!"

"I'm sorry. I didn't mean to—"

"I'm fine, Ava." He smiled. Real.

I stopped, staring at the joy on his face, so foreign and normal at the same time. Either I broke him, or I'd made him recall something. "What?" I asked.

"So tenderhearted. Every time you find your strength and speed, you feel terrible after you hit me."

That knocked the air out of my lungs. "Am I always me?"

He looked at me, as if he wasn't quite sure how to answer the question best. "Yes. You're always smart, a little rebellious, softhearted, fiery, and passionate. Not to mention competitive. I'm not always sure how you'll react to certain things, but I have a good idea. You're always you. I suppose that's one advantage I have in remembering everything first. I know who you are, who you'll be, how you've reacted in the past." He glanced at my hands. "Can you do it again?"

"The fire?" I stared at my palms and willed them to ignite.

Nothing.

I concentrated.

Nothing.

I tried to push the thought so hard tears dripped out of my eyes. Still nothing.

Nick touched my shoulders. "We'll keep working on it."

I looked up at him and breathed deep, realizing how tight my lungs felt. "What if I can't do it?"

He squeezed my shoulder encouragingly. "You can. I saw it. You can do it."

"In time?"

"Take the win, Ava." He motioned toward the back door, and I followed him inside.

Maybe he was right. I'd shot fire from my hands and moved faster than I ever thought possible.

Nick handed me a bottle of water from the fridge, and I downed half of it. He stopped for a beat, looking at me, then he sprouted a small smile. "It's nice to have you back, Ava." Then he headed to pick up the weapons, and I started to follow him.

The scar on his back caught my attention, and a memory flashed into me. He'd been stabbed while protecting me. It couldn't be the same scar—since I hadn't been born for his first death—but that didn't stop me from remembering. He'd been stabbed. Shot. Pierced by a sword. I fell to my knees as each memory flooded into me—emotions included.

Every time I'd lost him, a piece of me ripped from my chest.

Nick had died in my arms so many times.

Always saving me and Cade.

The memories continued pummeling me. And I sat crying in the rain. Screeching while I sliced open a monster's throat. Always I cradled his head in my lap and whispered, "No. Not again. Not now. Don't leave me yet."

And sometimes he touched my face. "We'll meet again, little sister."

The sound of the back door sliding open broke the loop of memories, but it didn't quell the tsunami of raw grief.

He was always so young.

"Ava?" He pulled my shoulders, but I couldn't get my sobbing self off the floor.

He wrapped me in a hug and pulled me close. "Hey, it's okay. What are you remembering?"

I looked up at him. Cleared the tears. "Nick?"

"What?" The worry in his eyes pulled at my heartstrings.

"Don't leave me this time."

He tucked my head close and kissed the top of it. "Ava, I will always protect you and Cade. I'm your big brother. That's what big brothers do."

"But don't die this time."

He held his breath a few moments. When he released it, the air seemed to falter a bit. "You know what? We'll defeat Psycho Chick, and then you and Cade will have nothing more to worry about."

"And you?"

He stood and offered a hand to help me up. I took it. "I will keep you safe because you're my little sister and I love you. But the burden of what sits on your shoulders—I will help you carry that as far as I can."

He . . . he loved me. I didn't know what to do with that. I couldn't breathe. A thousand pictures flooded through my thoughts of Nick, of Cade, of a woman I couldn't remember, a man I wasn't sure I knew, who looked like my brothers. I allowed the memories of all those people to flood me and slay my heart. I was loved. I'd always been loved. Nick told me they'd died forever, but I was starting to remember my parents.

An ember seemed to warm in my chest, and I wanted to laugh and cry. Nick would help me carry this burden. I swallowed my normal distance-increasing retort and let in one little piece of my true feelings. Just one. "I won't let you down."

The moment Nick's gaze met mine, a memory slammed into me.

I felt cold.

From the inside.

And shattered. As if someone had a ripped a piece of my heart out. Tears streamed down my face, and I sat in what looked like an underground tunnel. I'd buried my head into the warm and comforting embrace of someone.

"I'm so sorry, Ava."

That voice. I knew that voice. Nick's. He held me close, his strong arms the only thing keeping me from falling apart. Over and over, I whispered, "What have I done? What have I done?" But that memory seemed to stop, not like the others that faded as they ended. This one seemed frayed at the edges. As if something had torn away the rest of the memory. The part before it. The part after it.

I tried to recall what it belonged to, and the only thing I saw next was me standing in front of a grave. Nick on one side of me, Cade on the other. Many people had gathered. But it wasn't current. This had happened a long time ago. Somewhere ancient. I grabbed Cade's hand and squeezed. He looked up at me, his sad eyes stabbing pain through my core. His chin trembled, and I hugged him close.

Nick's hand on my shoulder caused me to face him. And I knew who had died. My heart dropped as the memory pushed more emotions my way . . . my mother.

Suddenly, a swirl of love whipped through me in a biting wind. Sorrow and sadness mingled with fond memories. I touched Nick's hand, still on my shoulder. And I faced him. "I can't do this."

Tears streamed down my face.

"You're not alone, Ava. I'm here."

Cade touched my arm, too. "We're both here."

"I—I'm so sorry!" I held in a sob.

Nick looked broken, but when he touched my arms—squeezed gently—strength and courage filled his features. "Ava, this is not your fault." He said each word with such conviction.

That thought gave my hope levity.

His eyebrows rose, and he chucked my chin. "Do you hear me?" His soft eyes pleaded for me to be kinder to myself.

My heart squeezed under the weight of my guilt. "She—"

"Loved you enough to die for you. Don't let her sacrifice be in vain. Don't blame yourself for it. Can you do that? Can you trust that I know what I'm talking about?"

I shook my head, a cold tear dripping off my skin. "How could you love someone enough to—"

"Ava, I love *you* enough."

The air left my lungs, and he wrapped his arms around me. I hugged him back tightly.

"Ava?"

That voice was Cade's, pulling me out of the memory.

A tear slid down my cheek. I was crying?

"Are you okay?" Both of my brothers, one on each side, asked at the same time.

"I'm fine. I—" My gaze snapped up to meet Nick's. "You remember everything?"

He nodded, concern in his eyes.

"And you feel like you know me?"

"I do know you." He squeezed my arms just like he'd done in the memory. "And I'll be here when you remember."

That comment knocked the air out of me. He'd be here. For me. I'd been waiting for this level of belonging my entire life. The tears wanted to start up again.

"Hey! He's not your only brother. I'm here for you, too." Cade leaned on the couch's arm and winked. "I just don't get into to the mushy stuff as much as this guy." He slapped his hand on Nick's back.

"Shut up." Nick reached over and grabbed Cade in a headlock.

"I was thinking group hug, but whatever." Cade punched Nick's side.

Sibling affection, or whatever it was, felt so normal. So real. I laughed and rolled my eyes, wiping away the remnants of past sorrow. "I have to go." I snagged a slice of pizza and bit in.

Cade finally extracted himself from Nick's grip and gave me a hug. "Be careful, please," he whispered.

I swallowed my bite of pizza. He'd remembered my date with Wyatt tonight. And he was worried. At least he hadn't said anything to Nick. Maybe he was starting to trust me.

But seriously, what was Nick so worried about. He'd met Wyatt. He was the kindest, gentlest— *"Wyatt went off. Bashed Scott's face in."* Patrick's words crashed into those thoughts like a wrecking ball, hard and heavy.

I shook the thoughts away. I knew this Wyatt. And this Wyatt . . . well, I liked him. A lot. I hugged Cade back. "I will. And you be good to Yuki."

"I promise." He smiled, sincere.

He let go and headed to the kitchen island. And my brothers waved as I left.

The feeling of warmth inside me started to grow. Was this really happening? Could I really belong somewhere?

I pulled the edges of my hoodie closed at my neck and jogged to the Fieldses'.

Maybe I could just pack up and leave with my brothers. We could run from Gwen until I was ready to face her.

But could I leave Wyatt? I wanted to give him a chance to tell his side of the story. Because I had the feeling he wasn't on Gwen's side at all.

And who was I kidding, Gwen would track us down.

Finally back at the Fieldses', I rushed through the front door, Jean and Dave smiling as I raced upstairs reminding them of my date tonight. I thought I even heard Dave chuckle.

All this . . . love. I hardly knew what to do with it, but for the first time in a long time, I didn't want to run. I wanted my family *and* Wyatt. That meant I'd stay and fight. Gwen would not ruin this for me.

I'd learn to control my fire.

## 32

AVA

I LOOKED IN THE MIRROR AGAIN.
Definitely going with the sparkly lip gloss. Why was I so nervous?

The doorbell rang. Heat spiked through my blood, and Ajax's deep barks shocked me out of my stupor. It was crazy how nervous I was. One more look at myself in my purple top and jeans. I pulled my lightweight black shirt over top, ran my fingers through my hair, took one last cleansing breath, and smiled at my reflection.

Then I headed down the stairs.

Wyatt stood at the bottom,  and his eyes widened magnificently. A slow smile stretched his lips, and all I could see was him. That casual outfit looked somehow more dressed up. I think he'd gotten a haircut. But what captivated me was the sparkle in his eyes.

He held out his hand to help me down the last few steps. Such a strange gesture, yet it suddenly felt so normal. I took his hand.

"Mr. Wilcox." I wanted to slap my hand over my mouth. Had I actually just said that? Heat flared in my cheeks.

"Ava." He didn't miss a beat, just steadied me as I fumbled my way down the last step. "You look amazing." He smiled and tucked my hand into the crook of his elbow.

"Thank you."

The whirlwind of Mr. and Mrs. Fields reminding us to be safe and have fun and come home on time passed so quickly—almost like a muffled version of reality—as my sharp focus remained on Wyatt. How he smelled—like the garden at the marquis's—at the strength in his arm beneath my hand. I didn't want to move away. Everything in me wanted to be touching him. And how his deep chuckle vibrated against the back of my hand. He squeezed his arm a little, like a tug on my attention, and looked down at me. "You ready?"

"Yes." I could not stop smiling. It was almost embarrassing. I followed Wyatt's gentle leading out the door.

My hand stayed in his arm until he led me to the car. "Are you hungry?"

"Yes." What was wrong with me? Could I say anything else? Why was I so wonderstruck?

He chuckled. "Good. I was thinking we could have dinner and then maybe I can take you to my favorite place."

"Really?"

He nodded and closed my door.

Dinner was divine. Falling into fast conversation with Wyatt came easier than expected. I felt like I knew him. I did. I just didn't remember all of it yet. After dinner he drove down to the beach. "You want to walk the pier?"

"Do I?" The pier at night, with its beautiful lights and archways lining the length of it. Not too windy tonight. "This is why you told me to bring a jacket?"

He smiled. "Let me know if you get cold."

I didn't think it would be possible to get cold with him. I followed him out onto the long cement walkway. The lighthouse far out in the distance, lines of lights on iron archways revealing the trail. The steady sound of the waves, more intense than their summer lapping. "It's beautiful here."

"I love it."

I looked over at him, taking in every detail. Awed by how familiar he seemed. "Why?"

"The water. The sand. It's so open and free and wild."

I slipped my hand into his and intertwined our fingers as if this was the most natural thing in the world. He glanced at me, and the lights revealed the desire in his eyes.

"My brothers don't trust you," I said.

He swung our joined hands a bit. "Do you?"

Trust. Such a heavy word. I could lie. I didn't want to. "I remember trusting you."

His thumb rubbed against the back of my hand, sending a tingle over my skin. "And do you now?"

I breathed deep. I wanted to. But I needed to know what he felt first. "I don't know yet."

"That's fair." He nodded.

"They think I should stay away from you."

He faced me, eyes tracing my face. "And what do you think?"

"If I asked you to leave—"

"I would."

"If I begged you to stay—"

"I would."

I felt odd right now. I wanted to know this devotion—I wanted to remember it. Feel it. My whole life I'd wanted people who would stick by me no matter what, and here they were—coming out of the woodwork. "Why?"

He tilted his head slightly and smiled ruefully. "I'm not sure you're ready to hear that answer, but suffice it to say I care about you very much."

The beating in my chest revved so fast I thought it might break through bone. It knocked on the door of my subconscious. I felt so loved. I wanted to hang on to those feelings tightly. As if I physically could, I squeezed my hand tight. My palms felt warm.

Too warm almost.

"Ava?" Wyatt snapped his hands away from me with a hiss, and I saw my fingers. Little sparks, like glowing embers with small, purple-tipped flames, flickered over my skin. There one moment and then gone.

I gasped. "Is that? Are you okay?"

"I'm fine." His eyes met mine. Intense, awestruck. "You found your fire." And then he gripped my shoulders, letting out a surprised laugh. "That's amazing!"

I couldn't stop staring at my hands, even though they looked normal now. Something about that fire felt different. I willed them to spark again. I closed my eyes, listened to Wyatt's encouraging voice, and felt for the warmth of the flame. Heat seeped into my palms, and I opened my eyes. There was definitely fire. I concentrated on making it grow, shrink. The flickering flame in my hands obeyed.

"I can control it!" I closed my hands, snuffing the fire. "Nick has been trying to get me to do that all week. Wyatt!" I gripped his sleeves. "If I asked you to train me—"

He straightened his spine and backed up a step. "Ava, I—"

"You're not willing?"

He grabbed both of my hands. "I'm willing. I—I just—wouldn't Nick be better suited to—"

"This happened here. With you. Nick is still training me. But if you did, too, I might be able to figure it out faster."

He still seemed reluctant. "I remember things Nick has told you in the past."

"Then show me. Help me. Please." I faced the water and held out my hands over the waves, dark in the night sky. "I need my fire or I'll never be able to defeat her."

He nodded once. "Okay."

COOL, EARLY-OCTOBER AIR KISSED MY cheek as I stepped outside after school. The next full moon was approaching, and Nick wanted me to help him on a hunt tonight—he said he thought Gwen would make her move on full-moon night. So I'd told Jean I wanted to sleep over at Yuki's this weekend.

Yuki caught up with me.

"I was just about to text you." My smile fell when I saw the broken look in her eyes. "What's wrong?"

"Do you have a minute?"

"Of course."

She dragged me to one of the benches under a tree that had lost most of its leaves already. Her finger picked at the green, peeling paint on the bench. "It's hard to explain."

"Try me."

She glanced up at me, and one corner of her mouth pulled down. Her eyes started to well with unshed tears. "He isn't what I thought he'd be."

"Cade?" My heart sank. "I thought things were going well. Did he . . . do something to you?"

"No!"

Well, that was a relief. I really didn't want to have to tear out Cade's throat because he broke Yuki's heart. But the way he'd been singing and floating this week, he'd fallen hard. I kind of felt bad for him. Yuki was going to shatter him to pieces.

She shook her head and dusted paint peelings from her fingers. "As you know, he took me on a date last week and was a perfect gentleman. And he's smart and funny. I—I just don't know if I'm ready for that."

"For smart and funny?"

She stopped and splayed her hand on the bench with force and looked up at me. "No. For someone I could see myself being with for the rest of my life. Growing old with."

"Whoa, Yuki. You don't have to decide these things right now."

"I know. But the thought of it. That he might want more. All it does is make me think how much more I don't have to give. I'm supposed to be having fun. Instead, I'm dwelling on the fact that my forever might not be very long."

"Yuki!" My heart stung as if she'd smacked it.

"I'm sorry, Ava. It's just the reality of my life."

"You're going to break up with Cade because you might die? That's—"

"Don't tell me what it is." Her eyes held a warning that told me to back off. "I don't expect you to understand. When I'm with him, I start thinking about the future. Then all I think is that it's a future I might not be able to have. It's supposed to be easy to go after high school boys and live my life because those relationships never last anyway. But it all feels so real, Ava." She looked away.

"This is real, Yuki. Everything you're living is real. And who's to say which relationships won't last."

She looked up at me. "I want to experience everything."

"I don't know when my time is, and neither do you. All you can do is live."

Her eyelids fluttered, a few tears clinging to them, but she smiled. "This is why I love you, Ava."

"I make you see the light in dark places?" I squeezed her hand.

"Yeah." She worried her bottom lip. "You don't have to understand.

But I have to do what I have to do. Just—I know you guys are friends. I don't want to make it awkward for you."

An ache seemed to hollow out a hole in my chest. I touched Yuki's hand. "I'm so sorry."

Suddenly, she sat up straighter and then picked up her bag. "I have to go. Sorry, Ava."

Before I had a chance to react, Cade rounded the corner of the bleachers. He saw me and waved, so I stayed on the chipped bench as he approached, his backpack hanging on one shoulder. "Have you seen Yuki?"

Her apology made sense now. She hadn't told him yet. I looked into Cade's hopeful eyes, and a piece of my heart broke for him. "Listen, I'm sorry to have to tell you this. Maybe you should stay away from her for a little while."

Just like that, the fire in his eyes winked out. He opened his mouth as if he wanted to speak and then closed it. I wanted to hug him. Tell him it would be okay. But how could I?

Instead, he frowned, and it did little to hide the hurt on his face. "What did I do?"

"Cade." I rubbed his arm, but he backed away, shaking his head.

"It's okay. If that's what she wants." He smiled, and it looked so real, it would have convinced me if I hadn't been the one to break the news to him. "I'll see you tonight." He didn't give me a chance to talk him out of leaving. Not that I would have. School grounds was too public a place for the emotions he carried.

And I understood that detachment. I also knew that masks didn't actually take away pain. They just covered it up so no one else saw. Later I'd let him know he didn't have to do this alone.

Head bowed and heart strained, I headed out toward my car. The sound of two harsh voices caught my attention. I whirled around to see Wyatt standing near a black car. Too many other cars in the parking lot blocked my view of the driver or his vehicle, but I knew the voice.

Nick.

Wyatt backed away from my brother's car a pace, hands in his pockets, glare in his eyes, and nodded once, tight. A spark of heat flared in my chest. What was Nick saying?

Then the engine revved and he sped off. I ducked behind the vehicle closest to me, but I got a good glimpse of tight-jawed Nick. A fire ignited in my gut. What had they been talking about?

I popped up, scanning the parking lot for Wyatt. He walked away with his head hung. I started in his direction in time to watch him stop and smash his fist into a parked car.

I froze, my pulse stuttering. *"Wyatt went off. Bashed Scott's face in."* He just shook his hand and kept walking.

A horn honked, and I realized I'd stopped in the center of the lot. My heart jolted back to life, blood slowly warming my veins again as I picked up my pace. I'd spent the last week secretly training with Wyatt almost every day. I'd seen nothing but the calm, patient young man from my memories. All that added up. Scott . . . that situation was different. He'd attacked Wyatt's sister.

I didn't care what anyone said. I cared what I'd *seen*. What I felt. Wyatt might have been a dark phoenix once, but if the darkness still resided in him, he fought it.

Still, I knew he was angry right now. More guarded than a moment ago, I caught up to him. "Wyatt!"

He stopped and faced me. "Hey."

"I thought you were going to train me after school today."

He sort of winced and pointed his thumb over his shoulder. "You know what, I totally forgot about this thing I have with my family today."

"So tomorrow?" Was he going to tell me?

He rubbed the back of his neck. "You know, I probably won't be available for a few days. I'm sorry."

I tried to tamp down my rising anger. The beating in my chest sped. Thrumming. Heating. "You're sorry?" My words came out hotter than expected.

His eyes widened, and he leaned back.

I encroached more. "You're sorry that you *won't* train me? All because my *big* brother threatened to—what? What did he even say,

Wyatt?" His name slipped off my tongue with more venom than I intended.

"Ava, relax." He motioned with his hands for me to calm down.

That only sparked more heat in my veins. I shook my head, disgusted. My words came out dark and deep. "Tell me what he said."

Wyatt's features hardened, and he stepped closer to me, lowering his head. "Nick is right. I am dangerous to you. Gwen has a power over me that I can't fight. If I stay away—"

"Wyatt." I gripped the lapels of his unzipped jacket in my fists as the anger in me melted into something much more volatile: fear. I suddenly realized that I did not want to lose him. This was why I guarded my heart, and he . . . he'd gotten past my walls. "You promised to train me. You said that if I asked you to stay—"

He tugged my hands free of his jacket. "Your training has been going well. Please, don't ask me to stay."

"Why not?"

"Because I will."

Hope filled my lungs, expanding pain. Why did it hurt so much to hope? "Then why leave? I can get Nick to understand. Don't you trust me?"

"Ava." His thumbs brushed against our still-joined hands. "I trust you. It's me I don't trust."

"Because of your darkness."

His Adam's apple bobbed, and he closed his eyes.

Wyatt wanted to control it. How could he if everyone kept showing him that they'd lost faith in him?

"Will you help . . . for me?" My voice broke on the last word.

Wyatt breathed deep. "I'll do anything for you."

My heart seemed to expand.

But his gaze grew serious. "I need you to hear my warning. Gwen is close. I can feel it. I've been on the lookout for her."

"Like Nick?"

He glanced at me sideways and squinted as if he was studying me. "Something like that."

"I'm going on a hunt with Nick tonight to make sure I'm ready to fight her. But I'd like to train with you once more."

He nodded. "Get in the car."

We drove in silence for a little while, and I studied the perplexed look on his face. As if he was wrestling to do the right thing. To control his temper.

He pulled into a nearly vacant parking lot at the beach. We both got out of the car, and the cool autumn air rushed off the water, chilling me to the bone. Someone had been here and made a campfire. I headed to put it out before flames caught the dune grass.

"Ava." Wyatt's voice seemed small and unsure in the wind.

I turned toward him, and he said, "If she's stronger than last time, the monsters she'll create will be harder to kill. Not as difficult as your average vampire maybe, but harder."

My stomach squeezed into a tight ball. I had no memory of previous monsters she'd created, but Nick had mentioned them. "So it's true, she's found a way to access Cade's power?"

He nodded. "That's why Nick is scared."

My throat tightened. "Nick said she was able to thwart my power usage temporarily once because of a special weapon she used."

"The Phoenix Quill. She found a piece of one. Nick burned it. The only way she can control your powers is to stab you with it."

I faced him, the reality of Gwen's coming starting to squeeze my insides. "Why are you so afraid of her?"

"You don't . . . remember?"

"I remember a lot. Enough. Like who you are."

He stared at me for a few heartbeats. "And?"

"I don't care." I stood in front of him, close. Wind off the lake blew the hair out of my face.

"And you still want me to help you?"

"If you're willing."

"Willing?" He half laughed and touched the side of my face so gently. I leaned into his palm. "You say the word, Ava, and I will help you do whatever you need."

"My Perseus, huh?"

That comment widened his eyes. The fire behind him sparked, taking my attention from Wyatt. I turned to face it, ready to bury it with sand, but the wood popped and cracked and flames shot high into the air with such force that Wyatt wrapped an arm around me and pushed me away from it. I fell on the sand.

"Ava, get out of here. Now." Wyatt tugged my sleeve and pulled me up.

"We have to—"

"Come on." Wyatt placed his hand on my arm in a strong grip. His eyes pleaded with me.

The flames grew. Danced. And changed to a grayish color with a sickly green smoke. I backed away a step, but a voice rose from the fire. "Ava, is that really you?"

Wyatt's hand trembled.

Firelight reflected in the wild fear in his eyes.

Quaking, I faced the blazing bonfire in front of me. A human form took shape in the flames and smoke, and though I couldn't really make out her features, I knew enough to fill them in. "Gwen?"

"You do remember me?" Her laugh was lyrical. And the fire seemed to move away from the logs, only a trail of sparks connecting her to the base. She was anchored. My pulse thrummed. Could I hurt her now? Was this really her? Could she be killed?

"I see you're still taken with your little pet."

A flare shot through me like someone struck a match across my skin. I stepped in front of Wyatt. I called the fire in me.

It exploded in my palms, orange and roaring.

I tucked my chin and stepped closer to her.

"Ava, what are you doing?" Wyatt's soft tug on my shoulder wouldn't stop me now.

"Oh, look. You want to play." Gwen's haughty voice grated on my nerves. No wonder everyone hated her. She sparked more flame in her fiery palms.

Mine was healthy and vibrant, orange and red and yellow. Nothing like her sickly, smokey green flames. I held out my hands and shot fire at her.

She breathed as the reddish blaze sailed toward her. Then with a puff of her dark fire, she blew mine out. Snuffed. Gone. I stared at my hands. At her.

Her laugh roared louder than the waves. "I know where you are."

"I'm ready for you!" I shouted, not sure of myself at all. But I couldn't let her see that.

"You and what army?"

She held up her hand, and fire blazed.

Wyatt stepped in front of me. "Will you run now?"

"No!" I tugged him away from her as she shot her flames toward us. We tumbled to the ground, but a biting heat in a strong wind pushed against me. Flattened me to the ground. Her face was above mine, dancing as the flames making up her form moved. "I will take everyone you love. And then I will kill you."

"Good luck," I bit out.

She backed away from me and sent a long tendril of smoke toward Wyatt.

I scrambled to my feet. But the green smoke twirled around Wyatt like a noose.

"Let him go!"

"I will. He's more useful to me alive. Aren't you, pet?"

Wyatt's face scrunched up, and he hunched over and cried out.

"What are you doing to him?"

Her eyes, dancing black flames, flickered to meet mine. "Kill her."

I scanned the beach, looking for any other signs of life. None. Who was she talking to?

Wyatt fell to his knees. "No!" His voice sounded pained.

Her gray-black fire slammed into him. "Kill her!"

"Never!" His eyes opened, the shame and guilt on his face clear. And he choked out, "R-run, Ava. Please."

"No." I ignited my hands once more and shot my fire, not at Gwen, but at the part of her she'd extended to hurt Wyatt.

She writhed back, screeching, and her eyes blazed as she glared at me. A massive flame shot straight toward me then exploded like a ball of fire. I put up my arms to shield my face and flew back off my feet, hitting hard on the wet sand of the shoreline.

My arm screamed as I tried to get up. It wouldn't move like I wanted it to. Shaking, I looked up to see if her next attack would come, but she was gone. The fire on the beach snuffed, covered in sand. And Wyatt raced from it toward me.

"Ava, are you okay?" He skidded to a halt next to me, his knees sinking into sand.

I sat up, clutching my arm. "I think it's dislocated."

"Let me help you." Wyatt looked into my eyes. The intensity in his showed his concern. "This'll hurt."

I braced myself for the pain, but it wasn't enough to stifle my crying out. As soon as it was over, Wyatt pulled me close and held me while I felt the pain ease away due to my healing ability.

"I didn't know she could do that," I whispered into his chest.

"Me neither." He breathed in a shaky breath. "You have to tell Nick what happened."

"I will." My heart stalled. She'd snuffed out my fire. Nick had to know. We should run. I was putting everyone in danger. She said she'd take all those I loved from me. My brothers. Yuki. *Wyatt.* "I'll see what Nick says. We might have to go into hiding until I'm stronger. I'll text you to meet me?"

He shook his head. "Ava, tonight I'm—"

I moved back so I could look at him. "What was she doing to you?"

He bowed his head. "She controls my darkness, Ava." He looked at me, eyes getting red. "That's why I can't be around you when she's there."

"But you fought her off. I saw you. You didn't let her win."

"I was completely useless."

I shot to my feet. "You were not!"

He stood slowly, dusting sand off his pants. "Yes. I was."

"No." I shook my head wildly. "You make me stronger. Look." I held out my hand and showed him the tiniest flame. A spark. It grew. "You believed in me when I didn't believe in myself."

He placed his hand over mine, causing me to put the fire away.

"Yes. And I always will. But Gwen is too strong for me. Please don't ask me to be there when you face her. I couldn't bear to let her control me again."

I placed my hand over his heart. This man who rescued me from a car crash and thought nothing of shielding my body with his, who mended Ajax's paw so gently, and who let people at school knock his books out of his hands to protect others—his temper didn't rule him. He was no dark phoenix. And tonight, he hadn't let Gwen control him. "I've seen it. You can control it. You aren't one of them, Wyatt."

"I want so badly to believe that." He looked into my eyes—pleading with me. "But the truth is, Gwen can control the darkness in me. If she gets close enough . . . I don't trust myself. I don't want to hurt you again."

Again? I didn't recall the first time, but right now, I didn't care, because this Wyatt—the one who saved me from *my* darkness—I trusted. I touched the side of his face, not caring that I was shivering from the cold. That all faded. It was just me and Wyatt, and I had to make him believe in the goodness inside him.

"You don't have to trust yourself, Wyatt. I'm not asking you to." I waited for him to really look at me. "But, please, trust me?"

A pained expression scrunched up his face. "If I hurt you—"

"You won't. *I* trust *you*." And as I said it, my soul echoed those words. He leaned into my palm, closing his eyes momentarily. "Do I always fall in love with you?"

He smiled softly. "Have you this time?"

"Remembering feelings and actually feeling them aren't quite the same, are they?"

"No."

"Then, I don't know how deep I am now, but I have fallen for you, Wyatt Wilcox. This time."

The intensity in his blue eyes—hot like a flame—melted my bones. I leaned closer to him, slid my hand from his cheek to his shoulder. The distance between us closed completely, and his lips met mine. And this moment mixed with other moments. Past moments. A thousand kisses flooded back to me. A thousand feelings. A hundred thousand moments. My heart nearly burst from feeling everything. The love. The heartache. But most of all, the knowledge that he was mine. He would give anything for me. And that filled me with hope as much as it hurt.

He pulled me closer, tighter, stronger.

And then he looked into my eyes and smiled. "I missed you."

I knew one thing at this moment: Gwen would take those I loved from me over my dead body.

# 34

CADE

I TOOK ANOTHER BITE OF FROSTED Flakes and someone knocked on the front door.

"Hang on just a second." I headed to the door.

At least I knew it wasn't Nick, because he would've used a key, which meant it had to be Ava, because no one else liked us. Well, no one liked my socially inept brother. Plenty of people liked me.

Except Yuki. That had come as a surprise, and it stung a little. Okay, a lot. I'd opened up a piece of real Cade to her. And then she'd checked out.

Typical.

Nothing I could do about it except reinforce some walls. Ava hadn't been any help. All she'd said was "Yuki is . . . complicated."

*You think?*

But Nick should really just give Ava a key already; she was over here more than she wasn't, training. She was making me look bad. Except that last hunt, I had taken out two wraiths and a vampire—on my own. Ava pretty much fumbled through a wraith attack, getting Nick stabbed again. It was painful to watch because I knew I'd made all the same mistakes.

The knocking intensified.

"I'm coming."

I opened the door a crack and did not expect to see Yuki standing on our porch, a notebook clutched to her chest, dressed in something very different from her normal not-a-uniform-but-looks-like-a-uniform outfits. My pulse raced. Had her avoiding game stopped?

I swung the opening wider and motioned to her outfit. "Are you wearing jeans? Because you look great in jeans."

"Hello to you, too," she said.

"Did I miss a planned meeting for our project?"

"No. You missed history class. I thought you might have skipped out early with a headache or something, and I brought you my notes." She lifted her shoulders and dipped her head low. Whoa. Was Confident Yuki rattled? I didn't think it possible.

I leaned against the doorframe, wishing I knew how to play her game. She'd said literally eleven words a few days after the date that she'd called "amazing" and "exhilarating," which I thought were pretty good reviews.

Then she turned suddenly cold and unavailable. Avoiding me expertly.

Ava wouldn't answer my questions about whether Yuki would ever call me back.

When Yuki finally passed me in the hallway at school, eight of the eleven words she'd said to me since the date were "maybe we should stay away from each other."

I'd believed that a pretty clear "I'm not interested" signal, until this very moment. And now I mentally kicked myself.

"Thank you." I held out my hand for the notes. "That was very kind."

She made no move to give me anything. "You're not even going to invite me in?"

I stepped aside so she could come in. "I thought you told me to stay away from you."

She hesitated, not stepping over the threshold. "I thought you were the type who wouldn't care if I said that."

Whoa. Okay. The "mixed signals" alarm sounded in my brain, leaving me confused. Maybe she'd been more okay with that glimpse of real Cade than I thought. "Are you going to come in?"

"Maybe this was a stupid idea."

"What? No. Why would it be a stupid idea?"

Her stare shifted slightly to a glare, and she slammed the notes into my chest. "Weren't you making out with someone else yesterday?"

Yeah, when I'd gotten the last three of the eleven words she'd spoken to me: "get a room." And to be fair, it was an unsuccessful attempt to ease the pain Yuki left. Explaining that to her didn't seem the best idea. I could just see that conversation heading south. "What do you care?"

Yuki glared and turned on her heel.

"Yuki—" I reached for her arm, not even sure why.

She whirled into me, breaking free of my grip before I could even release her. Then she grabbed my collar and pinned me against the open door with her forearm pressing into my windpipe.

"I wasn't expecting that." I smiled, my voice slightly choked. "First of all, I think you're overreacting. Second, don't you even want to hear my side?"

She dug her arm in, and fire seemed to ignite in her eyes. "Maybe I don't care."

She really knew how to cut deep. This was why I didn't let people in. I gripped Yuki's wrist and spun, extricating myself from her hold and backing up a step. "Maybe not, but you're here. I'm guessing that means you want to know." I headed inside.

A few moments later, Yuki followed, closing the door behind her. It didn't slam, which I thought noteworthy. "Cade, I don't know what came over me, and I'm sorry," she said.

I opened the fridge and poured a glass of orange juice. I held up the full glass, asking if she wanted any. She shook her head and set her bag on the kitchen island.

Then she looked down, holding one arm across her stomach, classic distance-increasing posture. "I shouldn't have told you to stay away." She looked up at me. "You scare me."

"Umm." I set the orange juice on the kitchen island, which she had conveniently wedged between us. "*You* just pinned *me* to the front door."

She closed her eyes, but smiled. "I'm really sorry about that."

Truthfully, she scared me, too. I knew her—past her. And if she was another phoenix, maybe she needed some guidance as the memories returned. I'd be lost without Nick—which I would never admit to him. I leaned my elbows on the kitchen island. "Does it help if I forgive you?"

Her gaze flickered to mine. "Yes."

"Good. You're forgiven, but don't tell anyone at school how easily I dropped a grudge. It's not good for my reputation." I tried a charming grin.

She moved around the side of the island. Closer. I stood up straight and froze as she kept nearing. She stopped inches from me. Her gaze didn't leave mine. Her eyes seemed a little sad. "That's a pretty heavy burden, trying to control what everyone else thinks about you. How's it working?"

I swallowed. "I . . . think I have no idea what you think."

"About you?" She moved in again. So close, I felt her body heat. Her intense eye contact melted my resolve, and I wanted nothing more than to kiss her.

Her arm reached around me, and I stilled, waiting for her to touch me. To invite me into her space. But she brought my orange juice glass to her lips and took a drink. Her eyes glued to me the whole time. Then she set the glass down. "I think I changed my mind."

"Why didn't you say so?" I knew she wasn't talking about the stupid juice. And I wasn't about to let this opportunity slip passed.

I leaned in and kissed her, soft at first. She wrapped her arms around me and pulled me in. I kissed harder. Cupping her head. Feeling her arms slide up my back. Across my neck. Into my hair. It was all Satsuma and familiar and cherry blossoms. And like something from a dream. Surreal and real at the same time. I didn't even know what Satsuma was until this moment. Which meant I knew her. I kissed her deeper. Sweeter. And she pulled me closer. Tighter.

When she backed away, her cheeks flushed and lips red, she smiled bashfully. She pressed her fingers against her lips, and her eyes practically gleamed. I'd never seen a girl look so beautiful after a kiss. She moved a step away, biting her lip.

"Yuki? Are you okay?"

"You feel so . . . forbidden."

Yeah. I got the same vibe. In fact I was forbidden. So was she. Phoenixes not being allowed to fall in love and all. At this moment, I didn't really care. "Is that a good thing?" My voice held an embarrassing tremble.

She giggled. "I think so. Yes. I—" Tears coated her eyes.

Oh no. Not a good sign. "Hey, what is it? What's wrong?" I took her hand. Had I misread everything again? Stupid idiot. Of course she wouldn't want me. Failure in each of my thousand lifetimes.

Her eyelashes fluttered. "I've never kissed anyone before."

I stared at her, relief flooding every vein. I just wanted to remember her beautiful, unsure smile right now. Her vulnerable, innocent eye contact. This moment. I never wanted to lose it. I rubbed my hand over her arm. "You had me fooled."

She sort of laughed.

I tugged her closer. "Thanks for letting me in."

She sucked in a breath, and it exhaled shaky. "Cade, I—I thought you were safe."

Something in my chest jolted painfully. "I'm not?"

"No. Because I thought you'd kiss me once and be done."

Why did that cut so deep? Right. Because I'd put that image out there. Maybe subconsciously, I knew about the stupid phoenix rule. Maybe that was why I always managed to sabotage anything good. "Is that what you wanted?"

"Maybe before."

Hope dared to rise, but I put it in a strangle hold. "And now?"

"I'm not sure what I want."

"One step at a time then." I touched her hair, tentatively. And she flickered in front of me, a wisp of a memory. Swirling cherry blossom petals surrounded her. A voice echoed on the wind. *You know this isn't right.*

And I was back in the kitchen, staring at Yuki and her soft smile. And something inside me craved her presence. This girl who saw through me. I needed her to feel safe with me. To know I'd never hurt her.

I cleared my throat, pushing emotion back behind its closet door. But I didn't put on my cocky mask. Yuki saw past it anyway. "You want to go for a ride?"

A smile and a hint of danger hit her gleaming eyes. "I thought you'd never ask."

Wow. Okay. I could really get used to this. I gripped her hand and towed her to the back door, handed her a helmet from a hook on the wall. "First, you have to tell me if you start to feel weak."

That soft, innocent look took over, and she nodded once. "I promise."

"Okay. And I will pull over the moment I feel nauseous." I paused. "We really are quite the pair, huh?"

She tilted her head sideways, hiding a shy blush. "Yes. I think we are."

35

AVA

"Now. Concentrate. And shoot." Nick's calm voice coached me.

I focused on the target Nick had placed at the end of the yard, letting the fear of what had happened yesterday with Gwen burn the sides of my heart and cause me to quake. I tried to call my fire. Embers, red and orange and yellow, glowed in my fingers, warmed my palms.

"Are you okay?" he asked, knocking me out of my concentration.

"What?" The spark of flame died, and I faced him.

He searched my expression with narrowed eyes. "You seem off. Something's bothering you."

I leaned away, sucking in a breath. "You can tell?" I always hid it so well.

The slight smile that curved his lips challenged me to try and hide from him. "I know you."

Did he? That thought opened the compartment inside me that housed anger like the opening gate at a horse race, and an explosion came out. "You talked to Wyatt behind my back."

Nick crossed his arms and widened his stance, as if bracing for more yelling. Maybe he did know me, because now that I'd unleashed the monster, it barreled at him.

"You trained with Wyatt behind mine. After I warned you—"

"You aren't my father."

"I know."

"You had no right."

"To protect you? It's not a right. It's my purpose."

"Oh." I flourished my hand. "Well, for your information, training with Wyatt goes very well. He is good at helping me find my fire. He's gentle, and he doesn't push me like you do. He—"

"Is a distraction."

"What?" Where did that even come from?

"You're in love with him. Don't get me wrong, I would have been fine with the two of you training together if I had known about it."

"It's not your business, Nick." I spat his name.

He breathed deeply, then finally spoke. "What do you remember, Ava?" His voice was quiet.

"A lot, including you sending him away to keep me 'safe.'" I used air quotes around the last word.

"Well, I remember." He raised his voice, which was something Nick rarely did. "And I am trying to keep you safe from Gwen. Once she's no longer a threat to you, to Cade, to Wyatt, then please, pursue that. But for now, while we're trying to defeat Gwen, please let me know if you're going to talk to people who might be on her side, voluntarily or not. After Gwen is gone, whatever you decide to do with Wyatt is up to you."

"Do?" My heart skittered.

"All I'm saying is Wyatt knows how dangerous he is. He knows when he's done fighting the darkness inside of him. He can only fight who he is for so long. I don't know how Gwen's demise will affect him." He paused, his eyes showing compassion. "Just let him go if he asks."

"Let him go?" I backed away from my brother, breath leaving my lungs like air from a punctured balloon. "If he asks? Why does it sound like you're telling me to . . . dispose of him?"

Nick swallowed, staring at me like he'd accidentally opened Pandora's Box.

"You are," I whispered. "That's the most disturbing thing I've ever heard anyone say."

"Ava, when you remember his fight—"

I wanted to yank my hair. "Have you never been in love, Nick? Never even tempted? It must be nice to be so cold-hearted that you don't even know what affection is."

Why couldn't I control my tongue? I grabbed my jacket off the chair. "If this is what family is, I'm sorry I ever thought I wanted it. *Alone* suits me much better."

I thought I saw a tiny wince. "Ava, I—Wyatt is a good guy. He's just not always in control. And that burden tears away at him. I'm sorry this is hard for you."

And my heart crumbled. Why did I hurt people who tried to get close to me? "You loved someone before, didn't you?"

A little pain and a little pride mingled in his features. "Your intuition is as sharp as ever, little sister. Use it to your advantage. It's your strongest asset."

I set my coat back down. "Wyatt can stand up to her."

"I love that you see the best in him, but the truth is—"

"The truth is, while we were at the beach yesterday, Gwen showed up in some strange ball of fire and told Wyatt to kill me. He resisted. So, yes, he can." Why was I still yelling?

Nick just stared at me. The only part of him that moved was his chest as he breathed in. He kept breathing in, though. Like an inflating balloon that was sure to pop any moment. Part of me wanted to step back, the other part wanted to trust him.

"Nick?" Contrasting a moment ago, my voice slipped out meek and quiet.

"When were you going to tell me about Gwen?"

"Today. Here. At this training session."

He breathed out, the air audibly shaking. He wasn't looking at me anymore. It seemed as though he was completely lost in thought. He started to walk away, toward the family room.

"Nick." I followed. "I swear, I was going to tell you. I—" Coming tears stung my eyes. He wouldn't answer me, just opened the weapons safe and started digging through it. "You're scaring me." My voice trembled.

He paused and faced me, everything about him a coiled spring. "You should be scared." I realized I wasn't the only one quaking. My blood frosted. "I had no idea she'd reclaimed that much of her power." He rubbed a shaking hand over his face. "She might be strong enough now. I've—" His voice broke, and it slayed me. "She's never been ready this fast before."

I would not let her win. I straightened my spine. "What do we do?"

"First, you have to let me in, Ava. Tell me everything."

I told him exactly where on the beach it happened, exactly what Wyatt had resisted. He didn't say anything.

"You think she'll come tonight." My insides hurt.

"It's a full moon. But I don't feel her that close yet. And she didn't reach out to you in person. I think we still have time. Not much. We can hold off for more if we—"

"No." My insides shook, and a tear leaked out of my eye. I could not tell him she'd snuffed my fire. He wanted me to trust him, but I wanted him to trust me too. And if I told him about Gwen beating my fire when she wasn't even at her most powerful, he'd realize I couldn't help him. That couldn't happen.

I just had to make my fire stronger. I had to buy time. "She'll only get stronger, too. We can pick a place to fight her and lure her there."

He breathed deep and seemed to pull himself together. He placed his hands on my shoulders. "I will be there with you. You understand? No matter what, I will be there."

My chest clutched. Even after the things I'd said to him? "And if it's tonight?"

His grip on my shoulders strengthened. "You will not be alone."

"Thank you."

"You use your fire." He leaned down and looked me right in the eyes. "You are stronger than you think. Your fire is stronger than you think. When you feel it's pushed the limit, remember that I'm here for you. Cade is here for you. And push harder. Can you do that?"

I looked at the target outside. "Yes." I squared my shoulders, and my fire burned in my hands, but it wasn't the angry fire I normally had. It was the same one I got when Wyatt trained me. Only it burned brighter. Hotter. And the tips of the flames glowed purple.

"That's right." Nick smiled. "You can kill her with that; I don't care how strong she is."

And I held on to that. Because I was going to need it.

The door opened, and I heard two very familiar laughs. Cade's and— "Yuki?"

"Hey, stranger." She smiled at me.

Cade ushered Yuki inside and shut the door behind her. "And this scary, brooding guy is my brother Nick." He motioned to Nick, who stood behind me.

Yuki smiled and extended her hand.

Nick took it, rather gently, but didn't say a word. Then her eyes widened, and a strange look—like a mix of confusion and fear—crossed her face. "I know you." Her eyes rolled back, and she fainted.

Cade and I both rushed toward her, but Nick caught her.

She fell limp in his arms.

"She needs a hospital!" I yelled. "She has a heart condition."

Nick looked up at me. Something had clearly left him shaken, and it showed in his eyes. "How do you know her?"

"She's my best friend." My pulse was pounding. We didn't have time for questions.

"She's a phoenix, isn't she?" Cade said. "I've had memories of her."

"What?" Why didn't he tell me?

Nick stood there staring at Cade for moments when I thought he should be taking my friend to the hospital. "She's not a phoenix, Cade. But I've met her before. In the past."

"If she's not a phoenix, then how—"

"Phoenixes have the power to heal one human from death. That person, however, will become stuck on that phoenix's life cycle."

I could hardly breathe.

Nick looked right at me. "Unless that phoenix kills them."

My heart quaked. Like that one human who had created the race of dark phoenixes. That meant Yuki was here because someone had healed her? Someone had broken the laws.

Cade stared at Yuki. "That means one of us brought her here?"

Nick glared at Cade. "No. One of you two. I suggest you remember which one."

# 36



ONCE YUKI WAS FEELING BETTER, I drove her home. "You sure you're okay?"

"Ava. Stop it. I'm fine." She sulked in the passenger's seat.

"Excuse me for being worried about my friend."

She sighed. "I'm sorry. I'm just exhausted." She offered me a small smile.

I pulled into her driveway. "You sure you're going to be okay tonight?"

"Now that I know I'm not crazy." She touched my hand. "Or alone."

That hit me hard. Alone. My whole life I'd thought I was alone. Now I wasn't, as long as I could kill Psycho Chick. Because if Cade died, I would die, and whether Cade or I had healed her, Yuki would die, too.

I couldn't let any of that happen.

I squeezed her hand back. "You're not alone."

She got out of the car and headed to her huge house, waving at me over her shoulder. It wasn't just Cade I was trying to save now. But did her sickness have anything to do with his dying? Nick didn't know.

Maybe I could heal Yuki. Nick said we all had healing capabilities for other phoenixes. Did that apply to humans on their cycles? Though I was determined to try, I didn't know how. Nick suggested I wait until after facing Gwen. Because of strength and all that. One look at Cade, and I'd agreed.

But if I failed, where did that leave Yuki?

I had too much at stake now. And something in my gut told me Gwen knew all about it.

My brothers. Yuki. Wyatt.

Wyatt. My pulse still buzzed as I thought of our time together this past month.

The faint tug in my brain told me a memory swirled near the surface.

A strange feeling of dread accompanied, and I swam in my own thoughts for a moment, terrified of what I would recall.

Then I realized I wanted to know. So I pulled over on a side street, parked, and sank into the depths of the memory, letting everything flood back.

I stood outside the marquis's estate amidst a crowd. It seemed all the servants had gathered. And the throb in my chest told me something was very wrong.

I clutched my arm across my stomach as they dragged poor Tommy out of the house and down to the tree in the middle of the field. My stomach roiled. They yanked his hair and pulled him faster than he could walk. Couldn't they at least be gentler to the poor boy? They knew Tommy had a bad leg.

"What's going on?" Wyatt's voice behind me caused me to turn. He stood with his jaw tight and fists clenched as Tommy's cries of "I didn't do it! I swear!" rang out in the thick, heavy autumn air.

I hugged my stomach tighter. "He stole the marquis's silver. There were three pieces missing—"

"No, he didn't." Wyatt started marching after them. He broke through the wall of servants, all standing in a way that showed me how sick they felt about this, and headed right after the men dragging Tommy to the tree.

"Wyatt." I grabbed his arm. "What are you doing?"

He faced me, his eyes harsh, pleading for me to understand. "He didn't do it."

"Do you have proof? Without proof, they'll flog you, too."

He expelled a deep breath, turned on his heel, arm slipping

through my grasp as he headed straight for Tommy, who was now strapped to the tree.

"He didn't do it!" Wyatt's voice cut through everything. The men turned. Only the side of Tommy's tear-streaked face was visible, but it filled with hope.

"Who did?"

"I don't know, but it wasn't Tommy," Wyatt said.

The man holding the whip took a step toward Wyatt and squared his shoulders. "He stole the silver. We caught him with it."

"He was returning it."

"Because he"—the man turned and aimed the whip at Tommy's back—"stole it!"

Wyatt darted forward as the man swung, and he flew in between Tommy and the whip, shielding Tommy from punishment.

The whip struck, tearing Wyatt's shirt and ripping a huge red gash into his back.

I covered my mouth with my hands.

Wyatt didn't move as the red stain spread on his tunic.

"Move or you'll feel the rest of his fifteen lashes."

"Fifteen?" Wyatt asked, still pressed against Tommy. He lowered his head and whispered something I didn't hear. Then rested his forehead against the tree over Tommy's head. "I'm not moving."

"So be it. Remove your shirt."

Wyatt threw his shirt to the ground and braced himself in front of Tommy.

Someone touched my shoulder, and I nearly jumped. Cade. And Nick stood with him. "Why is he so certain it wasn't Tommy?"

Tears streamed down my face as the red slashes kept ripping Wyatt's skin. "I don't know."

As soon as it was over, Wyatt fell to the ground, bloody and limp.

I raced through the crowd and knelt beside Wyatt, not noticing who walked past us to untie Tommy. All I could see was Wyatt hunched on the ground, bleeding, his back ripped up from the whip. "I need wine and oil. I need—" My voice shook.

"We're here," Cade touched my shoulder. He and Nick helped Wyatt to his feet and brought him to my quarters on the property.

Tommy, who couldn't stop sobbing, got me the supplies I needed to care for Wyatt.

After I'd disinfected and dressed every wound, he lay sleeping across the table.

I stared out the window at the setting sun. Nick and Cade were getting their weapons ready just outside, hidden from view, in case Wyatt woke. I'd planned to go with them—tonight's moon would be full, and almost full was bad enough. They'd be hunting werewolves—which weren't limited to turning one night a month like the legends typically said—but I couldn't leave Wyatt now. My worry for my brothers—going hunting alone—pulsed through me, but it shouldn't. They'd be fine.

Cade ducked in to ask how Wyatt was doing before he headed out with Nick.

Wyatt hadn't woken. Hadn't stirred.

I stepped outside to tell my brothers to be safe.

"You be careful too, Ava."

"I'll be inside. I'll—"

Nick leaned closer to me and whispered, "You're falling for him, aren't you?"

My face flushed. "Fallen, Nick. I—this is the real thing."

"Ava." He pressed his hands gently against my arms. "You know we are different, right? The code?"

"Mother said a phoenix could fall in love."

Nick's eyes darted away. "Yes."

I glanced at my brother. "Have you ever—"

"When a phoenix falls in love, it's for life. I've heard the same stories you have. I also know we have been forbidden—since the split of the dark phoenixes—to take on a soulmate that's not another phoenix."

My shoulders sagged. "You're forbidding me from seeing Wyatt?"

"No." His eyebrows rose. "He's a good man, Ava."

"I know. I was hoping you'd approve."

"Does he know what you are?"

I swallowed. Who I am. What I do. Hunt. Kill. Protect. Save. Destroy. Rebuild. Die. Live again. Repeat. "I'm tired of being alone."

"We have each other."

I faced my brother and knelt in front of him as we did when we asked something of Father with an abandon that showed we were ready to give our lives for our cause. I bowed my head. "I love him, Nick."

He crouched next to me, not what he was supposed to do. And the pain in his eyes was real and clear and raw. "Ava, you can be with Wyatt here, but you can't heal him when his time is coming. In the end, you have to leave him behind while you live on and on, over and over. Are you truly prepared for that, because if you aren't, you might want to reconsider."

"Is that what you did?" I asked him. "You left her behind?"

Nick blinked several times, his eyes starting to get red around the rims. "I don't wish that decision on you or Cade. That's all. I've been trying to keep you safe."

"By denying such a big part of life from me? By making me live in hiding and hunting at night? You really thought I would be able to run from life forever?"

"You don't remember yet, do you?"

"Have I fallen in love before?"

"No."

I whispered, "Cade has. Hasn't he?"

He nodded.

I stood. "That's why he hates you suddenly. He remembers?"

Nick winced. "I'm keeping you safe, Ava."

"Really? Because it seems like you're killing a part of me."

He opened his mouth, but I had nothing to say to him and didn't want to hear his response. I went back inside and shut the door on him.

The sun sank lower. My worry grew. Wyatt's eyes finally fluttered open, and I hurried to his side.

"Ava?" His voice came out gravelly, and he winced.

"Lie still." I touched his hand. "Would you like something to drink?" I had medicated wine ready for him.

"In a minute. Thank you." He closed his eyes, his features pinched.

I trailed my fingers over the back of his hand, trying to help ease any pain I could but feeling entirely helpless. If I used my healing ability, too many would notice. And my brothers and I wouldn't be safe here. "That was a very brave and selfless thing you did."

His eyes opened and pleaded with me. "Tommy's innocent."

"How do you know?"

"He was with me yesterday morning, chopping wood. Helping me carry it back toward the house."

"Tommy?" That surprised me. "You do know he has a limp."

He let out the faintest chuckle, and it warmed my insides to see him smile. "I'm aware. He can carry wood, though. And he wants people to know that he's able to do things. To hold his own around here."

I blushed. "I'm sorry."

"It's all right." He gripped my hand in his and brushed his thumb back and forth across my skin. "As we were walking to the barn, Tommy spotted something in the grass. A silver spoon. He said it belonged to the marquis. I told him he should return it." His thumb stopped moving. "He returned it, and that's what got him in trouble. My advice caused his punishment."

"That's hardly your fault."

"It's not Tommy's, either. He didn't deserve to be whipped."

I held his hand tight. "Neither did you."

He started to try and sit up.

"For heaven's sake, Wyatt. You shouldn't be moving."

He stopped short, hissing through his teeth, but his stubbornness won, so I helped him sit. "Thank you. My back is on fire."

I gave him the wine. "This will help."

He drank all of it, every movement slow and stiff. "What time is it?"

"Late evening. You slept for nearly the whole day."

"What?" His eyes snapped to life, and panic seemed to pulse into him. "I have to go."

"Tommy is taking care of your duties. My brothers are helping him. Don't worry about your chores. We're all pitching in after what you've done. So rest. Please."

He touched my cheek. "When did you learn to tend the injured?"

"I've been studying under the wise woman." I smiled. "And the wise woman thinks you should be resting."

He dropped his hand from my face and looked out the window. His body seemed to tense as if something out there were hunting him. Making him uneasy. I followed his gaze. Red bled into the sky, painting it a dozen colors.

"Ava?" Wyatt drew my attention back to him. "Do you have more of that wine?"

Of course not. I'd have to go back to the house to get it. It shouldn't take me very long. I touched his knee. "I'll be right back."

"Thank you."

I headed out the door, but his words stopped me.

"And, Ava?"

I turned toward him, my hand still on the doorframe.

He smiled. "Thank you for taking care of me."

"Of course. Sometimes Andromeda has to care for her reckless hero, Perseus."

He shook his head, that half smile still brightening his face. "I'm not a hero."

"You are to me. And Tommy." I raced to the house before he would see tears fill my eyes. I let the evening wind clear them.

When I returned, he was gone.

Where on God's green earth would he go? How could he even travel in his condition? I set the wine down and changed into my hunting clothes and gathered weapons from my chest of belongings.

Wyatt couldn't have gotten far with his back shredded like that, and I had a feeling he'd headed for the stables—who knew why. But my brothers would be out in these woods tonight with all kinds of monsters, and I couldn't have Wyatt, injured as he was, stumbling upon something made of nightmares.

I didn't need a light. My eyesight was good enough and the full moon bright enough. I headed toward the stables. "Wyatt?" I whispered.

Nothing.

A rustle behind me caused me to turn. Something in the woods. I raised my silver stake. Ready to protect this house from anything unnatural. I headed closer to the woods. Sniffing. Listening. Something shuffled behind me, and I spun around.

A howl broke the night. A howl I recognized.

The howls grew louder.

Oh, Wyatt. I could only hope he wasn't stupid enough to come out here.

I tracked the whooping howls of werewolves to a cave in the ground, hidden by twigs and a hedge, right outside the property border. The noise came from the opening, and I held my knife tight. I had a pistol with a silver bullet already loaded, but pistols took forever to fire. The stake was quicker. Easier. Even if I had to get close. I was ready. If only I knew where Wyatt had gone. My insides clutched at the idea that one of these monsters could get to him.

I tiptoed closer to the entrance. Sounds of pained howls and bones cracking told me exactly where I was. A werewolf den. And they were changing. Getting ready to go on a hunt. I clutched my knife tighter. Everything in my weapons stock was coated in silver for tonight.

Full-moon week.

All the creepy monsters did their worst this week. It was like the werewolves being there gave them a blanket of cover since most of us phoenixes were busy.

"You have to use the chains!" one strangled voice yelled, and I paused near the entrance to the cave. Paranoia rattled me, because that sort of sounded like Wyatt.

"Chains? For what, you idiot? You're coming to hunt with us." That voice caused my blood to freeze. Denton's cocky cadence danced over each syllable.

"I'm not hunting with you." The shaky voice came through the depths of the cave, and this time there was no question. It belonged to Wyatt. "Give me the chains."

What was he doing with werewolves?

"They won't keep you from escaping." Denton spoke low and ominous. "You can chain yourself to the rock all you want. Your werewolf form will figure out how to escape. It has two instincts. Survive and kill." The chains rattled, and Denton said, "It would serve you best to embrace what you have become."

"No, Denton, don't chain him. Let him run with us," someone else said.

I blinked back tears. Wyatt—my Wyatt—was a werewolf. I sank to my knees, clutching my weapon. Tears streamed down my face. I thought I'd fallen for a human, but it was worse. I'd fallen for a werewolf. A monster. A sob clawed to be let out of me, and I fought to hold it in. To remain quiet.

"No." Wyatt's scream was recognizable. He was changing. My resolve broke—a useless dam. Despite Nick's warnings, I had let myself feel. And Wyatt—he was nothing but a good, brave man. A soldier. And here he was—wait, Denton?

The new servants the marquis had hired used to be soldiers. He wanted them since the property was on the border and he had to protect England. Did he know some of them were werewolves? He must not. He'd hired my brothers and me to keep the monsters away.

Werewolves were good at hiding their scents, especially the older ones. But packs taught every member their secrets. Still, I should have scented Wyatt tonight. Cade would have. He was good at detecting them.

One grotesque beast clawed its way to the entrance. I hid behind the hedge, silver arrows ready. I shot, hitting its lung. He fell with a whine. The second was much louder. With my presence known, I wouldn't stand a chance here.

Three came to the tunnel entrance. They weren't exactly changed yet. Still in between. If Wyatt had just been bitten, I might still have time to give him the antidote—if I could reach him without giving myself away. Too late, they'd spotted me. I switched my crossbow for my knife and pistol.

A snarl rent the night, and I turned. Something in the haughtiness of this one's face told me it was Denton. "Looks like your little tagalong came." His voice was a growl.

A fourth werewolf exited the cave, healing scars all over his back. "Ava?" Wyatt's voice was strained. He was one of them.

My soul ached. I'd have to kill him.

My breathing stalled, and Denton managed to grab me in a crushing grip, twisting the arm that held my knife. "We can turn her and have a female." He brought his elongated muzzle toward my neck, and all I thought to do was look into Wyatt's eyes and plead with him to not be evil.

He stared back at me. Curling his grotesque fingers into a fist. "Let her go." His voice boomed out in a growl.

Denton laughed. "Or what?"

Wyatt leaped at him. Denton tossed me to the ground where three other werewolves pounced. I shot my pistol. One fell. But Denton had managed to knock my knife from my hand. I tried to reach another, but his grip was too strong. His fangs too close. How had I let myself become so distracted?

Denton roared and rolled off me, tussling with another werewolf. I lost track of which was which, but one finally landed a killing blow. And I was ready with my knife.

The surviving beast looked at me. Crouched low. Blood dripped off its muzzle. The growl resounded through my core, but I recognized him. Somehow, through the monster, I saw the man. And it was Wyatt.

"Wyatt?" I whispered and scooted back across the dusty earth. My elbows pushed me back as he continued to advance.

He lunged at me, mouth open. Teeth dripping with poison. Hot breath skated across my neck.

My blade touched his chest, but I couldn't push it in. I lowered the weapon. "It's me, Wyatt. It's Ava."

Slowly, he backed his head away, still towering over me. But he closed his mouth, looked at me, and something in his eyes seemed to flash blue for a moment. A sound like a gunshot in the distance made both of us flinch. His claws dug into my skin as he moved. Searing pain sliced through my neck. He faced me again, growling. I gasped and touched the wound.

He backed away from me and whined, ears laid back like a scared dog.

"Wyatt, it's okay." I sat up, but warm blood gushed through my fingers. It was deep.

He shuddered, crouching away from me, and bumped into a dead werewolf's body. He whined again.

I swallowed. "You killed him."

His eyes closed, and he turned his head away, shrinking back into the shadows. Everything I'd heard about werewolves taught they couldn't control their impulses. Their desire to kill. Even the kindest person in the world would kill if turned.

"Wyatt?" I stepped forward, one hand on my wound. Silver knife in my other hand.

He whined again. Then a cloud moved. As moonlight made his pupils smaller, a growl rumbled in his throat. He stalked closer, growling.

"I'm not going to hurt you!" I held out my hand and dropped the knife.

He stopped. Closed his eyes. Shook his head.

"The moon. It makes you lose your mind."

He seemed to realize what I'd said and retreated toward the cave. I should leave him, but if I did, would the animal side take over?

Slowly, he padded closer to me, and I froze. He sniffed my neck, but the wound was almost healed. I became hyperaware of his hot breath on my skin. The smell of blood. The carnage in the mouth of the tunnel. I looked up at him and the bit of blue leaking back into to the gold in his eyes.

Another shot rang out, closer this time. It had to be Nick and Cade. Wyatt growled.

I touched his shoulder. "Run. Hide. I'll protect you."

He darted into the cave, and I picked up my weapon and stood at the entrance.

"Ava!" Nick sprinted up to me. He hugged me close then looked me over as Cade raced closer. "You okay?"

I nodded, breathless. "They're dead. They're all dead."

"Were you bitten?" Nick touched the traces of blood on my neck.

"No."

He breathed out a heavy sigh, then started chuckling. "Nicely done, little sister."

Cade nudged one of the bodies. Then he bent down and stood up with a soldier's button in between his fingers. "Look at this."

Nick took it. "The soldiers. Wyatt came over with the group of them. Do you think—?"

"Yeah." Cade looked at me with sympathy in his eyes.

Nick winced. "Sorry, Ava."

"You don't know Wyatt was one of them."

Nick shook his head. "No. I don't. But regardless, I hope you're guarding your heart."

I glanced back at the mouth of the cave before following my brothers.

Then I was back in my car, parked not far from Yuki's, catching my breath.

Wyatt was a werewolf?

No wonder Nick wanted me to stay away.

I pressed my hand against my chest. If Wyatt wasn't a phoenix, that meant someone had brought him back. Me? I must have.

I'd fallen for a werewolf.

And I'd put him on my cycle.

I looked out the car window at the moon. Big and bright and full.

I nearly choked on a breath. Nick and Cade would be hunting tonight. I couldn't let them kill Wyatt.

# 37

## CADE

AVA HAD LEFT WITH YUKI, AND NICK couldn't stop pacing in the family room. I finally took to sitting on the couch, all of my questions falling on deaf ears, and waiting for him to sort through whatever had him so rattled.

He kept tapping his fist against his chin. And that scowl.

"Your face will freeze that way."

He finally looked up at me. "What?"

I thought of saying something snarky about him finally hearing me, but I'd just gotten his attention. "Why is the fact that one of us healed Yuki such a problem?"

"Because I was there when she died." He sank slowly into the chair across from me and wouldn't make eye contact. "She wasn't resurrected. In order for a human to be connected to a phoenix's cycle, that phoenix has to heal them and bring them back."

"Maybe I went back later?"

He shook his head. "No, you were with me, and you can't wait that long. That means that either you or Ava must have healed her previously."

"Previously as in a different lifetime?"

"No." He stood again, and I thought I'd lose him to the pacing, but he walked around to the back of the chair. "She was helping us find something to defeat Saki—Gwen."

"Did she? Find it?"

"It's called a Phoenix Blade." He shook his head. "And I think she did, but she died before she could tell us."

I stood up. "Do we need this thing? Ask her now. It's your chance."

Nick didn't respond or move, which told me he was still considering. He waved his hand in a circle as if trying to find the right words, while my pulse pounded impatiently. If Yuki knew a way we could defeat Psycho Chick, I wanted to help Ava before it was too late for both of us.

"There were these three artifacts. The blade was one of them."

"That's why you've been going to the library?" I asked.

He looked at me. "Yeah. There was a quill—I burned that—and a stone." He pointed to the kitchen island, which housed our strange supplies. "We found that, and there was—"

"The blade."

He nodded.

"Okay." I held out my hand to calm him. "I'll ask Yuki."

"Wait." He held up his finger, then he pulled out his phone and looked at it. He froze for a millisecond and swore.

"What's wrong?"

He looked up at me, eyes wild. "Gwen struck again."

"What?"

"Plans have changed. Kelsey's in trouble. Wait here for Ava." He grabbed his keys and coat. "Don't let anyone in. If you see a monster, kill it."

"Nick!" Just like that, he was gone.

Wait for Ava. Right. Because that's all I was good for. Wait for Ava. Stab a monster. Find Ava. But protect Ava? No. I could just imagine Nick thinking, *You're too fragile, Cade.* Even if he wouldn't say it. The way he looked at me, I knew.

I could hold my own. Maybe if they realized that, we could defeat Gwen.

A knock sounded at the door, and I pulled out my knife. Then I sort of laughed at myself for assuming a monster would actually knock on the door. But I clutched the knife tighter anyway.

The knock pounded again. "Nick? Cade! Come on, I know you're home."

I knew that voice. Knife in my left hand, I opened the door with my right—only a little, so Wyatt could see my face. "What do you want?"

"Can I come in?"

"Do you need an invite?"

"Funny." He pushed into the door with more strength than I was expecting, and I staggered back. He strode over the threshold and seemed to search the room. "Nick?"

"He's not home."

"Where is he?"

I couldn't rightly send Wyatt to Nick now, could I? Should I?

"Cade?" He sort of growled my name.

"He's hunting."

"Already?"

"Are you here to help us hunt tonight, *Wyatt*?" I decided to say his name with as much venom as I could muster because he hadn't showed up to help us yet, and I wanted to know why.

"I remember everything, Cade. My memories come back when I'm fourteen."

"Wait, really? Why do you stick around?"

He shrugged. "You mean why do I stay when Nick hates me?"

So my instinct was right. I put my knife away and crossed my arms, waiting for him to continue.

"Listen, I'm here because I found Gwendolyn. She's here under the name Gwen, and she's one of Kelsey's coworkers. I saw her tonight."

Whoa. Puzzle pieces clicking together. "Did you tell Nick?"

"I'm telling you. I just found out a half hour ago."

My blood heated. "She'll strike tonight, won't she?"

Wyatt's eyes narrowed. "I don't know what her plans are."

"Neither do I, but doesn't she normally strike on a full moon?"

Wyatt sighed heavily, as if something about my comment relieved him. Then I remembered him standing over me, telling me loyalty didn't suit me. I subtly placed my hand near my knife again, ready to pull it out. "Why did you think I asked you when she'd strike?"

Wyatt's eyes flicked to my hand.

I pulled out the knife with super-human speed, but he was just as fast. He grabbed my shirt collar and muscled me a step back. "What are you doing?"

"Trying to figure out your motive. I know you're one of them."

"One of . . ." He released me. "How much do you actually remember?"

"I'm still fuzzy on the details. But I know enough. You're a dark phoenix."

His eyes widened slightly, like there was so much more to the story. Of course there was. "No, I'm not, Cade."

I sighed and closed the front door. For some reason, I believed him. My memory might not have come through, but something in my gut told me to trust him. "I clearly don't remember enough."

"It'll come." For some reason, he sounded like a concerned friend.

"You aren't going to give me any hints, either, huh?" I headed into the kitchen. Wyatt followed. "It's probably not a good idea."

"If there was one thing you wished I remembered right now, what would it be?"

Wyatt sighed. "Gwendolyn has the ability to bring creatures of the dark under her spell. I'm afraid she might be targeting me again. That's why she befriended Kelsey. I might have to leave."

I stared at Wyatt, eyes narrowing. "Creatures of the dark? You mean monsters?"

"Cade, do you know what I am?"

"A light phoenix?" My voice cracked.

Wyatt shook his head. "I'm linked to Ava's life cycle."

I knew those words. "You mean she brought you back from the dead." I gripped the edge of the countertop as the whole room started to shake. Great.

"Cade?"

I heard Wyatt's voice clearly once. Saw his face in front of mine as I started to fall to the floor.

Then I passed through blinding pain and fell into the memory.

"Cade!" Nick hunched over me on the ground.

I tried to sit up, but my stomach screamed. A huge gash—oozing red through my ripped shirt. I glared at the monster in front of me. "This was my favorite shirt."

"Hold still. This will sting." Nick held a glass bottle. Werewolf antivenom. He poured some into the wound. That stuff always stung worse than I expected.

Ava stood between the monster and Nick and me. A look of determination set her face, and she held out her hands. "Why would you do that?"

"Ava, please. You can't rescue a monster." Nick's voice of reason wasn't going to get through to her. This I already knew. She was clearly in love, and that monster had thought he was protecting her when he'd lashed out at me. Right now he lay behind her, whimpering.

"Wyatt's not a monster." Tears leaked out of her eyes.

I stood, ignoring the pain in my side. "Nick," I placed my hand on my brother's shoulder. "Maybe you should—"

"Cade, you of all people know what must be done."

And something in my chest knew. And yet I didn't exactly agree. But Nick wouldn't listen to me. He never did. Even so, I grabbed his arm. "Don't do this."

"Nick?" Ava stared at him. "He's not a monster. He's not like the others."

Nick closed his eyes and looked away.

I snapped out of the memory and realized Wyatt must have moved me to the couch. He handed me a glass of water. I motioned to the bucket in his other hand.

He thrust it at me and I puked. I sat there a moment, my head still throbbing, not sure if I'd go again. "You're still here?"

"Of course," Wyatt said.

Not the response I expected. "How long was I out?"

"Twenty minutes."

"Can you hand me . . . ?"

"The dark chocolate? Where is it?"

It occurred to me then that Wyatt had likely been with us from then on. What time period? How many lifetimes had I known him? I motioned to the island. "Top drawer."

"Keep your head over that bucket. I'm not cleaning up your mess if you miss."

I had to chuckle. "Jerk."

Wyatt opened the wrong drawer and pulled out the box. He stopped, staring into it for so long I thought something in there must paralyze werewolves. Then I remembered it was a full moon and started to stand up, reaching for my knife. "What is it?"

He looked up at me. "Umm . . ." He shook his head. "When will Nick be back?"

"I don't know, but you might want to get out of here."

"You remembered?" He found the chocolate bar and brought it to me.

I sat with my back to the couch and the foul-smelling bucket at my side. "I know what you are." And the way he was acting toward me now, I wasn't sure what to think. "How many times have you tried to kill me?"

He winced and looked away, and a piece of me wished I hadn't asked.

"I'm sorry, Wyatt. I—"

"It's a valid question, Cade."

"Have you ever tried to hurt Ava?"

"I never tried to harm Ava on purpose. But Gwendolyn—will try to control me again."

"We won't let that happen."

"I don't want to hurt any of you."

I laughed. "Then you're a better man than I, because sometimes I want to strangle Nick."

He actually chuckled. "That's normal."

I tilted my head toward the kitchen. "What did you see in the box?"

He shook his head. "The Phoenix Stone. I wondered if Nick found out how to stop your headaches with it."

"What?"

"It's a stone that holds memories. We found it once, trying to see if it would help you. Trap your memories so Gwendolyn couldn't take them and steal your powers. Maybe he plans to give you back the memory he took."

My brother had taken a memory from me? Something in my gut twisted, and I narrowed my eyes. "What memory?"

Wyatt stood. "I'd love to stay and chat, but—"

"Now you're going to use that excuse."

He just stared.

"Unless of course you came here to kill me." I thought I'd try and lighten the mood.

When he realized I was kidding, he chuckled. "You're my best friend, Cade." Then he lost his smile for that searching expression. "If Gwen—"

My throat tightened. Best friend? I couldn't even remember that I had a best friend. But he seemed so sincere. "No, we'll stop Psycho Chick, you got it?"

He nodded. "You okay alone, because—?"

"Go."

He turned, almost to the door. "You be careful tonight."

I nodded. "You, too."

Ava had saved a werewolf. No wonder Nick was pissed.

## 38

NICK

I TOOK THE BIKE AND DROVE TO KELSEY'S house as fast as I could. I should have known that shadow puppet wouldn't be the only thing after her.

She'd texted me, panicking that someone was outside her house.

When I arrived and parked, I didn't see a soul. The house looked dark. I removed my helmet and strained my ears. One hand on a silver knife, the other ready to grab my gun, I crept toward the house.

Full moon night made it more difficult to sniff out individual monsters. So many of them were on the move. "Kelsey?" I headed around the back, taking the path with the stone pavers because it would be quietest, and stuck closest to the house.

"Kelsey?" I called again. Maybe I should text her in case she was holed up inside with a frying pan or baseball bat.

Movement caught my eye. Something in the shed out back. I turned my attention to it, and Kelsey popped up in the window. She waved me toward the shed.

I scanned the yard as I headed over.

She opened the door, grabbed hold of my arm, and practically pulled me inside. "You came?" Her whole body shook, and her eyes were wide. She didn't hold a frying pan or bat. Instead, she clutched a Maglite flashlight. One of the big, old, heavy ones. "Thank you."

"Hey." I slid my knife back into the sheath and looked into her eyes. "Why don't you tell me what's hunting you."

She released a shaky breath, and tears brimmed in her eyes. She started trembling worse. "You believe me?"

I swallowed and nodded.

She set the Maglite on the cracked coffee table and wiped her hands on her jeans as she sat on the tattered couch. "Remember that weird lizard creature you . . . killed behind the repair garage?"

A pit hollowed out in my stomach. "You saw that?"

Her eyelids fluttered. "I did not know what to think. I'd never seen anything like it."

"Most people haven't."

"I didn't want anyone to think I was going crazy, and I hoped I'd just forget about it. Then I saw you with that book. And Wyatt had the same one." Her hands shook. "I assume you and Wyatt are the same thing?"

All the air left my lungs as she slid a book across the coffee table. Then she pulled a piece of paper out from the pages. There was a drawing. A wolf. A moon. A creature of the dark.

"You know?" My words came out surrounded by air. "He's not usually very forthcoming."

"I'm a nosey sister." She stared at me, and her eyes narrowed. "How long have you known him?"

I sighed. "That's not important right now. What's hunting you?"

A distorted howl rose up outside, and I shuddered. Those weren't werewolves. Gwen was on the move tonight. Kelsey's warning had taken my attention, and I'd been too focused on that to sense Gwen. But now that I reached out for her, I could tell she was close. I had to get back to Ava and Cade. I had to take Kelsey with me.

I pulled my gun out of the holster beneath my jacket.

"What are you doing?" Her voice was breathless.

"Stay behind me." My heart raced. Cold sweat broke out.

Another howl—closer this time. I stood and motioned for Kelsey to get behind me. A growl shot up from the side of the shed. I raised my weapon and looked over my shoulder at her. She nodded, silent. A huge animal with white fangs and a long, grotesque muzzle jumped through the shed window. Glass rained down as its furry body—bigger than the average man—sailed through the opening. I unloaded.

Kelsey screamed and grabbed my shoulder. "Wyatt!"

"It's not your brother!" I yelled, but it was too late, she'd pushed into me. Three more climbed through the window, and a thumping sound banged against the door.

I swore and pulled out another clip. Shot the three inside. I pushed Kelsey behind me. They might want to capture me for Gwen, but what would they do to her? I had to keep her safe.

"Wyatt—"

"These monsters aren't your brother, Kelsey." I looked deep into her eyes and willed her to see my honesty. "I wouldn't hurt Wyatt. Not unless he asked me to. He's my friend."

She gasped and stared at me as though I were mad. Tears dripped from her eyes, and she shook her head. "I saw you kill that monster."

"You and I both know Wyatt isn't a real monster." I handed her my knife. "Here. In case they get too close to you."

"You can't possibly fight them all off." Her breathing quickened.

The door crashed open, two spilling over the threshold, and another wave entered through the window. Five in all. I shot one. Another. Three more. More replaced the fallen, and I lost count. And ammunition.

Drooling and growling, they stood blocking the exits. Not attacking.

"Kelsey, if I tell you to run—" I looked over my shoulder at her. At the tears in her eyes. Her quivering chin.

"I'm sorry." Liquid streamed down her cheeks. "She said you were a hunter. She said you'd kill my brother. I was protecting him. I—"

I expelled a breath, and my stomach twisted. My chest ached.

Her face scrunched up, and she covered it. "I-I'm sorry."

I turned toward the door.

Gwen.

My heart plummeted.

# 39

## CADE

NICK HAD TOLD ME NOT TO THINK
about Yuki. Did my fool of a brother know me at all? Naturally, Yuki
was all I could think about.

Since I saw the reasoning behind waiting for Ava, I tried to be
good. I picked up a box of frosted cereal and pulled out a bowl.
Dinner of champions.

And someone knocked on the door.

What was this, Grand Central Station? I ran to the door, hoping
it was Ava. It wasn't, but I moved aside, mouth dry. "Yuki. Are
you okay?"

"Yes." She stepped in, and I closed the door behind her. "No," she
amended. "I had a memory." She seemed really shaken, so I guided
her into the back room. We sat on the couch.

"Do you want to tell me about it?"

Eyes wide, she nodded.

I didn't like seeing her so scared, so I grinned. "Am I in it?"

She narrowed her eyes. "You are actually. And your weird
older brother."

Nick? Perfect. I stopped myself from slumping as I fought the faint
and clearly unfounded thought that Nick stole the thunder in my love
life often.

Then again, maybe it was totally founded.

She started to tell me. She said it was in Japan. Nick and Ava were there, fighting monsters and losing. We had to get Ava out of there. She paused and looked at me, seeming to study my face, and I swallowed, not wanting to move, not wanting her to forget a second of the memory. Because for some reason, I felt like I was there, too. And for the first time, this memory didn't hurt.

We were surrounded. And Gwendolyn—going by Saki—stood flanked by five monsters. The same werewolf/vampire hybrid thing I'd seen that night at the bonfire. Hugely muscled, like King Kong himself, over seven feet tall. Vampiric fangs, red eyes, snarling jaws. Mouths that opened far too wide to be considered normal.

She raised her hand, and another monster just like it broke out of the earth. How?

I slashed into another of her monsters, and it fell. They were weak, almost hollow, but she'd created them. With my stolen power—power I couldn't even use!

I ran toward her, but another monster blocked my path. I cut its head clean off, and it crumpled to the ground. And Gwen-Saki was gone. Where to? I whirled around in time to kill another beast. As it fell away, my gaze landed on Yuki. She fought valiantly, but there were too many. A monster with bloody jowls and red eyes lunged at her from behind.

"Yuki, look out!" I raced toward her.

She turned too late. The creature stabbed her through the heart with its long claws. She fell, hard, fast, motionless. I screamed, and it rang through my ears as it tore up my throat. I ran, calling all my speed, and struck the monster clean through with my silver-coated sword. The creature fell, and I raced past the disintegrating body to Yuki's side. I fell to my knees, crushing bruised and ruined *sakura* petals, and pulled her head onto my lap.

She tried to speak and ended up touching my arm. Blood trickled out of her mouth.

I looked back at Nick, fighting for Ava.

I—I couldn't let Yuki die. But I didn't have time. I had to decide now, without talking to Nick. Would he forgive me? Healing her would put her on my cycle. Make her attached to me in more ways than one. She'd fall for me. Forever. She'd love me instead of Nick.

I could feel Yuki's life force slipping, and it tugged at the power inside of me. And I looked at her. At the holes in her chest. The bright blood blossoming on her clothes. Sweat beading on her face.

She knew how to save my brother.

There was no other choice. Not one that could save Nick. He'd hate me for this. Her eyes glazed over. Her arms fell limp. And her chest no longer rose. I pressed my hands against her.

"Cade! No!"

Nick's shout registered, but I didn't care. I had to do this. Yuki knew how to find the blade. How to use it. She could help us. More than that, she belonged with us. After all she'd done, I wasn't going to let my brother stop me. I didn't care what he'd thought about the recklessness of love. He was stupid. I would save her.

And him.

My power rushed through me. Bright light glowed around both of us. I felt her mending. Coming back to me. Our fingers reaching for one another over an expanse of nothingness, like the painting on the Sistine Chapel ceiling, until Nick pushed me off her.

My head hit the ground.

The memory stopped.

I sat on the couch next to Yuki. My voice didn't want to work yet.

She looked at me, a tear in her eye that she wiped away. "You saved me?"

"Are you sure?"

"I feel it—in the memory, I mean."

Had she seen the same memory? "But you died."

"For a little while."

My heart slammed into my chest. I had saved her. Nick had told me not to fall in love, and I'd apparently fallen in love with Yuki. And saved her. I didn't care if Nick would be angry.

I looked into Yuki's eyes and grabbed her hands. "How much do you remember?"

"Well, I've been alive before." She shook her head. "Were those monsters real?"

I nodded. "Reapers. Saki—her name is Gwen this lifetime—she makes them from werewolves and vampires and, I don't know, dirt? But the Phoenix Blade. Do you know what that is?"

Her eyes met mine tentatively. "I-I don't know what you're talking about."

My blood thundered through my veins. Not yet. She'd remember. She had to remember. Because I still didn't know what it was or how it could defeat Gwen, which meant I had to get Nick to unlock that stone for me.

A strange shuffling noise echoed outside the window—unseen—and I looked at Yuki, pulse kicked to overdrive.

"Nick?" she asked.

"No." I crept toward the weapons safe and opened it. Shoved a loaded gun into my jeans. "He uses the door."

Yuki stuck behind me. She reached in and grabbed two katana swords. She arched an eyebrow. "You know how to use these?"

"You?"

She smiled. "What makes you think we need—"

I pressed my finger to my lips, signaling her to be quiet. I smelled something in the air that seemed off. "We have to get out of here." I took her hand and ran. We made it out the back door, but not to Yuki's car before three massive, dark figures outside the house jerked their attention toward us. The same creatures from the memory I'd just experienced.

"Those things?" Her voice shook. "They're here?" She handed me one of the swords.

I took it and shielded Yuki, praying I remembered how to use a katana in case these guys ate me out of bullets.

# 40

AVA

I WALKED THROUGH THE REEDS AND found a trail that headed down by the river where a small tree sat near a half-sunken dock that extended out into the water. The sound of someone rustling in the leaves caught my attention, and I noticed Wyatt by the water's edge. He wore a pair of blue jeans and seemed to be shoving another pair of jeans into a backpack. My lungs stilled. He must be getting his things ready because he'd be changing tonight.

Not wishing to startle him, I headed closer. But a memory enveloped me before I made it.

My hands pressed against the gaping wound in his chest. I was back outside the marquis's home with Wyatt, trying to get him inside. But he'd fallen to his knees. I'd been in this memory before. Only not this far. But just like before, he wasn't healing.

"Why aren't you getting better?" I'd removed the bullet. I checked the wound. Strange black lines seemed to spread out from it beneath his skin. My heart clutched. Was there nothing that could save him?

"Silver," he said, breathless.

I balled up my hands. I wasn't about to let Wyatt die. Not here. Not now. Nick would never forgive me. It didn't matter. Nick had already lost his chance, falling in love with someone he wasn't willing to heal wasn't my fault. He of all people should understand what happened when a phoenix fell in love. I wasn't going to lose Wyatt. "I have to get you out of here."

"Leave me. The poison. It will kill me."

"Not if I can help it. Can you stand?"

"Ava. It's no use. I—" He buckled over in pain.

"Who shot you?" I helped him lie down.

"I—I don't know. I—"

He fell to the ground and spewed blood. "S-silv . . ."

Silver. The bullet I'd removed was silver. But Nick and Cade wouldn't, would they?

"Wyatt?" I shook him, and he didn't respond. Just flopped onto his back. "Wyatt!" Tears streamed down my face, and something deep inside me broke open. It wanted to come out in a scream, a sob.

No. A balm.

My power.

I channeled everything to my hands, and they lit up from within. I pressed my palms against his gaping wound, and heat so bright and so deep filled the depths of me. My soul. My strength. This light consumed all of it, every crevice of my being, and with one surge, I pumped everything into him.

And Wyatt gasped. His eyes popped open. He gripped my hands.

"Ava. What have you done?"

"I saved you." I marveled at his closed wound. Nothing but a scar remained. And he was alive. "Come on!" I grabbed his hand and towed him up.

We made it inside and barred the door as the sounds of hounds drew closer. I leaned my back against the door, chest heaving.

Wyatt stood in front of me, staring at his healed wound. "Nick will never forgive you. I'm—I'm a monster."

"You're not." I pitched forward and grabbed his hand. "I've seen you. You're still you. As long as your heart pumps warmth, you will keep the darkness at bay." A tear slid down my cheek. "Besides, I wasn't about to lose you. Not now. Not ever."

He hugged me back. Crushed me so close I could feel his heart beating against my chest. Then he kissed the top of my head. "Thank you, Ava. For loving me enough to save me."

I hugged him tighter.

As the memory faded, the feelings didn't. They joined the ones I'd started making for him in this lifetime. I stared at this young man down by the river. The curve of his back. His muscular shoulders. My cheeks warmed. He glanced at me sideways and smiled.

I sucked in a breath. "You knew I was here?"

"It's hard to sneak up on me, Ava."

He started walking toward me. "How did you find me this time?"

This time? My mouth went dry. Lifetimes of finding him. It didn't seem normal. Falling this deep with someone I barely knew. "Do you remember the day I saved you?"

"Of course." His eyes grew intense. "You?"

I nodded, unsure of my voice. "You're always saving people, aren't you? That night at the accident site, when you shielded me, did you know who I was?"

"Yes."

"Do you remember the first time you saw me?"

"Yes."

No hesitation. No trepidation. Just yes. That warmed my soul. "So, how does your memory compare to mine?"

He looked down and scuffed his boots through the grass. "The first time I saw you, you had no idea I was even standing there." He glanced up shyly.

"What?"

"Do you remember the marquis's nephew?"

"Yes! Spoiled brat with more callers than he knew what to do with. He was seriously an Elizabethan version of the bachelor, parading women past one another."

"And he wanted you."

"No, he did not! I was a servant."

"The one girl he couldn't have." Those blue eyes pierced me. "Remember that day in the garden, while he was playing bowls. And he singled you out, saying he'd teach you to play?"

The wisteria had been in bloom, and the summer sun beat warm and friendly. My dress was heavy and cumbersome, and I missed my hunting clothes. And that man had tried to get me to take his arm. Not one, but three times. And I'd kept denying him and his cocky smile. He wanted more than I was willing to give. And it was so strange because I was not nobility. He could be flogged.

"The third time he tried to get you hold his hand—"

"A chestnut came from nowhere and hit him square in the forehead!" I started laughing. Wyatt laughed, too, and I looked into his eyes, brighter in the rising sun. "Tell me that wasn't you."

"You clearly weren't interested in his advances."

I could not contain my laughter. "You're kidding me! What if you'd missed?"

He shrugged. "I couldn't have you being spoken for before I even got to meet you."

"Oh? And what if I'd denied your advances?"

He stopped and stared at me, pulling me in with a gaze. "You didn't." His strong fingers laced between mine. He lifted my hand to his lips and kissed the back of it. Such a strange gesture except that it brought so much history full circle. "Do you regret that decision?"

"No." My voice seemed to be swallowed by the sound of the waves against the shore. My heart was like the sand, soaking in new memories, already damp with old emotions. And just when I thought my insides would burst from feeling so much, I looked right at Wyatt. "I'm supposed to save everyone from Gwendolyn. Nick says he thinks she'll come tonight. Maybe tomorrow."

Wyatt's eyes narrowed. "Are you asking me her plans, because I told Cade everything I know."

He had? "Nick thinks you should stay away from us when we fight her. He thinks you're dangerous."

"I agree with your brother on this."

I walked away from him, closer to the water, and immediately regretted it. He'd been shielding me from a bit of chill.

He followed. Stood behind me. Didn't put his hands on my arms to warm me like I wanted him to.

"I saw you stand up to her," I whispered.

"And you saw how hard it was. She wasn't even at full strength. The things she can make me do with a snap of her fingers . . . I can't let her get that hold on me again. Nick won't let it happen if he can stop me. We have an understanding."

My stomach dropped like a stone to the bottom of the river. "What kind of understanding?"

He was silent for so long that I turned to make sure he'd heard me. He glanced my way, and the sorrow in his eyes told me he'd heard. "Ava, the things I've done . . ."

"As a werewolf."

"It's still me." His gaze turned sharp. Like a blade.

"But it's not. You help people. I've witnessed it. In this lifetime. In other lifetimes."

"It's never enough to atone for what I've done."

I faced him fully. He looked so broken. "But that's not why you do good. Right?"

His smile was more of a wince. "Of course not. I just . . . There's a monster inside me. It's always clawing to get out. The darkness wants to overpower me."

"But darkness, no matter how deep, can't snuff even the smallest of light, Wyatt."

He sort of smiled. "Ava, that's what I love about you. When I—" His finger touched the side of my face and trailed over my jaw line, down my neck. Over the spot where he'd scratched me all those lifetimes ago. He swallowed. "Do you remember?" His voice broke.

I grabbed his hands. "You won't hurt me."

"That's the thing, Ava. I already have. I almost killed you."

"But you didn't!" I squeezed his hands. "You didn't, and you won't."

"You shouldn't put so much faith in me. The last time you did—"

"What did you mean when you said you and Nick have an understanding?"

"Ava, there's no doubt about the way I feel about you. But I don't ever want to hurt you again. I don't want to hurt anyone again. I made Nick promise something, and I'd like to ask you the same favor."

Something deep in my core shuddered.

He breathed in, shakily. "If I ever do anything to hurt you. If I ever do anything like what I"—he swallowed—"did before. Please, don't make me continue to be a danger."

I backed away from him. "What are you asking me?"

"You're the only one who can do it. You brought me onto your cycle. Only you can take me off."

"No!" The hurt in my chest threatened to choke me.

"Ava, all I'm saying is—"

"Stop!" I whirled away from him, tears threatening. Why would he want to leave me? The one person I'd chosen to be with forever, and he wanted to leave. I pressed my hands against my face to hide my tears.

"Ava, please listen to me." He grabbed my arm and turned me to face him. "I love you."

Those words made my heart stop.

He . . . ? I blinked rapidly, trying to catch up with the feelings exploding in my chest right now. He loved me. I shook my head. Why did everyone who said they loved me leave?

I pushed against him with the same force I tried to push back against the coming tears. "Then don't leave me!"

The words burned my throat. He pulled me in to him even as I pushed against him.

"I'm sorry. I just don't want to become the monster again." His chest heaved against me.

I looked up at him, the ache in my soul pulsing with each beat. "You won't."

"How do you know?"

"Because you called me your light in dark places. When you need a light, Wyatt—when you think the only thing inside you is darkness—remember that it isn't. As long as you love me, there's light. And as long as there's light, there's hope." I touched his chest with my palm. "I believe there's good in here. More than you think. Can you cling to that?"

His heart beat beneath my palm four times before he answered. "I can."

"Good. Then don't ask me to do away with you. My job is to hunt monsters. I know one when I see one."

"Yes, ma'am."

I smiled. "Don't 'ma'am' me."

He chuckled, and the sound was so freeing, it seemed to warm the wind.

I stared into his eyes, touched the side of his face, and coaxed him closer. His gaze traced my face. My lips. And I saw the longing inside as if he'd opened a door to his soul. He was trusting me. I let my walls fall, and I pulled him in and kissed him. His lips met mine, and warmth, nonexistent on this cold evening, exploded through every part of me. He wrapped his arms around me and held me close. Tight. His strong hands pressed against my back, my waist, my hips, as if he never wanted to let me go. He never had to. I held him back just as tightly while memories danced in my head.

Summer and winter and fall and stars. So many nights spent under the stars. His hand in mine. And those eyes. They drew me in. This kiss replayed all of it. But the memories rising to the surface most were from this lifetime. This Wyatt. The kiss ended, and I held him tight, looking into his eyes, my arms wrapped around his neck. Something about his expression seemed happy and sad all at once.

"What's wrong?"

"Nothing. Except that I have to go." I released him, and he picked up his bag. "Thank you," he said. "For giving me a chance. To atone."

A painful tug weighed my heart down. "Has there ever been a time in the past that I've chosen to not forgive you for your sins?"

He bowed his head. "Do you forgive me now?"

"Of course." I touched his face and nudged him to look at me. "I know enough. I know your heart. And it's good."

He started to shake his head. "Do you not remember? I slaughtered people." Tears filled his eyes.

I recalled his comrades, dead around me, and I ached as I realized what he must be remembering. "As a werewolf."

"The monster is still me."

"And that's why you can control it."

"I hope you're right."

AVA

WYATT RUBBED HIS THUMB ACROSS MY hand then let go. "I think you should go home tonight, Ava." He started backing away from me.

I grabbed his hand. "I'm coming with you."

"Ava."

"Don't try to stop me. You should know better."

"You want to be with a werewolf on his most dangerous night?" He sort of smiled.

I squeezed his hand. "I don't want you to be alone." And I didn't want him vulnerable in case Gwen tried to come after him.

He sighed. "Okay, but promise you'll—"

"I promise to stay safe."

He walked me to the car and got my door. As I slipped into the passenger's seat I asked, "Where have you been changing?"

"There's this abandoned cabin in the woods. There's a cellar. I set up down there. I have chains. I break my arm beforehand, and it slows the healing process enough to—"

"Wyatt!" I found it difficult to breathe. "This is why I need to come with you. Or bring you to my brothers' house. Nick has this room in the basement—"

He looked at me as though he wanted to protest, but he didn't say anything, just turned his attention to the road and pulled out of the driveway. I texted Nick to tell him where I'd be in case Gwen came looking. But I wasn't going to leave Wyatt tonight.

Wyatt drove through the woods to a rundown log cabin.

He pulled up next to it, and we got out of the car. I looked up at the quaint cottage. "Who owns this place?"

"I think my family still does. It was my dad's. He's in another state now, though."

I helped him take his duffle bag and my bag of weapons inside—just in case Gwen or her monsters found us. We walked inside. The scent of dust, wood, fear-drenched sweat, and a hint of blood filled the place. Wyatt lit a candle. The couch didn't look used—more layers of dust than I could count. Only footprints on the floor.

I set the bag down. "Wow. Cozy. Please tell me they have running water."

He winced.

I groaned. "You didn't tell me we'd be going back in time."

He chuckled. Then he set down the car keys on the dusty table. "If anything goes very wrong, take the car and go. I can find my own way home."

He motioned over his shoulder toward the door to what looked like a mudroom. "I have to go now."

I tugged his arm and pulled him to face me. "Wyatt, you're not alone tonight. Please don't act like I'm not part of this."

"Ava, I've been handling this alone for the past three years."

"I'm sorry."

A rueful smile hit his eyes. "It's not your fault."

Except that I had brought him to a new timeline. Over and over. And he'd had to go through the whole thing alone every time. I gripped my shirt collar with one hand and hugged my stomach with the other. "Is there anything I can do to help you . . . get ready?"

"No." He wouldn't look at me. "I want to go away until Gwen is gone. I can't let her control me again. I'm not strong enough to—"

"Yes. You are."

Something in his eyes changed. Became animalistic. Alert. Like Ajax when he heard a car door slam down the street. Glancing out the window, he stepped closer to me, hands gripping my arms firmly.

"Wyatt—"

His eyes met mine, and he placed his finger in front of his lips. A soft golden glow seemed to pulse around his pupils. His attention turned to the window, and he froze. Listening. Sniffing. "I need you to take cover." He let go of me and moved toward the door.

"Wyatt, I—"

He looked over his shoulder at me, his eyes gold, something in his face changing. He pointed to the closet. "She can't know you're here. Understand?" His voice came out gravelly—something I remembered from another time.

I nodded and backed into the closet by the door, keeping it cracked enough to see. Because if he needed my help, Andromeda wouldn't sit by like some buttercup.

He stalked forward, hand on the doorknob. His fingers elongated, claws grew out from them, clutching the knob. And a guttural growl rumbled in his chest.

From my slit in the closet door, his nose, morphing into a snout, became visible as he hunkered low. "I smell you." He growled.

Then he whirled around as something burst into the house from the back. Wyatt took off in that direction, smacking full force into a creature much bigger and stronger-looking than him. Wyatt looked more wolfish by the moment, but his claws were razors. They sunk deep into the creature's side as he snapped. The other beast— the wolfish-vampiric creature, opened its mouth much wider than possible, and its teeth elongated. It snarled, pushing Wyatt onto the ground and out of my view.

The snarling continued. Yelping and growling mingled. And I didn't know when to pop out of the closet. This was one of Gwen's all right, and if it got away and told her where I was, it could ruin my only chance to stop her. But Wyatt—

The growling stopped. Scuffling ensued. My heart lodged in my throat.

"Ava?" That voice, rougher than normal, still belonged to Wyatt.

I opened the closet door and raced out to see the ash on the floorboards. And Wyatt sitting there, wiping blood from his mouth. His face had gone back to normal, and his claws were receding. Turning into bloody fingers.

In three strides, I was wrapping him into a hug. "Are you okay? H-how are you able to change back?"

"Whoa. Hey, I'm okay." He nudged me to arm's length. "The moon isn't out yet, so I have some control." He paused. "I have to make sure it was alone. Please, please stay here."

The same logic from before, in the closet, wrestled through my mind again. "You have fifteen minutes."

"Technically"—he actually smiled—"I have seven and a half." He motioned to the window and the darkening sky. "It'll take some time for me to get . . . secured."

"Right." I let out a shaky chuckle. He gripped my arms with a gentle squeeze, then stood and raced out the door.

For six minutes, I fought pacing and strained to listen. Maybe I would sit by like some buttercup after all. I hated this.

"Ava?" My name preceded his entrance.

"Anything?"

He shook his head.

"Now what?"

He led me into the mudroom, carrying a candle, and opened a cellar door. Cold air rushed out, and he headed down the stairs. I followed.

The ground was packed dirt. The walls stone.

"This might not be much, but it's better than your brother's interrogation room." He lit more candles, revealing the room. Shadows danced on the walls. Light brought to attention the chains mounted into stone. Claw marks marred the floor. Bite indentations covered the leg of what seemed to be the fourth chair from the dining table upstairs.

I turned to see him remove his shirt. The bullet wound from ages ago—though it seemed like yesterday—stared back at me. The one the silver bullet had penetrated. I rubbed my hand over the small ridge. "Do you have scars, too, from the things that killed you in the past?"

"Just from the first time I died—like you."

"The first time." I looked into his eyes, and like with Nick, the memories barreled back into me. Wyatt dying. My grief.

I touched his side, the left, where I was certain he'd been skewered. He swallowed. His fingers trailed over my neck and sent a shiver over my spine. "Ava, I'm alive right now."

His words halted much of the grief. It still hurt, but I'd already grieved. I looked at him. Felt the love. I loved him. This Wyatt was the same Wyatt from the memories. All those emotions I wasn't sure I wanted to feel. I let them in.

Love poured into me, so foreign and familiar at once. Warmed me to my core. Made me feel alive.

His finger trailed up the side of my neck beneath my ear, along my jawbone. My pulse fluttered. And he turned me to face him. "I've lost you, too."

"I'm here right now, aren't I?"

"I wish you'd stop choosing to be here with me when I change. But at the same time, when you're here, you make it easier."

"Then I'll always be here."

The way he stared back at me made me step closer, as if annunciating my promise. His chest heaved. He bent closer so that his breath tickled my ear.

"Thank you." He brushed his fingers over my cheek, my neck. Then he kissed me. My heart thundered and thrummed and pounded. It was so full. Full of emotion. Full of love. For this man. Wyatt was Wyatt, no matter which cycle. No matter which decade or century. A tear slid down my cheek. What we had together was amazing, and I didn't want to lose him.

"Ava?" He wiped the tear away with his thumb, and I pressed my hand onto his, keeping his warmth against my face. "What's wrong?"

"Nothing. As long as I don't lose you, nothing is wrong." But something in the back of my mind sprang forward. "Who shot you that night?" I nodded toward the old scar.

He sighed as if this was inevitable.

My lungs shuddered. "Nick." My voice trembled in a whisper. "My brother killed you."

He shook his head. "Ava, look at me. I was already dead."

"No." I staggered away from him, the room seeming to tilt. "No. He—he knew!" My voice sounded airy. I swallowed, trying to ground myself in this reality. Here and now. And I looked at Wyatt. His round, wet eyes. A tug in my chest reminded me how I felt about him. "You aren't a monster. You are a hero, Wyatt. A hero. My brother is the monster." Regret coursed through every vein, and I looked up at him. "I—I have to stop him. He's—if Gwen—" I rubbed my hand over my face. "Tonight I stop Gwen. I free you for good."

"Ava, wait."

But I wouldn't wait. The part I didn't say to Wyatt was that I also had to stop Nick before he killed more creatures who didn't deserve to die.

## 42

CADE

I TWIRLED THE SWORD IN MY HAND, MY muscles recalled the movement. And my brain recalled the surge of cockiness. "Hey, boys, long time no see."

The new reapers growled. Round one took all my bullets. And shooting alerted these three dingy prowlers. I still hadn't made it out of the driveway.

The one on the left took a step.

Ava might have just cracked open her speed, but I'd picked mine up quickly. The only problem plaguing me was the stupid knack my powers had for shorting out at the worst possible moments.

That was where skill came into play.

I could only hope I'd trained hard enough, because now it wasn't just me on the line. Yuki still stood behind me. Monsters blocking our way to the car.

I held the sword in front of me. It blurred before me as I focused on the creatures. Waited for them to make the first move.

The one on the right started to spring forward.

Target locked. I dashed forward and cut down, slicing that beast's head clean off. Then I whirled around before the second one had a chance to move. I stabbed it through, pulled the sword out, and as it staggered, I chopped through its neck. The head rolled. Then I raced forward for the third. Adrenaline pumped through my veins, fueled my speed, covered every thought except one: get Yuki out of here alive.

Yuki stood, sword ready. But she wouldn't get a chance if I could help it. I climbed up the beast's back and stabbed through the skull. With a moan, it slammed into the ground.

I decapitated the last one just in case.

They turned to dust—blood and all—and I looked at Yuki.

"Look out!" She pushed me aside and let out a yell as she charged a final beast I hadn't seen. A different creature entirely. It looked almost like a living shadow of a very large snake with legs. Yuki stabbed deep, and the monster wrapped its clawed hand around the blade protruding from its stomach.

I swung to chop its head off, but it looked right at me. Those swirling gray eyes staring into me made me balk. "You're too late. She will kill you thissssss time. Her plan is already in motion. And it'ssssss all your fault."

Yuki pulled her sword free and swung. The creature's head toppled to the ground. Breathing hard, she turned to me. "What did that mean?"

I stared at her as feeling flooded back into me. I started shaking. "It means we go tell Nick she's coming. And to be honest, I didn't know those things could talk."

Yuki nodded. "I'm bringing the sword." But she blurred, and my head hit the grass.

I opened my eyes to a memory. I felt battered and bruised mentally, and I wasn't where I thought I'd be.

I walked down by the riverside with a beautiful woman on my arm. Red on the horizon over the water reminded me—she wanted to be here. To see the sunset despite my pleading that she should be in bed.

She looked up at me with eyes like green pools. Her golden hair fluttered in the breeze. A halo around her head. I leaned to kiss her. "Nick is going to kill me."

"As long as he doesn't kill *me*."

I gently stroked her cheek with my thumb. "He won't."

"He might. Making his little brother fall in love." Her smile tugged at something deep in my heart.

"Look." She turned away from the sunset to look at the darkest part of the sky. "First star of the night. Beautiful, isn't it? How such brightness travels so far through darkness just to show us its pretty light. It's like hope through a dark cloud." Her last word was choked off as she bent, coughing and holding her stomach tight.

I grabbed her, afraid she might fall over. Every muscle in her body was taut. She practically fell into me. I cupped her head close. "You're burning up. I told you not to come out here so ill."

"I wanted . . . to see . . . stars . . . again." The cough wracked her body. Her eyes blinked closed, and blood speckled her lips.

"Angelica?"

She fell against me. "Cade, you're like a star. When I look at you, you shine so bright." She smiled, her expression strange, eyes glassy.

"You can't die, Angelica. Don't die."

"I told you—"

"No. Yesterday you weren't this sick." It had happened so suddenly. My hope crumbled. Where was Nick? He was supposed to bring me the medicine she needed. He'd said not to get attached. That was why I'd kept the relationship a secret, but Nick was too astute. He'd figured it out.

I pulled her head onto my lap.

She curled into a ball, coughing again. Every muscle in her frail body tensed, and there was nothing I could do to help her. Blood dripped out of her mouth. She pressed her palm against my cheek, her touch weak and clammy.

"Cade?" Her voice seemed strained. "Promise me something?"

"Anything."

"Promise me you'll move on. Prom—" She coughed again.

No. I could do something. Who cared about the stupid phoenix laws?

She looked up at me. "I'm sorry I . . . won't be able . . . to meet your . . . brother."

Her head lolled to the side. Nick was coming. He'd forbid it. Forbid everything. He already did. I was already the brother who never did anything right anyway.

"Yes. You will." I set her gently on the ground and touched my hands to her chest. Dead. No. No, no, no. I could save her. Phoenixes weren't meant to be alone. The reason they'd made the law in the first place proved that. We craved companionship. I pulled every emotion that I'd ever felt for Angelica in our short time together to the surface.

My hands glowed. Warmth, light, and emotion poured out of me and flushed into her. Filled her. Filled me. All consuming, the light drenched both of us. She became a part of me, and I felt her pain. The poison attacking her. And just like I could heal my own body, I healed her.

"Cade?" Nick's voice muffled through the all-consuming presence of my power. "No!"

Nick's anguished cry blasted into me full force as everything came back clear and the light faded.

Angelica looked up into my eyes. "You—you saved me. You—I feel—how did you do that?"

"Cade." Nick's voice was measured. "Please, back away from her." He stood there with a wide-eyed Ava.

"What's wrong with you, Nick?" I pulled Angelica into me as tears streamed down her face. Down mine. We'd be together forever.

"Cade?" Nick crouched down to be eye level with me, but I held up my hand to keep him at a distance.

"I don't understand how someone like you—someone who cares about the poor and needy, someone so courageous that you protect humankind—could ask his own brother to let the woman he loves die."

Nick winced. "Of course I don't want you to suffer that kind of loss."

My tight grip on Angelica lightened. "Then you're okay with this?"

"If you want to fall in love, Cade, yes. I'm okay with it. But this woman—she doesn't love you. She tricked you. And she's—" He shuddered. "She's not who you think she is."

I looked into her deep, green eyes. "See, I told you. He doesn't know what love is."

"He does." Her face changed, and a strange smirk curved her lips. "And I pity him because he does. But you, you were putty in my hands.

Clay I molded. And now you will shatter." A piercing pain stabbed my gut, and I looked down to watch her pull a strange, red feather out of me. She stood and backed away from me. "The Phoenix Quill can kill any phoenix."

"No!" Nick raced forward, but she ran at him.

Ava skidded to my side, but Angelica threw the quill. It slashed open Ava's arm.

"It takes your healing powers." Angelica smirked. Then she said something to Nick. Something I didn't hear. And he stabbed her through.

Everything started to fade, and I looked up at Ava as she pleaded with me not to die.

When I came to, Nick knelt beside me and hugged me tight. "I'm sorry, Cade. I didn't know she'd gotten to you. I—I'm sorry she wasn't who you thought she was."

"What do you—"

Ava touched my arm. "That was Gwen, Cade."

Gwen? "I put a dark phoenix on my cycle? What will that do to me?"

Nick's expression seemed helpless—a look I'd never seen on my brother. "I don't know."

The memory winked out, leaving me in utter blackness. I wasn't awake. But I wasn't asleep.

I was numb.

All the brokenness stayed with me even as the memory faded.

I had loved . . . Gwen. Gwendolyn. Psycho . . . What about Yuki? Didn't I also love Yuki?

I'd put her on my cycle. Why? More urgently, what was missing from this memory? What had Nick put in that stone? I needed to understand everything.

I sat up and noticed Yuki sitting beside me, shaking my shoulder.

"You're awake." She hugged me tight.

I rubbed Yuki's back. "I need to get to Nick." I moved her aside and stood.

"Well I'm coming with you." She held up her car keys. "And I'm driving."

# NICK. MY OWN BROTHER.

He'd killed Wyatt.

Even after I'd begged him not to.

Did Cade know?

All Nick's talk about protecting me. And to think I had let myself believe him, love him even. Only to have him stab me in the back. He knew I'd loved Wyatt; that was the kicker.

I banged on the door.

No one answered. No one was home.

They were already hunting? I walked back to the car. Maybe Nick was looking for me at the cabin. I checked my phone, but there were no new texts. I got into the car and wiped tears from my cheeks. Nick had betrayed me.

I'd started to love him—I had let myself love him—and he knew about all these memories. He knew he'd betrayed me, and then he'd looked me straight in the eyes and asked me to help him. Told me he'd be there for me. And all this time he knew what Wyatt was. And that he'd tried to kill him.

My chest ached.

I leaned on the steering wheel and let the tears come. Even if Nick betrayed me, I couldn't let Cade die. I texted Wyatt: *When you come to, will you help me? I need to kill Gwendolyn. And I can't do it alone.*

Something nagging, like a memory, tugged at the corner of my mind. I pulled down a side street, turned off the car, and gave the memory my full attention.

It flooded into me. For some reason I knew this was France, a long time ago. I remembered that much.

Wyatt pushed my hair behind my ear and looked into my eyes. "I think Nick is finally coming around to the idea that you're not terrible."

"But I am terrible."

"Wyatt, you have to stop doubting who you are inside."

"Every month it's a struggle. And I don't—"

"You're not alone. Remember that." I placed my hand on his arm.

"Nick says you have to kill Gwendolyn."

"Yes. She is the last dark phoenix. And only I can kill her for good." I strolled along the bank, Wyatt's hand in mine.

He had to be nervous about tonight. About leaving us to go under Gwendolyn as a spy. Nick seemed to think it was a good plan. Cade didn't like it, though. He didn't like the idea of Wyatt getting that close to the enemy. He thought Gwen would see right through Wyatt's good heart.

I agreed. But Wyatt had decided in the end, and he'd sided with Nick.

I squeezed Wyatt's hand. "You're okay with Nick's plan?"

He nodded. "I'll be your spy. I'll get close to Gwendolyn—but I'll have to play a convincing role. Please know it's all for you."

I stopped walking and faced him. My pride swelled with love. "I trust you, with my life."

He breathed deep, his hands on my arms and a slight smile curved his lips. "That's a precious thing to trust me with. Especially when I'll be tapping in the darkest side of me."

I trailed my fingers over his jaw, and he leaned closer to me. My skin tingled with warmth. "Even the smallest light can pierce the dark. I'm your light, Wyatt. As long as I trust your heart, I'll keep shining. You'll come back to me."

His arms slipped around me. "I'll always come back to you."

I wrapped my arms around his neck and pulled him into me. He always kissed me with such passion that my heart fluttered and pounded at once. My body pressed against his, and all I could feel was his strong arms around me and every tingle pulsing through me that sparked anew with each deeper kiss.

I looked into his eyes, still holding him close. "Don't forget your Andromeda, Perseus."

He chuckled, his expression soulful. "Never. We'll take down this monster together, because my Andromeda is no helpless princess."

"Don't you forget it."

The memory pushed me three months into the future. I recalled the little home on the French Riviera. I remembered going over Nick's plan to kill Gwen—for me to kill Gwen. And I knew it was three months later, because that was how long it had been since I'd seen Wyatt.

He paced like a caged animal at the circus. Jumpy, distant, volatile.

I kept glancing at him, and the tight ball in my stomach wouldn't loosen. He darted his gaze away any moment I made eye contact with him. Five days till the next full moon, and he acted like he was about to change.

Nick pointed to the table where he'd set up little pebbles and sticks to represent us and the monsters Gwen had rallied. Our plan of attack. We were to sneak in tonight, two days before her planned attack. She wouldn't expect it, and Wyatt had told us where all the monsters would be.

"Are we clear?" Nick asked. "Cade and Wyatt and I will take out these monsters here."

"Stop using that word." Wyatt lunged at my brother.

Nick put his hands up. As Wyatt backed off, Nick pressed his hands into Wyatt's arms. "Hey, I need you to have a clear head. Can you do that, or do we put this off?"

"Tonight is the night she's mostly alone. She sends the werewolves away so they . . . attack in other cities. It keeps her location harder for you to find."

He'd already told us that.

"Do you need to sit this one out?"

I came up beside Wyatt and touched his back. "What's wrong? Are you going to change?"

He looked at me sideways, worry deep in his eyes, the same sorrow they held right before he changed. As if he wanted to ask forgiveness for all that he was about to do. "I—I think I'm just nervous. And I can't contain my emotions this close to—"

"I think you should sit this one out, buddy." Cade pulled himself up onto the table and sat there, dangling his legs over the side.

Nick narrowed his eyes and searched Wyatt's face. "Is there something you're not telling us? Has she done something to you? Hidden some information from us?"

Wyatt turned to Nick, opened his mouth, but said nothing. His hands gripped Nick's shirt, shaking. He tried to speak again. Then one tear dripped down his cheek.

My soul shattered.

Nick placed his hands on Wyatt's. "She did something to you."

Wyatt sank to the ground at Nick's feet. "I—I can't even tell you the truth. I'm trying."

Nick let out a frustrated growl and slammed his hand against the wall. Then he pinched the bridge of his nose. "Compulsion. It's a dark phoenix power. It's how they control monst—creatures of the dark."

I started to go to Wyatt, but Nick put his arm out to stop me.

He crouched next to Wyatt. "I never should have sent you in there as the spy. I'm sorry."

"Sh-she's already h-here. Run."

What? No. He—he couldn't have told her where we were. He . . . "Wyatt?"

He buried his head in his hands. "Please. Run."

Nick slammed open the back door. The three of us started to head out, but Gwen stood there, at least fifteen vampires, werewolves, wraiths, and reapers, and a few slithering shadows told me she had shadow puppets with her as well.

Werewolves? How?

She glanced at something behind us. "Good little pet."

I turned to see Wyatt slinking through the doorway.

I wanted to throw up. To spit at her. This disgusting woman. "He's not your pet." I clenched my fists.

But Gwendolyn patted her thigh, and, cringing, Wyatt slunk over to her.

No. A denial echoed in my hollow chest, and it hurt. There had to be a reason. An explanation. Wyatt had a plan. He wouldn't betray us. I met Gwen's hard gaze with a heat of my own.

"He's mine now." She snapped her fingers, and Wyatt screamed. He started changing into a werewolf. How was she doing that? My hope plummeted, and my knees weakened. Did she truly have control over him?

"Wyatt! Don't listen to her. Listen to your heart! Please!" My throat burned raw as I screeched. "You can't have him."

She chuckled. "Too late."

And I ran forward, dagger ready to kill.

But I didn't get my chance. Something in the memory seemed stuttered. Spliced. But that wasn't possible, right? I refocused, letting myself drift fully back into the memory. There. Cade stopped me from killing Gwen. I watched helplessly as he stabbed Gwen in the heart.

As she lay there, dying, her abominations ran. And Wyatt dashed away with all her monsters.

My mind swirled and pushed me into a new memory.

It grabbed hold of me with such force and raw emotion that a sob welled in my gut.

I was back in France after Wyatt had betrayed us and I'd spared his life. And he'd run. Nick and I had been tracking him, but what we'd found here made my insides feel shredded.

Blood.

Blood and bodies with ripped-out throats.

Claw marks cutting deep into skin.

I sank to the ground, clutching my stomach. Sobbing.

Cade knelt next to me, hand on my shoulder. "Ava, I'm—"

"Stop!" I pushed his hand away and curled into a ball, letting the sobs wrack me. "He did this," I whispered over and over.

Nick's voice cut through my crying. "And it was my fault. Not his. Not this time. I let him get close to her."

"This?" I still couldn't speak above a whisper. "This was my—"

"No, Ava." Nick clutched my shoulder, his soft voice in my ear. "We have to get Wyatt back before he's too far gone."

And as another sob tore through me, the memory dissipated. The emotion of it left me raw.

The reality of what he was capable of gutted me.

No wonder he'd been so tentative around me. He knew once I'd remembered what he'd done that I would . . . well, what would I do? Was he still this monster?

I PULLED INTO THE DRIVEWAY, AND YUKI jumped off the motorcycle. We both headed up the porch steps at Kelsey's house. No one was there.

I checked my phone and texted Nick again: *Where the heck are you?*

"Anything?" Yuki looked up at me.

"No."

"Please say you know where Ava is."

I shook my head as ice chilled my blood. If she had gone back to the house, would she wait? Hopefully she wasn't where I thought she was. "Let's go!"

We rode the bike home, just like we'd left it after slaughtering reapers here. And I raced inside, stopping dead in my tracks. "I remembered something very important." Truthfully, I'd been told earlier this evening, but no time for explanations.

"What?"

I didn't exactly trust my voice right now. I tried to steady it. "We can't trust Wyatt when it comes to Gwen. He—he betrayed us. And I . . . made a mistake with Gwen. It's my fault she's stripping me of my powers."

Yuki touched my arm, and something about the contact calmed my overdrive pulse. "It's okay, Cade. We can fix it now. I remembered something, too."

I pressed my palms against the kitchen island and tried to reset my breathing.

Yuki picked up the memory stone Wyatt had left on the counter. Her eyes widened. She stared at me. "Do you know what this is?"

"Yeah. My memory's trapped inside."

"Why?"

"Because Nick is stupidly secretive."

She pulled out her sword. "Then take the memory out."

I narrowed my eyes and tilted my head, taking in Yuki's sudden confidence. "Do you know how that works?"

An impish smile curled her lips. She held out her hand as if asking for mine. I placed it in hers. She flipped it over, so my palm was facing up. Then she placed her sword on my hand.

My heart sped, and I looked up at her.

"It needs your blood so it knows which memory is yours."

"Why didn't I think of that?"

She smiled at my sarcasm and slid the blade gently over my palm. I winced but tried not to move. As the blood pooled, she placed the stone in it, and the rock sucked up the red in my hand, swirling it inside. And I felt something unlock.

The memory started to seep into me.

I was at the mercy of Gwen in a shipyard in France, the day Wyatt had betrayed us and my mistake came full circle.

I lay on the ground, hard under my back. Everything felt cold as I stared up at the stars. And her face came into view.

"Caderyn."

I would have spit at her if it wasn't just going to land back in my own face. My shoulder and neck throbbed from where Wyatt had ripped me open. Three of her monsters muscled me to my feet and held me with my arms behind me.

"Leave him alone!" Ava raced up to Gwendolyn, and her dagger sailed for Gwendolyn's chest, lightning fast.

Gwendolyn caught Ava's arm, just as quickly. "You would kill your own sister. Your own brother?"

Ava flinched. "What?"

"Don't listen to her, Ava! Just do it." Nick's voice rose over the snarling and fighting.

Gwen's smile grew wicked. "Nick is a Taker. He can't kill me because I'm his twin."

My stomach roiled. She was my sister? I wanted to throw up. No wonder Nick called her disgusting. She'd—I'd kissed her!

Ava's voice shook. "No."

"Kill her, Ava!" Nick's voice drew closer.

Monsters blocked him from coming.

I tried to stand, but pain coursed through my body, sending me back to the dirt.

I tried to breathe. To feel . . . anything. If I killed Gwendolyn, it wouldn't end her for good. But it wouldn't turn Nick human, either. Only Ava could kill her for good. But it meant Nick would die, too.

My hand groped across the dirt, and I found my dagger. My fingers touched the hilt. Slow and sluggish, I wrapped them around the weapon. Then I summoned everything I had left. I sat up and plunged it into Gwen's heart.

She screamed and fell, dead. Her form swirled into a cloud of dark and zapped out of existence. One by one, her monsters started to screech and flee until we were the only ones left.

Ava stared at me wide-eyed. Then she pressed her hands against me and healed my wounds. "Why didn't Nick tell us she was our sister?" Her eyebrows pinched together. "How did we not know?"

"I have no idea." I touched her hand. "And because he's an idiot who thinks doing the right thing is more important."

Ava looked at me with her eyes round and full of tears. "Don't let Nick die."

I swirled out of that memory into another and another—just pieces of the same thread. The same information Nick wanted to hide from us. Some memories Nick had taken, but some . . . my father had stolen from me.

I stood leaning against the kitchen island holding the stone.

The pieces were filled in. The memory from Japan—me talking

with Yuki about something she'd found that could help Nick—that memory swirled back, too.

Yuki had found a blade that could be used to cut the tie between a pair of phoenix twins, in case one of them became evil. That meant, if we could get our hands on it, we could sever the connection between Nick and Gwen.

Ava could kill Gwen without sentencing Nick to death.

And the person who knew where it was had just remembered how to work the memory stone for me.

My heart clutched as hope dared to rise.

If Yuki could help us find the blade, I could save my brother. My fool brother. My insides squeezed. I couldn't let Ava kill Gwen.

"Cade?"

I swallowed, my throat tightening, and looked at Yuki, remembering what it was like to be loved. Memories of this feeling flooded back into me. Nick, Ava. Heck, even Wyatt. They all loved me. I had a family.

And I wasn't about to lose them. If I died, Yuki would die. Ava would die. Wyatt would die. And I was about to die if Ava didn't kill Gwen. "We need that blade."

Her mouth opened, and she widened her eyes. "I can't remember—"

"Can you please try?"

She nodded. I pressed my knuckles against my mouth.

"If Ava kills Gwendolyn . . ." Yuki's voice trailed off.

"You remember, don't you?" I cupped my face in my hands. "This is a disaster."

"Then we trap her. You know, take her hostage, until we find this blade."

I looked at Yuki and smiled. "You're a ray of sunshine, you know that? That might just work." I wanted nothing more than to kiss her right now.

She didn't give me the chance. "Let's go find Ava. Before your sister accidentally kills your brother."

"Right."

Thank heavens a text came through from Nick: *Meet us at the docks. Ava is here. Hurry.*

# 45



I WOKE WITH A START TO EARLY morning light, still in the car. Fresh tears threatened as I replayed the most awful moment of the memory that had unlocked to me: Gwen had controlled Wyatt. With one snap of her fingers, she'd made him change. She wasn't a full moon. How did she have so much power over him?

If she could control him, could I ever truly trust him? I shook the memory away, squeezing my eyes closed to make sure remnants wouldn't come back to haunt me.

Then I clutched the steering wheel tight, realizing I'd sobbed myself to sleep last night.

I'd left Wyatt alone.

I checked my phone to find that Wyatt had texted me back: *Meet me at the cabin?*

I sniffed residual tears away. Did I want to meet him now? Could I trust him? I'd remembered how much he loved me. How he was afraid to become the monster again. He deserved my loyalty. I would go meet him, but I wasn't going to allow him near Gwen, for his sake as much as mine, because he was right. He shouldn't be anywhere near Gwen. I should have trusted him. Should have listened.

The sun's early rays glinted between houses as I drove through town toward the woods.

Red and blue lights filled the streets. At least three police cars. What was going on? I had to find a different way around to get to the cabin. Blood pounded in my skull. What if Gwen found him first? I pulled into a driveway to turn around. Yellow caution tape fluttered in the wind. Police waved for a growing crowd of spectators to leave. People stood with their hands over their faces. Crying.

My breathing stalled. What was going on?

A car accident? There were no remnants of car parts. My heart whispered "no" because I knew exactly what caused this. A monster had been here.

Blood. I saw blood.

Blood on the curb.

Blood in the street.

How many families had suffered loss here last night?

My vision started to go black, and I sucked in air. I needed to breathe. I needed to get to the cabin and find Wyatt chained to the wall.

Then I caught sight of a body bag.

My throat constricted. Not just one. Cars behind me honked. I blocked their only way around this mess. But I saw four body bags.

I couldn't breathe. Couldn't think.

Eyes blurred, I drove straight for the cabin. As I wove through the long winding road through the trees, my heart beat in a prayer that Wyatt would be where I'd left him.

Blood-splattered trees.

Newly cracked limbs.

Piles of ash littered fallen leaves.

My stomach clenched, and I held in a sob. What had happened here?

I parked and got out of the car.

I prayed no more memories would come now. My fragile emotions couldn't take another one. I just wanted to find Wyatt.

I looked up, tears in my eyes, unsuccessfully trying to calm my thundering pulse. "Wyatt?"

No answer.

I ran around back and walked inside. "Wyatt?" Tears broke free. "Say something, Wyatt!"

On shaky legs, I raced down the cellar stairs—the door had been left wide open, spilling sunlight in. And the room at the bottom sat empty.

Chains, but no Wyatt.

Claw marks covered the dirt. Not just dirt. Blood covered the whole place. Spattered the walls, dripped all over the floor. The chair that had been here now lay a mess of splintered wood. I touched the ground and red came away on my fingers. My chest clutched.

I pulled out my phone, praying I could at least find him this morning.

"Come on, Wyatt. Pick up."

Someone answered.

"Wyatt?" My voice shook.

"Ava, at last we speak again." The room started growing dark in my periphery. I braced myself against the wall and pulled venom into my voice. "Gwen."

A tiny laugh accented her pleased smile. I could hear it in her voice. "Have you seen your lover's handiwork this morning? He spilled a lot of blood last night."

Blood . . . I couldn't breathe. Could hardly see. Pins and needles coursed through my veins. "What do you want?"

"You know what I want. You. Your powers. Your life."

"Where is Wyatt?"

"You saw where we had our little disagreement last night, I see. I wanted to make sure you were convinced."

"What have you done to him?" I screamed my throat raw.

She laughed, and I wanted to make her pay. "It's easy, Ava. Come alone, and I'll give you your brothers back. That's right. My monsters have Nick and his annoying friend Kelsey over by the loading dock. Kelsey is still alive because Wyatt, that tricky little wolf, got away last night, so I found Cade and what's her name . . . Yuki. And I have them here at Crane's Bargain Books—because it reminds me so much of home. Come and give me your powers, and I'll personally heal Cade. Then I'll tell my monsters to leave Nick and his friend alone. Don't, and I start killing. You and I both know Cade won't last another cycle. I told you I'd take all your loved ones, and *you* left them alone."

She ended the call, and I sank the floor, shaking. Fury built inside me. Mingled with fear. And hatred. Tears dripped hot down my cheeks.

I could not—would not—let her win again. She would not take everyone I loved from me.

I gripped my phone so hard my hand hurt. I calmed myself and stood. There was only one way out of this now. Pretend to give her my powers—which I honestly didn't know how to do—and kill her.

# AVA

My only option was to fight Gwen alone.

I headed back out to the car, and a rustling in the leaves caught my attention. I whirled around to see Wyatt headed my way.

Every emotion inside me pressed against the dam holding me together, and I ran to him. He met me with a worried expression, and I threw my arms around him. "You're okay?"

"I'm . . ." He hugged me tight and buried his face in my neck.

I couldn't hug him close enough. I had no idea if he'd remember what he'd done last night. If he'd even done it. Maybe that was all a ruse by Gwen the psycho. "Gwen knows where I am."

His breathing shook. "Sh-she sent more monsters here last night. After you left—"

"Are you okay?" I pulled back and looked at him, aware that a few tears had leaked out of my eyes. Bruising and scratches on his face, his arms, looked like they were slowly healing.

"Yeah." He thumbed away my tears. "Are you?"

No. For heaven's sake, no. I wanted to tell him, but I couldn't put Wyatt in the position of getting close to Gwen. Not after what I'd remembered.

But standing here, staring at him, my heart ached. Then I stepped back. "You're wearing clothes."

He let out a short, surprised laugh. "I normally do." Then he breathed deep. "I had clothes here. I went home to find Kelsey, but she's not there. I imagine she's searching for me, but I can't find my phone. I always leave it in my shed."

My heartbeat sped. It had to be true, then. Gwen must have Kelsey.

A thousand texts rang through my phone, making it buzz in my pocket.

Wyatt stared at me as if expecting me to answer it. I pulled out the phone and gasped and pressed my hand to my face as pictures came in. Pictures of Cade and Kelsey and Yuki and Nick. Bound. Gagged. Some of them bloody. All of them from Wyatt's phone. And one message came through: *You have one hour. I'm impatient.*

"Ava, what's wrong?"

I backed away from Wyatt. Was he lying? Had she already gotten to him?

"Ava?" His eyebrows pulled together, but he seemed more ready to bolt than to close the distance between us.

"It's Gwen. She has your phone." I held out mine so he could see the pictures.

His eyes widened. "We have to go save them. We—"

I grabbed his arm. "Wait. It has to be me."

"Ava." He held out his hands, and deep hurt seemed to cross his features. "Not alone. No."

My voice came out soft and unsteady. "Wyatt, I can't—you can't come with me."

"You have reason to not trust me, but I won't hurt you on purpose."

I'd seen what Gwen had done to him. "Y-you said you went home?"

"Yes." He drew the word out warily, as if trying to follow my train of thought.

"A-and Gwen was at your house? Did—" I didn't want to ask him this. But if she was using compulsion on him again . . . "Did she . . . see you?"

"No." He backed away, his features scrunching up. "You don't trust me."

I wanted to. I'd told him I would trust his heart. Forever. And yet,

Gwen controlled him. I stepped away from him. "It's close to a full moon. Just like before." My stomach clutched. "Do you know what happened in town last night?"

"Ava." He stepped closer to me, eyes pleading, arms out as if to calm me. "She sent her monsters to break me out last night, but that's all. I swear. Please believe me." His voice held a tremor. "I fought them off. Like at the beach. Ava, you said you believed I could control it. That was the only thing keeping me from losing it. Keeping me sane."

"Why don't you stay here?" A warm tear slid down my cheek.

"No. You can't ask me to stay here when you're alone. This is the most important fight you've ever faced. Your last chance. And she has my sister. My *mortal* sister."

I wanted to believe him so badly my heart squeezed in half.

I grabbed his hands. Gwen said she was with Cade and Yuki at the bookstore. "Wyatt, I think you'll be better off staying away from Gwen this time. She has Kelsey and Nick at the abandoned dock with some of her monsters. Cade and Yuki are with her."

"But you need help to defeat her. You don't think I can learn from my mistakes? You don't think I can fight her off? You—you said you thought I was strong enough. You—" He stared at me, blinking back tears. "I've made mistakes before, but you made me believe I could fight her off. You can trust me, Ava. I *know* I can resist her this time. I always come back to you."

It was a plea. I remembered what I'd said to him: *Even the smallest light can pierce the dark. I'm your light, Wyatt. As long as I trust your heart, I'll keep shining. You'll come back to me.*

"And . . . I need you to again." I looked into his wounded expression and prayed he'd be able to forgive me. "But right now, I only trust half of you." Even as I said it, my soul cracked in two. Because I wanted to tell him I trusted him so badly, it hurt.

He expelled a breath and backed away from me, his hands sliding out of mine. "Right."

"It's a trap, Wyatt."

Wyatt clenched his jaw. "I go after Nick and Kelsey. You go get

Cade and Yuki. I'll send Nick to you. And I'll stay away like you asked." His eyes masked over, hiding his soul. "You three can end this."

I nodded. "Go." My sorrow leaked out in my command.

He paused a heartbeat. "We all trust you, Ava. That's never been in question. But the reason you believe you have to face this alone is because you refuse to let yourself trust anyone."

Those words sliced something deep inside me. Could he be right? Was that why I always felt alone?

He sighed, turned, and ran. Didn't even look back.

And I knew I'd crushed his resolve, but it would be fine. Gwen wouldn't live long enough to torment him ever again. I got in the car and drove to the bookstore to face her alone. And end this for good.

# 47

AVA

I PULLED INTO THE EMPTY BOOKSTORE parking lot and looked up. The building always reminded me of some tiny Grecian palace with its columns and pillars. So vaguely familiar.

I swallowed, wiping my sweaty hands on my jeans. Silence greeted me. Too much silence. A CLOSED sign hung in the window, so it made sense that the parking lot was empty, but something felt wrong. Like a shiver in my bones. A monster baiting me from behind a tree.

I stepped out of the car. I had two daggers—one silver—my gun, and the crossbow and arrows. Who knew what kind of monsters she'd have created and brought with her.

My boots crunched against lose gravel. I sniffed. The air smelled off. Warmer than it should be, and slightly sour. Like old blood. I strained my ears. Then I heard labored breathing.

Chances were, Gwen wanted me to confront her, so all I really had to do was walk through the front door and find her, prepared for an ambush.

It sounded easy, but a slight breeze made me quiver.

Goosebumps dotted my arms. My stomach churned. As much as I knew I had to do this alone, I wished Nick were here.

Even Wyatt.

Why had I pushed them away? The betrayal—something in my gut told me I didn't have the whole story yet, that I wanted to hear their sides of the stories. But in my desire to keep everyone and arm's length, I'd jumped at the chance to distance myself.

To keep myself from getting hurt. Selfish, Ava.

And it hadn't worked. Now I was just alone and scared.

I'd sent Wyatt after Nick. I'd made him believe I didn't trust him. Didn't have faith in him. Didn't love him.

My heart squeezed.

If I was being honest with myself, I'd learned to love more people over the past few months than this whole lifetime. People I trusted. When all of this was over, I'd make it right.

I'd let them in. It wasn't right to make them prove they trusted me first. That, too, was selfish. Why couldn't I just admit that I trusted them?

My armor hadn't protected me at all.

I crossed the parking lot, sensing a shadow or two scurry across my periphery. Despite the sign, the front door was unlocked. I stepped in. There, just inside the door on the ground level, sat the top of a staircase. And the door leading to it happened to be conveniently propped open. How subtle.

A taunt? Maybe.

A trap? Definitely.

My throat tightened and I swallowed. The door opened easily.

The soft electric light was nothing but a bare bulb screwed into the ceiling with a pull chain. That swayed.

Someone had been by here very recently.

The skin crawled on the back of my neck, and every inch of me felt exposed.

I crept down the stairs. They didn't lead into complete blackness. That meant my trap waited. As I descended, the scent of dampness and soil surrounded me. It felt . . . oddly familiar. I couldn't recall why, but that was for the best. Memories could not distract me right now.

Three times I checked over my shoulder at a slight snuffling sound. Nothing. Her monsters were following, and how many hid in the cover of shadow, I wasn't sure, but with every step, more joined.

I stopped on the last stair and turned around, crossbow loaded and ready. "You don't scare me." A soft chuckle seemed to float on the breeze. I couldn't see who uttered it. I knew, though. A shadow puppet.

Stifling a shudder, I felt for its presence as Nick had taught me. Closed my eyes. Listened. There. I opened my eyes, aimed, and shot into darkness.

A strangled cry erupted, and the beast fell from the shadow clinging to the wall and lay on the stair. "She knows you're here," its voice rasped. "I wasn't alone."

My fear skittered like ice through my veins. I stepped up to the small, lizard-like being. It was hard to see, like a form in the dusk that's just out of sight. "Good. I can't take her down if she doesn't show up to the party."

It hissed. "She'll show up. And she'll devour you, phoenix of the light. Get ready. The darknessssssss is coming."

I straightened my spine as something in that threat tried to pull a memory but seemed unable to grab hold of it. Elusive. Almost like it was a memory I couldn't access yet. The creature's head lolled to the side, and in a puff of dust like coal, it disappeared.

I swallowed and faced the doorway, knowing Gwen and her monsters were on the other side.

I checked my gun, loaded with bullets made of silver and wood in case her vampire/werewolf hybrids needed both elements to take them down.

A cold shiver clawed through my blood. Hopefully Wyatt would send Nick in time to grant some backup, because I was starting to think this coming alone business was a bad idea.

I placed my hand against the doorknob, feeling the pulse of the other side.

It seemed quiet. Threatening, like a wild animal waiting to spring. But it also felt cold. As if the threat on the other side was more manipulative than anything.

I turned the knob and pushed.

The door swung open, and I stood ready with my gun.

The dimly lit basement made it hard to see exactly who was in front of me in the open, empty space surrounded by a crumbling-brick wall. A figure tied to a chair that had been tipped over lay across from where the staircase spit me out. Hands and ankles bound to the chair. It was a man, and he wasn't moving. My breaths came faster. Shorter. And I braced myself, weapon ready, and looked around the corners of the stairwell enclosure. Nothing.

I expected shelves of books—inventory for the store, at least. But the damp, dim area showed this was no place to keep anything sensitive to water. It seemed like a hollowed-out cave more than anything. The floor was mainly packed dirt.

An old root cellar perhaps?

Was there another way out?

I moved into the open space, certain to find Gwen and her posse lurking around an alcove. But all I saw was the mouth to an empty tunnel on one side, and the still form in front of me.

No one else was here?

Where was Yuki? "Cade?" Why wasn't he moving? Then I realized a puddle spread out from the figure on the ground. Blood.

"Cade!" I holstered my gun and raced over to him.

I expelled a breath when I realized this wasn't Cade.

"Nick." A deep ache spread through my chest as I reached him. Cuts covered his head, his face, and his arms. The blood spread out from his abdomen. I touched his shoulder. He didn't respond. "Nick!" I tried to calm my shaking fingers enough to check his pulse. It couldn't find it. But he couldn't be gone. Right?

"Why aren't you healing?" My voice barely made it past the tightening in my throat. I used my knife to cut his bindings. His limbs fell limp.

I pressed my hands against the gash in his side. I couldn't lose him now. "Nick, please don't die." I reached deep into my core and felt the love inside of me. It pulsed. Grew. Warmed me from the inside out.

And a golden light spread out from my hands. Like a sunrise bursting above the horizon. I closed my eyes and felt my power course through me, into him. Knitting his wounds, healing his bones.

I gasped. A hand grabbed my wrist, and I opened my eyes.

"Ava?"

"Nick! I thought you were—" I stopped as a sob tried to escape.

"I'm okay, thanks to you."

A flood of warmth shot through me, and I wanted to laugh and cry. He was alive. "What did she do to you?" I looked at his face. Blood still flecked his skin, but no more cuts.

"She made me drink venom. I couldn't heal on my own until it wore off—luckily you found me."

"Where's Kelsey? Cade? Yuki?" My voice trembled as ice-cold fear snuffed my short-lived relief.

He clenched his jaw, and his expression grew dark. "Gwen took them. She said you'd know where. Something about mistrust."

"Wyatt." My voice seemed so airy. I could hardly breathe. Guilt stabbed my heart deep. "She said you were at the docks. That she was here with Cade and Yuki." I pressed my shaking hand up to my mouth and everything inside me started to crumble. "I sent Wyatt there to rescue you and Kelsey. I sent Wyatt to the lion's den."

Nick's eyes rounded. "We have to get him out of there."

That familiar trickle of anger spiked through me as I recalled that my brother had killed Wyatt. My whole body shook, and I clenched my fists. "You are not going anywhere near him."

He glanced down and winced. "You must have remembered one of my past sins."

"As in plural?" I asked with more bite than I meant to, my old habits rising to the surface. Everything inside me wanted to trust Nick, screamed at me to trust him, but I couldn't yet. Not without answers. Hot tears formed in my eyes, and I wiped them away, glaring at him.

"You certainly remember how to cut deep, Ava."

"Me? *You* killed Wyatt. *I* can't trust you."

He grimaced and closed his eyes and bowed his head. "I'm sorry. You can trust me, Ava. Everything I have done has been to protect you."

"You're sorry? That's all? I don't have time for this. I have to get to the docks."

He raised his voice as I started to leave. "He was about to take out Cade's throat. Yes. I shot a werewolf, Ava. I stopped a werewolf from killing your brother. I'm sorry, okay? But you got what you wanted, didn't you? He's yours until the end of time. So let it go."

Then it hit me. I'd likely yelled at him many times about this. Every time I remembered. *My past sins*, he'd said. And here I stood rubbing his face in things I'd likely forgiven him for in the past.

Nick, who died for me over and over. Since then. Before then. The only constant in my life. My *family*. I needed him.

He looked at me. "I'm sorry I killed Wyatt. I didn't listen to you. I should have. You have good instincts. I won't fail you this time. I trust you."

He trusted me. Just like Wyatt said. Wyatt, who trusted me, and I'd sent him right to Gwen.

Nick gripped my arms. "You don't have to do this alone. You understand? I'm with you to the end."

And that right there melted my anger. All he'd ever done was protect me, and I'd believed the worst of him.

He looked into my eyes, and pride shone there like the sun. Warmed me from the inside out. "Ava, no matter what Gwen says to you—the lies she will try to tell you—you are stronger than she is."

"Then why have I never been able to beat her?"

"Because you forget your true potential. For some reason, you always push me away at first. Like you're afraid to feel loved. I don't know what it is, but you've embraced the love this time, haven't you?" His eyes searched my face, a glimmer of tears visible.

"Y-yes." My voice barely made it out.

"Good. Hold on to that." He gripped my neck, pulled me close, and kissed the top of my head. "And you have us. Me. Cade. And Wyatt will forgive you. We all love you. I love you."

"Why does it sound like you're saying goodbye?"

He chuckled, then winced a little. "Now, enough sentimentality. Let's end this?"

"Yes."

A creak announced the staircase door opening. Nick and I faced it, weapons ready, as one of Gwen's monsters paraded through. Other monsters pushed past it, flooding the cellar. We were surrounded.

"We've got this, okay? Your training will bring everything back. Trust me?"

I looked up at my brother and let myself be vulnerable. "I do."

"Atta girl." He smiled bright and pure.

Together, we faced the monsters.

And Wyatt walked through the door.

My heart crumbled.

"Don't kill him!" Kelsey's voice came through the stairwell next. A monster carried her in. Two others carried Yuki and Cade. Yuki fought and squirmed, so the monster hit her head. She went limp in his arms. My stomach dropped, and my heartbeat paused; when it started up, it hurt. Cade dangled in a monster's arms. Blood dripped from his nose.

I looked into Wyatt's eyes, hoping to find *my* Wyatt in them.

Gwen chuckled as she walked through the door. "It didn't take him long to decide." She smiled, sickly smug. "He's not yours anymore. So say goodbye."

WYATT STOOD NEXT TO GWEN. A SLOW smile stretched his lips that made my skin crawl. I recalled that smile. It wasn't mine. It was hers. He was hers. Again. An ache speared me.

"Wyatt?" My voice sounded so small and unsure.

"I thought you expected this much of me, Ava. Isn't that why you sent me away?"

He sounded more like Denton: cocky and self-assured. Not my Wyatt. A thought settled deep in the pit of my stomach. Would he ever be my Wyatt again?

Gwen chuckled. "Leverage was never something you quite understood."

Tears burned in my eyes, and I blinked them back. My skin heated. I called my fire, and it sparked to life in my hands. "What do you want?"

Gwen's eyebrows rose. "A pyrotechnics display? You're weak." She held up her hand and opened her palm. Fire—black as night and tinted with a sickly green color—burst to life. The flame rose high, making mine look like nothing more than a candle whose wick hadn't been trimmed. My stomach dropped, leaving a painful, hollow hole. How could I possibly compete with that?

Gwen laughed. "As we discussed, I want your power. I will be able to bring it to its full potential."

"You want my fire?" My voice was a whisper in the room.

"Ava, don't listen to her." Nick's steady voice broke against my doubt.

"No." Gwen shook her head as if she pitied my stupidity. "I want your Taker powers. If I become a Taker and a Giver, I can kill you. Kill Cade. And even Nick." Her attention shifted to Nick. "For good."

I clenched my fists, and my body shook as I glared at her. "I'll never give it to you!"

She sighed. "I'll entertain your little fight to the death. It's not like I have anything to lose. You, on the other hand, have everything to lose."

Nick stood closer to me. "I'll handle the monsters. You run to her as soon as you get the chance and take her out once and for all. Understand?" His eyes searched my face as if he feared I would let him down now. "Do not hesitate. You are stronger."

"We're surrounded."

He smiled, cocky, and for a moment, he looked more like Cade than I'd ever noticed. "Never stopped us before."

I stared at the monsters coming our way. There had to be at least twenty. His smile still sparked courage in me. His words rang in my soul. In my depths. Fueled my fire—and it grew. I pulled out my silver dagger and sliced into the first monster. It staggered, and I stabbed its heart. It fell dead. I recalled that this dagger was very potent. Good. I didn't have room for error. The next monster rammed me off my feet. As it barreled over me, I jumped up and jammed the weapon into its side. Another one turned to dust.

They kept coming. She called them out of the dust piles we were leaving. I would never make it to her if this continued.

"Are you afraid of me, Gwen?" I shouted.

As if my words had stalled time, the monsters parted, and I had a straight shot at Gwen.

"Afraid of you?" The disgusted look on her face morphed into a grin. "You really are simple."

"Don't underestimate what you don't understand." I made a break toward her, fire pulsing in my palms.

Her eyes widened. Whites visible. She wasn't ready to defend. I'd kill her. For good.

I thought of everyone she tried to take from me. All the lifetimes she'd cut short. The times she'd killed someone I loved. Of Wyatt. And fire pulsed into my hand. Hot. Strong. Fierce. She was a monster, just like her creations. I could kill a monster who wanted everyone I loved dead. I could do this!

As I moved, faster than her monsters, the flames grew and pulsed.

And I raised my hands. She was in my sights. The path of my anger. My vengeance.

I shot fire at her with both hands. It blazed, orange and red and yellow. Hot, like my anger. It reached farther than I'd ever seen it reach before.

This was it.

Her hand rose as if to shield her from my torrent of flame. Her fire spiraled out from her palms. A darkness filled her eyes. I recalled it from the time I'd seen her as a flame on the beach. Her fire, ashen swirls of black and green, raced out to meet my red-hot flames like a geyser of fire rushing at me. Her tendrils of smoke and fire billowed out from the sides, vines meant to choke and snuff.

As her power slammed into mine, my body jolted.

I kept my hands up, the steady stream of flames going.

I pushed back, hard. Reaching through every part of me. Fueled by my desire for vengeance. For freedom. My blood boiled. I roared as the fire shot like a hundred burning arrows, ripping through a piece of me, heading toward my enemy. Sweat dripped into my eyes.

She. Would. Die.

Black-and-green flames licked around the sides of my fire, dimming the color. Snuffing my power.

No! How was that possible?

I pushed harder. Tried to think of all the things she'd taken from me. A sob clawed inside of me. I wailed my desperation until it ripped through my chest.

Then something slammed into me so hard I flew backward, ramming into the crumbling brick. My head smacked against the hard surface. Overwhelming pain poured through me. As if all the sound in the room was suddenly zapped into oblivion, I heard nothing. But I felt everything.

My fire was no more than five feet in front of me, struggling to hold back Gwen's power. Too weak. Not enough. The wall started to crack as she kept pushing.

My throat felt raw from screaming.

I had nothing left.

My fire died.

And her flames hit me.

Sound returned, and I heard Nick shout my name. He pushed me, and I tumbled to the floor, Nick beside me. A swarm of Gwen's monsters separated us, caging Nick, and she walked toward me. "No fair. If I get no outside help, neither do you."

I stood, my bones mending, and wiped blood from my nose. "Since when do you play fair?"

"Good point." She snapped her fingers.

A sharp cry behind her made me stutter a step. I pulled the silver dagger from its sheath as someone crashed into me, sending me sprawling to the ground.

I looked up into Wyatt's eyes as he stood above me on hands and knees. He snarled, and his gleaming golden eyes simmered with the intent to kill.

"No," I whispered, and my soul cracked. Of course she would make me fight him.

WYATT TOWERED ABOVE MY PRONE body, growling and crying out as his bones started cracking. He was changing. She'd snapped her fingers, and he was powerless to stop the transformation from taking place. His nose elongated. Teeth grew to sharp points. His eyes pulsed gold, and wolfish features overtook him.

My breath shook. My heart ached. I put my hand on his chest and pushed, but he wouldn't budge. "She can't control you. Don't let her have a hold on you. Fight her, Wyatt. I know you can."

"Oh, Ava." Wyatt's eyes looked to be filled with mock pity, then he snarled. "This is me."

His words were a blade to my soul. I put my silver dagger away and pulled out a different one. I wouldn't kill him. I had to free him. He reared back and let out a horrendous cry as the change completed. I scrambled back from him.

But he caught me by the leg, his claws pressing against my jeans, and pulled me closer. Fangs protruded out of his snout, and he growled in my face. "Could you love this, Ava?"

Tears leaked out of my eyes. "Wyatt, that's not you."

He lunged toward me, wolfish teeth exposed. Claws ripped my shirt, dug into my skin, and he slammed atop me. My head banged into the hard floor, and I cried out. Tears dripped down my cheeks.

But I had the dagger. Slowly I moved my arm while maintaining eye contact. His eyes were wild. Raw. Afraid and angry.

"Wyatt."

He snarled and thrust his weight harder into me.

I showed him the dagger in my trembling hand.

"Will you finally kill me for good?" he mocked me. "Because of what I am?"

"I knew what you were when I chose you. I brought you here because I loved you."

"Loved." He scoffed.

"You have to fight this. You can. I've seen it. The love inside you makes you able to control it."

"What love?" he asked. "Everyone thinks I'm weak. No one believed I would be able to withstand her again."

"I do."

He squinted, and the claws digging into my arms seemed to release the smallest amount of pressure.

I pleaded with him to hear me. "You're stronger than she is. The love inside of you makes you stronger, remember?"

"This time that well is dry." He opened his jaws and snapped. Razor fangs bit into my neck. Saliva stung my skin. Burning, it dripped into me. I felt it pump through my blood like fire. Tears slid freely down my cheeks. My chest tightened. He'd broken his promise. He'd hurt me. I tried to hold on to sanity. I held to something else, Nick's words: *I need you. Cade needs you. And Wyatt would be lost without you.*

The air left my lungs in a rush. I'd pushed him away—right into darkness. He needed to see a light if he was going to have a chance to find his way back to me.

His snarling face stood inches from mine. "Could you love me now?"

"Yes," I whispered. "Yes. I can. I do. I always will. I love you. This monster isn't you."

He pulled back, his muzzle dripping with blood. My blood. His eyes flashed. Blue. Gold. Blue. Gold. Blue, gold, blue, gold. Then they shone bright. Gold. Yellow. Fire yellow.

I looked into those eyes and tried to find a connection to the real Wyatt. His heart. "You promised to protect me."

He whined.

"I gave everything for you. Against what my brothers ordered. Against everything. Because love is stronger. Love is stronger than her darkness. Than your darkness."

"I tried, Ava, and I failed."

Because I'd done that to him. "No. I failed you. Because I made you believe I thought the worst of you, but I didn't. I was only trying to protect myself. I didn't want the heartbreak if you didn't feel the same way. But it doesn't matter. Because I love you, Wyatt. Every lifetime. I love you. And you've always been there for me. You don't have to trust yourself. I trust you."

His eyes flashed blue. He shook his head, starting to change back. His eyes crushed closed. He whimpered. He rubbed his hand against his face and looked down at my blood on his palm. Hope dared to rise within me. "I'm sorry," he whispered.

Gwen snapped her fingers.

The sound echoed in the space between us.

Wyatt's pupils grew tiny, surrounded by rings of gold. And he snarled. "And now I bring you to her." He ripped the dagger from my hand and scooped me up.

Blood trickled over my neck. Why wasn't I healing? Werewolf saliva. Thankfully a surface wound, but I needed an antidote. I slammed my fists into his back, but it wouldn't break his hold.

"No! Ava!" Nick's desperate shout grabbed my attention, and I shifted enough to see him dangling in a monster's grip, clawing at its arms. He stabbed it, and it turned to dust. He landed on the ground and stood, facing Gwen.

"Brother dearest," Gwen said. "We can end this now."

Brother?

The word hit me.

She didn't mean that truly, did she?

Was she . . . my sister? No. She was a liar. None of that made sense. Why couldn't I breathe?

Three more monsters crawled up from ashes and pummeled Nick. Wyatt tossed me in front of Gwen.

Every bone in my body shook as I slammed against the hard-packed dirt. Werewolf venom burned in my veins.

"Ava, no!" The devastation in Nick's pained cry tore at my heart.

"Don't kill him yet. I want him to see this." Gwen stood above me now. I lay there, weaponless. She held a strange feather in her hands, and her lips drew into a wicked smile.

"Don't let her touch you with that! She'll take your powers. Ava!" Nick yelled, and I craned my neck to see the monsters holding him down. I looked up at Wyatt and his cold eyes.

Gwen bent over me. "Now you will give me your powers."

I felt something hard against my back, and hope lit inside me. The handle of the silver dagger. I slipped my hand beneath me. "You don't know me very well." I glared.

Her sick smile reminded me a bit of my own defiance. Her eyes, grayish-green, like mine, narrowed slightly. She really could be my sister.

"Why were you the favored one?" she snarled. "The last hope of phoenixes everywhere? They never should have put faith in someone as weak as you."

Weak? Who the heck did she think she was? She pushed her hand against my throat and leaned closer. "They should have loved me."

They? Is that what this was about? She'd never felt loved? I knew that feeling. That loneliness. I knew how to give her the tearing comment that would rip her apart at the seams. "Aww. Poor baby." I added venom. "No one ever loved you."

"That's where you're wrong." She pressed against my neck, and I knew I'd hit a sore spot. "Cade loved me." Gwen practically hissed. "Wyatt loves me."

I made sure she could see my glare.

"Cade?" Nick scoffed. "She's lying, Ava. Cade loved who she pretended to be. You're nothing but a pretender, Gwen."

Hatred burned inside me. "Wyatt doesn't love you, either."

"His darkness adores me. That's what scares you, Ava. You will never love that side of him. Me? I love him for what he's become. You fear him. He can smell your fear every time you're there while he changes."

"Shut up!" I glanced at Wyatt and his cold eyes. "Maybe Wyatt's darkness loves you. But I love *all* of him!" I pulled the silver dagger from behind me.

I stabbed, but she was faster. Her grip around my wrist pushed my hand to the ground, and she poised the quill above me. "Clever. That's all you've ever had. You're the weakest Taker in history."

"No!" Nick's shout registered in my ears. "Don't listen, Ava. Show her your fire."

My fire. Hadn't I already tried that?

"You have more to give, Ava! Unlock your true potential."

My true . . . ? A memory clawed at me, but I couldn't see it. It was like a dark spot in my brain. A memory that refused to open.

I shook it away and focused on what Nick had said to me earlier: *For some reason, you always push me away at first. Like you're afraid to feel loved. I don't know what it is, but you've embraced the love this time, haven't you? Hold on to that.*

Everything inside me warmed. He loved me. Wyatt. Cade. Yuki. All of them loved me. But I loved them back. I wanted to protect them.

This wasn't about vengeance. This was about saving those I loved.

My hands started to burn.

Glow.

Ignite.

The flame danced over my palms, encompassing but not burning. And the flame wasn't orange or red or any color of a normal fire. It was white and purple. Dark violet, light lavender, and every shade in between, with a blinding, white glow emanating in the center, like an opal.

"Yes!" Nick's voice registered, and then his strangled cry brought me back to sharp focus.

The pain in my body started to recede. Healing coursed through me, washed over me. Strength fueled my entire being, and I looked at the fire. My fire.

And an echo of a strange voice I barely remembered whispered in my being: *Such a beautiful flame, Ava.*

My mother's face flashed in my memory, and a pang shot through my soul. She looked like me. Her eyes showed so much love. Why hadn't I remembered her before? Her smile warmed my soul. Filled my heart. *Use your fire to protect. That's what a Taker does.*

I shook. I wanted to sob. I wanted to laugh. My own mother. She loved me. I stared into Gwen's face as the light from my fire dispersed the darkness. I slammed my palm against Gwen's chest and pushed with all my might as I sat up. Nothing could stop me now.

White-hot fire shot out of my hands and sent her flying backward. She slammed into the wall, and I held her there, like she'd done to me. Then I stood and turned, seeing the monsters look back at me with fear in their hollow eyes. I dug deep and sent a flash of flame with my other hand toward them. Toward the ones holding Nick down. My fire obeyed my will, targeting each of her creations. A white-hot blaze consumed them. And they shrieked as they turned to ash and dust. Then I faced Gwen.

But something inside of me flashed into my mind. A memory that started and stalled out just as it began. Gwen. In an underground tunnel much like this. My white flame about to pierce her. Then nothing. A truncated memory.

Why?

I let go of the steady stream of fire for a moment and stared at her. She slumped to the ground but then stood up. Pulsed her own black flame in her hands.

Hands on fire, I pulled a flare to the surface. It crackled in my palms, and I aimed it at her.

She smirked. "I can't believe you're so eager to kill your own sister. Your own brother."

"No, Ava!" Yuki's tight shout registered. "Don't do it. She's Nick's twin."

My heart seemed to stall, and I flinched. "What?"

"If you kill Gwen, you kill Nick," Yuki's voice strained.

I stepped back. A tingle shot through me, clouding my vision, making me see black spots. I would kill Nick? The flames in my hands dimmed.

"Ava, don't hesitate. Just end her!" Nick yelled, but his cry fell on numb ears. How could I kill him? My own brother?

I sucked in a shuddering breath and glanced at Nick. Tears blurred my vision.

"Ava! It's okay." His voice shook.

No. It wasn't okay.

I would not lose him, too. Hot, searing pain shot into me, and I slammed into the ground, Gwen's fire pushing me there. Not again. I lifted my hands and held back her flame. Then I shot my own. The explosion knocked her back.

We both stood. "You might be stronger this time," she said, "but I am not afraid to kill you." She lifted her hands and pointed them at me.

Nick reached me and pulled me out of the way, around the stairwell's corner. "Now, Ava."

I looked into his eyes. I'd just gotten him back. I'd just learned to trust him, all of them. And now I had to say goodbye . . . forever?

"There has to be another way," I said.

Nick pushed me, and a stream of black fire shot where I had been standing. It scorched the brick behind me. Gwen turned to strike me again, but Wyatt flung himself into her. Sent her sprawling to the ground.

All the air left my lungs as Gwen grabbed him by the throat and pierced him deep with . . . the quill!

I raised my hands to shoot fire at her, but Wyatt stabbed Gwen in the chest with my dagger.

She gasped and fell backward.

Wyatt knelt over her, the quill protruding out of his middle, hand still gripping the dagger's hilt. "Don't you dare," he said quietly, ripping the quill from himself and ramming it into her.

"No!" she screeched.

Then he fell. A thunder of pain started in my soul and resounded through my whole being.

Gwen's scream went silent as her body disintegrated into a black ball of flame that dropped to the earth and winked out. I knelt over Wyatt, blood seeping from his wound. His chest rose and fell shallowly. I pressed my hands up to him, and they lit with white light. Pulsed healing into him. He didn't open his eyes at first, but he morphed back into a man in nothing but torn pants. Then his wounds began to close. Heal. And his breathing evened out. He opened his eyes, scared and wild. And he scrambled away, but I grabbed his arm.

"It's okay. It's me."

"Ava?" He touched the spot on my neck that he'd ripped open. It was healed. "How?"

"How indeed." Nick dropped beside me and pulled me into a hug.

All I could think was I hadn't killed Gwen. That meant she wasn't dead for good. She'd come back. And Cade? Was this Cade's last cycle? I couldn't even form a coherent thought anymore.

AVA

Nick pressed his hand against my healed wound. "Your fire did this? How?" He looked into my eyes. "Are you okay?"

Far from it. I trembled.

"Here." He handed me a vial of werewolf anti-venom. "Drink it, I guess?"

Since there was no wound to pour it into, his thought process made sense. I gagged it down. Then I looked at my brother as shame heated my face. I hadn't killed Gwen. That meant she would still come back. But it also meant I'd saved Nick. "Does this mean we failed?"

"Hey." He hugged me tight. "You did not fail, Ava. You used your fire." He shook as much as I did.

"I don't want you to die." Tears gushed out of my eyes. How was I going to fix this?

He froze, and I pushed against his chest to see what he was looking at.

Wyatt had moved. He huddled against the wall, shivering. I tugged on Nick's arm. "It was my fault," I whispered. "Don't hurt him."

I stepped closer to Wyatt. He seemed smaller. I crouched near him. "Wyatt, I know you didn't betray me. I mean before I sent you to her. Did you?"

"No." He whined as if something inside was ripping him apart. He shook his head and a growl rumbled in his throat. He was fighting it. "And I didn't kill those people. The only blood on my hands from last night is from Gwen's monsters."

My chest cracked. I'd hurt him. I touched his face as more tears coursed down my cheeks. "I believe you. I'm so sorry. I should have believed you earlier. I should have trusted all of you." My throat was thick. "You make me stronger. I thought I could do this alone, but I couldn't. You—you saved me."

"I didn't mean to kill her." He looked so small and hopeless. I leaned in and wrapped my arms around him. Pulled him close to me. "I know. And I'm so sorry I made you believe I didn't trust you. I wanted to keep you safe. But I shouldn't have split us up."

"Ava?" Nick's voice trembled.

I let go of Wyatt and whirled around to see Nick kneeling beside Cade. I ran to him, every part of me shaking.

Nick had untied everyone, and they all clustered around Cade.

Cade, who wasn't moving. An ache spread through my veins. Was he breathing?

Nick's jaw clenched as he shook Cade's arm. "Cade!"

"Let me." Yuki moved closer. She gently pushed Nick away and touched Cade's head. "Cade?" her voice hummed, soft and quiet.

His eyelids fluttered, and he opened them, breathing in deep. He glanced around. "Whoa, why is everyone staring at me?"

Nick leaned closer, eyebrows pulled together. "How do you feel?"

He sat up and looked at Yuki. "I thought it was a fluke." He glanced back at Nick. "When she touches me, the headaches go away. I-I can have a memory without puking."

Nick turned his inquisitive gaze to Yuki.

She sort of shrugged.

"Yuki is tied to Cade?" I asked.

She nodded. "I remember him healing me."

"But you died anyway?" Nick rubbed his face in his hands. "We can figure that out later." He turned to Cade. "How do you feel?"

He moved his hand, phoenix fast, but slow for Cade. He swallowed. "I think I'm weaker."

"But you still have powers? Gwen didn't take them all?"

He shook his head.

Nick breathed a shaky breath. "Then we have time." He looked at Yuki. "Something about her makes you whole?" He crouched in front of Cade. "I think her being here has bought you some time."

"How?" Yuki asked. "Is it enough time to find the blade?"

My heart stuttered. "What blade?" I looked at Nick.

"It's a mythical weapon that's said to be able to break the connection between twins." Nick shook his head as if it were a long shot.

I touched his arm, all my hope rising. "So I could kill her for good and not lose you?" My throat closed up and I swallowed. I would have to give him a piece of my mind, but not right now. Not while everyone was just happy to be alive.

"In theory."

"What he means to say is yes." Cade stared at him the way I felt. The innocent, little-boy look in his eyes. He wanted to know why his brother would leave him. Then he felt amazed that his older brother would die for him. He turned to Yuki. "Can you find it?"

"I'll do whatever it takes."

"Good enough for me." Cade looked at Nick. "Well?"

He nodded. "We find the blade. Next time we meet Gwen, we kill her for good."

"When will that be?" Cade asked.

Nick sighed. "I don't know. But I do know that she unlocked phoenix-like powers she shouldn't have, such as sending a projection into a fire to talk to someone." He glanced at me. "If she has unlocked others, she might be able to control when and where she shows up again."

Cade narrowed his eyes. "Meaning?"

"Meaning it could be this lifetime."

"I will be ready." I looked into Nick's eyes.

Nick shook his head. "We."

That cracked open the door to the cage I'd locked around my hope. "Yes." My voice was airy, then stronger. "*We* will be ready." I opened my other palm and showed him the flame. The white-and-purple fire.

"Whoa!" Cade stared at it. "What did I miss?"

Nick beamed at me. "You did it."

"I couldn't have done it without you." But something inside of me tugged sadly. I looked at my hands. "You didn't tell me that my killing Gwen would kill you."

"You wouldn't have done it, Ava."

I grabbed my brother's arms and looked into his eyes. Mine started burning. "You're right."

"Ava." He let out a very small laugh, the kind that said he was overwhelmed with relief and very serious about what he was going to say. "I wanted you and Cade to be safe. I will always protect you. I never meant to turn you into a monster. Takers are always so sweet and kind. You wouldn't think they'd be phoenix killers. That's what I love so much about you. You're always willing to see the good in others."

I pulled him close and buried my face in his leather jacket, not caring about the drying blood. "You're my brother, Nick. If I had known killing her would kill you, I never would have attempted it."

He breathed in a shuddering breath.

"Don't you understand? I've wanted family my whole life. But you wanted that, too, didn't you? You wanted to have a family. To feel loved?"

"Ava, someone has to love first."

I squeezed him tight. "Yes. But both have to be willing to accept love. And I love you back. That's why we're going to find this blade."

He paused for an eternity. "Thank you."

After he let me go, I couldn't help it. I launched forward and wrapped Cade in a hug, too. "I'm just glad you're okay." More tears wanted to come. I wiped them away.

"Whoa, Ava. What's gotten into you?" He chuckled.

"Shut up and hug me, you idiot."

He did. "Thank you." He hugged me tighter. "For wanting to save me."

I looked up at him. "You're my brother."

"I've always wanted a sister."

"You have not." I playfully punched him.

"You're right. But I should have always wanted a sister."

Nick motioned to the cellar door. "Shall we?"

"Yes." I turned to find Wyatt. He'd gravitated closer, and Kelsey stood in front of him protectively.

"You two coming?" I extended a hand, which made Kelsey relax.

Wyatt stepped around his sister. His body shuddered, and he breathed in. His chest heaved as he looked at me, like he wanted to say something. Anything. But wasn't sure what to say. Wasn't sure what to feel. Or how I would feel.

He didn't need to say anything. And he deserved to know how I felt. I wrapped him in a tight hug.

Only a slight hesitation delayed his return embrace. Then it was forceful. Like he needed it as much as I did. Maybe more.

"Ava, I'm so sorry. I didn't mean to put Cade at risk. I—I bit you! I don't even know—"

"Hey, you don't have to apologize." I looked into his eyes, and he winced away from my gaze.

I knew this Wyatt. I remembered this Wyatt.

"Please don't shut me out." I touched his cheek.

Slowly he turned his attention to me and offered up my silver dagger. "I think it's time. I-I think you should kill me."

# 51

## AVA

"WHAT?" I BACKED UP FROM WYATT, staring at the dagger's bloody handle, and my heart jumped into my throat. "No!"

"Wyatt! No!" Kelsey's cry echoed my own.

"Ava, I killed people. I hurt people. You." His voice trembled. Tears coated his eyes. "I've never hurt you on purpose before. And I—"

"No." I pushed the knife away. "Wyatt, don't ask me to do this," I whispered, throat tight.

Cade approached us. "Wyatt, Ava's right. That wasn't you. At the docks, I saw what that Psycho did to you. You were protecting your friends. Your sister."

He let out a harsh laugh. "That's what you guys don't understand. It was me. That *is* me." He glanced at Nick as if he were a lifeline. "Nick gets it. He's the only one willing to do the right thing."

"Wyatt?" Kelsey raced over to him, but he backed away from her. "You didn't kill those people. Gwen told me she had her monsters do it. She said you wouldn't hurt anyone. You—"

"I bit Ava's neck! I could have killed Cade."

"Wyatt." Nick's voice made me turn, and heat spiked through my blood. I would not let him hurt Wyatt.

He clenched his jaw. Then he looked at Wyatt. "You hurt Ava tonight."

Wyatt closed his eyes and sank to the ground, elbows on his knees, head in his hands. The knife he'd tried to give me clattered to the floor between his feet. "I know. And I don't want to be that monster again."

I sat beside him, moving the knife away from his reach. "You won't be."

But I wasn't the only one to say it. Nick's voice clearly rang out with mine. I looked up at my brother. He'd picked up the knife and crouched next to Wyatt.

"Nick!" Kelsey touched his shoulder. He gazed up at her, that soft look in his eyes that I'd seen when he spoke to me as a little girl. Then he slowly placed the knife in his belt and turned his attention back to Wyatt. "Because we're going to make sure she doesn't get ahold of you again. All of us."

"You mean . . ." Kelsey stared at Nick.

My brother nodded. Looked right at me. "I wasn't right. Ava was. This whole time, you were, Ava. I'm sorry I didn't listen." He turned to Wyatt. "You hurt Ava, but it was a surface wound. Even under her control, you reined it in. You fought it. You didn't take Ava's second weapon. I know you felt it when you picked her up."

Wyatt frowned, but slowly his head lifted and he met my brother's stare.

"You're not a monster, Wyatt."

Wyatt squeezed his eyes closed. I slid my hand across his shoulders and pulled him into me. Then I looked at Nick and mouthed, "Thank you."

Kelsey hugged Nick. "Thank you," she whispered. Then she reached out and grabbed Wyatt's hand. "You promised not to leave me." She pulled him in for a hug next.

"Does this mean we get to use that interrogation vault once a month as a guest room?" Cade asked.

Nick chuckled slightly.

Wyatt's shoulders shook, and he actually smiled. "I'm not using your stupid interrogation room."

Everyone joined in the laughter, letting the tension crumble.

Kelsey bumped her shoulder against Wyatt's. "You might want to consider it. Gwen sort of trashed the cabin."

"Come on." I grabbed his hand. "Let's get out of here."

I crawled out onto the roof of my brothers' house. My foster parents were thrilled that I'd connected with my biological brothers. Jean had tenderly touched my face and told me she was happy to see the light in my eyes. Then, on my seventeenth birthday, she and Dave told me they'd make sure Nick got legal custody if that's what I wanted.

I'd cried some of the happiest tears in my life—well, this cycle anyway.

Deciding to stop pushing everyone away was a work in progress, but I'd started.

And I still had everyone I loved.

A shuffling against the roof tiles made me turn, expecting to see Cade up here again, staring at the stars with me and popping Combos like they were candy. But it was Wyatt.

Considering I hadn't seen him much the last few days—he'd missed school, which I totally understood—I wanted to run to him and throw my arms around him. Instead, I smiled and waited for him to approach. I remembered enough to know that letting Wyatt come around after something like this was better than pushing him too fast.

He stood beside me. "This seat taken? Or would you rather be alone?"

I patted the shingles. "Haven't seen you around. Kelsey is here every night."

"She's trying to figure out how to help defeat Gwen when she comes back." He didn't look at me while he spoke, still ashamed, it seemed, of everything he'd done while fighting Gwen's influence.

I motioned at the sky. "Stars are out."

He nodded.

I scooted a little closer to him, smiling at the way he gave me a slightly surprised look. "Andromeda is bright this evening."

"She's always bright."

I glanced over at him and his soft eyes. Intense eyes. He wasn't looking at the stars. He seemed captivated by me.

Heat hit my cheeks. "You know that constellation there." I drew his attention to the sky. "Perseus. He's a hero. Rescuer of those in distress. Mighty warrior."

His gaze traced my face. "Yeah?"

I nodded, still looking at the stars, but aware of his attention on me. "Against all odds, he faced his demons and won."

"Ava—"

I looked right at Wyatt, and he closed his eyes. Bowed his head. I leaned into him. "He had help from his friends."

"I'm sorry."

"For what? Wyatt, you don't have to say you're sorry. You—"

"For asking you to . . . I never should have. I didn't think it through. I was trying to protect people I love. And I didn't want to hurt you again."

I sat up straight so I could read his expression. "You remember what you do when you're . . . well, you know?"

"Yes. What I do. Who I am. Who I was under her spell. The feeling of helplessness. All of it. I don't always know while it's happening, but I remember later."

"I'm sorry you have to remember that." I gripped his hand tightly. "But I need you to know something."

He looked back at me, seemingly afraid to ask the question and curious all at once.

I squeezed his hand. "You're worth fighting for."

His chest rose, and he started to turn away from me. I pulled him back to face me. "And I won't stop until you're free."

"Free?" The word was almost a whisper.

"Yes. From this prison you have to enter once a month."

"Why would you—"

"Because I love you, Wyatt."

"Even now?"

I rested my head against his shoulder. "I chose to save you out of love, and nothing is going to break that bond. Not now. Not ever."

I had a family now. My whole life I'd been struggling to have others love me enough to make the tough sacrifices, enough to accept me for who I was and to stop pushing me away. In reality, I had been doing the pushing. But if Nick taught me anything, it was that family is worth making sacrifices for. So I'd chosen this family, and they'd chosen me right back.

We were willing to protect one another. That was what mattered.

That was what Gwen would never be able to break.

Love would bind us. And I could think of nothing stronger.

# ACKNOWLEDGEMENTS

IT TAKES A VILLAGE TO WRITE A BOOK. This is something I learned this year at a writers' conference. I had always felt so ashamed that I secretly *needed* people to help me with this career that I'd always pictured a solo mission. It's not. I need support, feedback, hugs, people to fangirl with me and people who believe in me. And I am truly blessed. I get to do what I love because of you.

So when I say "thank you," please know that it is from the bottom of my heart. From the most sincere place in my soul. I want to write until the day I die. Those of you who make that possible, thank you.

First and foremost, I thank my Savior, who gave me the desire and passion for this career. And then he put this amazing "village" of people who love me right out my front door.

I thank my husband, who puts up with my deadlines and excited ramblings about the "next story" and creativity that is so different than his own.

I thank my kids for their fresh perspective, encouragement, and enthusiasm. You mean the world to me. I love all of you to Krypton and back!

My family, Mom, Dad, and Molly, Jamie, Keanan, Evie, and Cilia, I couldn't do this without your constant support. I mean that. HUGS! To my niecelings, who I hope will someday read this book.

My in-laws, Dale and Linda, bless your hearts for taking care of my kids when the deadlines are tight and for displaying my books proudly on your shelves.

And my friends. I said I was blessed, and I am. I have so many writer and non-writer friends who provide an amazing support group. You guys read my rough drafts, remind me that I can do this, and sometimes, when I need it, you make unicorn poop cookies with me, remind me with a hearty "form Voltron!" or "Wonder Women unite!" that I'm not alone, and even cry with me. And when I celebrate highs, you are the first to squee over my newest covers, gush over my favorite characters, and remind me that you told me so.

Nadine, you were my first mentor, and without your encouragement and support, I would not have made it this far into my career. Your light shines bright. Keep shining.

Lindsay, Avily, Catherine, Jamie, Nadine, and Sara, you are the writer friends I go to for everything. Thank you for being my people. A writer is lost without her people!

To YOU, my wonderful readers, THANK YOU! These books are for you. And they are not whole without you! You bring them to life.

And a special thank you to my editing team: Lindsay! Jamie! Tera! I could not have done this without you!

To my agent, Steve Laube, who believes in my stories and pulled my first ever manuscript out of the slush pile, thank you. Sincerely.

And to all of you who believed in me thus far, your encouragement is treasured. Thank you.

# About the Author

S. D. GRIMM HOPES TO WRITE STORIES for always. Her first love in writing is young adult fantasy and science fiction, which is to be expected from someone who looks up to heroes like Captain America, Wonder Woman, Spider-Man, and Nightwing, has been sorted into Gryffindor, and identifies as rebel scum. Her patronus is a night fury, her spirit animal is eevee, her lightsaber is blue, and her favorite meal is second breakfast. She is represented by Steve Laube of the Steve Laube Agency, and her office is anywhere she can curl up with her laptop and at least one large-sized dog. You can learn more about her upcoming novels at www.sdgrimm.com.

www.ingramcontent.com/pod-product-compliance
Lightning Source LLC
Chambersburg PA
CBHW061631190726
48289CB00006B/1559